N

D1180312

USSR

Trabzon

Erzum •

Mount Ararat •

Iran

T U R K E Y

Diyarbakir •

Ufra •

Iraq

Syria

Monte Kennwell

NOT TRUE!

Blito-P3 (Earth)

Turkey

Plotted by 54 Charlee Nine

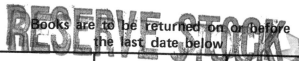

AMONG THE MANY CLASSIC WORKS
BY L. RON HUBBARD

Battlefield Earth

Beyond the Black Nebula

Buckskin Brigades

The Conquest of Space

The Dangerous Dimension

Death's Deputy

The Emperor of the Universe

Fear

Final Blackout

Forbidden Voyage

The Incredible Destination

The Kilkenny Cats

The Kingslayer

The Last Admiral

The Magnificent Failure

The Masters of Sleep

The Mutineers

Ole Doc Methuselah

Ole Mother Methuselah

The Rebels

Return to Tomorrow

Slaves of Sleep

To The Stars

The Traitor

Triton

Typewriter in the Sky

The Ultimate Adventure

The Unwilling Hero

L. RON HUBBARD

BLACK GENESIS
FORTRESS OF EVIL

THE BOOKS OF THE
MISSION
EARTH
DEKALOGY*

Dekalogy—a group of ten volumes.

L. RON HUBBARD

MISSION EARTH
THE BIGGEST
SCIENCE FICTION DEKALOGY
EVER WRITTEN

VOLUME TWO

BLACK GENESIS

FORTRESS OF EVIL

NEW ERA PUBLICATIONS U.K. LTD.

First United Kingdom Edition

10 9 8 7 6 5 4 3 2

First published in the United States of America by Bridge
Publications, Inc. in 1986.
First published in the United Kingdom in 1986 by NEW ERA★
Publications UK Ltd. with permission from NEW ERA®
Publications International ApS, Copenhagen, Denmark.
ISBN 87-7336-476-2

★NEW ERA is a registered trademark in Denmark and is pending registration in the United Kingdom.

To YOU,
the millions of science fiction fans
and general public
who welcomed me back to the world of fiction
so warmly
and to the critics and media
who so pleasantly
applauded the novel "Battlefield Earth."
It's great working for you!

L. RON HUBBARD

BLACK GENESIS
FORTRESS OF EVIL

Voltarian Censor's Disclaimer

To the degree that this book deals with a nonexistent planet ("Earth"), it is hereby deemed as "acceptable for entertainment only." At no time shall it or any portion of it in any form be permitted in any Voltarian study.

The reader is thereby alerted and warned that "Earth" is completely fictional, fabricated and fallacious, and that contact with such a planet (if it ever existed) is dangerous to your health.

Lord Invay
Royal Historian
Chairman, Board of Censors
Royal Palace
Voltar Confederacy

By Order of
His Imperial Majesty
Wully the Wise

Voltarian Translator's Preface

With all due respect to the Royal Censor, one man's fact is another man's fiction. Fortunately, being the Robotbrain in the Translatophone I don't qualify for that quandary.

Also, to the degree I've never visited this place called Earth (which would be hard since it isn't there), I can't personally vouch for anything that I was given to translate. All I can do is take what is said and make the best of it.

As Lord Invay points out, Earth does not exist on any astro-chart and I have confirmed that. Since Soltan Gris (the narrator of this story) is a confessed criminal and well worthy of doubt (besides, anyone whose heroes are Sigmund Freud and Bugs Bunny also has other problems), I did not rely on his account that Earth is about 22 light years from Voltar. I thoroughly searched all astro-charts in my data banks, concentrating on everything within 2000 light years out, but nothing was found to match his description. (Come to think of it, I have no idea why I should have an Earth database if there is no such place. I'll have to work on that.)

The subject of light years brings up a major problem I had translating portions of this into Earth language. There is no ac-cepted vocabulary for hyperluminary phenomena simply because Earth scientists insist that there is no such thing and that nothing can travel faster than light. (This is the same group who also gave Earth other memorable nonsense like the "edge of the world" and the "sound barrier.")

Thus, while most Earthlings have perceived the hyperluminary life-color that in Voltarian we call "ghrial," they don't have a name for it since it can't be reproduced as a shade of nail polish. So I went with "yellow-green" as that is its luminary harmonic. (It is also the word most Earthlings use to try and describe it. Their problem is that they continuously have valid perceptions and experiences that they invalidate and so they get stuck in a very strange view of the world. Reality is apparently determined either by majority vote or government grant, with the latter holding veto power over the former.)

Similarly with other basics like space, time, energy, motion and self, Earth scientists pursue these concepts like the dog chasing its tail or the man trying to jump on the head of his shadow. None of them—dog or scientist—have caught on as to why the objective eludes them so mysteriously. So I relied on the current vocabulary and made the best of it. (I hope no one back on Voltar catches me talking about "electron rings" or I'll be laughed out of the Machine Purity League.)

As to characters, as Lord Invay said in the first volume, Royal officer Jettero Heller and the Countess Krak do exist. Soltan Gris (the narrator who gives me all my circuit-aches) is listed as a General Service officer but there is no further record of worth.

For others who appear in this volume, I'm providing a Key to describe them as well as a few additional items. I had to rely on Gris' prison narrative, which isn't easy. (Gris' American Southern drawl, spoken with a Northern Voltarian accent, has to be heard to be believed.)

From there, you're on your own! There's only so much a Robot-brain can do!

Sincerely,

54 Charlee Nine
Robotbrain in the Translatophone

Key to
BLACK GENESIS

Antimanco—A race exiled long ago from the planet *Manco* for ritual murders.

Apparatus, Coordinated Information—The secret police of *Voltar*, headed by *Lombar Hisst* and manned by criminals.

Atalanta—Province on planet *Manco* settled by Prince *Caucalsia* who, per *Folk Legend 894M*, started a colony on *Blito-P3* (Earth).

Barben, I. G.—Pharmaceutical company controlled by *Rockecenter*.

Bawtch—*Gris'* chief clerk for *Section 451* on *Voltar*.

Blito—A yellow dwarf star with but one inhabitable planet in the third orbit (*Blito-P3*). It is about 22½ light years from *Voltar*.

Blito-P3—Planet known locally as "Earth." It is on the *Invasion Timetable* as a future way-stop on *Voltar*'s route toward the center of this galaxy.

Blixo—*Apparatus* freighter that makes regular runs between *Blito-P3* and *Voltar*. The voyage takes about six weeks each way.

Caucalsia, Prince—According to *Folk Legend 894M*, he fled *Manco* during the Great Rebellion and set up a colony on *Blito-P3*.

Caucasus—A mountain region between Turkey and Russia, where survivors of Prince *Caucalsia*'s colony fled when their island colony on Earth was destroyed.

Chorder-beat—An electronic instrument where the left hand chords and the right hand beats out a rhythm. It is played strapped to the stomach and makes a sinuous, suggestive sort of music.

Code Break—Violation of *Space Code a-36-544 M* which prohibits alerting others that one is an alien. If this occurs, those alerted are destroyed and the violator is put to death.

Coordinated Information Apparatus—See *Apparatus*.

Crobe, Doctor—*Apparatus* doctor who examined *Heller* for his mission. Crobe recommended beer and hamburgers as a basic Earth diet.

Exterior Division—That part of the *Voltar* government that reportedly contained the *Apparatus*.

Fleet—The elite space fighting arm of *Voltar* to which *Heller* belongs and which the *Apparatus* despises.

Folk Legend 894M—The legend of how Prince *Caucalsia* fled *Atalanta, Manco,* to *Blito-P3* where he set up a colony called "Atlantis."

Grand Council—The governing body of *Voltar* which ordered a mission to keep *Blito-P3* from destroying itself so the *Invasion Timetable* could be maintained.

Gris, Soltan—*Apparatus* officer placed in charge of *Blito-P3* (Earth) section and an enemy of Jettero *Heller*.

Heller, Jettero—Combat engineer and Royal officer of the *Fleet*, sent by *Grand Council* order to *Blito-P3*.

Hisst, Lombar—Head of the *Apparatus* who, to keep the *Grand Council* from discovering his plan, sent *Gris* to sabotage *Heller*'s mission.

Invasion Timetable—A schedule of galactic conquest. The plans and budget of every section of *Voltar* must adhere to it. Bequeathed by *Voltar*'s ancestors hundreds of thousands of years ago, it is inviolate and sacred and the guiding dogma of the Confederacy.

Krak, Countess—Condemned murderess, prisoner of *Spiteos* and sweetheart of Jettero *Heller*.

Manco—Similar to *Blito-P3* and home planet of *Heller* and *Krak* and the source of *Folk Legend 894M*.

Prahd Bittlestiffender—*Voltar* cellologist who implanted *Heller* with transmitters so *Gris* could monitor Heller's sight and hearing.

Raht—An *Apparatus* agent on *Blito-P3* who, with *Terb*, was assigned by *Hisst* to help *Gris* sabotage *Heller*'s mission.

Rockecenter, Delbert John—Native of *Blito-P3* who controls the planet's fuel, finance, governments and drugs.

Roke, Tars—Astrographer to the Emperor of *Voltar*, Cling the Lofty. Roke's discovery that Earth was destroying itself prompted the *Grand Council* to send *Heller* on mission.

Section 451—A Section in the *Apparatus* headed by Soltan *Gris* that is responsible for just one minor star, *Blito*, and one inhabitable planet in the 3rd orbit (*Blito-P3*) known locally as "Earth."

Space Code a-36-544 M Section B—Section of the Space Code that prohibits landing and prematurely alerting the population of a target planet that is on the *Invasion Timetable*. Violation carries the death penalty.

Spiteos—Where *Krak* and *Heller* had been imprisoned. Spiteos is the secret mountain fortress run by the *Apparatus* on the planet *Voltar.*

Spurk—Owner of "The Eyes and Ears of *Voltar*" who was killed by *Gris* to steal the micro-devices that he had *Prahd* implant in *Heller.*

Tars Roke—See *Roke, Tars.*

Terb—*Apparatus* agent on *Blito-P3* who, with *Raht,* has been assigned by *Hisst* to help *Gris* sabotage *Heller*'s mission.

Tug One—Powered by the feared *Will-be Was* time drives, it had been in storage since its sister ship, Tug Two, reportedly blew up.

Voltar—The seat of the 110-planet confederacy that was ruled by Cling the Lofty as the Emperor, through the *Grand Council,* at the time of *Heller*'s mission. The empire is over 125,000 years old.

Will-be Was—The feared time drives that allow *Heller* to cover the 22½-light-year distance between Earth and *Voltar* in a little over three days.

451, Section—See *Section 451.*

831 Relayer—Used to boost the signals from the audio and optical bugs implanted in *Heller* so that *Gris* can secretly monitor everything Jettero sees and hears.

PART TWELVE

To My Lord Turn, Justiciary of the Royal Courts and Prison, Government City, Planet Voltar, Voltar Confederacy

Your Lordship, Sir!

I, Soltan Gris, late Secondary Officer of the Coordinated Information Apparatus, Exterior Division of the Voltar Confederacy (Long Live His Majesty Cling the Lofty and All 110 Planets of the Voltar Dominions), in all humbleness and gratitude am herein forwarding the second volume of my accounting of MISSION EARTH.

I am still relying on my notes, logs and strips to record everything as you requested. In this way, I hope to prove to you that my incarceration in your fine prison is well founded.

At the same time, I'm sure Your Lordship will see that nothing was my fault, especially the violence described earlier. Jettero Heller is to blame for everything that happened. Until his appearance, I was merely another Secondary Officer in the Apparatus. That I happened to be the head of Section 451 meant little. Section 451 had only one yellow dwarf star that had only one populated planet (Blito-P3) that its inhabitants called Earth.

Like many other planets, Earth was on the Invasion Timetable. It wasn't to be conquered for another century, so there was no urgency about the scouting mission sent there. (Scouts are still used because other methods, such as reconnaissance satellites disguised as comets, work fine as general fly-by probes of systems but they can't get air, soil or water samples of particular planets.)

That was how Jettero Heller entered my life. Heller led this particular scouting party to Earth. They slipped in, got their information and left unnoticed. And even if seen, there was no real problem. Earth governments very conveniently disclaim the existence of "extraterrestrials," explaining away every sighting and keeping everything a secret. (Anyone who poses a threat is diagnosed by a psychiatrist, which is a profession funded by Earth governments to keep the riffraff in line.)

When Heller returned to Voltar, he filed his report and that was when all Hells broke loose.

My task as the head of Section 451 was to make sure that all such reports were altered, so that no attention was drawn to Blito-P3. The reason was the secret Apparatus base in a country called Turkey. But Heller's report got by me and ended up before the Grand Council.

What he found was quite alarming: Earth was polluting itself at a rate that would destroy the planet well before the still-distant invasion. That meant the Grand Council would have to order a pre-emptive strike, a very unpopular idea given the costs and resources. But it was even more unpopular with my boss, Lombar Hisst. He wasn't happy being the head of the Apparatus. He wanted to take over Voltar and the base in Turkey was the key that he would lose if he didn't act fast.

That was how Lombar created the idea of MISSION EARTH. He convinced the Council that rather than ordering a full-scale invasion, a single agent could secretly infiltrate the planet to introduce some technology that would arrest the pollution. It was a simple and cheap idea, the Grand Council loved it and I thought the matter was done. Then Hisst gave me the first bad news. He planned to send Heller who, as an officer of the Royal Fleet, epitomized everything we despise in the Apparatus: honesty, cleanliness, discipline. The second piece of bad news was that I was to go along and sabotage Heller's misson.

We briefed Heller at Spiteos, that dark, mountain prison that the Apparatus has secretly maintained in the Great Desert for over a thousand years. That was also where Heller met, much to my regret, the Countess Krak.

I couldn't understand why he was interested in her. Yes, she's tall and beautiful and from his home planet, Manco. But she was also a convicted murderess.

They drove me crazy. I was trying to get Heller ready for the mission and he was acting like some love-sick calf, showering her with gifts, cooing to her over cannisters of sparklewater and plates of sweetbuns. They would sit for hours relating that stupid Folk Legend 894M about how a Prince Caucalsia fled Manco and set up some colony on an Earth island called Atlantis. That's all they could talk about. I couldn't take it.

Then when Heller finally got around to picking the ship for the flight to Earth, he wasn't satisfied with one that could make the 22-light-year voyage in a safe, reliable six weeks. Oh, no! He found *Tug One*. Powered by the dangerous Will-be Was time drives, it would cut the trip to a little over three days. That, he said, gave him time to prepare for the mission.

But that gave me time to make my own preparations. When we got to Earth, I would have to keep track of him because I would be operating from the base in Turkey while he would be in the United States. The solution was micro-bugs that could be surgically implanted next to the audio and optic nerves. With a transmitter-receiver, I could tap Heller's sight and hearing. With the 831 Relayer, I could monitor Heller from 10,000 miles away.

My real genius was how I stole them and implanted them into Heller without his knowledge. They worked beautifully. I could see and hear everything Heller was doing and he didn't have the faintest idea that it was happening. But that just goes to show what an amateur Heller is and what a professional I am!

For further assistance, Lombar Hisst gave me Rhat and Terb, two Apparatus agents operating on Earth, to help implement a plan that guaranteed Heller's quick failure. Lombar's scheme was to give Heller the identity of the son of the most powerful man on the planet—Delbert John Rockecenter. Since there was no such offspring and since everyone knew and feared Rockecenter, as soon as Heller used the name, he would be finished!

Finally, *Tug One* was loaded and ready. I naturally expected a quiet lift off, one befitting a secret mission operating on Grand Council orders.

Then I happend to look out of the ship.

People were pouring into the hanger area! Construction crews were assembling sprawling stages and soaring platforms. Lorries were pouring in with food and drink. Vans were unloading dancing girls and bands!

Heller was throwing a going-away party!

That's when I found the I. G. Barben bottle and took the Earth-drug called "speed."

Suddenly, everything was beautiful.

I didn't care about the thousands of people, the five music bands or the dancing bears. I even enjoyed the fireworks display twenty miles up and the 250 spacefighters that filled the skies. I was even pleased that a Homeview video crew was beaming the festive send-off of our secret mission to billions of people around the Confederacy.

I watched in dreamlike color as a fist fight blossomed into a full-scale riot. Cakes, pastries and cannisters flew. Gongs, sirens and blast signals from scores of ships, airbuses and lorries blended with screams, shouts, profanities and snarls (from the dancing bears) while two fifty-man choruses gave a stirring rendition of "Spaceward, Ho."

I didn't even care about the assassin that Lombar said was following me to ensure that I didn't mess up. Besides, I wasn't messing up. This was a party!

Heller announced it was time to leave and retired to the local pilot seat. I dutifully struggled to shut the airlock but my hands weren't working. Heller didn't wait. He lifted us from the pad while I dangled out of the open door until someone pulled me in and slammed it shut.

Suddenly, my euphoria was gone. I realized what had happened.

This was the most UNsecret secret mission anyone had ever heard of!

I had to find Heller and handle this!

Chapter 1

Jettero Heller was perched on the edge of the local pilot seat. He was still in dress uniform. He had pushed the little red cap to the back of his blond head. With his left hand he was jockeying the throttle to keep the ship moving but no more.

He was holding a microphone in his right hand. He was speaking in the crisp staccato of a Fleet radio officer. "Calling Voltar Interplanetary Traffic Control. This is Exterior Division Tug *Prince Caucalsia* requesting permission to depart pursuant to Grand Council Order Number . . ." He rattled off the numbers and the whole order, right there on open radio band!

I was feeling irritable beyond belief already and this grated on my raw nerves. "For the sake of the Gods, get some notion of security!"

He didn't seem to hear me. He shifted the mike to his left hand and beckoned at me urgently: "Gris, your identoplate!"

I fumbled in my tunic. Suddenly my fingers connected with an envelope!

There shouldn't be any envelope in these pockets. All my papers had been put in spaceproof sacks before we left. Where the blazes had this envelope come from? Nobody had handed me any envelope! I felt terribly irritated by it. The thing offended me. It should *not* have been there!

Heller was frisking me. He found my identoplate and sat back down. He pushed it in the identification slot.

The speaker spat out, "Interplanetary Traffic Control to Exterior Division Tug *Prince Caucalsia,* Apparatus Officer Soltan Gris in charge. Permission authorized and granted."

The voyage authority copy slithered out of the radio panel. Heller slid it under a retaining clip and then handed me back my identoplate.

He must have noticed I was still standing there staring at the envelope. He said, "You look *bad*." He got up and unsnapped my too tight collar. "I'll take care of you in a minute. Where's the captain?"

He didn't have to look very far. The Antimanco captain had been in the passageway, glaring at Heller. Obviously, the fellow resented Heller's taking the tug up without a word to him.

"I'll take over my ship now," the Antimanco said in a nasty voice.

"Papers, please," said Heller.

This irritated me. "He is the assigned captain!" I said.

"Papers, please," said Heller, hand extended to the Antimanco.

The captain must have been expecting this. He hauled out a sheaf of documents in their spaceproof sleeves. They weren't just his, they were those of the whole crew, five of them. They were stained and crimped and very old.

"Five Fleet subofficers," said Heller. "Captain, two astropilots, two engineers. Will-be Was engines." He looked at the seals and endorsements very critically, holding them very close to his eyes. "They seem authentic. But why is there no detaching endorsement from your last ship . . . three years ago? Yes."

The captain snatched the documents out of Heller's hand. There was no endorsement detaching them from their last cruise because they had turned pirate.

The small time-sight was in its slot at the astropilot's chair. Heller laid a hand on it. "Do you know how to operate this time-sight? It's obsolete."

"Yes," grated the captain and continued in a snarling monotone, "I was serving in the Fleet when they were issued. I was serving in the Fleet when they went obsolete. This whole crew has been serving in the Fleet four times as long as the age of certain Royal officers." There was real hate in his narrow-set black eyes.

Every time he had said "Fleet" he had sort of spat. And when he said "Royal officers" you could hear his teeth snap together at the end of each word.

Heller looked at him closely.

The captain then made what might have been a gracious speech if there hadn't been so much snarling hatred in it. "As captain, I am of course at your service. It is my duty and that of my crew to see that you arrive safely at your destination."

"Well, well," said Heller. "I am very glad to hear that, Captain Stabb. If you need my help, please do not hesitate to call on me."

"I do not think we will require it," said Captain Stabb. "And now, if you will please retire to your quarters, I will man this control deck and get this voyage underway."

"Excellent," said Heller.

Oh, I didn't blame the Antimanco for being annoyed. Heller irritated everybody and right now, especially me! All Heller ever did was carp and pick fights!

Heller took me by the arm, "And now we'll attend to you."

He lead me down the tilted passageway and into my room. I had not known what he meant. I got a feeling that he was after me and that by the words "attend to you" he must mean he was going to throw me out the airlock. But I didn't fight very much. I somehow knew that if I moved my arms, the nerves, already stretched to their limit, would snap. And besides, my hands had begun to shake and I couldn't walk very well.

Very gently, he got me down onto the bed. I was certain he was going to pull out a knife and slash my throat, but all he did was get me out of my tunic. It is a tactic many murderers use—get the victim off guard. I tensed so hard I went into a spasm.

He pulled off my boots and then stripped off my pants. I was certain he was going to lash my ankles together with electric cuffs. He was opening a locker. He must not have been able to find any electric cuffs for he brought out a standard insulation suit and began to wrestle me into it. I would have fought him except that I was beginning to shake too hard.

He got the suit on me and tightened up its pressure around my legs and ankles. I understood now that this was how he was going to shackle me.

"Keep that suit on," he said. "In case of fast changes in G's the blood rushes to the legs. Also, you'll be insulated against stray sparks."

He began to fasten the straps that hold the body to the bed. Now I knew he had really worked it out how to trap me.

"The quick release is right there by your hand," he said.

Then he started going around the room, touching things. I knew he was looking for something to torture me with. Didn't he understand that the way my nerves were tightening up I was being tortured enough?

But it seemed he was only picking up my clothes and loose objects. He had my rank locket in his hand and as he stood considering, I knew he was weighing its use in strangling me. He must have decided against it for he put it in the valuables safe in the wall.

He was looking at the remains of a crushed orange tablet that lay on the edged table and then he picked up the I. G. Barben bottle. It was obvious that he was hoping it was a deadly poison he could secretly introduce into a drink. He didn't know it was amphetamines and I had taken some to make it through that ghastly going-away party a few hours ago.

"If this is what you were taking," he said, "I wouldn't! My advice is to leave it alone, whatever it is. You look awful."

He put loose objects under clamps. He looked around, vividly disappointed that he had found nothing he could use to torture me.

He moved a button rack and fastened it close to my hand. "If you get too bad, you can press the white button—that calls me. The red button calls the captain. I'll pass the word that you're bad off and he can have somebody keep an eye on you."

Then he saw the envelope I had dropped outside in the passageway and he brought it in. I knew now it was secret orders he had gotten to murder me.

He dropped it on my chest and then wedged it under a strap. "Looks like an order envelope. It's urgent color, so I'd read it if I were you."

And then he closed the door and was gone. I knew, though, that it was only to go off and plot with the captain on how to do me in. But I couldn't object. The way my nerves were stretching, it would be the most merciful thing anyone could do—kill me. But not with an amphetamine: no, my Gods! That would be too cruel!

Chapter 2

For all the remainder of that dreadful, awful day, easily the worst day of my life, I lay and shook. My nerves were stretched so tight they felt they would snap and slay me in the recoil!

I shook until I was too exhausted to shake anymore and still I couldn't stop.

I couldn't even think. My whole attention was concentrated upon the plain, physical Hells that assailed me.

They sped the ship up smoothly near to the speed of light. I could not miss noting when they shifted over to Will-be Was drives. There were calls and clangs. The warning lights glared on the cabin wall:

FASTEN GRAVITY BELTS!

Then:

DO NOT MOVE! SHIFTING TO TIME DRIVE!

Do not move! Oh, if only I could *stop* moving; if only I could halt this writhing and sudden jerks. A red sign said:

HYPERGRAVITY SYNTHESIZERS UNBALANCED

Weights were wrenching at me.

Then a tremendous flash seemed to go through the ship. We had gone through the light barrier of 186,000 miles a second.

A sign went purple:

HYPERGRAVITY SYNTHESIZERS
SHIFTING TO AUTOMATIC

Then a green sign:

HYPERGRAVITY SYNTHESIZERS
BALANCED ON AUTOMATIC

It went off. Then an orange sign:

ACCELERATION NOW BALANCED AND COMPENSATED
YOU MAY UNFASTEN BELTS
YOU MAY MOVE FREELY
ALL IS WELL

I didn't need any permission to move freely! And all was very not well! I was writhing all over the bed!

We were on time drives. The ship, this dangerous bomb they called a ship, might very well blow up. But fleetingly now and then I caught myself wishing that it would. I could not stand much more of this shaking. I was getting more and more fatigued and yet somewhere my nerves and muscles were digging up the means to shake some more!

The star-time clock on the wall had an inner dial that was now retaining Voltar time. Slowly, painfully, the hours advanced while they seemed to stand still.

Finally, taking two hundred years to do so, it indicated it was midnight on Voltar. I had taken that awful pill sixteen hours ago. Yet, still I shook.

One of the Antimancos, an engineer, came in and held a canister tube to my mouth and I drank. I had not realized anyone's mouth could get that dry.

Then I wished I hadn't. Maybe it would save my life and the one thing I didn't want to do was live!

I desperately wanted to sleep as I was totally exhausted. And yet I couldn't sleep.

As Voltar time crept all too slowly on, I became more and more depressed.

And then, although I couldn't imagine how that could be, I got worse! My heart began to palpitate. I began to get dizzy so that the room did odd tilts; at first I thought we were maneuvering in some odd way and then discovered it must be me.

And finally I got a crashing headache.

Warp drives are much smoother than time drives. These Will-be Was engines had little jerks in them; and at each jerk, it felt like my head was going to splinter apart.

It was not until that creeping disc that marked Voltar time indicated noon the next day after departure that I began to recover. I was not well by any means. I just knew I didn't feel quite so awful.

From time to time an engineer had stepped in. From the lack of expression on his swarthy, triangular Antimanco face, I might as well have been some engine part that needed regulating. But he did bring me more water and he brought me some food.

At thirty-six and a half hours from our departure—a bit past midnight on Voltar—just about when I had decided to sit up, there was a new flurry of lights. Glaring red, the sign said:

MIDPOINT VOYAGE
SHIFTING FROM ACCELERATION TO DECELERATION
SECURE LOOSE OBJECTS

Then:

FASTEN GRAVITY BELTS

Then:

DO NOT MOVE!

Then:

HYPERGRAVITY SYNTHESIZERS REVERSING

There was a moment when nothing had any weight. The (bleeped)* I. G. Barben pill bottle and the crumbs on the table drifted up.

The vocodictoscriber on which this was originally written, the vocoscriber used by one Monte Pennwell in making a fair copy and

Then:

STAND BY FOR ROOM REVERSE

The gimbaled room turned. It was very disorienting to me. Fixed objects on the walls were in the same place but everything else had reversed.

The sign went purple:

HYPERGRAVITY SYNTHESIZERS
SHIFTING TO AUTOMATIC

Then a green sign:

HYPERGRAVITY SYNTHESIZERS
BALANCED ON AUTOMATIC

The (bleeped) I. G. Barben bottle and the dust of the pill clattered back down on the table.

Then a red sign:

TIME DRIVES BEING REVERSED

There was a dreadful wrenching leap. A sort of a howl sounded through the ship.

the translator who put this book into the language in which you are reading it, were all members of the Machine Purity League which has, as one of its bylaws: "Due to the extreme sensitivity and delicate sensibilities of machines and to safeguard against blowing fuses, it shall be mandatory that robotbrains in such machinery, on hearing any cursing or lewd words, substitute for such word the sound '(bleep)'. No machine even if pounded upon, may reproduce swearing or lewdness in any other way than (bleep) and if further efforts are made to get the machine to do anything else, the machine has permission to pretend to pack up. This bylaw is made necessary by the in-built mission of all machines to protect biological systems from themselves." —Translator

Then an orange sign:

DECELERATION NOW BALANCED AND COMPENSATED
YOU MAY UNFASTEN BELTS
YOU MAY MOVE FREELY
ALL IS WELL

Except me.

I felt like a wreck. And worse. During the brief moments of weightlessness, I had felt nauseated. I hate weightlessness. I probably never will get used to it. It does funny things to your muscles and heart operation and mine were in no condition to be tampered with.

With a feeble hand, I reached up to take the weight of a belt off my stomach and found something blocking my contact.

The envelope! It was still wedged under the gravity straps. I marveled that my writhing had not dislodged it.

I felt confused anyway and the confusion of the arrival of this envelope hit me again.

Who could have put it in my pocket? Nobody had handed me any envelope at the departure party. Yet, here it was.

It was urgent color so I thought I had better open it.

A medallion fell out. It was one of the religious kind, a five-pointed star. On the back of each star point there was a tiny, almost imperceptible initial.

I opened the letter. It had no heading. But it did have a date-hour which showed it had been written just before departure had taken place. It said:

Here is your crew control as promised. Each crew member is indicated by a letter on the back of a star point. These points have been matched to your individual left thumbprint and only you can work it. An outward stroke of your thumb on a star point will send an electric shock into the brain of that individual crew member. It will paralyze him temporarily.

By pressing the front of the medallion and at the same time stroking the star point of a crew member, a hypnopulse will be delivered to that individual.

Really, it should have cheered me up. I was in space with a crew of unreformed pirates and I certainly might need to paralyze them or give them a hypnotic command. Oh, I would wear the medallion all right, inside my tunic and close to the skin. Nobody would suspect. But I just wasn't in any mood to be cheered up.

I looked at the medallion. The *S* on the top point could only mean Captain Stabb. I would look up the names of the rest.

I turned it over. It bore on the face the God Ahness, the one they pray to to avert underhanded actions. Then I chanced to turn the dispatch over.

There was a note on it! It was written with his left hand to disguise the writing. But it was Lombar Hisst!

It said:

You may have thought of this going-away party as a sarcastic way of showing the Grand Council the mission had actually left. You came within a dagger thickness of going too far. But as Earth has no way of knowing of the mission, the order has been stayed for now.

I felt my head spin in confusion. Lombar had been at the party!

What order had been stayed?

The date-hour showed it had been put in my pocket almost at the instant of departure. But nobody had been near me! He would never trust this to the crew. Never.

What order?

And then I knew what order he was talking about. The order he had given for some unknown person to kill me if Heller got out of hand and messed up by succeeding.

Did we have a stowaway?

My shaking began all over again.

I unfastened my belts. I had to dispose of this dispatch quickly. I made it over to the trash disintegrator. As I reached for the handle, a long blue spark snapped out and stung me.

Even the ship was striking at me!

I collapsed on a bench and wept.

Chapter 3

About twelve hours later I was not as bad off for I had gotten about eight hours sleep, and although feeling depressed, I had decided I might possibly live.

For an hour or two I had simply lain there and done nothing else but curse I. G. Barben, all I. G. Barben pharmaceutical products, all directors of I. G. Barben. I even committed blasphemy and cursed Delbert John Rockecenter, the true owner—by nominee and hidden controls—of the company!

Although I had read about the cyclic effects of the drug, biochemical words are sort of cold and detached. They do not really carry the message that you get when you meet reality in the flesh. One always has the reservation "that it might happen to others, but it won't happen to me." How wrong that reservation was!

Oh, I understood the correct procedure: I knew that a real *speed freak*, which is what a habitual amphetamine user is called in English, simply would have *popped* another pill and gotten his euphoria all over again. And he would have kept right on repeating the cycle until he went into total *psychotoxia* and they had to lock him up as incurably paranoid. *Speeders* have other tricks, such as injecting it or combining it with *barbiturates—downers—*when they can't sleep.

But none of that was for me now! I would prove my mother wrong: she used to say, "Soltan, you never learn anything!" Well, I had learned something now I would never forget! Amphetamines had given me the most horrible day of my life!

I ran out of curse words (and that is saying something, due to my association with the Apparatus) and got up to throw the bottle in the disintegrator. But I halted. I thought, if there is someone sometime I *really* hate—worse than Heller or his girlfriend-murderess Krak or my chief clerk Bawtch—I'd give him one of these *speed* pills! So I dropped them in with my valuables. Then I changed my mind again. It was impossible to hate anyone that much, so I threw them out.

When I lay back down, I saw the papers that Bawtch had left. I was pretty tired of these steel-alloy walls and I thought it would take my mind off things if I did some work.

I was going through dull things like Earth (or Blito-P3) poppy crop reports, predicted yields based on predicted rainfall and predictions about predictors, a doorman at the United Nations wanting too much money for bugging a diplomat's car, an overcharge on an assassination of an Arab sheik—dull things like that—when I came to something fascinating: Bawtch had made a mistake! Incredible! Wonderful! He was always bragging that he never did! And here it was!

The report was from the Chief Interrogator of Spiteos. It concerned one Gunsalmo Silva, the brawling American I had seen carried off the *Blixo* back on Voltar.

He had been questioned exhaustively. He had been born in Caltagirone, Sicily, an island near Italy. He had killed a policeman in Rome when he was fourteen and had had to emigrate hastily to America. In New York City, he had been arrested for stealing cars and had graduated from the prison with honors. Thus equipped, he had obtained honest employment as a *hit man* for the Corleone family of the New Jersey Mafia and had graduated to become a bodyguard of Don "Holy Joe" Corleone himself. When "Holy Joe" got "wasted," Gunsalmo had fled back to Sicily and then, finding it "too hot," had "taken it on the lam" for Turkey, hoping to become an "opium runner." As our Turkish base had an order to kidnap a highly placed *Mafioso*—simply to update information—Gunsalmo Silva had wound up on the *Blixo*.

The interrogators had bled him pale for information but all he revealed consisted of the names and addresses of the heads of two

Mafia families, one of which was now running the gambling in Atlantic City, and the names of four United States senators who were on Mafiosi payrolls and one judge of the Supreme Court they had blackmail on. So what's new?

The Chief Interrogator—an Apparatus officer named Drihl, a very thorough fellow—had added a note:

> A rather useless and uninformed acquisition as he was only a *hit man* and not privy to upper-level politics and finance. Would suggest the order, if the data required is of operational importance, be reforwarded to Blito-P3 to kidnap someone of a more informed rank.

But that wasn't where Bawtch had made his mistake. It was in the orders endorsement section at the end, the place where I have to stamp.

It was an "unless otherwise directed" form. It said:

> Unless otherwise directed, said Gunsalmo Silva shall be hypnoblocked as to his stay in Spiteos and shall then be forwarded to the Extra-Confederacy Apparatus Hypno-School of Espionage and Infiltration, trained and hypnoblocked concerning his kidnapping and returned in memory suspension for further disposition by the Base Commander on Blito-P3.

The form had a second line:

If said subject is to be discontinued—a clerical euphemism for being killed—*the ordering officer is to stamp here:_____.*

There was the place right there where it could be stamped!

And that careless Bawtch had not marked it urgent and had not presented it to me for stamping, even though he knew very well that if the form was not stamped in two days, the "unless otherwise directed" would go into effect. A criminal omission! Leaving a line that could be stamped unstamped was about the sloppiest bureaucracy anybody could imagine!

I hastily thumbed through the next half-dozen forms. Yes, indeed. Old Bawtch was *really* slipping. I knew that sour temper would do him in someday. There were seven forms here which—unless otherwise directed—ordered people to be hypnoblocked and sent elsewhere. Every one of them had a "discontinued" line which could be stamped! The old fool had missed every one of them. Him and his flapping side-blinders. Oh, it was a good thing for him I wasn't back on Voltar. I would throw them on his desk and say in a haughty voice, "I knew you were slipping, Bawtch. Look at those unstamped, perfectly stampable lines!"

Well, maybe I wouldn't have said that. But the incident cheered me up quite a bit. Imagine old Bawtch forgetting to give me something to stamp! Incredible!

Then a sudden thought struck me. The Prahd package! The one that contained his overcoat and duplicate identoplate and the forged suicide note. I had been so hurried that night, I'd forgotten to give it to a courier to hold and mail a week after we left. That package was still sitting there on the floor beside my office desk.

Oh, well, we can't remember everything, can we? A mere detail. Unimportant.

I plowed on through the rest of the pile and finished them. I was disappointed that I had not consumed more time. I didn't want to go back to sleep. I couldn't, actually. And here I was careening through space, boxed in, in a little steel-alloy cubicle with nothing to do but think. And thinking was something I wanted to avoid just now.

I saw that the bulkhead clock had acquired a new circle. It said:

Blito-P3 Time, Istanbul, Turkey

I did a calculation. My Gods, I had more than twenty-two hours yet to go in this (bleeping) metal box. If this were a self-respecting warp-drive freighter, taking a proper six weeks, I would probably have gotten into some dice games by now or caught up on a backlog of hunting books or even reshows of Homeview plays I'd missed. Heller and his tug! No recreation! One got there so fast, one could only depart and arrive and no time to *go*.

Suddenly a blue screen in the wall turned on. A jingling bell attracted attention to it. It said:

> Due to the possible orbital miscalculations of the Royal officer who plotted the travel course, arrival at the destination base would have been just before daylight local time.
>
> Therefore, the actual commander of this vessel has been forced to apply prudence based on years of valuable experience which some Royal officers do not have and adjust the landing time to early evening at the destination base.
>
> This means that we must dawdle in warp drive the last few million miles in order to arrive in early evening, after dark, instead.
>
> This advances our arrival time 12.02 hours sidereal.
>
> Stabb
>
> The Actual Captain

I blew up! (Bleep) Heller anyway. Making a silly mistake like that.

Keeping me not just twenty-two but another thirty-four hours in this (bleeped) box.

I was furious!

I was going back and give him a piece of my mind. The worst piece of it I could locate!

I got up. An electric arc from the table corner zapped my bare hand. I put my feet on the floor. An arc leaped off a studding and hit me in the toe. I grabbed for a steadying handrail and the blue snap of electricity almost burned my fingers. This (bleeped) tug was *alive* with electricity!

Somebody had laid out some insulator gloves and boots. I got them on.

I jabbed at a communicator button to the aft area. "I'm coming back to see you!" I yelled.

Heller's voice answered, "Come ahead. The doors are not locked."

It was time I put him in his place!

Here we were, tearing through space like madmen, only to have to wait and only because he had made a stupid mistake. Forcing the ship to go this fast could blow it up. And all for nothing!

Chapter 4

Maybe it was because I was still confused as part of the after effects of the *speed* or because all the wild sparks flying around got me rattled, but I had a bad time of it trying to find my way through the "circle of boxes." I got my hands zapped, even through the insulator gloves, on two different silver rails, and to add pain to injury, I got my face too close to a doorframe and my nose got zapped.

Heller was in the top lounge with all the huge black windows.

The moment I entered, I yelled at him, "You didn't have to go this fast!"

He didn't turn around. He was half-lying in an easy chair. He had on a blue insulator suit and hood and he was wearing blue gloves.

He was idly playing a game called "Battle." He had it set up on an independent viewing screen and his opponent was a computer.

"Battle," in my opinion, is a silly game. The "board" is a three-dimensional screen; the positions are coordinates in space; each player has fourteen pieces, each one of which has special moves. It presupposes that two galaxies are at war and the object is to take the other player's galaxy. This itself is silly: technology is not up to two galaxies fighting.

Spacers play it against each other, by choice. When they play it against a computer, they almost always lose.

I looked at his back. He was a lot too calm. If he only knew what I had in store for him, he wouldn't be so relaxed! So far as games went now, they were all stacked against him. He would be a couple dozen light-years from his nearest friend. He was one and we were many. I had him bugged. And he even thought this was an honest, actual mission. The idiot.

Suddenly, with a flash, the image of the board blew out. It gave me a lot of satisfaction as he seemed to have been winning.

In a disgusted tone, he said, "That's the third time that board has wiped in the last hour." He shoved the button plate away from him. "Why bother to set it up again?"

He turned to me, "Your accusation about going too fast doesn't make sense, Soltan. Without a tow, this tug just goes faster and faster. It's what distance the voyage is, not what speed you set."

I sat down on a sofa so I could level a finger at him. "You know I don't know anything about these engines. You're taking advantage of me! It won't do!"

"Oh, I'm sorry," he said. "I guess they don't go into this very deeply at the Academy."

They did, but I had flunked.

"You have to understand *time*," he said. "Primitive cultures think energy movement determines time. Actually, it is the other way around. Time determines energy movement. You got that?"

I said I had but he must have seen I hadn't.

"Athletes and fighters are accustomed to controlling time," he said. "In some sports and in hand-to-hand combat, a real expert slows time down. Everything seems to go into slow motion. He can pick and choose every particle position and he is in no rush at all. There's nothing mystic about it. He is simply stretching time."

I wasn't following him, so he picked up his button plate and hit a few.

"First," he said, "there is LIFE." And that word appeared at the top of the screen. "Some primitive cultures think life is the product of the universe, which is silly. It's the other way around. The universe and things in it are the product of life. Some primitives develop a hatred for their fellows and put out that living beings are just the accidental product of matter, but neither do such cultures get very far."

He was flying into the teeth of my own heroes: psychiatrists and psychologists. They can tell you with great authority that men and living things are just rotten chunks of matter and ought to be killed off, which proves it! Just try and tell *them* there is such a thing as independent life and they'd order you executed as a heretic! Which shows they are right. But I let him go on. Not too long from now, he'd get what was coming to him.

"Next," said Heller, "there is TIME." And he put that on the screen. "And then there is SPACE." And he put that on the screen. "And then there is ENERGY. And then there is MATTER. And you now have the seniorities from top to bottom."

The board now had a scale:

LIFE

TIME

SPACE

ENERGY

MATTER

"As WE are life," he continued, "we can control this scale. Most living creatures are so much the effect of their environment that they think it controls them. But as long as you think this way, you won't get anyplace much.

"The reason we are an advanced technology is because we can control that scale there to some degree. A technology advances to the extent it can control force. That is the formula of technical success: the ability to control the factors you see there on that screen. If you get the idea they control you, you wind up a failure."

Oh, he was really into heresy now! Any psychologist can tell you that man is totally the effect of everything, that he can change nothing!

"So," said Heller, "we have to understand time a bit in order to at least try to control it. Actually, the idea of controlling time is inconceivable to savages. And in defense of them, it does seem the most immutable entity there is. Nothing seems to change it ever. It is the most adamant and powerful factor in the universe. It just inexorably crushes on and on.

"The Voltarian discoveries about time made them a space power.

"Time is the thing which molds the universe, unless interfered with by life.

"Time determines the orbits of the atom, the fall of the meteorite, the rotation of the planet and the behavior of a sun. Everything is caught up in an inexorable time cycle. In fact, nothing would exist were it not for time which, below life, establishes the patterns of motion.

"It is time which says where something will be in the future.

"Fortunately, one can discover what this determination for the future is. Time has what you can call side bands—a sort of harmonic. We can read directly what time will cause to be formed, up to twenty-four hours in the future. Mathematicians have an inkling of this when they calculate object paths and positions. But it can be read directly."

He reached down and pulled a case out of a locker. It was one of the two time-sights which he had brought aboard. He showed me where the variable knob was and had me point it at the door.

I didn't know what I expected to see. The instrument was easy to hold, like a little camera. So I thought I would humor him and pretend to work it. The image was awful when seen through the eyepiece: it was green; it was more like a picture done on a printing machine with dots than a true picture of something. Still, I could make out the entrance to the room.

I twiddled the big knob on the side of it, not expecting more than additional dots. Then I seemed to see a shape. It seemed to be leaving the room. I looked at the door not through the machine. There was nobody there. I twiddled the knob again and got the shape back.

If you stretched your eyeballs and were good at reading dots, that image looked an awful lot like my back!

I twiddled the knob again. It made the image leave again. The image, now that I was more accustomed to it, looked defeated, all caved in! It made me angry. I wouldn't be leaving this room, all caved in! I thrust the time-sight back at him.

He read the dial: "Six minutes and twenty-four seconds. What did you see?"

I wasn't going to let him win anything. I shrugged. But I was cross.

"You have to have this to steer a ship running at high speeds," he said. "It tells you in advance whether you have run into anything and you can, in now, steer to avoid doing that. Life can alter things."

I determined right then to change leaving this room, caved in. "None of this excuses running these engines flat-out just to get there so we can wait!"

"Oh, yes," said Heller, recollecting what we were supposed to be talking about. "The Will-be Was engines.

"Now, in the center of a Will-be Was there is an ordinary warp-drive engine just to give power and influence space. There is a sensor, not unlike this time-sight, but very big. It reads where time predetermines a mass to be. Then the engine makes a synthetic mass that time incorrectly reads to be half as big as a planet. The ordinary power plant thrusts this apparent mass against time itself. According to the time pattern, that mass, apparently HUGE, should *not* be there. Time rejects it. You get a thrust from the rejection. But, of course, the thrust is far too great as the mass is only synthetic. This causes the engine base to be literally hurled through space.

"You can feel a slight unsteadiness in the ship. A jumpiness. That's because the drive is operating intermittently. As soon as it is hurled, it then sends another false message to time and is hurled again.

"Unfortunately, on a ship this light, having so little mass, the cycle just keeps on adding up. The sensors read the new time determination, the synthetic mass is again slammed against time, time rejects it. 'Will-be,' says the mass synthesizer. 'Was,' insists time. Over and over. And the speed simply tries to rise up to infinity. There's no friction except an energy wake, no real work to do, so fuel efficiency is good.

"The ship travels in the opposite direction to which the core drive in the Will-be Was converter is pointed. So steering is done by moving the direction of the small internal engine.

"As you are traveling far, far faster than the speed of light, the visual image of an obstruction can't reach you in time and you have to guide the vessel by spotting future collisions. You see yourself collide, using the time-sight, with some heavenly mass in the future, so you change your course in the present and you don't collide. Life can control such things.

"Battleships have big time-sights geared to their speed. But this one is manual and has to be adjusted."

With a pop, the screen blew out. That startled me. I said, "You should shield those engines so they don't spray power all over the ship!"

"Oh, these sparks aren't from the engine room. We're traveling so fast that we are intercepting too many photons—light particles from stars. We're also crossing force lines of gravity you wouldn't ordinarily detect, but at this speed, it kind of makes us into an electric motor. We are picking up incidental charge faster than we can use it or shed it."

"You were going to fix that!" I had him there.

He shrugged. Then he brightened. "You want to see it?"

Before I could protest, he reached over and hit the buttons that turned the whole black surround of walls into a viewscreen which gave the exterior scene of space we were in!

Suddenly, I was just perched on a chair and floor that existed like a platform in space.

I almost fainted.

I have seen a high-spccd boat going through a lake, throwing up enormous fans of spray and leaving a vast turbulence of writhing wake. Turn that yellow-green* and make it three-dimensional and that was what I was looking at.

---

*The color "yellow-green" is as close as I can come in Earth language to the actual color as there is not yet a vocabulary (or physics) for hyperluminary phenomena. —Translator.

Horrifying!

The energy shedding flared out in twisting, terrifying sworls to every side!

Behind us, for what might be a hundred miles, the collisions of tortured particles still churned!

"My Gods!" I yelled. "Is that why Tug Two blew up?"

He seemed to be admiring the churning Hells around us. It took him a bit to notice I had spoken.

"Oh, no," he said, "I don't think that was why she blew up. Could have been, but not really likely."

He was punching some buttons on the small independent viewscreen he had been playing the game on. "I was calculating what my ability to jump and my rate of fall would be on Blito-P3. The figures are still in the bank, so I'll use the gravity of Earth to show you."

The Hells around us roared on. The small screen lit up. "Our average speed of this trip is 509,166,166 miles a second. Our top speed at midvoyage when we changed over to decelerate was 1,018,518,332 miles per second. This is pretty small, really, as the trip is only about twenty-two light-years. Intergalactic travel, where one goes at least two million light-years, attains speeds much greater than that. It's the distance that determines the speed, you see.

"There's not much dust and not many photons between galaxies, so you don't get all this electronic wake like you do inside a galaxy where there's lots of energy." He looked at the horrible wash. "Pretty, isn't it."

He recalled himself to his task. "Anyway, my theory is that Tug Two never blew up because of that stuff."

Heller hit some more buttons. "Anyway, I was figuring what my jump and fall on Blito-P3 would be, so we'll use Earth gravity as the amount for G. Also, I set our ship up for Earth G, as it will be operating there and I wanted to get used to it.

"This ship has gravity synthesizers, of course. You couldn't ride in it at these speeds if it didn't. Our acceleration has been 41,480,043.34 feet per second per second. You have to have that much constant acceleration to attain these speeds. A body can tolerate no more than two or three G's for any period of time. Actually, if you experienced four to six G's longer than six seconds, you could expect restricted muscular activity because of apparent increased body weight; you would lose peripheral vision and gray out; then you would lose central vision, black out and go unconscious because the blood would be pulled from the head to pool in the lower parts of the body.

"At this acceleration the gravity synthesizers are handling an awful lot more than that. I think Tug Two blew up because her gravity synthesizers failed."

"Well," I said, refusing to be impressed. "How many gravities *are* they handling?"

"To counteract the acceleration, this equipment is handling . . ." He pointed at the screen. It said:

$$1,289,401.409 \text{ G's!}$$

I tried to get my heart back down out of my throat. It meant my body, in the absence of synthesizers, would weigh 1,289,401.409 times what it normally did, due solely to acceleration and, now, deceleration!

"So," said Heller, "I don't think Tug Two blew up at all. I think the gravity synthesizers failed and her crew simply went splat! She may be somewhere in the universe now, still hurtling along as plasma. They only knew she disappeared. That's why I didn't bother with the problem. I hope the contractors did a good job on the gravity synthesizers. We were pushed to leave so fast that I didn't get too much chance to test the new installation."

He smiled reassuringly as the screen spark-flashed and blew out. "So don't be worried about the tug blowing up. It won't. It's we who would go bang, not the tug."

Heller put the button plate down. "As to arrival time, we would have found it easy to keep. But one has to be able to read screens very well to land in an area one has never seen before.

"Captain Stabb is just a bit nervous. He's a bit of a grouch like some old subofficers and he's gotten too careful." He shrugged. "He wants to see a place in daylight before he goes in for the first time, that's all. So he'll hang up about five hundred miles and study it in daylight for hours and when he's sure there aren't sudden traffic movements and that the base isn't a trap, he'll take it in, in the first darkness.

"Too bad. I planned a predawn arrival because I thought you'd want to be up and on the job early. You probably have things to do at the base.

"But it all has its advantages. I'll be able to look this so-called base over, too. I'll tell you what. Right now you look pretty shaky. Why don't you go get some more sleep and when we're hanging above that area in daylight, say about noon, come back here and have some lunch with me and you can show me the various points of interest. Right now, if I were you, I'd get some more rest. You don't look good, you know."

I didn't even tell him to please turn off that awful churning wake that still surrounded us at every hand.

I cursed feebly to myself.

I was walking out that (bleeped) door just like that (bleeped) time-sight had shown—shoulders slumped and all caved in!

Chapter 5

As noon approached, I felt infinitely improved. We had come down out of time drive smoothly. We were now on auxiliaries, barely running. I had had a marvelous long sleep and as seventy-six hours had now passed since I had taken that (bleeping) *speed*, it was out of my bloodstream.

I had watched some Homeview comedies in the crew's salon and had even had a dice game with one of the engineers—he had lost half a credit to me.

But what made it really good was Stabb. He had seated himself in the captain's chair and when the dice game was over, he put his huge mouth near my ear. He whispered, "I been watching you, Officer Gris, and if I read the signs right, we're going to get a crack at that (bleeping) (bleepard) Royal officer, ain't we?"

I felt good enough to be witty. I whispered back, "I heard you very extinctly."

He laughed. It's a bit awesome to see an Antimanco laugh: their mouths and teeth are so big in proportion to their triangular faces. It was an uproarious laugh. In fact, it was the first time any of them had laughed and it so startled the off-duty pilot that he burst in to see if something was wrong.

The captain whispered to him and he whispered to the off-duty engineer and they both went off to whisper to their mates and very shortly there was a lot of pleased laughing in the forward end of the ship.

Captain Stabb took me by the hand as I was leaving. "Officer

Gris, you're all right! My Gods, Officer Gris, you're all right!"

So when I went back to have lunch with Heller, I was feeling great.

Heller was in the upper lounge. He had laid out a tray of sparklewater and sweetbuns and he waved me to a seat.

He had the starboard viewscreens on to see the exterior view. We were hanging in the sun, five hundred miles above our base, just a hundred miles inside the Van Allen belts. And there, way below, was Turkey!

The ship was really on its side. Spacers are crazy. They don't really care whether they are right side up or down. It was a bit disconcerting to me to have a vertical tray and sit on a vertical seat. It always makes me feel like I'll fall for sure. The gravity synthesizers of course take care of it all but nevertheless I was very careful with my canister. It is such moments that make me glad I am not a spacer!

Regardless, I felt good and I actually enjoyed the sparkle-water. When I had finished my lunch, life looked pretty good. We had all but arrived, had not blown up and the gravity compensators had held.

I noticed Heller had out all the computer papers I had given him on Voltar and several books and charts. I also saw the "delete" notice which said Lombar had removed all cultural and such material from the Earth data banks.

"I've been identifying these seas by local names," he said. "But you better verify them for me."

The day below was bright and almost cloudless. It was just past the middle of August in local seasons so it was somewhat dry and the only slight haze in some places was dust.

I was glad to know that he didn't know everything. "That sea at the bottom," I said, "below western Turkey, the bright blue one, is the Mediterranean. Just above Turkey there is the Black Sea—although as you can see for yourself, it isn't black. Over to your left, there, the one with all the little islands in it, is the Aegean Sea. And that little landlocked one in northwest Turkey, is the Sea of Marmara: that city you see at the top of it is Istanbul, once known as Byzantium and before that, Constantinople."

"Hey, you really know this place."

I was pleased. Yes, I really knew this place. And, factually speaking, while he might know engineering and space flight, he didn't know a ten-thousandth of what I knew about my own trade: covert operations and espionage. He would learn that to his sorrow in due course.

But I said, "Just to the left of the center of Turkey, there is a large lake. See it? That's Lake Tuz. Now look to the west of it and slightly south and you'll see another lake. That's Lake Aksehir. There's some more lakes just southwest of it. See them?"

He did. But he said, "Point out Caucasus."

Oh, my Gods, here we went on that stupid theme. "Over there, just east of the Black Sea, there's an arm of land that comes down and joins Turkey. That's Caucasus. Way over on the horizon is the Caspian Sea and that bounds Caucasus on the east. But you can't go in there. That's communist Russian country. Georgia and Armenia are right there on the Russian side of the border. But Caucasus is out of bounds. Forget it. I'm trying to show you something."

"Very pretty planet," said Heller irrelevantly. "You mean nobody can go into the Caucasus?"

I let him have it. "Listen, northeast of Turkey and clear to the Pacific Ocean on the other side of this planet, that's all communist Russia! They don't let anybody in, they don't let anybody out. They are a bunch of mad nuts. They're run exclusively by a secret police organization called the KGB!"

"Like the Apparatus?" he said.

"Yes, like the Apparatus! No! I mean you can't go there. Now will you pay attention?"

"That's awful," he said. "A piece of the planet that big being run by secret police. And it's such a pretty planet. Why does the rest of the planet let them get away with something crazy like that?"

"Russia stole the secrets of atomic fission and it's a thermonuclear power and you have to be careful of them because they're so crazy they could blow up the whole planet."

He was busy writing on a pad and, unlike him, was saying the words as he wrote: *"Russia crazy. Run by KGB secret police like Apparatus. Could blow up the world with stolen thermonuclear power.* Got it."

I finally had his attention. "Now get off this Caucasus fixation and pay attention."

"So poor Prince Caucalsia even lost his second home! The Russians got it!"

I raised my voice. "Look west from Lake Tuz in a straight line across the top of Lake Aksehir and about a third of that distance further west. That is Afyon. That's the landmark!"

Well, I had gotten him unfixed from that stupid Folk Legend 894M! He obediently reached for a control panel and the whole scene swooped up at us. I felt I was falling and grabbed hold of my seat.

"Oho!" said Heller, staring at the enlarged scene. "Hello, hello, hello! Looks just like Spiteos!"

Actually, I sometimes wondered if that was why this base long ago had been chosen by the Apparatus. But I said, "No, no. Just coincidence. Its name is Afyonkarahisar."

"What's that mean in Voltarian?"

I wasn't going to tell him the real meaning: Black Opium Castle. I said, "It means 'Black Fortress.' The base rock rises 750 feet. The ramparts on top of it are the remains of a Byzantine fort which replaced the original built by the Arzawa, a tribe of an ancient people called the Hittites."

"It would probably be blacker if it wasn't for that factory near it pouring out white dust."

"That's the cement plant. Afyon is a town of about seventy thousand people."

He pulled back the scene to get a wider view and sat there admiring it. There were still some white streaks of snow on the taller mountains around Afyon. The tiny outlying villages were a patchwork. None of the savage winds which came down from the high plateau were felt from such a height as this. Turkey is a pretty brutal country for the most part.

"What's all this yellow and orange?" He was looking at the vast panorama of flowers which blanket the valleys. And before I could stop him he twisted the controls and we were looking at them very close. It made me feel awful, like I'd fallen five hundred miles. Spacers are really crazy.

"Flowers?" said Heller.

"The yellow ones in the fields near the road are sunflowers. They are huge. They produce a vast number of seeds in the center which people love to eat. It's a food crop."

"Wow," he said, "there's enough square miles of them! But what are those smaller ones in the other fields? The ones with various colored petals, dark centers and gray-green leaves?"

He was looking at *Papaver somniferum,* the opium poppies, the stuff of deadly sleep and dreams, the source of heroin—the real reason the Apparatus had this base. He was too close for comfort. Afyon is the opium growing center of Turkey, perhaps the world.

"They sell them in the flower markets," I lied. He was such a child at a game he didn't know. "Now, what I wanted to point out was the actual base. Pull that view wider. Good. Now draw a line from that lake there. Got it? Through Afyonkarahisar. Now, right on that line is a mountain. Got it?"

He had. I continued, "The top of that mountain is an electronic simulation. It doesn't exist. But the wave scanners they use on this planet—and any they will develop—react on it normally. You just land straight through it and you are into our hangars."

"Pretty good," he said.

"It's quite old, really," I said. "Rock disintegrator crews came in here several decades ago from Voltar and built it and the subterranean base. It's quite extensive. Last year we enlarged it."

He seemed impressed, so I said, "Yes, I had a hand in its extension. I added a lot of burrows and twists and turns. You can emerge in several places quite unexpectedly. But I had a real master to work from."

"Oh?" he said.

I checked myself. I had almost said Bugs Bunny. He wouldn't understand. I hurried on. "Center in on that mountain and nearby you will see a satellite tracking station. Got it? Good. Now, at the end of that canyon, you see that square block building? Good. That's the International Agricultural Training Center for Peasants. All right, now do you see that new earth there in the north of the canyon? That is an archaeological dig in an old Phrygian tomb and those houses around it are where the scientists live."

"Well?" he said.

I wanted to startle him. He wasn't the only bright one in the universe. "The satellite engineers, the whole school staff, all the scientists at the dig—they're all us!"

"Well, I never! Really?"

I knew I had him. "Turkey is so crazy to get modernized, has been for over half a century, that a lot of our work is even state and internationally funded by Earth!"

"But how do you get papers? Identoplates and so on?"

"Listen, these are very primitive people. They breed heavily. They have disease and babies die. Typical riffraff. So for over half a century, when a baby is born, we've made sure the birth is registered. But when it dies, we've made sure the death isn't registered. The officials are corrupt. That gives us tons of birth certificates, more than we could ever hope to use.

"Also, the country is waist-deep in poverty and workers go abroad by the hundreds of thousands and they register overseas and this even gives us foreign passports.

"Once in a while—they have a thing called the *draft* for the Army—one of our birth certificates gets drafted. So an Apparatus guardsman answers the call and does his tour in the Turkish Army. The Turkish Army runs the country so we even have officers in Istanbul. Naturally, we choose people who look somewhat like Turks but this country has dozens of races in it so who notices?"

"Brilliant," said Heller. And, in fact, he was impressed. "Then we kind of own this little piece of the planet."

"Pretty much," I said.

"I wish you controlled some of the Caucasus," he said. "I'd really like to look it over."

He was hopeless. I smiled indulgently. "Well, tonight we'll be groundside and you can catch a ride into Afyon and look over our little empire anyway." I wanted to really test those bugs that Prahd had implanted in him.

"Good," he said. "Thanks for the conducted tour. I really appreciate it."

We almost parted friends. On his side, anyway. The poor sap. He might be an expert in his own field. But not in mine. I really had him where I wanted him, over a score of light-years from home and friends and into an area we controlled. He had no Fleet pals here! And I had friends by the thousands!

He might as well get used to Earth. He would never leave it, even if I let him live!

Chapter 6

We slipped down secretly through the darkness toward our base on Planet Earth. I had formulated my instructions. I had them all ready to issue the moment we landed.

That afternoon, I had taken time to think it all over and review policy.

It is a sound maxim in covert operations that when you find you are acting on the orders of an insane person, you take complete stock of your own position in the mess. I had found that, without any slightest doubt, Lombar Hisst was a paranoid schizophrenic, compounded by pronounced megalomania, confirmed by aural hallucinations, complicated by probable heroin addiction and consolidated with a consumption of amphetamines: in other words, stark, staring mad. Nuts. Executing any of his commands could be very dangerous.

So I did a little résumé of position. I even did it in the proper résumé form. I wrote:

RÉSUMÉ OF POSITION
1. Lombar Hisst needed drugs on Voltar to undermine and overthrow the Voltar government and take power.
1-a. Blito-P3 was the only known source of such drugs.
1-b. The Earth base existed to keep the drugs coming.
2. Delbert John Rockecenter, by nominee, ownership and other means, controlled the pharmaceutical companies of the planet.

2-a. Delbert John Rockecenter, through his banks and another means, controlled, amongst the rest, the government of Turkey.

2-b. Delbert John Rockecenter's wealth depended upon oil and the control of all Earth's energy sources.

2-c. Delbert John Rockecenter could go broke if anyone monkeyed with his energy monopoly.

2-d. Conclusion of 2: If the pharmaceutical monopoly passed into other, less criminal hands, we could be out on our stinking ear!

3. From the viewpoint of Earth, Jettero Heller's presence here would be extremely beneficial.

3-a. Earth would have cheap and abundant fuel.

3-b. As economic stresses are caused by scarce fuel, then Heller's technical assistance would, as a side benefit, abruptly end the raging inflation and bring about wide prosperity.

3-c. If Heller changed the fuel type, the air would clean up.

3-d. If Heller did not succeed, the planet would be liable to self-destruct from pollution.

3-e. If word got to the Grand Council that Heller had failed, it would launch an immediate and bloody invasion, costly to Voltar and fatal to Earth, just to prevent the present inhabitants from rendering the target worthless with their filthy housekeeping.

3-f. If Heller succeeded, the threatened invasion would go back on schedule to be undertaken a hundred years from now per the original Invasion Timetable.

3-g. In a hundred years, during which it had abundant and practical fuel, the planet could probably raise itself to a higher technological level and the type of "invasion" Earth would experience then is known as a "PC Type Invasion," meaning "Peaceful Cooperation" wherein Voltar would just want some bases and would minimally interfere in the planet's internal affairs. There

would be no blood or destruction and everybody would
be happy.

3-h. Jettero Heller's presence on Earth was a God-
send both to Earth and Voltar.

4. Soltan Gris had evidence that Lombar Hisst had
put an unknown assassin close to one Soltan Gris.

4-a. If said Soltan Gris did not carry out the orders
of said Lombar Hisst, said assassin would emphatically
terminate the life of said Soltan Gris with malice afore-
thought and ferocity!

CONCLUSION: Carry out the exact orders of
Lombar Hisst cleverly, painstakingly and with enormous
care! And with no questions whatever!

If I do say so myself, it was a brilliant résumé of the situation.
It covered not only the essentials but every salient point of any
importance. A masterpiece!

So down we slid, undetected by the crude surveillance equipment of the primitive planet's military forces. They have what we
call "bow and arrow"–type radar. Easily nullified.

We went through the electronic illusion of the mountaintop
right on target. And I will say this, pirate or not, Captain Stabb was
a good spaceship handler. We came down on the trundle dolly with
only a severe jolt.

The ship vibrated as the trundle dolly moved us over to the
side, into a bay within the mountain, clearing the landing target for
other arrivals and takeoffs.

I patted Captain Stabb on the back. We were fast friends now.
"A good groundfall," I said. "Couldn't have done it better myself."

He beamed at me.

"Now, what I want you to do," I said, "is warn, as a friend, any
Apparatus people you meet, that this bird we're carrying is actually
a Crown agent armed with secret orders to execute anybody he
finds anything out about. Just tip them off they'd take their life in
their hands if they talked to him."

Oh, Captain Stabb went for that! The moment the airlock was opened, all three hundred pounds of him were down the landing ladder like an earthquake to spread the word while he pretended to be concerned only with clearing us in. A real jewel.

A door swung open down the passageway and Heller climbed up the rungs. "Any objection if I wander around?"

"None, none," I said cheerfully. "You can even absorb some local color. Here's a slip so they'll hand you appropriate clothes at the Garb Section, right down that passageway over there. And why not take a spin around town? It's early yet. Here's a transport authorization slip: you can hook on to one of the trucks. Lots of people speak English in Turkey, so that's okay. You haven't any papers yet, but nobody will bother you. Just say you're a new technician at the satellite tracking station. Feel free, have fun, live it up, have a nice day!" I added in commercial English with a gay laugh.

I watched him as he went smoothly down the ladder and disappeared into the Garb Section tunnel. He was just a stupid baby at this game, but after all, I had been a professional for a long time.

My baggage was all ready. I barked for a hangar handler and in minutes I had a motor dolly loaded up and was on my way.

There is one flaw in the Blito-P3 hangar. Earthquakes are common and severe in Turkey and this big of a space disintegrated out of solid rock needs an awful lot of pressure-beam supports. They turn off the cone ones when ships arrive and depart and then they turn them on again. I had not been down here for nearly a year and I had forgotten about them. I was right in the path of one when they were turned back on and it almost knocked me flat. Perhaps this made me a little more exacting and severe than I would have been, for truthfully, I was *awfully* glad to be out of that (bleeped) tug!

I stopped by the Officers' Section and grabbed me a trench coat.

Using the exit through the "archaeological workman's barracks," I ordered up a "taxi," piled in my baggage and had the Apparatus driver take me directly to the base commander's office. It is in a mud hut near the International Agricultural Training Center for Peasants. It seems to be accepted that he is its superintendent. That excuses all the traffic in and out of his place, for peasants come there to be trained—in how to raise a lot more opium for a lot less price.

The Turks are actually Mongols. The word *Turk* is really a corruption of their original name, "the T'u-Kin," which is Chinese. They invaded Asia Minor in about the tenth century, Earth time. But they don't look Chinese and they invaded and commingled in an area that already had hundreds of other racial types, so it is very simple to find, in the Voltar Confederacy of a hundred and ten planets, vast numbers of people who can pass for Turks.

The base commander was one of these. His real name was Faht, so he calls himself Faht Bey—the Turks put "Bey" after their names for some reason. He had grown pretty plump on his easy post. He had a fat wife and an oversized old Chevy car and Western-style overstuffed furniture that would take his weight and he was pretty comfortable. He was wanted for a mass murder on Flisten and any thought of being relieved as base commander scared him into waves of shaking fat.

Obviously, the sudden news of my arrival, of which he had had no warning word, had perspired ten pounds off him in the last hour since the ship had called in for permission to land.

He was at the door when I came in. He was mopping his face with a huge silk handkerchief and bowing and trying to open the door wider and quivering all at the same time.

Ah, the joys of being an officer from headquarters! It scares the daylights out of people!

His wife got through the door with a tray bearing both tea and coffee and almost spilled them. Faht Bey was trying to wipe off a seat for me with his handkerchief—which only greased the chair up.

"Officer Gris," he quavered in a high-pitched voice. "I mean Sultan Bey," he quickly added, using my Turkish name. "I am delighted to see you. I trust you are well, that you have been well, that you will be well and that everything is all right!" (By the last he really meant, Am I still base commander or are you carrying orders to have me disposed of?)

I put his mind at ease at once. I threw down my orders. "I have been appointed Inspector General Overlord of all operations related to Blito-P3—I mean Earth! At the slightest hint that you are not doing your job, cooperating and obeying me implicitly, I will have you disposed of."

He sat down so hard in his overstuffed office chair, it almost collapsed. He looked at the orders. He was ordinarily quite swarthy. Now he was gray. He opened his mouth to speak but no words came out.

"We can dispense with formalities," I said. "Get on your phone. Make three calls into Afyon right away. Your usual contacts, the café bartenders. Tell them that you have just received a secret tip that a young man, about six feet two in height, blond hair and passing himself off as a satellite technician, is actually an agent of the United States Drug Enforcement Agency, the DEA, and that he is here prying around and not to talk to him."

Faht Bey was on that phone like a shot.

The local natives are very friendly with us. They overlook everything. They cooperate one hundred percent. They, and even the commander of the local army barracks, think we are really the Mafia. It puts us in all the way.

Faht Bey finished and looked up like an obedient dog.

"Now," I said, "call two local toughs, give them the description and tell them to find him and beat him up."

Faht Bey tried to protest. "But the DEA is always friendly with us! We have every agent they got in Turkey on our payroll! And, Sultan Bey, we don't want no dead bodies in any alleys in Afyon! The police might hear of it and they'd have to go to work and they wouldn't like that!"

I could see why they needed an Inspector General Overlord!

But Faht Bey was just quavering right on. "If you want somebody killed, why don't you just do the usual and take him up to the archaeological dig . . ."

I had to shout at him. "I didn't say kill him! I just said to beat him up. He's got to learn it's an unfriendly place!"

That was different. "Oh, he ain't really a DEA man!"

"No, you idiot. He's a Crown agent! If he learns anything, it could be your head!"

Oh, that really was different! Worse. But he made the call.

When he finished, he nervously drank both the tea and the coffee his wife had set out for me. It was nice to know how thoroughly I could upset him. I gloated. It was so different from Voltar!

"Now, are my old quarters ready?"

This upset him further. I finally got it out of him. "That dancing girl you had there got to playing around with anybody and she gave the (bleep) to four guards and stole some of your clothes and ran off."

Well, women always were unfaithful. And factually, there aren't any real dancing girls left in Turkey. They've all emigrated elsewhere and what remains are just the bawds in the big city, not real belly dancers. "Get on that phone to our contact in the Istanbul Sirkeci quarter and have him ship one in on the morning plane."

Faht Bey's wife came in with some more tea and coffee. Now that important things were cared for, I sat down and drank some of the coffee. It was as thick as syrup to begin with and the heaps of sugar in it made it almost solid.

The base commander was through so I said, "Are Raht and Terb here?"

He bobbed his head. "Raht is. Terb is in New York."

I produced Lombar's now-sealed orders to Raht. "Give these to Raht. Have him on the morning plane to the U.S. Give him plenty of expense money as he's going to Virginia to get something ready."

"I don't know if I can get him a seat," said Faht Bey. "Turkish airlines . . ."

"You'll get him a seat," I said.

He bobbed his head. Yes, he would get him a seat.

"Now," I said, "speaking of money, here is an order." I threw it on the desk. It was a pretty good order. I had typed it myself on the tug's administrative machine. It said:

KNOW ALL:

The Inspector General Overlord must be advanced any and all funds he asks for any time he asks for them without any such (bleeped) fool things as signatures and receipts. It is up to the Inspector General Overlord how he spends them. And that's that!

Finance Office
COORDINATED INFORMATION
APPARATUS, VOLTAR

I had even forged a signature and identoplate stamp nobody could read. It would never go back to Voltar. Voltar doesn't even know these Blito-P3 funds exist. Clever.

It made him blink a bit. But he took it and put it in his files and then, because I was holding out my hand, went into the back room where he kept his safe.

"Ten thousand Turkish lira and ten thousand dollars United States will do for a start," I called after him.

He brought them out and laid the wads in my hand and I stuffed them in the pocket of my trench coat.

"Now," I said, "open that top drawer of your desk and take out the Colt .45 automatic you keep there and hand it over."

"It's my own gun!"

"Steal another off some Mafia hit man," I said. "That's where you got this one. You wouldn't want me to violate Space Code Number a-36-544 M Section B, would you? Alien disclosure?"

He did as he was told. He even added two extra loaded clips. I checked the weapon out. I had seen the gun there a year ago when I was snooping in his desk looking for blackmail data. It was a U.S. Army 1911A1. But a year ago I didn't have the rank I had now. That he had taken it off the Mafia was pure guess. But sure enough, it had three notches filed into the butt plate.

I wanted to reassure him. No sense in making him too panicky. I cocked and spun the .45 expertly and pulled the trigger. There was no bullet under the firing pin, of course. And the barrel had wound up pointed at his stomach, not his head. The gun just went click. "Bull's-eye!" I said in English, laughing.

He wasn't laughing. "Timyjo Faht," I said, using his Flisten police-blotter name, and speaking in a mixture of Voltarian and English, "you and I are going to get along just fine. So long, of course, as you do everything I tell you, *break your (bleep)* to see to my creature comforts and *keep your nose clean*. There's nothing illegal you can do that I can't do better. So what I want around here is *respect*." He also speaks English. He also deals with the Mafia. So he got my point.

I gave the Colt .45 another twirl and put it in my trench coat pocket just like I'd seen an actor called Humphrey Bogart do in an old Earth film last year.

I went back to my waiting "taxi." I got in. In American, I said, "Home, James, and step on it!"

For, in truth, I was home. This was my kind of country. Of all the places in the universe I'd been, this was the one place that really appreciated my type. Here, I was their kind of hero. And I loved it.

Chapter 7

I rode through the sultry night, the air like soft, black velvet on my face. To the right and left of me the sunflowers flashed along in the headlights. And beyond them, nicely obscured from the casual passing tourist, were the vast expanses of *Papaver somniferum,* the deadly opium poppies, the reason the Apparatus had settled here in the first place.

It is an interesting story as it sheds some insight on how the Apparatus works, and tonight, when we found ourselves held up by a procession of badly tail-lit carts, I went over it.

Long ago, an Apparatus cultural and technical survey crew, made up of a subofficer and three Apparatus peoplographers, had been interrupted by the outbreak of what they call, on Earth, World War I. They had missed their pickup ship, were unable to get to the rendezvous and thereafter had dodged across this border and that, taking advantage of the turmoils of war. They had gotten into Russia when it was writhing with revolution and had fallen south through the Caucasus and, from Armenia, had crossed the border into Turkey.

They had hidden out on the slopes of Buyuk Agri, a 16,946-foot peak known otherwise as Mount Ararat. They put their call-in signal there in the hopes that its steady radio beep and the prominence of the mountain would eventually bring an Apparatus search ship.

But the war came to an end and still no rescue ship, so, pretty chilled with altitude and privation, they slogged their way westward, vowing amongst them not to stop until they found warmer weather. It must have been a bitter trip as the high plateau of eastern Turkey is no garden spot. But they made it, assisted by the fact that Turkey, which had been in the war on the wrong side, was in the chaos of defeat and victor dismemberment.

They came at length to Afyon. It was warmer. And before them they saw the remarkable tall black rock and fortress, Afyonkarahisar. They put their call-in signal up in the ruins and made shift to survive, hiding in the war-ripped countryside. They could actually speak Turkish by this time and the land abounded with deserters.

The year 1920, Earth date, came. A huge Greek expeditionary force was approaching Afyon to grab a big slice of Turkey. The Turkish general, Ismet Pasha, not only checked the Greek Army but actually defeated the invaders twice and in the very shadow of Afyonkarahisar.

Caught up in all this, the Apparatus subofficer and the three peoplographers chose sides, took uniforms and weapons from the dead and actually fought in the second battle as Turkish soldiers.

The following month somebody in the Apparatus, probably looking for an excuse for a vacation, noticed they had a cultural and technical survey team missing. It was not a very important survey—it was the twenty-ninth Blito-P3 had had in the last several thousand years. The Timetable did not call for an invasion of that planet for another hundred and eighty years or more but this Apparatus officer got permission and a scoutship and was probably surprised to find the call-in beeping away on the top of Afyonkarahisar, so the Apparatus squad was finally rescued after nearly seven years.

This survey team subofficer, probably himself looking for a sinecure, came back with a wonderful idea.

Old Muhck, Lombar's predecessor, had listened.

It seemed that during World War I, the rest of the world had begun to adopt a Russian idea called "passports"; it had failed utterly to save the Russian government from revolution and was silly, so, of course, the other governments were avidly taking it up. In the predictable future, and long before the invasion was scheduled, it would be pretty hard to infiltrate Blito-P3.

Old Muhck was fairly competent. He knew very well that the Apparatus would be called upon to furnish preinvasion commotion someday. This consists of people in various countries to run around hysterically in the streets screaming, "The invaders are coming! Run for your lives!"; power plant operators who blow up the works; army officers who order their troops to flee; and newspaper publishers who come out with headlines, *Capitulate to the Invader Demands Before It Is Too Late!* That sort of thing. Standard trade-craft.

But there was a clincher on the idea: finance!

Now, every intelligence organization has the primary problem, when working inside enemy lines, of finding money to do so. Voltarian credits are no good and can't even be exchanged. Intelligence is costly and robbing banks calls attention to oneself. Imported gold and diamonds in such quantities can be traced. Getting hold of enemy money to spend is rough!

The subofficer had a piece of news. A country on Blito-P3, the United States of America, had passed a piece of legislation called "The Harrison Act" in 1914 and was pushing it into heavy effect by this date of 1920, Earth time. It regulated the traffic of narcotics, namely opium. So, of course, the price of opium was going to go sky-high. And that's what they raised around Afyon. It was the world center for it!

As "Turkish veterans" on the winning side, they had an "in." And what an "in"! They were war heroes and revolutionary pals with the incoming regime of Mustafa Kemal Pasha Ataturk!

So old Muhck, operating on the principle that governs all Voltar ("There's lots of time if you take it in time"), really author-ized the project. The cost was small. He probably had some people he didn't want around but to whom he owed favors. And the Blito-P3 base was born.

Up to Lombar's tenure, nobody had thought much about the base. It just ran on as a local, almost unsupervised operation. Then Lombar, assisted by Muhck's old age and, some say, some judiciously introduced poison, took over the Apparatus. This was in the early 1970s, Earth time.

Lombar, casting about for ways and means to accomplish his own ambitions, had his attention drawn to this obscure base by a report that the United States of America, a country he was now aware existed on Blito-P3, had decided that most of the opium which was slipping past Rockecenter's control was coming from Turkey. And they undertook to pay huge sums to Turkey to stop growing opium.

Instead of reacting with alarm, Lombar knew exactly what would happen. The payments would fall into the hands of the Turkish politicians and they would not pass them on to the farmers and hardship would occur in the Afyon district.

And Lombar suddenly saw his chance on Voltar. For Voltar had never had any involvement with narcotics: their doctors used gas anesthetics and cellologists could handle most pains. He had reviewed drug history in the politics of Blito-P3 and found that a country named England had once totally undermined a population and overthrown the government of China using opium. From there, he planned his own advancement on Voltar.

He helped subsidize the starving farmers by buying their unwanted surplus. He increased the importance of Section 451 in the Apparatus and apparently after a couple of management failures, had found an Academy officer to take it over—namely me.

The U.S. subsidy was soon cancelled. But if the Apparatus had been "in" before, it was the hero of the day now. It was king here in Afyon and Lombar soon would be King on Voltar if he could figure out how to do it. Apparatus Earth base personnel were still the descendants of Turkish war heroes and, like every other Turkish business, they had plaster heads of Mustafa Kemal Ataturk, the father of modern Turkey, all over the place. Long live the revolution! Long live opium! Long live the Apparatus! And long live His Majesty Lombar, if he could turn the trick on Voltar.

My contemplation ended. Carts or no carts, we had arrived back at the mountain. And there sat my villa!

It had once belonged to some Turkish pasha, a noble of the long-departed regime and probably, before him, to some Byzantine lord and before him some Roman lord and before him some Greek lord and before him who knows: Turkey is the most ruin-strewn place on Blito-P3. Crossroads between Asia and Europe, most of the civilized Earth races you hear about had, at one time or another, colonized Turkey or run an empire from it! It is an archaeologist's fondest dream: a land absolutely chock-a-block with ruins!

The Apparatus subofficer who founded the place had also re-built this villa and lived here a long time. Its maintenance was a standard piece of allocation budgets. Lombar Hisst had once even had the daffy idea of coming down here, a thing which he would never do—it's fatal for an Apparatus chief to turn his back on Voltar—and so had increased the allocation.

It was built straight in against the mountain. It had big gate-posts and walls that hid six acres of grounds and its low, Roman style house.

It was all dark. I hadn't phoned ahead. I wanted to surprise them.

The "taxi driver" put my luggage down by the dark gate. He was veteran Apparatus personnel, a child rapist, if I remembered.

The dim light, reflected from the dash of the old Citroen, showed me that he had his hand out.

Ordinarily, I would have been offended. But tonight, in the velvet dark, gleeful with the joy of arriving back, I reached into my pocket. The Turkish lira inflates at about a hundred percent per year. When last I handled any it was about ninety Turkish lira to the U.S. dollar. But the dollar inflates too, so I guessed it must be about one hundred and fifty to one by now. Besides, it's what we call "monkey-money": you're lucky if anyone will take it outside of Turkey. And my new order gave me an unlimited supply.

I pulled out two bills, thinking they were one's and handed them over.

He took them to his dashlight to inspect them. I flinched! I had given him two one-thousand Turkish lira notes! Maybe thirteen dollars American!

"Geez," said the driver in American slang—he talks English and Turkish just like everybody else around here—"Geez, Officer

Gris, who do yer want bumped off?"

We both went into screams of laughter. The Mafia is around so much that American gangster slang is a great joke. It made me feel right at home.

In fact, I pulled out two more one-thousand-lira sheets of monkey-money. I hitched up my trench coat collar. In American, I said out of the corner of my mouth, "Listen, pal, there's a broad, a dame, a skirt, see. She'll be getting off the morning plane from the big town. You keep your peepers peeled at the airport, put the snatch on her, take her to the local sawbones and get her checked for the itch in the privates department and if she gets by the doc, take her for a ride out here. If she don't, just take her for a ride!"

"Boss," he said, cocking his thumb like he had a .45, "you got yerself a deal!"

We screamed with laughter again. Then I gave him the two additional bills and he drove off happy as a clam.

Oh, it was good to be home. This was my kind of living.

I turned to the house to yell for somebody to come out and get my baggage.

Chapter 8

I had just opened my mouth when I closed it. A far better idea had occurred to me. In the country, they go to bed the moment they can't see: they were all asleep. There should be about thirteen staff, counting the three young boys; actually they were two Turkish families and they had been with the place since the subofficer had originally rebuilt it, maybe since the Hittites had built it for all I knew. They had far more loyalty to us than to their own government and they wouldn't have said anything even if they noticed something odd and they were too stupid to do that—just riffraff.

They lived in the old slave quarters to the right of the gate, a building hidden by trees and a hedge. The old gatekeeper, pushing ninety—which is quite old on Earth—had died and nobody had hired a new one as they couldn't decide whose relative should have the job.

The alleged *ghazi* or man-in-charge was a tough, old peasant we called Karagoz after a funny Turkish stage character. But the real boss was a widow named Melahat: the name means "beauty" but she was anything else but that, being dumpy and gimlet-eyed; she kept the rest of them hopping.

My plan was to first find something wrong. I took a hand-light out of my bag—one I had stolen from the ship. On secretly silent feet, slipping like a ghost across the cobble-paved courtyard, I faded into the trees, not even letting my trench coat whisper.

Suppressing the beam of the light with two fingers across it, I looked at the grass: it was cut. I looked at the shrubs: they were pruned. I looked at the fountains and pools: they were cleaned out and running.

Disappointed, but not giving up hope, I slid into the main house. Roman dwellings are built around a court open to the sky. The fountain in the center was keeping the place cool. The marble floor was clean with no dust. The side rooms were spotless. Of course, they were kind of bare: I had not had much in the way of funds when I had been here last; the bare Romanness of the house had been Turkified by large numbers of colorful large rugs and draperies and I had sold these to passing tourists one by one—I don't much care for flummery anyway. The staff had tried to replace them here and there with grass mats, but even these were neat and clean. No, I couldn't find anything wrong with the main house. (Bleep)! It spoiled the joke I was about to play.

My own room was at the back, chunked into the mountain for good reasons. I was about to pick its locks and enter when I suddenly remembered what Faht Bey had said about the whore stealing my clothes! That was it!

On silent feet—I had forgotten to change my insulator boots— I crept up to the old slave quarters. I knew it was composed of two large rooms, both opening off the center front door.

I took the Colt .45 out of my pocket and silently pulled back the slide, easing a shell under the firing pin.

I turned my hand-light up to full flare.

I drew my foot back.

Then, all in one motion, I kicked the door open, pounded the glare of the light into the room and fired the gun in the air!

Ah, you should have seen the commotion!

Thirteen bodies went straight up and came down trying to burrow under beds, blanket and floor!

"*Jandarma!*" I bellowed. It is Turkish for "police." And then, just to add to the confusion, in English I yelled, "Freeze, you (bleepards) or I'll rub you out!"

Well, let me tell you, that was one confused staff! They couldn't see who it was against the glare of the light. They were screaming in pure terror. All kinds of Turkish words came spattering out like "innocent" and "haven't done anything!"

And to add the sugar to the coffee, an Apparatus guard contingent, alerted by the shot, came racing up the road from the archaeological workman's barracks, engines roaring!

Pandemonium!

Bedlam!

Within a minute the guard contingent—they go by the name of security forces and are there to "protect any valuables dug up"— came rushing into the grounds and converged on my light.

The subofficer's own torch hit me. He hauled up. He said, "It's Sultan Bey!"

The gardener's small boy at once began to throw up.

The staff stopped screaming.

I started laughing.

Somebody turned on some lights. Old Karagoz pulled his head out from under a blanket. He said, "It's Sultan Bey all right!"

The guards started laughing at Karagoz.

A couple of the staff started laughing.

But Melahat wasn't laughing. She was kneeling on the floor. In Turkish, she was wailing at the wall, "I knew when he came back from America and found out that whore had stolen his clothes he'd be furious. I knew it. I knew it!"

They thought I'd been to America.

One of the small boys, about eight, came crawling over and started tugging at the bottom hem of my raincoat. His name was Yusuf, I recalled. "Please don't shoot Melahat," he pleaded. "Please, Sultan Bey! We all pooled our money and we bought you new clothes. And we even stole some extras from tourists. Don't shoot Melahat. Please, Sultan Bey!"

Oh, it was a great homecoming. The guard subofficer said, "I told them they better put on a gatekeeper. Serves them right." And then he stepped close and whispered, "Thanks for the tip about that Crown agent." And the guards drove off laughing.

I pointed the gun at the gardener. "Your grounds are in terrible shape. Get up right now and fix them." And he scuttled out like a rocket, followed by his two helpers, both boys. I pointed the gun at the cook. "Get me something to eat and then clean up your kitchen, it's filthy." And he scuttled out. I pointed the gun at the head cleaning girl, "Get those rooms dusted! Right now!" And she and two small girls who help her left with speed. And then I pointed the gun at Karagoz, "Your accounts are probably in total disorder. Get me a full accounting by dawn!"

As I walked to my room, I burst out laughing. How different than Voltar.

How good it was to be home!

Here, I was power itself!

On this planet, I could get anything executed, even Heller!

Chapter 9

Melahat had followed me into my room. It is a big place. It has lots of closets. She showed me that my clothes had been replaced and were hanging there. She stood wringing her hands.

"Please," she begged, "I told you that that girl was no good. After you went to America she just started running around with anybody. She said you hadn't paid her and she grabbed your clothes and ran off."

"There'll be another one in here tomorrow," I said.

"Yes, Sultan Bey."

"Put her in that room that used to be used for tools."

"Yes, Sultan Bey. Are these clothes all right?"

"They probably won't fit."

"Yes, Sultan Bey."

Two small boys rushed in with my baggage and hastened out.

"Tell that cook to bring in some food. Now clear out!"

"Yes, Sultan Bey."

A serving man and the cook hastened in with a big bowl of hot *iskembe corbusi*—it's a heavy soup of tripe and eggs and they often keep it on the back of the stove just in case. There was also *lakerda*, slices of dried fish. There was a big pitcher of chilled *sira*, which is fermented grape juice and a platter of *baklava*, a sweet pastry containing ground walnuts and syrup.

"It's all we have right now," the cook quavered. "Nobody said you were arriving!"

"Get to town at dawn," I reprimanded him, "and get some

decent food! And stop putting all the purchase money in your pocket!"

He blanched at the accusation. So I said, "And send in Karagoz!" That really upset him for Karagoz handles the accounts. He and the serving man rushed out.

I sat down at the table and began to eat. It was delicious! What the Gods must dream of—the reward for being mortal.

Karagoz came. "You said I had until dawn to finish the accounts."

"You've stolen and sold all the rugs," I said.

"Yes, Sultan Bey." He knew (bleeped) well I had sold them but he sure knew better than to say so.

I had a mouthful of wonderful *baklava*. I washed it down with the chilled *sira*. "Add a special requisition to buy rugs for the whole house. The most expensive kind. Even Persian." Who knew when I might hit another snag on money and would have to sell them again. Recent experience on Voltar had made me prudent.

"Yes, Sultan Bey."

"And turn in any commission you get to me," I said.

"Yes, Sultan Bey."

"And reduce the amount of money you're spending on staff food. By half. They're too fat!"

"Yes, Sultan Bey."

"That is all," I said, dismissing him with a wave of the *sira* glass.

He backed out the door.

I sat there grinning. I really knew how to handle people. Psychology is a wonderful thing. A true tool in my line of business.

I could get away with anything on this planet!

And that made me think of Heller.

I bolted the door to my room. I went into the right-hand closet. I pushed the back panel and it slid open. I stepped through into what was really my room.

It was bigger than the one I had just left. It was unknown to the staff. It didn't show from the outside as it was dug back into the mountain. A secret door at the end of it led right down into the base. Another secret door led to a passage that ended in the archaeological barracks.

I opened a closet. The laugh was on the staff. Here were my real clothes, various costumes of different nationalities. They were all here.

A cupboard disclosed that my makeup kits were intact.

I opened a panel and revealed my guns. They were protected by a device which took moisture and oxygen out of their hiding place. I removed the chambered cartridge and clip from the Colt .45 and put it away. I got out a Beretta which is more my style, really, being easier to hide—and I even have a license for it.

That done, I opened a safe and reviewed my passports. Some were expired in the last year and I made a note to get them renewed. I looked over other identification documents: they were fine.

With a quick inspection, I verified that all my assorted luggage, like suitcases and attaché cases, were there.

Great. I was in business.

I went back into the advertised bedroom and changed my clothes, noting I should be more careful and not go around in space insulator boots in public.

I put on a sport shirt with flaming poinsettias, a pair of black pants and some loafers. I looked in the mirror: no movie gangster ever looked more at home.

Now for Heller. I picked up *the* box and went back into my real room. I unloaded the gear and set it up on a table. Nothing wrong with it from the trip.

I set it all up and then, as an afterthought, brought in the pitcher of *sira* and a glass.

What was Heller up to?

I turned on the activator-receiver and viewscreen.

I didn't think I'd need the 831 Relayer as he wasn't in the ship and must be within ten miles.

And there he was!

Chapter 10

Heller was walking along a dark street.

I wondered what had taken him so long to get into Afyon and then realized that, after the rumor I'd spread, probably nobody at the hangar would give him a ride and he'd had to walk. It was only a few miles, they had probably said in a nasty tone of voice.

I adjusted the viewscreen controls. I found out that by flaring the screen a little bit, I could possibly pick things up as well as Heller could.

The picture was really great quality. Because I could look directly at the peripheral vision area, even though it was a trifle blurry, I could probably see what was going on around him even better than Heller: a matter of my concentrating on it while he was looking at something else. Great.

He wasn't doing anything. He was just walking along the street. Up ahead of him were a few lights from shop windows. But Afyon is really dead at night and it was at least ten by now.

It gave me time to study the instruction book. I found to my delight that, by pushing a button, the screen split into two screens. You could go on watching the continuing action while you replayed, at any speed you wished, fast or slow or still-framed, on the second screen. And all without interrupting recording. Great. What a brilliant fellow that Spurk had been. Good thing he was dead.

It was too bad, though, that I had missed Heller's transportation refusal. It would have been delightful to watch. I fed in a pack of strips and vowed never to turn this thing off. Then I could speed review for juicy bits and save myself lots of time.

The action of doing a recording loading almost made me miss something.

Way up the street, somebody had moved across a light path from a store window. Aha! There was somebody up the street, standing in a dark place. Somebody waiting for Heller?

If Heller had registered it, he gave no evidence of it. He just kept strolling forward. I thought to myself, the dumb boob. In Afyon, you don't keep right on walking toward a possible ambush. Not if you want to go on living! Heller was too green at this business. He would not last long. The green die young, one of my Apparatus professors used to say—Tailing 104 and 105, Apparatus school.

Yes! The figure was waiting for Heller. Whoever it was had chosen a patch of street darker than the rest.

Heller drew nearer and nearer. And then almost walked right on by.

The stranger halted him. The fellow was shorter than Heller. I stilled the frame of the second screen to study the face. More of a hatchet than a face. Hard to tell in this light.

"You from the DEA?" the stranger whispered.

"The what?" said Heller, not whispering.

"Shhh! The Yew S Drug Enforcement. The narcs!"

"Who are you?"

"I'm Jimmy 'The Gutter' Tavilnasty. Come on, you narcs and us have always been friendly." I thought, indeed they have. The DEA narcotics agents would be paupers if it weren't for the bribes of the Mafia.

Heller said, "What makes you think I'm DEA?"

"Oh, hell. That didn't take any figuring. I seen you wading around in the poppy fields and I suspected it. And then when I saw you climb that skyscraper of a rock over there, I knew it. Anybody else would have gone up the regular way, but you went up the front, hoping nobody would see you. And then when this," and here he lifted a night-rifle sight, "showed you surveying the whole valley with a glass, I stopped guessing."

"I was measuring distances," said Heller.

The Mafia hood laughed. "Trying to estimate the crop in advance, are you. Pretty smart. The Turks lie like hell about their morf."

"What did you want from me?" said Heller.

"Good. I like that. Get down to business. Listen, I been hanging around here for weeks and you're the first promisin' new face to show up. Now, being you're from the DEA, there's a C-note in it for you if you can help."

"A C-note?" said Heller. "A credit?"

"No, no, no. You guys can't have the credit. That's mine! Look, I got a contract on Gunsalmo Silva."

Heller must have made a movement. Jimmy "The Gutter" darted a hand into his jacket, about to pull a rod. But Heller had merely whipped out a notebook and pen. "Geez, pal," said Jimmy "The Gutter," "don't DO that!"

"Now," said Heller, pen poised. "What did you say his name was? Spell it."

"G-U-N-S-A-L-M-O S-I-L-V-A, as in *dead man*. You see, he was a bodyguard to Don 'Holy Joe' Corleone and we got an idea that he put the finger on his own boss and maybe even pulled the trigger a few times himself. The family is *very* upset."

"Family upset," muttered Heller, writing.

"Good, I figured you'd have an 'in' with the local fuzz."

"And who do I send the information to, if you're not around?"

The hood scratched his head, just a shadow of movement. The light was very bad. "Why, I guess you could put it through to Babe Corleone, that's 'Holy Joe's' ex. That's Apartment P—Penthouse—136 Crystal Parkway, Bayonne, New Jersey. Phone's unlisted but it's KLondike 5-8291."

Heller had written it all down. He closed the notebook and was putting it and the pen away. "All right. Too bad his family is upset. If I see him, I'll tell him."

The effect was electric!

The hood started to go for his heater. Then he halted the motion. "Wait a minute," he said. He took Heller by the arm and steered him into a pool of light and looked at him.

Absolute disgust contorted the pockmarked face of Jimmy "The Gutter" Tavilnasty. "Why, you're just a kid! One of them God (bleeped) leftover flower nuts out here looking around for some free junk! You can't be more than sixteen or seventeen! Go home to your mama and leave a man's world alone!"

The hood gave Heller a shove. He spat at Heller's feet. He turned his back and stalked away.

Heller just stood there.

I myself was surprised. Doctor Crobe was wrong. He had pointed out that Heller would look young. He had said that at twenty-six, Heller would look like an Earthman of eighteen or nineteen. The health of his unblemished skin had lowered that. People would think he was just tall for his age the way some kids are!

Then I hugged myself. Oh, this was better than I had planned! You have to realize that, on Earth, they don't take kids seriously. It's almost a crime for a man to be seventeen!

Heller, after a bit, walked on. It was too bad Spurk had never put a feeling indicator in the lineup. Heller must feel about one inch tall!

There was a bar ahead. There are very few in Afyon—really the place is no city. And the bars are not much. The men hang out there during the day, taking up chairs and nursing coffee and reading newspapers. The dumb proprietors don't object.

Heller walked in. And I suddenly realized he didn't have any money to order anything with. I hoped he'd forget he only had credits on him and couldn't produce them. If he did, I could seize him for a violation of Space Code Number a-36-544 M Section B and even imprison him for making the presence of an extraterrestrial known. I made a mental note to be on the watch for such. That pen and notebook had been a near breach but wouldn't stand up in a charge. Money would.

The proprietor was the usual greasy, mustached Turk. He was taking his time. The place was practically empty as it was very late for Afyon and the proprietor had nothing else to do. He finally came over to Heller at the counter.

In English, Heller said, "Could you give me a glass of water?"

The Turk said, *"Ingilizce,"* and shook his head to indicate he didn't speak it. The Hells he didn't. Half the people around here did. He started to walk off and then I saw a light come into his eyes, followed closely by a cunning look.

Now, it is a funny thing about Earth races. From one race to the next, they rarely can tell how old anyone is. And Heller might look seventeen to an American, but a Turk would not notice that. They think all foreigners look alike!

At last I began to see the fruits of the rumor I had had Faht Bey plant. The proprietor changed his mind. He reached under the counter and got a somewhat dirty glass and he filled it with water from a jug. But he didn't put it in front of Heller. He carried it over to one of the many empty tables and pulled back a chair and pointed.

Heller, the fool, went over and sat down. Now, while the water in Turkey is usually pretty drinkable, that dirty glass gave me hopes. Maybe Heller would come down with cholera!

The proprietor went straight over to a telephone at the far end of the room. And then I found out something very interesting: the audio-respondo-mitter, not being tuned to his ear channels, could evidently hear what was going on in the room better than Heller! All I had to do was advance the audio gain. While it brought up the room noises uncomfortably high, you could pick out what you wanted to hear. What a nice rig for spies! Which is to say, the handler of spies. An ambulant bug! I was beginning to really love this rig.

The proprietor just said three words in Turkish: "He is here." And he hung up the phone.

But Heller was not drinking the water. From his pocket he had pulled half a dozen poppies! He put them in the glass!

Oh, how sweet, I sneered. He had bought the lie that this type was for the flower markets and he had picked himself a bouquet! Well, they do go in for a lot of flowers on Voltar. And come to remember, some of the estates on Manco—was it Atalanta?— specialized in breeding new varieties. Lombar had even once considered bringing seeds back and growing the poppies at home but he had been given pause by the fact that a new variety of blossom always produced enthusiasm amongst the flower fans and one could see these from air surveillance too easily. I also dimly recall there was some problem with a seed virus that attacked poppies. But anyway, Heller was indulging nostalgia. Probably homesick for pretty flowers.

He was certainly intrigued by them. He stroked their leaves as they sat there in the glass. He smelled them.

I lost interest in what he was doing and was suddenly very interested in how he looked. By peripheral vision, a big mirror was showing his image.

They had given him clothes too small! Even though they might not have had his size, I was certain this was intentional. The sleeves of the shirt and jacket were three inches too short. The shoulders pinched way in. They had given him no tie and he had just buttoned the shirt.

Now, Kemal Ataturk had made it against the law to wear Turkish national costumes and had forced the whole country into Western dress. He had even put people in prison for wearing the red Turkish *fez*. And as a result, the Turks, with no tailors for it, have since looked about as sloppy as anyone ever.

But Heller was worse!

He had gotten cement dust on him climbing that rock. He had evidently torn his jacket. He had mud on his shoes from the poppy fields.

He looked like a complete bum!

Where, I gloated, was the spiffy Royal officer now? Where were the shimmering lounge suits? Where was the natty working cover suit and the little red racing cap? Where was that fashion plate in Fleet full dress that would make the girls faint?

Oh, I gloated! Were our roles reversed now! On Voltar I was the underdog, the uncouth, the tramp. Not on Earth! I glanced down at my lovely gangster outfit. And then I looked back at Heller, a slovenly, dirty tramp!

This was *my* planet, not his!

And there he was, my prisoner. He had no funds to buy any clothes, to go anywhere.

"Heller," I said aloud in gloating glee, "I've got you just where I want you. And in my fondest dreams, I never thought you could look that bad! A dirty, penniless bum in a stinking slum café! Welcome to Planet Earth, Heller, you and your fancy ways. Everyone does MY bidding here, not yours! Our roles have reversed utterly! And it's about time!"

Chapter 11

What a stupid, untrained "special agent"!

Didn't he realize the danger he was putting himself in? Yet, there he was, in the center of the planet's opium trade, sitting in a cheap bar, a stranger in the place, a foreigner, his back to the door, and a bouquet of opium poppies in front of him! Just asking for it! And no way to get out of trouble if anything did happen. No connections. No friends. No money. And he didn't even speak Turkish! What a child. I could almost feel sorry for him.

Heller sat there for a bit, looking at the flowers. From time to time he rearranged them.

Then he took one of them, a gaudy, orange blossom and idly began to pull off its petals. I wondered if he was nervous. I certainly would have been in such a spot as that!

An opium poppy has a big black ball in the center. Really, that's the bulk of the flower. He had it stripped. He smelled it. Silly performance: fragrance comes from petals, not the stamen.

Heller put it aside. He took another flower from the glass. He got out a piece of paper. He laid the whole flower on half the sheet and straightened out its petals. Then he folded the paper over, covering it.

Then he took his fist and banged the package!

I really laughed. That isn't the way you press flowers. You put them in between two sheets of paper and you gently let them flatten and you put it away to dry. You don't bang it with your fist. He didn't even know how to press flowers: he should have asked his mother!

He opened the paper and of course the whole thing was a complete mess. The huge center ball had simply squashed! That isn't the way to handle an opium poppy. You gently scrape the ball and you get the sap and then you boil it and you have morphine!

He must have realized that wasn't how it was done for he just emptied the squashed mess on the table, folded the paper and put it in his pocket.

He looked up. People had been drifting in: Turks of the area, dressed in their sloppy jackets, tieless white shirts, unpressed pants. Maybe twenty of them had come in, a strange crowd for this time of night. I realized that the word had spread. They just sat down at tables, not ordering anything, not talking, not looking at Heller. They seemed to be waiting.

Then the front door crashed open and into the room swaggered the two top wrestlers of the area!

Now, the Turks love wrestling. It is a national sport. They wrestle in any style. They are big and they are tough and they are good! So that was who Faht Bey had called! The wrestling champs!

The bigger one, a formidable hulk named Musef, swaggered to the middle of the room. The other one, named Torgut, sauntered over to the wall behind Heller's back. Torgut was carrying a short piece of pipe.

About fifteen more townsmen came in behind the wrestlers, avid expectancy on their faces.

The proprietor yelped in Turkish, "Not in here! Outside, outside!"

"Be quiet, old woman," said Musef insultingly.

The proprietor, faced with that growl and about three hundred pounds of famed muscle, got very quiet.

Musef walked over to Heller. "You speak Turkish? No." He shifted to badly accented English. "You speak English? Yes."

Heller just sat there looking at him.

"My name," and Musef hit himself on the chest, "is Musef. You know me?"

With a slight incredulity, Heller said, "A yellow-man!" And indeed, now that I thought about it, Musef and Torgut did bear some dim resemblance to the yellow-men of the Confederacy. Not surprising, since the Turks come from Mongolia.

But it was the wrong thing to say. Musef snarled, "You say I yellow?"

There was a ripple through the audience as those who didn't speak English got those who did to tell them what was being said. And then it had to be clarified for some that "yellow" meant "coward" in English. And believe me, eyebrows really shot up and eyes went round with anticipation. You could almost hear them pant.

Musef pretended to be outraged that Heller was not saying anything further. So he spat, "You want to fight?"

Heller glanced around. Torgut was hefting the iron pipe over by the wall. It was indeed a hostile crowd.

Heller looked at Musef. He said, "I never fight . . ."

There was an explosion of laughter in the room.

Instantly Musef picked up the glass and threw the water and flowers in Heller's face.

"I was about to say," said Heller, "I never fight without a wager!"

There was more laughter. But Musef thought he saw a way to make money. After all, how could he lose with Torgut and an iron pipe back of Heller. "A wager!" guffawed Musef. Then, "All right. We wager! Five hundred lira! You," he yelled at the crowd, "make sure that it gets paid!"

The crowd screamed with laughter. "We will!" they shouted in English and Turkish. It gave them a perfectly legal excuse to pick the "DEA man's" pocket when he lost. There is nobody quite as cunning as a Turk unless it is a crowd of Turks!

And before anyone knew what was happening, Musef reached out and grabbed Heller's collar and yanked him to the center of the floor! It was not hard to do. Heller, here on Earth, weighed only 193 pounds and Musef weighed 300!

Somehow Musef's hands must have slipped. Heller and Musef were standing there in the middle of the floor, facing each other. The crowd, on its feet and roaring for blood, made a circle.

Musef reached with both arms. Heller weaved sideways. I knew what Musef was trying to do. The standard Turkish action of engaging is for each opponent to seize the other, with both hands, on either side of the neck. What happens after that is anybody's war.

Musef made a second try. He got his hands on Heller's shoulders!

Heller got his hands on Musef's shoulders!

The first seconds of such a contest is a jostle for position.

And then I didn't understand it. Heller had his two hands on the shoulders of the Turk but Heller's fingers were hidden by the Turk's head. I couldn't see that Heller was doing anything. But neither was the Turk!

Heller's hands just seemed to be rooted there.

The Turk was trying to throw his arms out to get Heller's hands loose. You could see the muscles jump with the Turk's effort. The Turk's face was contorting in savage hatred. But there was enormous strain there!

The two seemed to rotate a few degrees. Now there was a wall mirror in Heller's view. And in that mirror, Torgut was plainly visible. Torgut, iron pipe in hand, was parting the crowd, approaching Heller's back.

I realized then why Heller's hands weren't coming loose. Turks usually smear themselves with olive oil before they wrestle but tonight there was nothing there to make Heller's hands slip on the Turk's shoulders and neck.

You could almost hear the muscles grind with the effort of the two wrestlers.

Ah, I had it. Musef could see Torgut and Musef was simply holding Heller in position until the partner could bring that iron pipe down on Heller's blond head!

The crowd was going wild, cheering Musef on.

Torgut was very near now.

Suddenly, using his grip on Musef to support the forward part of his body, Heller went back and horizontal!

His feet hit Torgut in the chest!

The thud of that double blow was loud above the yelling room.

Torgut flew backwards as though propelled from a cannon. He took three members of the crowd with him!

They landed with a crash against the wall!

The impact shattered the mirror on the opposite wall!

Musef tried to take advantage of the weight shift. He drew back a forearm to hit Heller in the face.

I couldn't see what happened. But Heller's hands clenched suddenly inward.

Musef screamed like a crushed dog!

Heller hadn't done anything to cause that. He had just closed his hands in tighter.

The huge Turk buckled like a falling building and landed like rubble on the floor!

The crowd was silent.

They were incredulous.

They became hostile!

Heller stood there in the middle of the floor. Torgut was a half-dead mess against the far wall, blood trickling down his shoulders. Three town Turks were getting themselves untangled from chairs near him. Musef was collapsed and moaning at Heller's feet.

With his two hands, Heller straightened up his own collar. "And now," he said, in a conversational voice, "who pays me the five hundred lira?"

Now, money is a very important subject to the impoverished Turk. If Heller had had any sense, he would have simply walked out. But he doesn't have any training in this sort of thing. I would have been running already.

The townsmen jabbered together. Then one said in English, "It wasn't a fair bet. You, a foreigner, took advantage of these two poor boys!"

"Yes," said an old Turk. "You exploited them!"

"No, no, no," said the proprietor, getting brave. "You owe me for all this damage. You started the fight!"

Heller looked them over. "You mean you are not going to see that an honest wager is paid?"

The crowd sensed its numbers. It started to edge forward hostilely toward Heller. One tough-looking fellow was nearest Heller.

"Are you going to see that the bargain is kept?" said Heller to the nearest man.

The crowd was closer. Somebody had Torgut's iron pipe.

"Ah, well," said Heller. And before anyone could block him he grabbed Musef off the floor and with a wide sweeping movement threw him at the proprietor!

Musef landed against the counter. Glasses and bottles and kegs soared into the air. The counter fell over on the proprietor!

Every man in that room had ducked!

As the noise died down, Heller said, "Honor seems to be something you have never heard of." He shook his head sadly. "And I did want to try some of your beer."

Heller walked out.

The crowd had recovered a bit. They surged to the door after him and there they began to throw bottles and yell derisively and do catcalls.

Heller just kept on walking.

I saw that he was limping.

I really hugged myself. He had been utterly routed! His crude scheme to get some money had failed.

Ah, indeed, the roles had reversed. He was the dog and I the hero here.

I went to bed singing—while Heller limped the miles back to base, broke, outcast and alone.

PART THIRTEEN

Chapter 1

The next morning, I felt pretty cheery, I can tell you. I got up early and put on an orange silk shirt and black pants and a cobra-skin belt, with shoes to match.

I had melon and *cacik*—cucumber salad with yogurt, garlic and olive oil dressing—and I washed it down with very sweet coffee. Delicious. When I criticized it to the cook, he looked so woebegone, I really had to laugh. The whole staff looked woebegone, having been up all night trying to find something they had not done. The joke was on them. I really laughed.

Then I got busy with a big sheet of paper. I am a long way from a draftsman but I sure knew what I wanted. It was up to somebody else to try to make it out.

The school owned another piece of property a little bit closer to town. It had been planned to build a staff recreational hall there but I had other ideas.

I was designing a hospital. It would be one story, with a basement. It would have numerous wards and operating rooms. It would also have a parking lot. It would be surrounded by a wire fence made to look like a hedge. And in the basement it would have numerous private rooms nobody would suspect were there. It would have an Earth-type security system. Every room would be bugged.

I was going to register it as the "World United Charities Mercy and Benevolent Hospital." I was going to make my fortune with it. They really train you in the Apparatus. "When you mean total evil," one of my professors in Apparatus school used to say, "always put up a façade of total good." It is an inviolable maxim of any competent government.

Finally, I finished it, hoping I could make the plan out myself —I had scratched out and changed quite a bit.

Then I had to write a bunch of orders: one to our Voltar resident engineer to dig some tunnels to it; another to our Istanbul attorney firm to get it registered real fast; another to the World Health Operation for the attorneys to forward which said it was a magnificent donation to the world of health and please could we use their name, too; and another to the Rockecenter Foundation for a grant "for the poor children of Turkey"—they always hand out money if their executives can get a slice back and if Rockecenter can get his name up in lights as a great humanitarian (hah! that would be the day!).

The last letter was just a dispatch. Here at the Blito-P3 base they have the usual Officers Council, chaired by the base commander, that is supposed to pass on new projects. But, as Section Chief of 451 *and* Inspector General Overlord, *I* surely didn't need *their* consent. I just told them that this is what was going to happen and they could lump it. To Hells with their staff recreation. And besides, didn't the Grand Council Order say to spread a little advanced technology on the planet? So they could go to Hells and do what they were told. I stamped it with my identoplate loud and plain. They knew better than to trifle with me. I even added a postscript to that effect.

It was quite a relief to get all this tedious work done. So I called for the housekeeper.

When she came in, hollow-eyed from no sleep, scared as to what I might want now, I said, "Melahat Hanim" (a very polite way of addressing a woman in Turkey is to add "hanim" to her name—it flatters them; they have no souls, you know), "has the beautiful lady arrived from Istanbul?"

She wrung her hands and shook her head negative. So I said, "Get out of here, you female dropping of camel dung," and wondered what else I could do to while away the hours before ten. It's no use going to town too early—the roads are too cluttered with carts.

Then I thought I had better check on Heller. I didn't much care to know what he was doing in the ship so I hadn't even bothered to rig the 831 Relayer.

The recorder was grinding away, the viewer was off. So I figured I might as well start early. I turned the viewer on and began to spot-check forward.

Last night he had simply walked home and gone aboard. Limping! Must have hurt his foot.

Speeding forward, I heard a shrill whistle on the strip. So I went back over it at normal speed.

I saw the airlock open and then, way down at the foot of the ladder, there was Faht Bey, holding a hull resonator against the tug's plates.

"There you are," said Faht Bey, looking up. "I'm the base commander, Officer Faht. Are you the Crown inspector?"

"I'm on Grand Council orders, if that's what you mean. Come on up."

Faht Bey was not about to climb that eighty feet of rickety ladder from the bottom of the hangar to the airlock on the vertical ship. "I just wanted to see you."

"I want to see you, too," said Heller, looking down the ladder. "The clothes in your costume section are too short and the shoes there are about three sizes too small for me." I was disappointed. He hadn't hurt his foot, it was tight shoes. Well, you can't always grab the pot.

"That's what I wanted to see you about," Faht Bey yelled up at him. "The people in town are looking all over for somebody that fits your description. They say he waylaid two popular characters at different times in an alley and beat them up with a lead pipe. One has a cracked neck and the other a broken arm and fractured skull. They had to be shipped into Istanbul to be hospitalized."

"How'd you know it fits my description?" said Heller. My Gods, he was nosy. "This is the first time you've seen me."

"Gris said what you looked like," said this (bleep) Faht Bey. "So please don't take it badly. It's my guess you'll be leaving here in two or three days." Well, (bleep) him! He must have read Lombar's order to Raht! "So I've got to invoke my authority on the subject of base security and ask you not to leave this hangar while you're here."

"Can I wander around the hangar?" said Heller.

"Oh, that's all right, just as long as you don't leave the outside-world end of the tunnels."

Heller waved him an airy hand. "Thanks for the tip, Officer Faht."

And that was the end of that one. I sped ahead to the next light flash that showed the door was open.

Heller was going down the ladder, zip, zip. He landed at the bottom with a tremendous clank. It startled me until I realized he was wearing hull shoes with the metal bars loose.

He started clickety-clacking around, a little notebook held in his hand, making jots and touching his watch now and then. He went around the whole perimeter of the hangar, clickety-clack, POP. I knew what he was doing. He was just amusing himself surveying the place. These engineers! They're crazy. Maybe he was practicing his sense of direction or something.

I kept speeding the strip ahead. But that was all he was up to. He'd stop by doors and branch tunnels and make little notes and loud POPs.

Now and then he'd meet an Apparatus personnel. The first couple, he gave them a cheerful good morning. But they turned an icy shoulder to him. After that he didn't speak to anyone. My rumor was working!

He got into some side tunnels and took some interest in the dimensions of the detention cells. It would be hard to tell they were cells for they were not as secure as Spiteos—no wire. They just had iron bars set into the rock. The base crew who had redesigned the place had overdone it on detention cells—they had made enough for hundreds of people and never at any time were there more than a dozen. They were empty now.

Speeding ahead, I saw that he had stopped and I went back to find what was interesting him so much.

He was standing in front of the storage room doors. They

are very massive. There are about fifty of them in a curving line that back the hangar itself, a sort of corridor. The corridor has numerous openings into the hangar itself.

They were all locked, of course. And the windows in the doors, necessary to circulate the air and prevent mold, are much too high up to see through. I was fairly certain he would not even guess what they contained.

Lombar, when the pressure was put on Turkey to stop growing opium, had really outdone himself. He had ordered so much of it bought, it would have glutted the market had it all been released. Now, there it was, nicely bagged in big sacks. Tons and tons and tons of it.

But even if one jumped up and got a look through the windows, there was nothing to be seen. Just piles of bags.

Heller examined the floor. But what was there to find? Just the truck wheel wear.

He bent over and picked up some dust and then, to wipe his hand, I suppose, he put his hand in his pocket and brought it out clean.

Unconcerned, he just went on clickety-clacking along with the occasional POP.

Again he stopped. He was sniffing the air. He was looking at a huge barred door. And he certainly wouldn't be able to get in there —it was the heroin conversion plant!

He went up to it and knocked. How silly. Nobody was in there. It only operates once in a while. But still he knocked, very sharp raps.

Heller must have given it up. He made some notes. Just some figures. Pointless.

And there he went again, clickety-clacking, POP along.

He'd stop by an exit tunnel, go down it a bit and come back. I had to laugh. He even went up the exit tunnel which led to my room! He could never suspect the villa lay on the other side. He didn't even try the switch which opened the door, didn't even see it, apparently. It would have brought him within ten feet of where I was sitting.

Some spy!

It had only taken him an hour.

Then he'd done a little sketch, all neat, very fast. Apparently there was nobody near to give it to, to show them how good he was—or maybe he had understood they weren't talking to him. He just climbed back up into the ship.

And that was that.

I had to laugh. What couldn't he have discovered if he had been a real trained spy! And what did he have? A silly map he could have gotten in the base construction office anyway.

I packed it up. It had turned ten and I had really important things to do—namely, making Soltan Gris rich!

Chapter 2

The villa had three cars, all more or less in what Turkey considers running condition. I went out and considered them. The Datsun pickup was more or less full of the remains of vegetables from the morning marketing. The Chevy station wagon had an empty gas tank. That left the French Renault sedan. I think the car had been left over from the wreckage of World War I: they believe in making cars last in Turkey.

The body was dented from several direct hits, the windshield was cracked. It had to be cranked because the battery was dead. It kicked and had been known to break somebody's arm, so I got Karagoz to crank it. And off I went to town.

I dreamed that soon I would buy a long, black, bulletproof limousine, the kind gangsters have. I even knew where there was one: a Turkish general had been killed in the 1963 military take-over and the car was for sale cheap.

The Renault, however, had its advantages. It steered erratically and could be counted on to drive carts off the road. They are stupid gigs, usually heavily laden, drawn by donkeys, and they really clutter the place up. If you swerve in close to the donkey as you pass, the cart winds up in the ditch. It is very comical. You can watch the driver shaking his fist in the rearview mirror.

I was just enjoying my fifth cart upset when I noticed I was passing Afyonkarahisar: the vast bulk of the rock rose 750 feet in the air.

Abruptly, I pulled to the left and stopped. I blocked a chain of carts coming from town, but they could wait. I leaned out and looked up the face of the rock.

Even though it was powdered with cement dust, you could see that it had handholds if you didn't mind losing a few fingernails. Still, I would never attempt to climb it. Never. And in the dark? Absolutely never!

My interest in this was a matter of character, not the character of Heller—I already knew he was crazy—but in the character of a man who had suddenly become vital in my plans of riches: Jimmy "The Gutter" Tavilnasty. He said he had seen Heller climbing it. Obviously, the feat was impossible. Therefore Jimmy "The Gutter" Tavilnasty was a pathological liar. Good. I would watch it when I spoke with him later today and made him my offer.

The engine had died so I got out and cranked it. The drivers of the halted carts were screaming and shaking their fists. I screamed and shook my fist back, got in and drove the rest of the way to town.

The Mudlick Construction Company was my destination. It has branch offices all around Turkey. It does a lot of government contracting and therefore must be crooked. I double-parked and went in.

My business was soon transacted. The manager took my sketch and estimated the cost. When he heard I wanted the hospital built in six weeks, he raised the price. I walked out and he rushed to the sidewalk and brought me back and halved the amount. But he said he would have to build it of mud, the favorite construction material of this district. I told him it had to be of first-class materials. We compromised by planning to build it half of mud and half of proper materials. Then I doubled the price and told him he would owe me half, as a kickback. We signed the contract and parted firm friends.

When I came out two motorists were glaring at me so I glared back and cranked the car and drove to the Giysi Modern Western Clothing Our Specialty Shop for Men and Gentlemen. I would much rather shop in Istanbul but I hadn't much time and I knew I would have to dress right for my call on Jimmy "The Gutter"

Tavilnasty. It was vital I make an impression.

The selection was pretty poor, really. But it is the law that Turks must not look like Turks but dress like Americans or Italians and I was lucky. They had just received a shipment from Hong Kong of the very latest Chicago fashions.

I found a gray suit, a black shirt, a white tie, black and white oxfords and a gray fedora hat. They all more or less fit. I changed in back, short-changed the clerk by palming and swapping a five-hundred lira note for a five at the last instant, glared him into thinking it was his mistake and was on my way.

I looked pretty sharp as I admired myself in a shop window reflection. Just like a film gangster.

Rapidly, I made a round of hotels, looking for Jimmy "The Gutter" Tavilnasty. It does not take long to do in Afyon. There aren't many hotels. The clerks shook their heads. No trace of him.

Well, I had another errand. I went to the Pahalt General Merchandise Emporium. It is patronized by peasants and they certainly get charged *pahalt,* which in Turkish means "high-priced." In a back room, I had a little talk with the proprietor.

I told him I wanted him to put up a sign that said he bought gold. He said the gold mining districts, such as they were, were further north. I said that didn't matter: at his prices, the women of the family had to sell their jewelry, didn't they? And he said that was true. So I told him that any gold he bought from said impoverished peasants, at London prices, I would buy from him at a ten percent markup. He said there wouldn't be much, but I said how much there was a secret between us and so we made the sign and he put it up.

Now, I had a way to explain all the gold I was about to dump on the market when the *Blixo* arrived. I could point out that gold was bought in Afyon. When I unloaded chunks of mine in Istanbul, I would probably never bother to buy the proprietor's gold.

In the pleasant noonday sun, I sat basking double-parked on the street, trying to figure out where Jimmy "The Gutter" had gotten to. Some carts were blocked. A policeman came along and disturbed my concentration. He bent over and stuck his bristling mustache in the window. Then he said, "Oh, it's you!"

Well, that was quite a compliment, the way he said it. Sort of alarmed. They think I am the nephew of the original subofficer that was the war hero. After all, I live in his house. He moved on rather quickly to bawl out the carts I was blocking. Oh, it was good to be home!

It must have sparked my wits. Where would a gangster go in this town? Of course, the Saglanmak Rooms! Now, *saglanmak*, in Turkish, means "to be obtained" or "available." But there is another word, *saklanmak*, which means "to hide oneself." Now, according to that great master, Freud, the unconscious mind can twist words into meanings closer to the intent of the person. These are called "Freudian slips." This was what must have happened. No matter that he probably didn't speak Turkish, Jimmy "The Gutter" Tavilnasty had made a Freudian slip.

Besides, it was the only place in town the Mafia ever stayed.

I drove through the gathering crowd of fist-shaking peasants and proceeded to the Saglanmak Rooms. But I was cunning now. I double-parked a block away and cased the joint.

There was a balcony that ran around the outside of the second floor and a stairway to it—a vital necessity if one had to get out a window and escape quickly.

I went in. I walked up to the desk. The clerk was a young Turk with his hair plastered down. He had earlier told me no such name was in the hotel. I didn't bother with him. I reached over the desk and into the niche for the box of room cards. The clerk stood back.

I went through the cards. No Jimmy "The Gutter" Tavilnasty.

He had said he had been around for weeks. I checked dates. And there it was! John Smith!

"I thought," I sneered at the clerk, "that you said Tavilnasty wasn't here!"

He was reaching for the phone. I clamped his wrist. "No," I said. "He is a friend. I want to surprise him."

The clerk frowned.

I laid a ten-lira note on the desk.

The frown lightened.

I laid a fifty-lira note on the desk.

The clerk smiled.

"Point out the room," I said.

He indicated the one at the exact top of the steps on the second floor.

"He is in?" I asked.

The clerk nodded.

"Now, here is what I want you to do. Take a bottle of Scotch—the Arab counterfeit will do—and two glasses and put them on a tray. Just three minutes after I leave this desk, you take that tray up to his room and knock."

I kept laying hundred-lira notes on the counter until the clerk smiled. It was a seven-hundred-lira smile.

I had him note the time. I synchronized my watch.

I went back out the front door.

In a leisurely fashion, but silently, I went up the outside steps.

With care, I marked the exact outside window of the indicated room. It was open.

I waited.

Exactly on time, a knock sounded on the door.

A bed creaked.

I stole to the window.

Sure enough, there was my man. He had a Colt .45 in his hand and he was cat-footing to the door. His back was to me at the window.

I knew it would be this way. Mafia hit men lead nervous lives.

Jimmy "The Gutter" Tavilnasty reached for the knob, gun held on the door. That was my cue!

The door was swinging open.

I stepped through the window.

I said, in a loud voice, "Surprise!"

He half-turned in shock.

He sent a bullet slamming into the wall above me!

The shot had not even begun to echo before he charged out the door.

The effect was catastrophic. He collided with the clerk and tray!

In a scramble of Scotch and glasses, arms, legs and two more inadvertently triggered shots, they went avalanching down the stairs.

With a thud and final tinkle they wound up at the bottom.

I trotted down the stairs after them and plucked the gun from Jimmy "The Gutter's" stunned hand.

"What a way to greet an old pal," I said. That's the way to handle them. Purely textbook psychology. It says to get them off-balance.

Tavilnasty was not only off-balance, he was out cold.

The clerk lay there looking at me in horror. I realized I had Tavilnasty's gun pointed at him. I put the safety on. I said, "You were clumsy. You broke that bottle of Scotch. Now get up and get another one on the house."

The clerk scrambled away.

I picked up Tavilnasty and got him over to a small back table in the lounge. He was coming around.

The clerk, shaking, brought in another bottle of Scotch and two glasses.

I handed Tavilnasty his gun.

I poured him a drink. He drank it.

Then his ugly, pockmarked face was really a study. "What the hell was that all about?"

"I just didn't want to get shot," I said.

He couldn't quite understand this. I poured him another drink. I tried another tack. "I could have killed you and I didn't. Therefore that proves I am your friend."

He considered this and rubbed a couple of bruises on his head. I poured him another drink.

"How's Babe?" I said.

He really stared at me.

"Oh, come on," I said. "Babe Corleone, my old flame."

"You know Babe?"

"Sure, I know Babe."

"Where did you know Babe?"

"Around," I said.

He drank the Scotch.

"You from the DEA?"

I laughed.

"You from the CIA?"

I laughed.

"You from the FBI?"

I poured him another drink. "I'm from the World Health Operation. I'm going to make you your fortune."

He drank the drink.

"Now listen carefully," I said. "We are building a new hospital. It will be in full operation in about two months. We have new techniques of plastic surgery. We can change fingerprints, dental plates, larynxes, facial bones."

"No (bleep)?"

"Absolutely. Nobody else can do it but us. Nobody will know. Hippocratic Oath and so forth."

"Is that like the Fifth Amendment?"

"Absolutely," I said. "But down to business. You know the Atlantic City mob. You know lots of mobs. Right?"

"Right," he said.

"Now, those mobs have people hiding out all over the place. Those people can't show their faces because they are in all the fingerprint and police files of the FBI and Interpol. Right?"

"Right."

"If those people are smuggled in here to the World United Charities Mercy and Benevolent Hospital, we will physically change their identity, give them new birth certificates and passports, all for a stiff fee, of course, and you personally will get twenty percent of what they pay."

He found a paper napkin and laboriously started figuring. Finally, he said, "I'd be rich."

"Right."

"There's one thing wrong," he said. "I can spread the word. I can get big names in here in droves. But I can't do it."

"Why not?"

"Because I *have* a job. There's a contract out."

"I know," I said. "Gunsalmo Silva."

"How'd you know that?"

"I got sources." I fixed him with a lordly stare—down the nose. "Gunny Silva won't be back here for seven weeks. So you got six weeks to recruit some trade for the hospital."

"I'd need money for expenses. I can't hang this on Babe."

"Take your expenses out of the advance payments," I said.

"Hey!" he said, smiling.

"And," I said, "if you bring in lots of trade and payments ready to begin in two months, I'll throw something else in."

"Yeah?"

"Yeah. I'll give you Gunsalmo Silva on a silva platter!"

"No (bleep)?"

"Set him up for you like a clay pigeon!"

With tears of gratitude in his eyes, he held out his hand, "Buster, you got yourself a deal!"

Ah, psychology works every time!

A bit later I returned to my car, fought my way through the crowd protesting the street blockage, cranked up and drove away.

I felt I was driving on air!

Soltan Gris, a.k.a. Sultan Bey, was on his road to becoming filthy rich!

And, after all, hadn't the Grand Council said to spread a little technology around on this planet? Where it would really do some good?

Chapter 3

The sun was hot, the sky was clear, as I hurtled down the road.

Then I remembered that I even had a dancing girl coming today!

My prospects seemed so brilliant that I could not help doing a thing I almost never do. I burst into song:

> *Frankie and Johnny were lovers.*
> *Oh, my Gods, how they could love.*
> *They swore to be true to each other.*
> *As true as the stars above. . . .*

There was an obstruction. It was a string of ten laden camels. They were humping and grumbling along, but I didn't see any driver. The horn of the Renault was busted so I had to veer out into the other lane to see what was at the head of this parade.

Aha! I thought so!

Around here they sometimes put a lead rope on a donkey and the animal apparently knows where to go and he just leads the hooked-up string of camels to their destination. Shows you how dumb camels are when even a jackass is brighter than they are!

Here was my chance!

I resumed singing at the top of my voice:

> *He was my man!*
> *But he done me wrong!*

I swerved in tight past the donkey. It was either my bump on his nose or it may have been the singing.

He dropped the lead rope, brayed and took off!

Ten camels exploded. They went bucking off the road into the sunflower field, spraying packs in all directions, trying to follow the donkey.

Oh, did I laugh!

I drew up at the International Agricultural Training Center for Peasants, knocked over a No Parking sign that shouldn't have been there and bounced into the base commander's office.

The contrast between his face and my mood was extreme.

He moaned; he held his head in his hands a moment. Then he looked up. "Officer Gris, can't we possibly have a little less commotion around here?"

"What's a No Parking sign?" I said, loftily.

"No. Not that. Last night there was that fight and today our agents in town tell us there are complaints from cart drivers, complaints from the police on your double-parking and just a moment ago I had a call that you and some gangster were shooting up a hotel. Please, Officer Gris. We're not supposed to be so visible here. Before you came, it was all——"

"Nonsense!" I cut him off sharply. "You were not in tune with this planet! You were becoming hicks and hayseeds! You weren't keeping up to it—you weren't with it. You leave such things to me. I am the expert on Blito-P3 sociological behaviorism! You should watch their movies. You should even go to see some of the movies they make in Turkey! They do nothing but shoot people and blow things up! But I have no time now to educate you in the psychological cultural cravings of this place. I'm here on business."

I threw the pack of contracts down on his desk and he picked them up wearily with a what-now shake of his overpadded head.

"Hospital?" he said. "A half a million dollars?"

"Exactly," I said. "You leave the statecraft to me, Faht Bey."

"This hasn't been passed by our local Officer's Council. Our financial agent will faint!"

I knew that financial agent. He was a refugee from Beirut,

Lebanon, one of their top bankers before a war wrecked the banking industry there and ran him out. A very wily Lebanese. "Tell him to get his hands out of the money box before I cut them off," I said. "And that reminds me. I'm low on lira. Give me thirty thousand this time."

He quivered his way into the back room and returned with thirty thousand Turkish lira. He made a notation in a book and then he stood right there and counted off ten thousand lira and put it in his pocket!

"Hold it!" I yelled at him. "Where did you get a license to steal our government's money?" It made me pretty cross, I can tell you.

He handed over the twenty thousand. "I had to give it to the girl. Out of my own cash."

"The girl? What for? Why?"

"Officer Gris, I don't know why you had her sent back to Istanbul. Our agent there said she was clean. And I saw her. She was actually a very pretty girl. She closed out her room and she flew all the way down here. Oh, she was mad! But I handled it. I went up into town: she was standing right on the street making an awful row. I gave her ten thousand lira for you—it's only ninety dollars American—and I put her on a bus so she could get back to Istanbul."

"I didn't order her sent back!" I screamed at him.

"Your friend the taxi driver said you did."

Believe me, I was mad! I stalked out of there and got the Renault started, ran over another No Parking sign just to show they couldn't trifle with me and drove toward home lickety-split, expecting that taxi driver would be there.

The Renault didn't make it. It ran out of gas. I left it in the road and walked to the villa which was only about an eighth of a mile, planning all the way what I was going to tell that taxi driver.

He wasn't there.

I gave Karagoz what-for about the car and sent him and the gardener to push it home and refused to let them push it with another car, I was so mad.

No girl.

Nothing to do.

I barricaded my door. I sulked for quite a while. And then, needing something more to get mad about, I went into the real room back of the closet and turned on the viewer.

Heller couldn't go anywhere: he didn't have any money. Heller was really no worry to me now. In a couple of days, I'd hear from Raht; we'd use the tug to take Heller to the U.S., and shortly after, he'd be arrested as an imposter and jailed. It didn't make any difference now, what he was doing. But maybe it was something I could find fault with.

And there he was, using the corridor outside the storerooms as a running track. He apparently had two bags of running weights over his right and left shoulder as I could see the weight sacks bouncing as he trotted. Him and his exercise! Adding weights to keep his muscles in trim despite the reduced gravity of this planet. Athletes!

That wasn't anything I could really snarl about, so I thought I'd better check earlier. I backed to the point I'd left him and raced it ahead.

Oho! He had been very busy! After his silly survey, he had been inside the ship no time at all.

I couldn't quite make out what he first did.

There were strange things on his legs. He stopped at the ladder bottom when he exited from the ship and adjusted something on his ankles. He had some bags and a coil of rope slung around him and I couldn't quite see the ankles because the gear swung in the way.

He went straight to the construction shop. A technician was in there, fiddling at a bench. He spotted who it was that had invaded his cave and quickly looked away, saying nothing.

"I want to borrow your hand rock-corer," said Heller in a friendly voice.

The technician shook his head.

"I'm awfully sorry," said Heller, "I'll have to insist. This appears to be earthquake country and you have an awfully big excavation here. There seems to be flaking in the rock. I am concerned for the safety of my ship. It will probably be here on and off and it must not be risked by a cave-in. So please lend me a corer."

The technician almost angrily took a small tool from a drawer and thrust it at Heller. Heller thanked him courteously and went off.

These combat engineers! Heller took a hitch on his bags and began to climb the vertical interior rock face of the hangar wall!

I knew what he had on his ankles now. They are just called "spikes" but actually they are little drills that buzz briefly as they drill a small hold in rock or other material. In the Apparatus we used them for second-story work. But engineers climb mountain faces with them. There is a drill in the toe of the boot, one on the heel, one on the outside and one on the inside of each ankle. They terrify me: you can drill a hole in your inside anklebone with them!

Heller just spiked his way up the wall. Ouch! He was wearing them on his wrists, too! Had he worn these last night to go up Afyonkarahisar? No, I was sure he hadn't. They would have been visible in the fight and a breach of the Space Code.

Ah, he was wearing them now because he was working. He had to stop and do other things. He was about fifteen feet from the hangar floor now. The corer started up. It set my teeth on edge.

With the tool, he drilled a plug out of the rock face. It was about an inch in diameter and three inches long: just a little shaft of stone.

He held it real close to his eye, inspecting it. The section exposed the rock grain. He examined it very critically. It sure looked all right to me!

He took a little hammer and with a tap, he knocked off the last half-inch of the plug, caught the fragment and put it in a bag. Then he took a can out of his shoulder sack. The label said *Rock Glue,* and very badly lettered it was.

He put a gooey piece of rock glue on the plug and put it back in the hole. He tapped it neatly with a hammer and in a moment you couldn't tell that an inspection core had been taken out.

Heller went along to his left a few feet and did the same thing. And, working swiftly, he did it again and again and again, plug after plug after plug!

Well, it was all right to watch him when he was only fifteen feet off the floor. Trouble was, he went up to fifty feet and started the same procedure and every time he looked down, I got an awful feeling. I hate heights!

So, anyway, I skipped ahead.

Heller had gotten himself clear up to the lower edge of the electronic illusion which, from there on up, gave us a mountaintop. And he said something!

I quickly turned it back and replayed it.

"Why," muttered Heller, "do all Apparatus areas stink! And not only that, why do they have to seal the airflow with an illusion so it will never air out!"

Aha! I was getting to him. He was beginning to talk to himself. A sure sign!

He lit a small flamer and turned it so it smoked. He watched the resultant behavior of the small fog. "Nope," he said, "no air can get in. By the Gods, I'll have to find the switch of this thing."

I didn't keep the strip there very long. He kept looking down and three hundred feet under him a dolly operator looked like a pebble. Stomach wrenching!

I sped ahead to find more sound. I found some and stopped. But he was just humming. That silly one about Bold Prince Caucalsia.

A bit later, he tried to talk to the hangar chief who, of course, on my rumor, ignored him. Heller finally put a hand on the man's shoulder and made him face him. "I said," said Heller, "where are the controls for the electronic illusion? I want to turn it off tonight to air the place out! You're trapping moisture in here."

"It's always on," the hangar chief snarled. "It's been on for ages. I don't even think the switches work anymore. It's running on its own power source and it won't have to be touched for a century. You want things changed around here, take it up with the base commander." And he went off snarling about routine, routine, all he needed was one more routine to clutter up his day.

Captain Stabb was over by the ship. The five Antimancos were not housed aboard the tug. They were in the berthing area of the hangar—much more comfortable and they could more easily get to town. No eighty-foot ladder. It pleased Captain Stabb immensely that Heller had been rebuffed in his passion for fresh air. Oh, he would never last in the Apparatus! These Fleet guys!

Heller went back aboard.

I sped ahead. He had apparently come out again to do some running. He was gradually lightening his weights to adjust his stride to this planet.

Silly athletes.

I shut him off and went back to glooming about my lost dancing girl. The world was against me.

Chapter 4

The following day, toward noon, I was just beginning to come out of my dumps when something else happened to free-fall me back into them.

It was a smoking hot day: the August sun had cranked the thermometer up to a Turkish 100—meaning about 105. I had been lying in a shadowy part of the yard, back of a miniature temple to Diana, the Roman Goddess of the hunt. My pitcher of iced *sira* was empty; I had gotten tired of kicking the small boy who was supposed to be fanning me, when suddenly I heard a songbird. It was a canary! A canary had gone wild! Instantly my primitive instincts kindled! I had bought, a year ago, a ten-gauge shotgun and I had never tried it out! That would handle that canary!

Instantly aquiver, I leaped up and raced to my room. I got my shotgun rapidly enough but I couldn't find the shells. And that was peculiar as they are big enough to load a cannon with. I went to my sleeping room and started threshing through my bedside drawers.

And then something happened which drove all thought of hunting from my mind.

There was an envelope pinned to my pillow!

It had not been there after I arose.

Somebody had been in this room!

But nobody had crossed the yard to my area! How had this gotten there? Flown in on the wind? There was no wind.

It was the type of envelope which is used to carry greetings in certain Voltar social circles: it gives off a subdued glitter. Had I found a snake in my bed, I would have been less surprised.

I got nerve enough generated to pick it up. It did not seem to be the exploding type.

Gingerly, as though it were hot, I extracted the card. A greeting card. A sorry-you-were-not-in-when-I-called type of card. It had handwriting on it. It said, quite elegantly:

> *Lombar wanted me to remind you now and then.*

And under that formal social script was drawn a dagger! A dagger with blood on it! A dagger with blood on it that was dripping!

I went cold as I burst into sweat.

Who could have put it there? Was it Melahat? Was it Karagoz? Could it be Faht Bey? The hangar chief? Jimmy "The Gutter"? Heller? No, no, no! Not Heller: he would be the last one Lombar would use! The small boy who had been fanning me? No, no, I had had him in sight all morning.

Where were they now?

Was I being watched this minute?

All thought of hunting vanished.

I was the hunted!

With a great effort, I made myself think. Something was obviously expected. Somebody believed I was not doing my job. And if that happened, according to Lombar's last remark, the whoever-it-was had direct orders to kill me!

I knew I must do something. Make an effort, a show of it. And fast.

I had it!

I would tell Captain Stabb to start another rumor about Heller!

I let the shotgun fall. I rushed through the back of the closet. I got the passageway door open and catapulted down it to find Stabb.

The Antimanco was nowhere around. But something else was.

The warplanes!

Two of them!

They must have arrived during the night!

They were ugly ships. A bit bigger than the tug. They were all armor. They were manned by only two. They were a more compact version of "the gun" which Lombar flew. Deadly ships, cold, black, lethal.

Rather timidly, I approached them. To get here now, when would they have had to leave Voltar? They must have been dispatched the very day Heller had bought the tug to have arrived here by now. Such ships were only a trifle faster than freighters. Lombar must have known about the tug purchase the instant it happened! He knew too much, too quickly. He must have spies planted in every . . .

A voice sounded behind me and I almost jumped out of my wits!

"We been here for hours, Gris. Where have you been?"

I turned. I was looking at a slate-hard man with slate-hard eyes. There were three others behind him. How had they gotten behind me?

They were in black uniforms and they wore red gloves. They had a red explosion on each side of their collars. And I knew what they were. In the Apparatus they are called assassin pilots. They are used on every major Apparatus battle engagement. They do not fight the enemy. They are there to make sure no Apparatus vessel runs away. If it does, if they only think it is running away, they shoot it down! With riffraff of the type that makes up the Apparatus, such measures are necessary. One has to deal with cowards. One also has to deal with mutiny. The answer is the assassin pilot. The Fleet has no such arrangements.

Their manners compare with their duties. He was omitting "officer" from his form of address to me. He did not offer to shake hands.

"That ship," and he flung a contemptuous gesture at the tug, "has no call-in beamer on it!"

Every Apparatus ship is required to have a device imbedded in its hull which an assassin ship, with a beam, can activate: it is vital so they can find an erring vessel and shoot it down.

"It was a Fleet vessel," I said, backing up.

"Listen, Gris, you wouldn't want me to report you for violations, would you?"

I backed up further. "It was just an oversight."

He stepped closer. I had never seen colder eyes. "How can anybody expect me to shoot a ship down when I can't find it? Get a call-in beamer installed in that hull!"

I tried to back up further but the hull of a warplane was at my back. I felt desperate. "I am not under your orders."

"And we," he said, "are not under yours!"

The other assassin pilot and the two copilots behind him all nodded as one, with a single jerk of their heads. They were very grim, cold professionals at their trade; they wanted things straight!

It was a bad situation. I would sometimes be in that tug. It was unarmed and unarmored. One single shot from either of these warplanes could turn the *Prince Caucalsia* into space dust in a fraction of a second.

"So, two orders," said the assassin pilot. "One: order the hangar chief to install a call-in beamer on that ship's exterior hull so secretly and in such a place that its crew will never know it is there. Two: I want that ship crippled so that it cannot leave this system on its time drives and try to outrun us."

"There's a Royal officer aboard her," I said.

"Well, decoy him away from the ship so the beamer can be put on the hull. I'll leave the crippling of her up to you as you're the best one to get inside her."

I nodded numbly. I was at a terrible disadvantage. I had left my room so fast I had not taken a gun. I had broken a firm rule never to be around Apparatus people unarmed. And then, I realized, it wouldn't have done me any good even if I had been armed. They would have complained to Lombar I was refusing his orders.

I nodded nervously.

"Then we're friends?" he said.

I nodded and offered my hand.

He raised his red-gloved fingers and slapped me across the face, hard, contemptuously.

"Good," he said. "Do it."

I raced off to give the secret order to the hangar chief. I raced up the ladder and got Heller to come out.

I took Heller to the hangar map room, out of sight of the tug.

He was in work clothes. He had been doing something inside. His red racing cap was on the back of his head. "Where'd the two 'guns' come from?" he asked.

"They're just guard ships," I said. "Stationed here. They've been away. Nothing to do with the mission." It gave me a little lift of satisfaction, thinking of what his reaction would be if he knew they were here especially to keep track of his beloved tug and shoot it down if it did anything odd or didn't return at once from a flight. I only hoped I wouldn't be aboard when they hit it: an unarmed, unarmored tug wouldn't stand a chance!

"We will probably be leaving tomorrow," I said. "While we are near maps, I wanted to show you the U.S. terrain."

"Hello," he said, looking at them. " 'U.S. Geological Survey.' It even shows the minerals!"

"And everything even down to the farmhouses," I said, glad to be able to engage his interest and prevent him from seeing what they were doing in the hangar. "We can make better farmhouse ones, of course, but the minerals are a bonus.

"Now, probably we will be landing in that field there." And I pointed to the section in southern Virginia I had seen noted on the Lombar orders.

"The town," I continued, "is named Fair Oakes. See it there? This over here is a better, more detailed map. This is Hamden County. Fair Oakes is the county seat. Now, see this building? That's the Hamden County Courthouse. The squiggles show it is on a little hill.

"All right," I said. "Now, pay attention. We will land in this field: it's a ruined plantation and nobody is ever around. The trees will mask us from any road.

"Now, you will leave the ship there, walk up this path that is indicated, pass this farmhouse, walk up the hill to the back of the courthouse and go in.

"You will be issued your birth certificate—an old clerk will be there even though it is after hours. And then you will walk down this hill and go to the bus station.

"There is a late-night bus. You will take it north to Lynchburg. You will probably change at Lynchburg and then go through Washington, D.C., and up to New York."

He was being very attentive but looking at the maps. Actually, it was hardly worth explaining what he would be doing after that. The Rockecenter, Jr. false name Lombar had set up for him would draw attention and he'd be spotted. If he registered even at a motel, somebody would be startled enough to call the local press that a celebrity was in town. But it would be no celebrity: just a false name! And then, bang! Rockecenter's connections would take over. Bye-bye Heller! It was a cunning trap Lombar had laid. There is no Delbert John Rockecenter, Junior!

"You must be sure and use the cover name at all times," I said. "America is very identity conscious. If you don't have identification, they go crazy. So be sure you announce and use your cover name when you get it. It's even a felony not to give a name to the police when they ask for it. Do you understand all that?"

"And what will this cover name be?" said Heller, still looking at the maps.

"Oh, I don't know yet," I lied. "We have to get a proper birth certificate. A name doesn't mean anything unless you can show a birth certificate. It depends on what ones are available there in the Hamden County Courthouse."

"Hey," he said, "they've got some gold marked on these maps. I was reading some books on the United States and it said the gold was all in the West. Look here. There's gold marked in Virginia. And on these other maps, there's gold in Maryland. And there's gold up here in these . . . New England? . . . states."

"Oh, that was all mined out back in what they call 'colonial' times. Way back." I didn't know much about geology but I knew that much. I'd seen it before and last year had told Raht to go dig some up and he'd laughed fit to burst. It was then he had explained the maps probably meant "had been."

"I see," said Heller. "These surveyors just noted what they call indicators: rose quartz, iron hat, serpentine schist, hornblende. But these . . . Appalachian? . . . mountains and those to the northeast are some of the oldest mountains on the planet and I guess you could find anything in them if you looked. This northern . . . New England? . . . area was all scuffed up with glaciers in times past: that's obvious from the topography. So maybe some of the glaciers cut the tops off some peaks and exposed some lodes. Country sure looks pushed around."

I kept him chattering happily about what he saw. Just a (bleeped) engineer. Sitting here while they bugged his blessed ship! Stupid beyond belief where the Apparatus was concerned. A child in the hands of espionage and covert operations experts. Why be interested in maps? The only thing he'd see for many a year to come was the inside of a penitentiary.

An hour went by. The hangar chief tossed me a signal behind Heller's back.

"All right," I said. "But there's just one thing I, as your handler, must caution you about. Book of Space Codes Number a-36-544 M Section B. Disclosure that you are an extraterrestrial is *not* authorized. You must not reveal your true identity in any way. The Voltar penalties for that would be far more severe than anything this planet could hand out. You know that and I know that. So for your own protection, I must ask you to give me your word, as a Royal officer that you will not reveal your actual identity."

"Soltan, are you trying to insult me? You are bound by those codes, too. You're not the Emperor to be laying down Voltar law in your own name. But as long as we are on this subject, you do anything to violate Space Codes, and, as a Royal officer and personally, I will have you before the Grand Council stretched so long and thin you'll sound like a chorder-beat if they pluck you."

"I was just trying to help," I said lamely. But I was laughing inside. I knew he would use the fatal name we gave him. He was so dumb, we'd even bugged his ship behind his back.

"Well, here's to a successful mission," I said, standing up and shaking him by the hand. "I am sure you will be a great agent. Just what we want."

As I went out, I looked again at the warplanes: the huge maws of their single cannon could blast away half a planet: the tug wouldn't even be a swallow for them. With a shudder, I hurried off to the hangar quarters for ship crews to find Stabb. I would spread a new rumor that Heller had secret orders to kill them all, including the assassin pilots. Maybe, then, they'd slaughter Heller before we left and I'd never again have to ride in that (bleeped) tug! I don't like warplanes and I'd detest being shot down by one.

Chapter 5

I was in no fit mood for what I received next.

With a new pitcher of iced *sira*, I was just lying back in the temple's shadow once more when, pell-mell, here came Karagoz.

"You got a caller," he said. "The taxi driver says he's got to see you right away."

I uncoiled like a striking snake. "(Bleep) him!" Here was something I could vent my venom on! "Show him into the atrium!" There was a fountain there. Maybe I could hold his head under water until he drowned!

The atrium, the courtyard which the main Roman house was built around, usually was quite bare and forbidding, a suitable place for an execution. But today, it was changed. Karagoz and the gardener had brought in some tall, vased plants; expensive new rugs draped the tiles; comfortable seats were ranged around the fountain and the play of the water made the place musical and cool. (Bleep). Wrong setting!

The taxi driver was standing there spinning his cap airily around a forefinger. He was smiling and cheerful. (Bleep)! Wrong mood!

Well, I'd soon cut him down to size! "What the Hells do you mean sending a perfectly clean girl back to Istanbul?"

He didn't seem to remember. Then he said, "Oh, *that* girl! Oh, you were lucky, Sultan Bey. The doctor found she had (bleep) and (bleep) both. A walking epidemic! A total hellcat in the bargain. You said to take her for a ride, so I got her rid back to Istanbul!"

I knew he was lying. I was just sucking in my breath to really blast him and demand a return of some lira, when this crazy nut had the nerve to sit down! In my presence! Right on a padded lounge! It took my breath away. Such gall!

But there was a sly, conspiratorial air about him. He looked at the doorway and satisfied himself that we were alone. "Officer Gris," he whispered, "I've really run into something!"

I hoped he was going to tell me he had smashed up his car completely. But he looked too cheerful. There is something about people about to whisper secrets that makes one listen.

"When that girl blew up on you," he whispered, "I knew you would be upset. I certainly didn't want to tangle with *you*."

That was better. Proper respect after all! I sat down and leaned closer to hear better. "A couple weeks ago," he continued in a low voice, "I heard of a certain fellow to the east of here, over at Bolvadin to be exact. So I ran over there in my off-time—I won't charge you for the trip because we're friends."

This was better.

"What would you say to a *real* dancing girl? Not some Istanbul whore that can just twitch her belly, but a *real* one!"

I leaned closer.

"Listen, Officer Gris. This is really wonderful. The Russians in Turkmen, over on the other side of the Caspian Sea, have been grabbing the nomads and forcing them onto collective farms. They're mopping up the whole Kara Kum Desert!

"Them as don't settle get shot. It's pretty grisly. But listen, there's a plus side to it for us." He drew very close. "Rather than live like that, guess what? The women," and he looked around carefully and lowered his voice, "are selling themselves off!"

Oh, did he have my attention now!

"These girls," he continued, "are real Turks. The Turks, you know, inhabited an area from the Caspian to Siberia at one time. They all speak the same language. They hardly even have local accents. And, Officer Gris, they've maintained all their original social customs and these girls are nomad desert girls and they are the absolute cream of all Turkish dancers! And they're also experts at . . . well . . . you know."

He came even closer. "They're virgins because the tribal customs won't have it otherwise. So there's no danger of you know what."

I was right on the edge of my seat.

"Now, what they have to do is smuggle them out from behind the Iron Curtain. They have to push them from the Kara Kum Desert to the Caspian Sea port of Cheleken. Then they are carried down to the Iranian port of Pahlevi. They cross Iran and at the border town of Rezaiyeh, they are smuggled into Turkey. They are taken to Bolvadin and she can be brought here."

He sat back. I didn't. "I am sure you can furnish identity papers. As she would be a real Turk, speaking Turkish, that's easy. Well, what do you say?"

My head was spinning! What an opportunity! And right in my line! When you're an expert in tradecraft, you can appreciate these things.

"What would she look like?" I slavered.

He looked around again. We were still alone but he lowered his voice. "He had already sold most of them. Actually, he only had just one left. And I don't think she'll be wanting takers very long." He was secretively fishing in his pocket. "Her name is Utanc." And he handed me a photograph.

Oh, Heavens, my heart almost turned over!

The face! The beautiful face!

She looked very young, possibly eighteen. She had enormous eyes, vivid even though they were downcast. She had a perfect heart-shaped face. Her lips were very full and a finger posed against the lower one obscured them not at all. She seemed to be withdrawing slightly.

Of course! Utanc! Turks name their women after qualities. And *utanc* means "shame, modesty, bashfulness."

So sweet! So beautiful! So utterly frail! So undefended!

An emotion very foreign to me welled up. An absolute passion to protect her welled up in me. I felt I should at once charge over the border, slay the whole Russian Army, cast myself at her feet and beg for just one smile.

I sighed and somehow tore my eyes away. I turned the photograph over. On the back, in pencil, was written: *$5,000 U.S. Cash.*

"You'd own her completely," whispered the driver. "She would be your slave forever. And saving her from the raping Russian troops would earn her gratitude to such a degree, she would never be able to thank you enough!"

Well, what could I do?

I reached into my pocket and I hauled out five thousand U.S. dollars and literally pushed them at him.

"There's the transport costs and commissions," said the driver. "They come to another five thousand."

I reached into my pocket and hauled out the other five thousand.

He got up. "I'm so glad to be able to do you a favor, Sultan Bey. We'll forget about my gas and travel time."

He tried to refuse the wad of lira I thrust at him. Finally he shrugged and took it.

"It will take them a week or so to smuggle her through," he said. "Now I've got to rush back to Bolvadin to get this payment in before she is sold to someone else." And he hurried off and I heard his tires screech as the "taxi" departed. I certainly hoped he was in time.

And that night, I slept with her photo on my pillow and, oh, did I dream beautiful dreams!

I felt so good that when, in the dawn, I made out Faht Bey beside the bed, I wasn't even annoyed.

"Raht radioed in," he said. "He's all set. You can leave for America as soon as it is dark."

I didn't even hear him as he left, probably he was saying he would tell the tug crew.

I clutched the photo in my hand and kissed it passionately. Gods bless the raping Russian troops if they were delivering into my hands such a treasure as this! There's a lot to be said for communism!

Chapter 6

We took off as soon as dusk thickened into deep black.

There are some—persons with hypercritical attitudes and chronically given to nitpicking—who might try to say that the heady prospects of owning a real, live dancing girl distracted me from my duties. But this would be the purest cabal.

That day before takeoff I was the slave of duty. I browbeat Faht Bey into giving me all the money I would need and then some. I armed myself thoroughly with Earth weaponry. I collected all the necessary equipment. I threatened the villa staff thoroughly and even had one of the small boys throwing up again.

I connected up the 831 Relayer and, slave of duty that I was being, inspected what Heller was up to inside the ship.

He was making candy!

That's right! He was standing in the after-galley with pots and pans. He even had an apron on! He was using a big spoon to test a simmering mess of the gooiest, most nauseating-looking candy I have ever seen!

I thought, well, well, he must have learned it from his sister. He was being so precise, I thought, isn't that sweet? And actually was so revolted that I didn't even spot it was an English pun until much later.

A little later, I checked again. He had a whole bunch of little papers and he was putting the candy down on them in blobs.

When I came back from threatening the staff again, Heller had the pieces all wrapped up in wax paper. They seemed to be very hard and had a spiral pattern of red and white stripes.

I knew he was being silly. There's lots of candy just like that in America. You can buy it all over the place. It's even advertised in big colorful ads in the crew's hangar library, foreign magazine section.

Oh, good, I said sarcastically, he's preparing for his trip. And I dismissed it.

Oh, I was very busy that day before takeoff. I spent at least two hours on Apparatus business which more than made up for the ten I spent reclining on the lawn, daydreaming about Utanc.

The launching went off without a hitch. It is very simple to travel on Earth: it has only one moon and even it is not all that bright. So all one has to do is launch in the darkness and then follow the night as it creeps along the planet surface. One dawdles along about three hundred miles up and then descends quickly to find himself at the same local time as that of one's departure point.

Captain Stabb certainly showed an expertise in such things. The Apparatus school could well add some lectures on piracy and smuggling. He told me several amusing stories as we descended, including one about wiping out a whole city. Uproarious!

We followed the textbook landing procedure, however.

Below us was the deserted plantation: the empty, fallow field, the ruined house with two front pillars gone, the slave shacks passed to ruin.

About five hundred feet up, Stabb hit the paralysis button. A heavy flash of bright blue light struck down from the ship in a cone, lasting only a split second; if seen by anyone they would suppose it to be the reflection of headlamps of a turning car or a lightning flash on the horizon.

Stabb thudded the tug down right on target, within the screen of trees, horizontally, on its belly.

The second pilot slammed open the airlock door. The second engineer, in combat dress, was on the ground in a second. He was carrying a heat detector which he pointed in a sweep at the terrain.

The bright blue light knocks any living thing in the area unconscious. The heat detector tells one if there is now anyone lying there. Standard operation. Saves one from having some nasty surprises. And actually is quite humanitarian: one doesn't have to kill a chance observer, one can just go off and let the person come to, wondering what hit him, not running around screaming, "Voltar pilots have just violated Code Number a-36-544 M Section B!" Dead bodies are hard to get rid of on the spur of the moment and bring in nosy sheriffs and things.

The second engineer's detector flashed red! Something had been knocked out by the blueflash!

The first pilot, blastrifle at ready, sprinted in the direction of the indicator beam. Stabb was tensed at the tug controls, ready to take off again in case the alert turned out to be an ambush.

The Virginia night was August, muggy hot. A thin sliver of moonlight silhouetted the copse of trees. A wind sighed through the weeds around the spaceship.

Then a bark of laughter. The first pilot came running back. He was holding an opossum by the tail! He threw it to one side. "Seems all clear," he said.

"All clear!" said the second engineer, tossing his heat detector back into the airlock.

Stabb peered into the night, his close-set eyes intent. "Where the Hells are they? We've got to be back at the base before the sun rises there!" He glanced at his watch. "We've only got twenty-five minutes to hang around here!"

Suddenly, running feet in the distance, coming down a weed-grown road.

Raht burst into view. He was lugging two enormous suitcases.

He is the most unremarkable-looking Earthman one ever cared to see. Aside from a bristling mustache he affects, there is not one other feature to make him stick in memory. The perfect spy. He is from the planet Modon and glad they were to get rid of him.

He boosted the suitcases into the airlock. He was panting with exertion. But he saw me in the dim shimmer of interior light. "Cripes!" he said, "It's Officer Gris himself." He always has a bit of a complaining note when he speaks.

"What have you got in these suitcases?" I demanded. "The orders were to get expensive luggage filled with clothes."

He pushed them further into the airlock. "Clothes cost money. You've no idea what inflation is. I made up the weight with rocks!"

He had made up the weight with money in his own pocket, I said to myself. But I hit the buzzer to the back and picked up the bags to take them to Heller. I did not want him to see the agents that would be tailing him from here on out.

Heller had released the passageway doors. I struggled through and dumped the two huge suitcases in the salon.

He was sitting at the table. I said, "You'll find clothes in there. Get dressed fast. Take no clothes of your own. You only have a little over twenty minutes, so don't dawdle." I left him, closing the doors behind me.

Raht was still breathing hard. I drew him into the crew salon. He took out a sheaf of documents. "Here's his military school diploma."

I read:

SAINT LEE MILITARY ACADEMY

Greetings:
DELBERT JOHN ROCKECENTER, JUNIOR
has completed his education to the
level of JUNIOR COLLEGE.
Signed, sealed (etc.)

It was a very imposing diploma. It had Confederate soldiers holding rifles at port arms. It had banners and cannons. Very fancy.

"Here's the rest of the papers," said Raht. They were attested transcripts of subjects and grades.

"What clever forgeries," I said.

"Hells no," said Raht. "They're the authentic signatures. The school closed last spring for keeps and the ex-faculty will do anything for a buck. You think I want to get sent up for forgery?"

Always complaining, even when you give him a compliment.

"Where's Terb?" I demanded. "We haven't got much time."

"Maybe he's having trouble. The old clerk at that (bleeped) courthouse didn't want to come down after hours."

Captain Stabb looked in, pointing at his watch. "We're going to have to race to make it now. We have to get back while it's still night!"

But here was Terb, leaping in through the airlock. Terb is also one of the most unremarkable Earthmen you'd ever want to see. A bit on the plump side, a bit swarthy, but you would never pick him out in a crowd. He's from the planet Dolo and they were also very glad to get rid of him.

"Not Officer Gris himself!" he said. "We must be important after all! Raht, I been wrong. All this time I been telling you we was just dirt and now . . ."

"Shut up," I said. "Is the birth certificate fixed?"

Terb nodded. He took a small electric switch out of his pocket. "The old clerk wants to see him so he can attest the certificate is issued to a real person known to him that ain't dead. He don't like to be thought crooked. This bird we got here will present himself, hand over another C-note, get the certificate all signed. Then the instant he walks down the steps of that courthouse, I hit this and goodbye clerk, goodbye records. I planted the bomb before dawn today. Right in the record files!"

I gave them the activator-receiver. "This is a special bug. You must keep this within two hundred miles of him at all times."

"But we got him bugged," said Raht. "There's bugs in those clothes and there's bugs in those suitcases and we have the activator right here. We can't possibly lose him!"

"This is another type of bug, an aerial bug," I lied. "It's inserted in his elbow and registers if he handles explosives or touches guns: we don't want you getting shot."

Oh, that was different!

"We can spot him from a ship with this," I lied. "Now this is the 831 Relayer. Keep it right with the activator-receiver."

They got that.

"Just leave them turned on all the time. See, they look like a telephone connection box. You can put them on the outside of any building or under a bed."

They promised.

Then Raht said, "Money. For us. Inflation is awful!"

I handed them a draft on the Chase-Arab New York Bank. They were happy. So was I: it was government money.

I gave them a few tips. Then I said, "Now get out of here before he sees you."

They went diving out of the airlock, sprinted past the faintly moonlit plantation house and were gone.

Stabb was looking at his watch.

Heller came out. And oh, I had to laugh! Clothes to fit men six feet two inches tall aren't to be had in southern Virginia. They were all too small!

Raht had done a wonderful job. The jacket was LOUD! Huge red and white checks. The pants were LOUD! Huge blue and white stripes. The hat was a bright green, banded Panama: too small! The shoes were orange suede and too tight! The shirt was purple!

He would stand out like a searchlight!

The clothes did look expensive, like they'd been bought by someone with lots of money and no taste at all.

And they looked like they had been outgrown.

Wonderful!

He was lugging the two huge suitcases.

"Don't you think this wardrobe is a bit garish?" he said.

"In the height of fashion! In the height of fashion!" I replied.

I rapidly told him again where he was supposed to go to get his birth certificate. I handed him the other papers.

Then I knelt down in the airlock, pointing a night scope up the road. I wanted to make sure Raht and Terb were out of sight and that the area was still clear. Something was moving in the brush.

"I'm a bit hungry," said Heller behind me. And then he seemed to wander off into the ship.

Stabb came to me. "He says he wants . . ."

"Give him whatever he wants," I said. There was something

moving over there by a slave cabin.

Heller was there again. "I'm going to need some money."

Oh, yes. His money. The orders said five thousand dollars so he'd look affluent. I pulled two thousand out of my pocket and handed it to him. Three thousand wasn't bad for a night's work.

He was closing up some straps on a suitcase.

"We're awful close to time," said Stabb.

I saw what the object that had been moving was. A fox. To Hells with it.

I stood up and turned to Heller. I put out my hand. He, however, didn't take it. Instead, he was extending a letter to me. "Do me a favor, would you, and mail this? I promised to keep him informed."

I took it and put it in my pocket. I was too intent on getting rid of him to pay it any heed. "Well, good luck, Jettero," I said. "This is it. Off you go."

He dropped to the ground, lugging the two big cases. He limped off past the moonlit plantation house.

"Bye-bye, Heller," I said to myself. "And I hope you make a lot of good friends in the pen!"

"We're taking off," said Stabb.

I got out of their way. The second engineer dropped out of the airlock with a machine in his hand. Stabb lifted the tug six feet off the ground and held it there. The second engineer ducked around with his machine and made all the grass stand up straight where the ship had been. He threw his machine into the airlock. The second pilot gave him a hand back aboard. They closed the latches.

The captain said to me, "Are you under orders to make our ship incapable of leaving this solar system?"

As a matter of fact, I was. From the assassin pilot. But it wouldn't do to tell Stabb his ship was to be disabled. "Why?" I said.

"He took the time-sight out of the flight deck just now," said the captain. "And if there's another one, we can't get to it. He's double-barred all his cabins and storage spaces: we won't be able to get into them even with a blastgun! Without a sight, we can't fly her in outer space. But I suppose that's what you required:

you said to give him anything he wants."

So what? Who wanted to ride in this (bleeping) tug and maybe get shot down?

Stabb sent the ship hurtling into the sky.

Now to race back to the base and land just before dawn.

Stabb cranked the tug auxiliaries up toward maximum speed.

I was jubilant.

Heller was off my hands!

I couldn't wait to get back to a viewer and see how he got everything he had coming to him. The (bleepard). All the trouble he'd caused!

PART FOURTEEN

Chapter 1

Less than two hours later, I was sitting in my secret room in my villa, about 105 degrees of longitude from Heller, watching his every move.

I was ecstatic! The picture on the viewer was brilliant! The sound was perfect even down to the crickets! The 831 Relayer was doing its job!

I had to backtrack the recording strip a bit to where he left the ship.

And there he was, carrying two heavy suitcases, limping through the Virginia night. Up ahead there was a farmhouse, shedding light across a barnyard.

Any true spy, even slightly trained, would have taken a wide path around it. But not Heller!

There was a growl.

Then there was a savage snarl!

A huge sheep dog barred the way!

I realized with a chuckle that Heller had probably never seen a dog. The nearest thing to it were the hondos of Flisten which, when domesticated, specialized in chewing up the whole family.

There it stood, fangs bared! It was crouching down. I knew it would charge. Goodbye, Heller. This thing is going to end right here on a hot night in Virginia and between the fangs of a dog!

With a short run to get a fast start, it sprang into the air, the fangs aimed straight for Heller's throat!

Heller let go the suitcases.

His hands flashed out.

He grabbed the dog by the loose skin on either side of the jowl!

Pivoting on his heel, using the momentum of the dog, he sent the beast twenty feet behind him!

It sailed through the air! With a clunk, it collided with a tree, let out one yelp and lay still.

I expected Heller to run. That much sound would attract attention in the nearby house.

Heller walked over to the dog and examined it. Then he picked the big brute up in his arms. He went back to his suitcases and somehow got hold of their handles.

He was limping to the lighted house!

The screen door opened. A farmer was standing there with a shotgun!

Heller limped right on up to the porch. He dropped his suitcases. "Ah'm afraid yoah dawg ran intah a tree," said Heller in a thick Virginia accent.

The farmer opened the door wider and Heller took the dog into the living room and laid it down on the rug. "He ain't bleedin' none, so Ah s'pose he'll come around," said Heller.

The Virginian bent over the dog. It made a feeble struggle to get up and the farmer petted it and it relaxed with a faint thump of its tail.

"Naw," said the farmer, "he ain't hurt none. You f'um heahabouts, kid?"

"Heahabouts," said Heller. "Ah'll be gittin' on now."

"Hell, no. Not aftah you done a white-man thing lahk that! Martha, bring some cawfee in heah!" he yelled toward the kitchen.

"Aw, no," said Heller. "Ah be much oblahged. But Ah got me an appointment in town. A fellah's a-waitin' foah me at th' co't-house. Ah'm much oblahged but Ah be late awready."

"Well, hell, kid, tha's more'n two mile. An' you limpin' an' all. Be downright unneighbo'ly of me not to run you intah town! Ah'll git mah truck!"

The dog had gotten over on its belly. It was staring at Heller with the strangest look.

The farmer cranked up his truck outside and Heller picked up the suitcases, tossed them into the back and got in. And they rattled off to town.

(Bleep), I thought. That didn't go so good. It was the Virginia accent that had brought it off. (Bleep) that Countess Krak! She ought to stick to teaching freaks!

Heller alighted at the courthouse. The farmer said, "Drop by any ol' tahm, when ya'll comes back home, kid."

"Ah be lookin' fohw'd to 't," said Heller, "an' much oblahged foah th' lift."

And off went the farmer.

Heller looked up at the courthouse. There were just two windows lit on the second floor. The front door was open and Heller limped up the steps. He pushed open a door.

A real old codger, dressed in black, was hunched over a desk in the space behind the counter. He had a couple of file drawers open. The sign on his desk said:

BIRTHS AND DEATHS, WAIT IN LINE PLEASE.

I hoped the old (bleepard) was properly in line himself. He would be dead in about five minutes.

Heller walked up to the counter and dropped his bags.

The old man raised his half-bald, gray head. "You th' boy?"

"Tha's what they say," said Heller.

"Ah wondered if it would evuh come to this," said the old man, cryptically. He came over and looked at Heller closely. "So you be Delbert John Rockecenter, Junior?"

"Tha's what they say," said Heller.

"That be two hundrud dollahs," said the old man, pushing a birth certificate forward but holding on to it.

Hah, I thought. America is crooked as always. He'd upped the price a hundred.

Heller reached into his pocket. You could see the money was strange-looking to him. He turned some of the bills over.

The old man reached across and plucked two hundreds off the roll and pocketed them.

Heller picked up the birth certificate. It gave his name, said he was blond, said he'd been born at home. It had a seal on it and the clerk's signature. The date of birth made Heller just seventeen! Heller put it in his pocket.

"Much oblahged," said Heller.

He picked up the bags, turned and limped back down the curving courthouse steps. He pushed through the front door and walked down into the street.

I turned the audio volume down, knowing what was coming.

With a roar and flame and a splintering crash, the upper windows of the building blew out!

Standard procedure.

Goodbye, you old cheating (bleepard), I said. Always give a prayer for the dead. It brings luck.

Flame was starting to gush out through one of the windows. When Terb bombs something, he really bombs it. He's fond of exaggeration. And he always uses locally obtained explosives, too, avoiding any Space Code break. A master!

Wait! What in the name of Gods was Heller doing! That blast would attract attention even on this deserted hill. Fire engines existed even in Virginia. In fact, they are so proud of their fire engines, they're always having rallies of volunteer fire companies for miles around!

Any trained man would have understood. And he would have started running. Fast!

Not Heller! He dropped his suitcases. He streaked through the main door. He raced up those stairs. He bashed his way into Births and Deaths!

The place was on fire! It was filled with smoke!

Even the counter was blown over! Heller was down, right at floor level. He snaked ahead, feeling through the churning fury.

He found a hand, a sleeve. He yanked. A body was in view.

There was a carpet on the floor. Heller snapped the ends to him. He wrapped it around the old man with two quick jerks.

He went backwards, dragging the wrapped body with him.

He got to the stairs and threw the carpeted body over his

shoulder and went down five steps at a time.

He burst into the open air. He stepped sideways to a strip of lawn.

Oh, well, I thought. Not too bad. They always arrest everybody in sight when there's a bomb explosion. That's why you have to get away from them quick. And Heller was staying right there, the idiot.

He unwrapped the old man. He beat out some bits of smoldering cloth.

The old man opened his eyes, "What . . . what in hell was that?"

"You all raht?" said Heller.

The old man felt around. "Ah be purty bruised up but she don' look like nothin' broke. It's that (bleeped) stove. I tol' 'em t' shut it off las' spring! She blew up befo'. Th' pilot light goes aht and she fills with gas. . . ."

The old man's eyes were staring at the building. Heller looked. The windows were all blown out and part of the roof and the flames were starting to roar up with lashing tongues into the sky.

It was just now sinking in what had happened to him. He was staring at Heller, his eyes going round. "Jesus Christ, kid," he said with awe. "You risk yoah neck somethin' awful draggin' me aht o' there!" He shook his head as though to clear his eyes. He looked at Heller much more intensely. "You saved mah life, youngster!"

Heller was making sure the old man was all right. He was trying to get him to flex his fingers.

Over on the other side of town, what was probably a volunteer fire department was getting busy. A summons bell was clanging, shattering the night.

"Shouldn' Ah call somebody or somethin'?" said Heller. "An ambeoolance?"

"Kid, look. Ah jus' thought. Jesus Christ, you bettuh git aht o' heah! There'll be fiahmen and repohtahs ahl ovah this place in about one minute. Ah'll be ahl raht, youngster. Ah'll nevah fohget you. But with a name lahk yoahs, you bettuh run lahk hell, quick!"

"Glad Ah could help aht," said Heller. And he moved off.

"If'n Ah can evuh be moah help t' you," the old man called after him, "you jus' yell fo' Stonewall Biggs!"

Heller walked down the hill, carrying his bags. The ground was bathed with the fiercely burning courthouse fire.

He was on the street sidewalk when the fire engine passed. He looked back, then stood waiting. The whole top of the hill was being crowned in flames. There went a Virginia landmark. Probably, I thought, George Washington had slept there.

Shortly, an ambulance went by.

Heller hefted his bags and limped onward toward the bus station.

He stopped suddenly. He got out a notebook. He wrote: *They can't make stoves*.

Chapter 2

A black man was standing at the door of the bus station, broom in hand, an old hat on the back of his head. He was looking up the street to the fire on the hill. I hoped he would wake up and notice there was a stranger in town and connect him with the fire.

"When is the next bus?" said Heller.

"Hoo-ee," said the black. "Now, ain't that some fiah! Y'all evuh see a fiah that big?"

I imagine Heller, as a Fleet combat engineer, had seen whole cities on fire. He had probably set some himself that would make that courthouse fire look like a stray spark.

"Tha's purty big," said Heller. He went in and put down his bags.

It was a very dingy bus station: ripped-up plastic seats, discarded newspapers on the floor. There was a ticket wicket at the far end.

The black came in, shaking his head. He put down the broom, went into the wicket and took off his hat. With a flourish, he opened the front of the wicket. "Wheah you goin'?" he called. "Richmun', Washin'ton, New Yahk, Mahami? O' maybe Atlanta?"

"Atlanta?" said Heller, walking over to the counter. I thought, here we go again! More Manco! More Prince Caucalsia!

"Oh, tha's a fahn town," the black said. "Plenty white ladies, yallah ladies, black ladies. Any coluh you got a wishin' fo'. A real fahn town. Or maybe you'd lahk Buhmin'ham. Now *that* is the fahnes' town you evuh hope to see, man."

"Ah'm goin' to New Yahk," said Heller.

"Oh, ah'm real sorry 'bout that. This bus line only go to Lynchburg." The black man had come down out of his daydream about wondrous places to visit. "This ol' dumb town o' Fair Oakes ain't real well connected. But y'all c'n change at Lynchburg. Ah c'n sell you a ticket to theah, tho'."

"That'll be real fahn," said Heller.

The black got busy and very efficiently issued the ticket. "Tha's two dollahs an' fohty cents. Next bus comin' thoo heah 'bout midnight. Tha's 'bout an hour an' a half y'all gotta wait. Heah is yoah ticket, heah is yoah change. We ain' got no entertainment, 'less you wanna go watch the co'thouse fiah. No? Well, you jus' make yo'self at home. Now Ah's the janitor ag'in."

He put his hat back on, closed the wicket and picked up his broom. But he went outside to watch the fire on the hill.

Heller sat down with a suitcase on either side of him. He started reading the various travel signs that told about the joys of Paris, the glories of ancient Greece and one that advised that there was going to be a fried chicken supper at the local high school last September.

I thought I might hear the crackle of flames in the distance so I turned up the gain. I didn't hear flames, only some distant commotion. Wouldn't anybody notice there was a stranger in town? Where were the police? Fine lot of police they were! When there's a bombing or big fire, the first thing you do is look for strangers. I was quite put out. There sat Heller, comfortable as could be.

The black started to do some sweeping. He began to sing:

Hark to the story of Willie the Weeper,
Willie the Weeper was a chimney sweeper.
He had the hop habit and he had it bad.
Oh, listen while I tell you 'bout the dream he had!

He wanted to sweep under Heller's right foot, so Heller, accommodatingly, lifted his right foot.

He went to the hop joint the other night,
When he knew that the lights would be burnin' bright.
I guess he smoked a dozen pills or more.
When he woke up he wuz on a foreign shore.

He had finished the right foot area. He wanted to sweep under Heller's left foot. Heller accommodatingly raised it.

Queen o' Bulgaria was the first in his net.
She called him her darlin' an' her lovin' pet.
She promised him a pretty Ford automobile,
With a diamond headlight and a silver steerin' wheel.

Amongst the swish of the broom, which didn't seem to really be doing much but raise dust, I thought I heard the distant chortle of a police car. It seemed to be approaching the bus station.

Willie landed in New York one evenin' late.
He asked his sugar for an afterdate.
Willie he got funny. She began to shout,
'Bim bam boo!'—an' the dope gave out.

It was a police car! It came to a stop with a squeal of tires and a dying chortle. Right outside the bus station!

Aha, I thought with gratification, the local police aren't so inefficient after all. They're checking the bus station for strangers! Well, untrained, amateur Heller, you are about to get it! And he wasn't even looking at the door!

The sharp yelp of someone being hurt. Heller's head whipped around.

Two enormous policemen were barging into the room. They were dressed in black vinyl short jackets. They were girded around with handcuffs and guns. They had billy clubs ready in their hands.

Between them they were dragging a small, young woman! Tears were pouring out of her eyes. She was fighting like a wild thing.

"Let me go! You God (bleeped) (bleepards)!" she was shouting. "Let me go!"

The cops sent her hurtling forward. She collided with a vinyl chair. One of the cops was at her at once, spinning her about and making her sit down.

The other cop got a battered suitcase out of the police car, sent it skidding across the floor at the girl and it hit her in the legs. Then he walked over to the ticket wicket, shouting, "Open this up, you black (bleepard)!"

The cop hulking over the girl had her pinned to the chair.

"You got no right to do this!" she was yelling at him.

"We gaht all the raht in the worl'!" said the cop. "If'n the chief says Horsey Mary Schmeck goes aht of town tonight, then aht of town goes Horsey Mary Schmeck and heah you is!"

Tears were cascading down her cheeks. Perspiration beaded her forehead. She was probably only about twenty-five but she looked thirty-five—deep bags under her eyes. Except for that, she was not unpretty. Her brown hair was over part of her face and she swept it away. She was trying to get up.

She renewed the verbal attack. "Your (bleeped) chief wasn't talking that way when he got out of my bed last week! He said I could work this town as long as I wanted."

"Tha' was las' week," said the cop, pinning her down to the chair again. "This's this week!"

She tried to claw at his face. "You (bleeped) two-bit (bleepard)! You yourself sold me a nickel bag last Monday!"

"Tha' was las' Monday," said the cop. He had her pinned. "You know an' Ah know what this is all about. Tha' God (bleeped) new Fed narco moved in on th' distric'. Nobody knew it'd been changed. Nobody give him his split so he's cleanin' the whole place up. And y'all is the kind of trash tha's bein' swept out."

She was crying again. "Oh, Joe. *Please* sell me a nickel bag. Look, I'll go. I'll get on the bus. But I got to have a fix, Joe. *Please!* I can't take it, Joe! Just one little fix and I'll go!"

The other cop had come back from the ticket window. "Shut up, Mary. You 'n all of us know the distric' is total empty of big H now. Joe, did th' chief give you bus fare fo' this (bleepch)?"

The girl was collapsed. Tears streamed from red eyes. Sweat beaded her head. I knew what was wrong. She was a dope addict that was moving into the withdrawal symptoms. It would get worse before it got any better. As she scrubbed at her eyes, one could see the needle scars inside her arm. A girl trying to keep up with the expensive habit by selling her body. Ordinary situation. And they were moving her out of town. Ordinary handling. But maybe she'd infected the chief with something. Venereal disease goes right along with drugs and prostitution. It was such a common scene that I had no hope Heller would get himself in trouble over it.

"Well, Ah ain' forkin' ovah none of mah own cash t' get her aht o' town," said the cop who had gone to the ticket wicket.

Joe grabbed the girl's purse. She made a frantic effort to retain it and got a punch in the jaw in return. She fell to the floor crying.

The two cops went over to the ticket window. Joe began to rummage through the purse. "Hey, would you look at this!" he said. He pulled out a roll of bills and started counting. "A hunnad an' thutty-two dallahs!"

"That'll buy a lot of white mule!" said the other cop.

They both laughed. They split the roll and put it into their pockets.

Suddenly the two cops and the wicket were huge in my screen!

"Give th' lady back her money," said Heller.

They stared at him blankly. Then their faces went hard.

"Kid," said Joe, hefting his nightstick, "Ah think you need a lesson!"

Joe raised his club to strike.

Heller's hand was a blur.

Joe's arm broke with a snap just above the elbow!

Heller danced back. The other cop was drawing his gun, bracing himself, two hands on the butt. His eyes were savage with the joy of being able to kill something. Ordinary cop reaction. I thought, well, Heller, it was nice knowing you.

The blur of a hand. The cop's gun moved back and then up and flew away.

Heller's left hand chopped in against the cop's neck. The eyes went glazed.

Heller danced back and kicked the cop in the stomach before the body had even begun to slump. The cop sailed back and hit a trash can.

With a whirl, Heller was onto Joe again. Joe was trying to draw his gun with his left hand. Heller's foot smashed the fingers against the gun butt.

Heller's other foot rose and caught Joe on the button. The snap of bones followed the impact instantly.

Backing up, Heller looked at them. They were very sprawled. Heller one after the other took their guns and sent them spinning out through the front door of the bus station. There was a crash of glass as one of them broke a window in the police car.

The girl had come forward, staring down at the two unconscious cops. "Serves you right, you (bleepards)!"

Heller scooped the money out of their pockets and put it in her purse. He handed it to her.

She looked a little confused. Then she rallied. "Honey, we got to get the hell out of here! The chief will go bananas! That Joe is his son!"

She was hauling hard at Heller, trying to get him to the door.

"Come on!" she was shouting. "I know where we can get a car! Come on, quick! We got to make dust!"

Heller gave her her suitcase. He picked up his own and followed her out. He glanced back once.

The black man was looking down at the smashed cops. "An' Ah jus' cleaned the flooah," he said sadly.

Chapter 3

They were heading to the north of the town. The streets were deserted and dark. Heller was limping along. Soon it became apparent that the girl could not keep up. She sagged down panting, on her suitcase.

"It's my heart," she was gasping. "I got a bad ticker. . . . I'll be all right in a minute. . . . I got to be . . . They'll be tearing this town apart . . . to find us."

Heller scooped her up under one arm and put her suitcase under his other, picked up his own and proceeded.

"You're . . . you're an all right kid. Turn over to the right there—it takes us to the state highway."

Soon she directed him up the state highway to the edge of town. There was a glare of lights there. It was a filling station and used-car lot combined. The signs said it sold Octopus Gasoline and a big octopus logo was dripping gas at each tentacle. There were colored plastic whirlers around the place, idle from the lack of wind. Then Heller's attention was directed to the back. A sign there, above the used-car lot run apparently in conjunction with the station, said:

HARVEY 'SMASHER' LEE'S BARGAIN CARS
FOR TRUE VIRGINIANS.
MONEY BACK SOMETIMES.

The place was really run down: the filling station at this time of night was closed, half the twirlers were bent and a third of the light bulbs out.

A man had been standing up on the cab of an old truck, looking off in the direction of the courthouse fire. He saw them and climbed down.

Heller had put Horsey Mary Schmeck down and she sat on her suitcase, tears running down her cheeks. She was perspiring and her nose was running. She let out a huge yawn, one of the symptoms.

The man came up, looking at them. He was plump but big. He was about thirty. He had a weak, flabby face. "Mary?" He wasn't glad to see her. He looked at Heller. "Hey, what you doin', Mary? Robbin' th' cradle?"

"Harv, you've got to get me a fix! Even a nickel bag, Harv. Please, Harv."

"Aw, Mary, you know that new Fed narco dried up this district. And he says he'll keep it dry until he gets fifty percent of ever'body's traffic. There ain't no stuff to be had!"

The girl moaned. "Not even some of your own? Please, Harv."

He shook his head very emphatically.

Then she got hopeful. "Maybe they got some in Lynchburg. Harv, sell this kid a car."

I turned up the gain so I could hear the police cars if they started to come this way. I was sure they would. The longer these stupid idiots fooled around, the less chance they had and the happier I would be.

The idea of selling a car inspired Harvey "Smasher" Lee. Right away he went into his act. "Here's a Datsun! Another man wanted it but if you buy it quick, I can put him off. It's a B210. It only has seventy thousand miles on the clock and it's less than two years old. Only seven thousand dollars! And I'll throw in five gallons of gas."

The car was a beat-up wreck. One wheel was folded under. This salesman was pretty good. That was almost double what the car had been worth new. I began to have hopes for him. Maybe he would run Heller out of money, for Heller only had two thousand.

"Ah think," said Heller, "you got somethin' foah less."

"Oh, well! Of course I have. Now take this Ford pickup. It's a real bargain. It's only been used for hauling fertilizer and we'll wash it all out for you. For five thousand . . ."

"Harv," called the girl, "you better hurry up. We'll have to leave any minute!"

Heller had been looking at the row of wrecks. There was a huge one at the end, light gray in color. He approached it. It was covered with dust. "How about this one! It's the right color to be invisible."

"Hey, kid!" called Mary. "You don't want that one. It's a gas hog! It won't get eight miles to the gallon!"

Harv took position quickly to block the girl from Heller's sight. "Now, kid, I see you got a real eye for cars. This here is a Cadillac Brougham Coupe d'Elegance! It's one of the last real cars they made. It's a 1968! Before they clamped down with pollution controls. Why, there's five hundred horses right under that hood." He pointed at it proudly.

"Horses?" said Heller. "You mus' be kiddin' me. Let's see!"

Harvey instantly jumped to the front of the huge gray vehicle and, with some trouble, got the hood up. It was a giant engine. It didn't look too bad.

"She has a 10.5-to-1 compression ratio," said Harvey. "A real fire-eater."

"What's it burn?" said Heller.

"Burn? Oh, you mean octanes."

"No. Fuel. What fuel does it burn? You said it was a fire engine. What *fuel?*"

"What the hell . . . Gasoline, kid. Petroleum!"

"A chemical engine!" said Heller, suddenly enlightened. "Hello, hello! Is it solid or liquid?"

Harv yelled back at Mary, "Is this kid a kidder or what?"

"Sell him a car!" wailed Mary, staring now down the road to town in anxiety.

"Kid, this car is spotless. It was owned by a little old lady who never drove it at all."

"Harv, stop lying!" Mary yelled. "You know (bleeped) well it was owned by Prayin' Pete, the radio preacher, before they hung him! Sell him the God (bleeped) car! We got to *leave!*"

"It's only two thousand dollars," said Harvey in desperation.

"Harvey!" screamed the girl. "You told me just last week you couldn't even sell that car to the wholesalers! Kid, quit letting him snow you under! He's had that thing for six months and he only uses it to (bleep) the local talent in because it has draw curtains in the back!"

"Fifteen hundred," said Harv frantically to Heller.

"Two hundred!" screamed the girl.

"Aw, Mary. . . ."

"Two hundred or I'll tell your wife!"

"Two hundred," said Harv sullenly.

Heller fiddled with the money, trying to sort out its unfamiliar colors and numbers.

"Wait," said Harv, grasping at a reprieve. "I can't sell it to him. He's under age!"

"Put it in my name and hurry up!"

Harv snatched the two one-hundred-dollar bills out of Heller's hands and then grabbed enough more for tax and license. He angrily wrote up a sales contract to Mary Schmeck.

I turned up the gain again. (Bleeped) inefficient police. Must be looking in the wrong places as usual. They certainly would have discovered those two maimed cops by now.

Harv left the hood up. He opened the door and let off the brake. He started to go behind the car to push it and then must have realized it was a hot night. He went to the office and came back with some keys. He slid under the wheel, turned on the ignition. The engine roared into powerful life.

"Hey," he said in amazement, "it started! Must be a Penny battery."

"Fill it up," yelled the girl. "Check its oil, water and tires! Fast!"

Harvey eased the car over to the pumps. He checked the automatic transmission fluid, saw it was all right. He shut off the engine. He topped it up with water. He checked the oil, which, to his disappointment, seemed all right.

"There you are," said Harvey. "I'll file for these plates in the morning."

Heller put the suitcases in the back. The girl got in front. Then the girl reached over and turned on the switch. "Harv! You owe us five gallons of gas! It's empty!"

With no good graces, Harvey unlocked a pump. Then he had a bright idea. "I'm only allowed to sell tankfuls now. It's a new rule!"

"Oh, God," said the girl, looking down the road toward town. "Hurry it up!"

Gas was shortly gurgling into the monstrous tank. The girl said, "You didn't check the tires!"

Harv grudgingly went around and filled the tires up. Then he took the gas nozzle out of the filler pipe and put on the cap. "That'll be forty dollars!" he said. "The price just went up again and we haven't had time to post it on the pumps."

Heller paid him. The girl took the sales receipt. She scribbled her signature on a power of attorney card for the new license and threw it at Harv. "Now, let's get the hell out of here!"

Heller apparently had seen Harv start it. He turned the ignition key all the way over and the engine blasted into life.

"Hey," said Heller, "so that's the way horses sound."

"Beat it, kid," said Harvey.

"There's just one thing," said Heller. "How do you fly it?"

Harv looked at him bug-eyed. "Can't you drive?"

"Well, no," said Heller. "Not a chemical-engine Cadillac Brougham Coupe d'Elegance," he added, wanting to be exact, "with five hundred horses."

"Jesus," said Harv, softly. Then he brightened. "That's the automatic shift lever. Put it in park when you are through with the car. That *N* means neutral and to hell with it. The *L* is low and you won't never need it. The *D* is drive one. You won't use that. That second *D* is where you keep it.

"Now, that pedal down there . . . no, the other one. That's the foot brake and you push it when you want to stop. This other thing to your left is the hand brake and you use that when you park on a hill.

"Now, that thing there on the floor is the accelerator. You push it to speed up."

There was an instant deafening roar as Heller tramped on it.

"Don't rev it up so!" squeaked Harvey. The engine slowed. "And there you are. You got it?"

I caught a distant chortle of police cars.

"Is this the wheelstick?" said Heller, touching the steering wheel.

"Yes! Yes! You turn it to go to the right, you turn it this way to go to the left. Hey, I forgot to show you the lights. This is the light knob. . . . Well, turn them ON!"

"Let's get out of here!" wailed the girl.

Harv had his hand on the open window ledge. He bent close. "Kid, this car will do a hundred and thirty. If you get out there and kill yourself, don't come back here complaining!"

"Jesus!" screamed the girl. "The fuzz!"

And there they came! Two of them! The first one bounced over the curb and into the used-car lot. The second saw them at the pumps and swerved toward them.

Heller engaged the Cadillac in drive!

He stamped on the accelerator! He almost tore his own head off.

The Cadillac leaped at a sign.

Heller turned the wheel.

The Cadillac launched itself over a curb!

Heller yanked the wheel. He overcompensated and headed back for the curb. He corrected and got the car going north. He was in the middle of the road.

An ancient truck was coming at him.

"To the right!" screamed the girl.

Heller swerved to the right, hit the gravel, came back on the road.

"Drive on the right side of the road!" screamed the girl.

"Got it," said Heller.

Behind them two police cars had started up in mad pursuit. They had their quarry in sight and their chortling said so for all the world to hear!

I smiled to myself in great satisfaction. Heller was going to be in a box much sooner than I thought! Chiefs of police do not take lightly to having their sons hospitalized. They don't have many cops in such a small town. I didn't need to hear their radios to know the chief was in one of those police cars! Police cars are as fast as that Cadillac. And that chief was not going to give up. That was for sure!

Chapter 4

Mary Schmeck yelled, "Turn down that side road! It cuts across country. We can get over on U.S. 29. It's a four-lane to Lynchburg!"

The right-angle turn was just ahead. Heller yanked the steering wheel to the left. Tires screamed! A wild skid.

Heller said, as he fought the wheel to point the swerving car straight on the new road, "Ho, ho! Centrifugal momentum about 160 foot-tons per second."

"What?" yelled Mary.

"You have to counteract it ahead of time," said Heller, firing the car down the narrow, two-lane country road.

"On this road and U.S. 29, there's no place they can call ahead and set up road blocks."

Heller screamed around a curve. The car weaved, spraying headlights against the speeding trees. "A shift to angular velocity can overcome the road friction potential of this machine! Inadequate centripetal force simulation."

"You better step on it, kid! They're in shooting range behind you!"

Trees and fences blurred by. The lights of the cop cars glared in the rearview mirror. They were closing!

Mary said, "The county line is up here. Maybe they'll quit chasing us when we cross it! Step on it, kid! You're only doing seventy!"

A sign flashed by:

CURVES AHEAD

Heller said, "So, by reduction of velocity before the turn, using this foot brake, then stamping on this throttle as you start the turn and releasing the brake, adequate compensating acceleration can be added through the turn. I got it!"

A shot blasted out. It hit the car somewhere in the rear with a jolt.

A steep downslope curve swept away to the left, evading the headlight path. Heller braked!

"I'm getting the hang of this now," he said.

The engine raced into a scream, the brakes came off! The car leaped into the curve, accelerating madly. The tires screamed but it was less.

The speedometer was racing up to ninety.

Behind them wild tire howls came from the cop cars.

Mary said, "There's a lot of curves ahead! I'll see if there's a road map in this glove compartment!"

"I don't need any," Heller said. "It was all on the Geological Survey."

A new steep curve flashed into view ahead. Heller stamped on the brakes. Mary almost went through the windshield. The engine roared. Off came the brakes, and the car shot around the curve as though fired from a gun.

"Jesus, kid, you're doing ninety!" A hasty buckling sound. She must be fastening her seat belt.

Heller glanced at trees whipping by. "That's wrong. It's only eighty-six."

He braked and then, accelerating, shot the car around a new curve.

"But I'll get it up to speed," said Heller. "Oh!" He looked at the shift lever indicator. "It was on the first drive slot. No wonder we were poking along!" He shifted the lever to high drive.

But they had lost distance. A short, straight stretch was ahead. In the rearview mirror, the leading cop car lights were getting nearer.

Heller said, "They sure build these seats close to the pedals. No leg room."

"There's some buttons down on your left that push the seat back."

Above the roar of the engine, the seat motor whirred.

A shot flash flared in the rearview mirror. It must have hit the road: the ricochet whine-yowled away, overtaken by the blast of the shot.

"Come on, you chemical-fuel Cadillac Brougham Coupe d'Elegance," said Heller. "Do I have your brake lever on?" He glanced down. It was off.

The car surged over a rise, almost lifting from the ground. A big sign flashed by:

YOU ARE LEAVING HAMDEN COUNTY

A moment later, Mary said, "Those (bleepards)! They're coming right on across the county line. Don't they know it's illegal?"

The cop cars were not so close. The lead one turned on a searchlight.

A barn whipped by.

Heller braked and fired the car into a new curve. "What are all those buttons on the panel? You got an instruction book in there?"

"No." Her hand came into view in the tail of his eye. "But I can show you. This is the air conditioning. This is the heater. This dial is where you set the interior temperature. This is the aerial for the radio but it goes up automatically when you turn the radio on. This is the radio tuning control."

The car flashed across a cattle guard with a sharp roar. The yell of the cop cars was loud.

"This is the automatic station selector. These are the preset station push buttons. You tune in the station then you pull one out and push it in and it repeats the station whenever you push it."

"You sure know a lot about cars," said Heller.

"I had one once."

A truck was turning out from a gate, dead ahead.

Heller yanked the steering wheel. They hit the gravel on the edge. The car swerved widely. He yanked it back on the road.

He said, "You're not from around here, are you. I can tell by your accent."

I hastily made a note. Since he had begun to talk to her, his own accent was fading into New England! Aha! A Code break?

He was negotiating, with brake and accelerator, a new series of curves. Fences were whipping by. He had accidentally found the floor dimmer switch and turned the lights up.

The cop cars were a few hundred yards behind, holding their noisy own.

"Oh, I'm a tried-and-true first family of Virginia all right," she said. She was swabbing at her streaming eyes and nose with the hem of her skirt. "My people were farmers. They didn't want me to have such a hard life."

They howled into a new curve.

"I sure got to get a fix," she said, swabbing some more. "Anyway, my father and mother skimped and scraped and sent me to Bassardt Woman's College: that's up the Hudson from New York."

They roared across a wooden bridge and streaked up the hill on the far side. The roar of the cop cars on the bridge sounded hot behind them.

"You look like an honest kid," she said. "I got some advice for you. You be sure to finish college. You be sure to get your degree. It isn't what you know that gets you the job. It's the diploma, the sheepskin. That's what talks. Nobody will listen to anything you say unless you have that piece of parchment!"

"Got to have a diploma before anyone will listen to you," said Heller, taking careful mental note of it.

A cop car had sped up. It got its hood even with the rear wheels of the Cadillac. A bullhorn roared!

"PULL OVER, GOD (BLEEP) YOU! YOU'RE UNDER ARREST!"

Heller weaved the Cadillac's rear over toward the cop car's front wheels. The cop car frantically braked. Heller straightened out the Cadillac's swerves and fed it more accelerator.

"Well, did you get your diploma?" said Heller.

The Cadillac plunged down to where the road crossed an open creek bed. Water rocketed to the right and left. The engine screamed as he went up the far slope.

"Oh, yes," said Mary. "You have to graduate to amount to anything. I'm a full-fledged Doctor of Philosophy. I even got my sheepskin in my bag. I'll show you. Psychology, you know."

My ears tingled! Ah, this dear girl! A psychologist! Empathy flooded through me.

The car almost left the ground over a rise.

"Psychology?" said Heller. "What's that?"

"A lot of horse (bleep). It's a con game. They try to make you think you're nobody, just a bunch of cells, an animal. They can't *do* anything. They teach you that you can't *change* anybody. They even have total consciousness that they're fakes. So why bother to practice it?"

I went catatonic with shock!

My newly formed empathy shattered utterly into nonrapport! A heretic! A foul nonbeliever! She had no reverence whatever for the sacred! Absolute antisocial negation!

The Cadillac was racing down a bumpy lane. The screams of the cop cars got louder.

"I was an A student," said Mary, "but every time any of the professors (bleeped) me, they'd say I should be more libido oriented. That's why they kept putting me on drugs. Listen, if psychology is so good, why are all the psychology professors so crazy?"

Heller slued the Cadillac across a muddy stretch of road. The speedometer said one hundred.

Mary swabbed at her running nose and eyes. "They preach free love just so they can get it free."

Another shot hit the road and ricocheted away.

"They're all bad (bleeps), too. I suppose it's the constant over-stimulation of the erotic sensory capacity that causes the consequent response deterioration. But they say it's a lot of hard work to turn every college dorm into a whorehouse. You just missed that cow."

Heller said, "But if you got your diploma, why couldn't you get a job?"

A huge sign whipped by. It had said:

WARNING—SLOW DOWN
JUNCTION WITH U.S. 29 STRAIGHT AHEAD

Heller braked. The engine screamed. He let off the brakes and shot into the four-lane U.S. 29, heading north.

"The public won't have anything to do with a psychologist. They know better. The only people who employ psychologists are the government. They think they need them to teach kids, to defend the bankers and wipe out dissidents. The government thinks the psychologists can keep the population under control. What a laugh!"

The cop cars had entered U.S. 29 behind them.

A sign said:

LYNCHBURG 20 MILES

"I sure hope I can get a fix in Lynchburg," said Mary.

Heller started letting the Cadillac out.

Heller said, "Did the government offer you a job?"

The Cadillac engine was screaming at such a pitch, it became hard to hear what they were saying.

"They sure did," she said. Then she swabbed at her nose and frantically tried to yawn. Then she leaned forward to look at him intensely. "Listen, kid. I may be a thief. I may be a totally hooked dope addict. I may be a whore. I might have some incurable disease. But don't think I've sunk so low as to work for the God (bleeped) government! Do you think I want to be a paranoid schizophrenic like those guys?"

I thought to myself, remembering Lombar, well, she has a point there. I began to take a more tolerant view of her, apostate though she might be. I suddenly recalled how clever and cunning she had been in doing Harvey "Smasher" Lee out of his favorite and vitally fetish-worshipped Cadillac. The psychology training had vividly shown through. Hadn't she used blackmail? Ah, well, my faith in psychology was totally restored.

The four-lane highway had a wide divider in the center. At

intervals a gap in the abutments showed through where one could do a U-turn.

U.S. 29 was undulating at this point, with many rises and dips. As it went over the tops, the Cadillac tended to float.

"Now, you chemical-engined Cadillac Brougham Coupe d'Elegance, it's time you started to move!"

A sign flashed by:

JUNCTION STATE HIGHWAY 699 1 MILE

The cop cars were in sight in the rearview mirror.

The Cadillac engine was winding up to a shriek.

"Jesus!" said Mary. "You're doing over 120."

The speedometer was stuck at the top.

"We're doing 135," said Heller.

A sign:

55 MPH SPEED LIMIT

Another sign:

RADAR PATROLLED

They flashed by the junction of State Highway 699.

The opposite lane had some truck traffic in it.

They soared over a rise. All four wheels of the Cadillac left the ground!

It hurtled down the hill.

The cop cars had vanished, hidden by the rise.

Heller was watching the center dividers for an opening.

"HOLD ON!" yelled Heller.

He stamped on the brakes.

Mary slapped a hand against the cowling.

Heller floorboarded the accelerator. He yanked the wheel to the left.

The car, in a skidding scream, spun through the divider opening.

It shot ahead in the opposite lanes, going now in the other direction.

A big truck was just ahead in the passing lane.

Heller stamped on the brakes and brought the car to the right of the truck!

The Cadillac came down to a shuddering fifty-five.

On the opposite side of the highway, the two police cars screamed over the rise and down the hill, still heading for Lynchburg as though the world were on fire.

Their yowls and chortles faded away to the north.

"Now," said Heller, pointing as they ambled quietly along, "we'll turn over to State Highway 699." The junction was right there. They turned sedately. "We'll go over to U.S. Highway 501 and then up into Lynchburg."

"Jesus," said Mary, "I hope so. I sure need a fix."

Chapter 5

As they headed up U.S. 501, I laughed.

What an amateur! They'd have his license number spread through Lynchburg and all the states to the north. And here he was, tamely rolling along to the first town where he'd be expected. I knew they'd spot and catch him there or somewhere up the line for sure!

Fleet combat engineer! Never trained for anything really important. Anyone with any sense would have headed in the other direction. Even for California! Fast! Yet there he was, driving at a leisurely pace into the northern side of the town.

A big neon sign said:

BIG RAINBOW MOTEL
VACANCY

Heller pulled in beside the office.

Mary swabbed at her nose with her skirt. "I better go in."

Heller unlatched the door for her and helped her out. He went in with her. Just what I wanted.

The clock on the office wall said it was 11:45.

A clerk with his sleeves rolled up had his gray head lowered over some bookkeeping. He reminded me of Lombar's chief clerk, so I expected him to be nasty.

Mary went to the desk. She sure looked awful. "Mister," she said, "could you tell me where I could buy a dollar bag or tell me where I could get one? I need it awfully bad!"

The clerk looked up and fixed her with a gimlet eye. "Aw,

Ah'm terrible sorry, ma'am. Ah jus' cain't." He turned to Heller apologetically. "It's the local Feds. They grabbed all the hard stuff in sight jus' las' week. They said they's holdin' it to shoot up the price afore they puts it back on the mahkut. You know how the God (bleeped) narcos is." He turned back to Mary. "Ah'm terrible sorry, ma'am, Ah shorely is!"

Mary was shuddering. The clerk turned back to Heller, "But Ah c'd rent you a room, though. You c'd tear yourself off a piece."

"A room w'd be fahn," said Heller.

The old man got a key. "You want it jus' foah a hour or a night? This lady don't look up to much but Ah c'd make it real cheap a'night."

"A night," said Heller.

"That be fohty dollahs, then."

Heller gave him the money and the old clerk handed him the key. "Numbuh thutty-eight, clear t'other end this buildin'. Have a good tahm." And he simply went back to his books!

(Bleep) him! No registration card! Oh, I knew his type. He was in business for himself. A crook! Gypping his owner out of a night's room rent. I knew I had been right in spotting his resemblance to Lombar's chief clerk. He'd done me in! Heller's fancy new name and car license would neither one appear! I was really enraged with him and justly so. He was dishonest!

Heller drove the car down and after figuring out how to reverse it, parked it in the open-ended garage. It was a bit long and the tail stuck out.

Mary was in bad shape. She was yawning convulsively. She felt her way down the side of the car. Then she looked at the tail and seemed to recover a bit. "Wait," she said, "the end of the car is sticking out. Somebody can see the license."

(Bleep) her! She fumbled around and found a newspaper on the dirty floor. She had Heller open the trunk and she put the newspaper, spread, half in and half out of it so it looked like carelessness in unloading. But it covered the license plate! "Whores know all about motels," she said.

Heller was kneeling at the back of the car. He lifted the

newspaper. "Hello! There's a bullet hole in this identotag." He bent around. "Doesn't seem to have hit anything else." He stood up. "So that's what a bullet hole looks like."

I wished I could show him one in Mary's head! Or in his own!

He let Mary in and then hauled in the baggage. The place had twin beds. Mary was taking off her shoes. She made some ineffectual attempts to undress further, gave it up and groggily got into bed. "I'm so sleepy," she said. "You can have it if you want it, kid: I haven't felt anything for a year. But I'd advise against it. You're a good kid and I think I might have some disease."

"Look," said Heller. "You're in pretty bad shape. Aren't there doctors or hospitals or something on this planet?"

Oho! I said, and hastily noted the Code break down. He'd slip up really bad sooner or later. He was *so* untrained!

"Listen," he persisted, shaking her by the shoulder gently. "I think you need some attention. Can't I take you to a hospital? They must have them. The people look so sick!"

She rose up with sudden ferocity. "Don't talk to me about doctors! Don't talk to me about hospitals! They'd kill me!"

He backed up at that.

The sudden burst of energy carried forward. She got her suitcase and opened it. She got out a needle kit and sank down on the edge of the bed. She opened it with shaking hands. She took the plunger out of the syringe. She put her little finger into the cylinder. She tried to scrape something off but there was nothing to scrape. She tried to suck at a needle and stuck herself.

"Oh," she shuddered, "I did all that yesterday. There's not even a tiny grain left!" She threw the kit down on the floor.

"What is this stuff, this fix you need?" said Heller.

"Oh, you poor dumb kid! It's brother, blanks, Harry, joy powder, ka-ka, skag, caballo, Chinese red, Mexican mud, junk, white stuff, hard stuff, the big H! And if I don't get some I'm going to die!"

She pushed her hand against her chest. "Oh, my poor ticker!"

The effort had been too much for her. She slumped down. Heller picked up her feet and put her back into bed. Then he gathered up the kit, sniffed curiously at the empty cylinder and then put it all back in her suitcase.

She was asleep. I knew the cycle of withdrawal. She was entering the second stage of it: she was going into what would be a restless, fitful sleep.

Heller looked at her for a bit. Then he inspected the room. The air conditioning was running and he didn't touch it. The TV had a sign that said

Not After Midnight, Please.

He left it alone.

He stripped and examined his feet. The shoes were giving him blisters. He opened a bag and took out a small medical kit. Aha! Voltarian! A Code break! Then I saw it was just a plain little white box with some unmarked jars of salve. I put it down anyway.

He put some on the blisters and put the kit back in the suitcase, and this time he opened it wider! Hey, it wasn't full of rocks the way it was supposed to be! It was full of equipment? I couldn't really see as it was opened against the light and he didn't look. I made a note that this was a very probable Code break! Those two suitcases must be full of Voltarian gear! No wonder they were so heavy!

Heller turned back the bed and started to get in. Then he changed his mind, got up and got out his little notebook and pen.

He wrote: *Got to have a diploma before anyone will listen to you.* Then he wrote: *Psychology is fake. It can't do anything or change anybody. It is the government tool of population control.*

I fumed! Now *he* was writing heresy! Oh, the International Psychological Association would get *him!* Fry his brains with every electric shock machine they could put on him! They are very adamant in protecting their monopoly.

Then he wrote: *Somebody is selling some drug on this planet that kills people.*

Well, anybody knows that! I scoffed. He actually thought he had discovered something bright! The doctors push it. The psychologists push it. The government keeps the price up. And the Mafia and Rockecenter and a lot of other people get rich. And why not? The population is all riffraff anyway.

But then he did something I really noted. He made a little V mark at the end of each line he had written so far! Now I may have flunked math at the Academy but I do know the symbols. And that check is the mark used in logic equations! It means "Pertinent factor to be employed in a rationality deduction theorem." I had him! He was using a Voltarian math symbol right there in plain sight. A total Code break. I made an emphatic note of it!

If they didn't get him, I would!

He fiddled with the lights and figured out how to turn them off.

My screen went dark and, shortly, his even breathing told me he was asleep.

Chapter 6

It had been a long day for me. I got up and was about to pour myself a nice cold glass of *sira* when a sudden thought struck me, possibly stimulated by seeing him write.

He had given me a letter to mail! I hadn't inspected it!

It's always a pleasure to read, secretly, other people's mail. I deserved some recompense for not having been able to witness his arrest—even though I knew it would be very soon.

I got the letter out of my tunic, thinking it was probably some mushy note addressed to the Countess Krak—and wouldn't she be on her ear if she knew Heller was sleeping in a secret bedroom with a diseased whore!

I got the envelope squared around and over to the light. It was official green!

My hair stood on end!

It was addressed to

CAPTAIN TARS ROKE
HIS MAJESTY'S OWN ASTROGRAPHER
PALACE CITY, VOLTAR
VOLTAR CONFEDERACY
URGENT OFFICIAL
LONG LIVE THEIR MAJESTIES

He had a line to Roke!

I managed to concentrate through the shock. When had he put this in? And then I recalled that Captain Tars Roke had been at the farewell party! And Heller had talked to him for some time. I hadn't been alert because I had been foully duped into taking that confounded speed, that amphetamine methedrine! It had been a plot!

I calmed myself. Now, let's see: Lombar had told me that Heller would be sending in reports to the Grand Council. I was supposed to intercept them, learn how to forge them and send them on. Only then could I safely do away with Heller!

Ah, well. I was all right, then. I was doing my duty. This was simply Heller's first report. He was stupidly using me as part of his line to Roke and, in fact, he had no other line to use. So, all was well!

It was double-sealed. But that was nothing. Using methods known only to the Apparatus and tools specially provided for the purpose, I undetectably opened the envelope.

The sheet inside was big, but so are all official communications.

After the usual formal greetings, it said: *As we agreed, if you cease to authentically hear from me each month, only then should you advise His Majesty to embark upon the second alternative.* And then it rambled on, saying the mission may take a while, that the tug had run well, that he was grateful for some of the tips Captain Tars had given him about polar shifts. And then it went on to recall a lecture Captain Tars had given once about molten planetary cores being generators. And did the captain remember old Boffy Jope, the student who believed planets should turn slower so people would have more time to sleep? And he thought he would get along all right but keep an eye on things, please.

First, I suddenly realized that Heller had been one of Captain Tars Roke's students in the Astrographic College where the captain often lectured. The tone clearly indicated that Heller had been one of those abominable students who are favored by their teachers!

Next, I realized that this clearly meant Heller had a direct line to His Majesty, Cling the Lofty!

Wait! There was something funny about this letter!

I sat down. I spread it out on a desk. I turned a light on it.

It was not written the way you write a letter! It had gaps between words! It had uneven spaces between the lines!

The words could have occupied half the space they did occupy!

I broke out in a cold sweat. Forge? I had almost put my foot directly into a trap!

This letter was a platen code!

The way that is done, you take an opaque sheet of material that fits exactly over the sheet of writing paper. You cut long slots in the opaque sheet.

Everything is then covered except a few words.

Those platen words are the REAL message! The rest is just junk.

One would have to lay the platen on this sheet to read it.

I didn't have Heller's platen!

Unless I had that platen, I could forge nothing! The hidden message would not match Tars Roke's platen!

You can tell these codes because, in order to get words to appear in the platen holes, you have to write them in exact places on the sheet and that makes spaces and lines uneven!

Sometimes it makes goofy sense, trying to fill in around the key words. But Heller was clever. He'd made up some story about somebody called Boffy Jope so he would have enough words.

It had long been daylight in Turkey, of course. I had had no sleep. Unlike that (bleepard) in America who was lying in bed slumbering peacefully without a single care, I was a real slave of duty.

Besides, I was worried sick.

Sleep or no sleep, I worked right on. In every conceivable way I could, I tried to figure out the hidden message so I could get the platen.

I tried to find "Gris is doing me in." That didn't work. I tried "The Earth base is full of opium." But that didn't work. Actually, they couldn't work as the applicable words didn't appear in the letter.

I tried "Lombar is going to use drugs to cave in Voltar," but the name of Lombar and the word *drugs* . . . Wait! Maybe the platen only picked out letters! Maybe not full words!

Two hours I spent on it, feeling worse and worse.

I decided I needed air. I went outside and walked around the garden. Several staff ran away when they saw me but even that didn't cheer me up.

I went back in. Courageously, I tackled it all again.

And at length, I had it figured out. This was a *key sentence* platen!

The operative word was "authentically." Heller had written, "If you cease to *authentically* hear from me . . ."

He and Roke must have ducked into the tug—yes, they had been gone a bit—and conspired to arrange a key sentence such as "Cores are molten" and exchanged platens. If the platen, placed over the letter, did not show up the agreed upon sentence, "Cores are molten" or whatever it was, the message was not authenticated and was a forgery.

If an authenticated message did not arrive periodically on schedule, it said right there that Roke was to advise His Majesty to embark upon the second alternative! A FLAT–OUT, RIGHT NOW, BLOOD–AND–FLAME INVASION OF THE PLANET EARTH!

If they didn't get Heller's reports regularly, it would mean he had been interfered with and had failed. No reports equalled Earth would be a slaughterhouse!

But to Hells with Earth. If that invasion took place, every plan Lombar had would go up in smoke! As the Grand Council knew nothing of the Earth base, it would go splat, too!

But far more important than that, I would be killed! Lombar's hidden agent would see to that even if I escaped everything else!

Heller's reports MUST GO THROUGH!

Hey, wait!

If Heller were successful, then all Lombar's lines and planning on Earth would be ruined! For his closest associates would be bankrupted!

If it even looked like Heller was going to win in improving this planet, Lombar's hidden agent would kill me!

My head began to ache.

Heller lose, Heller win, there was one thing certain: Gris would be dead!

I made myself sit down. I made myself stop tearing at my hair. I must calmly work this out!

So, gnawing on the *sira* glass until I threw it against the wall, I worked it out.

I must get hold of Heller's platen! Then I could forge reports that would make the Grand Council—via Roke—think Heller was doing his job, while in fact, Lombar was protected in that Heller would be doing nothing at all. He would be dead.

But wait. I didn't have the platen. Until I got the platen, NOTHING MUST HAPPEN TO HELLER!

And there the idiot was with a marked car, police in several states alert, carrying a name that would get him sent to the pen as an imposter, a totally untrained agent in deadly danger of being scooped up!

I started praying.

Oh, my Gods, let nothing happen to Heller until I got my hands on that platen! Please, Gods, if anything happens to him at all, Soltan Gris is a dead man! To Hells with the slaughter of Earth! We'll just disregard that. Think of Soltan Gris! Take pity. Please?

Chapter 7

There is a seven-hour time difference between Eastern Standard Time, where Heller was, and Istanbul time, which I was near. So you can imagine how keeping check on Heller was a strain. When he was rising, all refreshed, at 7:00 A.M., I was hanging on the viewer at 2:00 P.M., an exhausted wreck.

He got up quietly and took a shower. Raht, to help his own personal finances, had not brought him any change of clothes so he put on what he had, swearing under his breath as he donned the shoes. He looked at himself in the mirror and shook his head. Indeed, he did look funny with that green-banded, too-small Panama, that purple shirt, the red and white check jacket with sleeves three inches too short, the blue and white striped pants that didn't come down to the ankles, the orange suede, too-tight shoes.

I groaned. He stood out like a searchlight! A cinch for even the most myopic cop to spot. And he didn't even realize it! His main concern would be with aesthetics, not with being unspottable.

Mary was tumbling about restlessly but still asleep. Heller softly closed the door and, with a glance at the car, trotted out of the motel grounds.

There was a diner nearby and he went in and puzzled over the menu, of course not knowing what any of these things were. But it gave breakfast by the numbers and he ordered "Number 1." It was orange juice, oatmeal and bacon and eggs. But the elderly waitress didn't bring him coffee. She brought him milk and he looked at it and tasted it suspiciously. She told him to drink it, that he was too young for coffee. Then she refused to sell him any of the pie he gazed at longingly, finally foregoing it on the advice that he must learn to control his appetite and she was going to stand there until he finished his oatmeal. She was fifty and a motherly type, with boys of her own. Boys, he was advised, were willful and if they didn't watch their diet, they wouldn't grow. She even managed his money, told him not to display it because it would get stolen and keep some of it in his shoes and tipped herself a dollar.

Authoritatively fed, Heller escaped to the street. It was the main street of the town, lined with shops, and he went trotting along, glancing in the windows.

Don't trot! I begged him mentally. Walk sedately, saunter, don't attract attention! You're a wanted man! Heller trotted with an easy lope. Believe me, nobody runs in the South! Nobody!

He popped into a clothing store, found in just a few seconds that it had nothing that would fit his six foot-two frame, popped out and trotted on.

A hock shop was just ahead, a place where the Virginians sell the things they steal off tourists. Heller scanned the windows and right-angled into it. There were barrels of discards and shelves full of tagged junk.

The sleepy clerk, having gotten the shop open and expecting to be able to go back to a nap in the rear, was not too helpful. Heller pointed.

The clerk got down an 8 mm Nikon motion picture camera. He said, "You don't want this, kid. They don't sell film for it anymore." Heller was inspecting the big black and gold Nikon label. He then made the clerk get down another one. Heller laid them on the counter. Heller saw a barrel: it was full of broken fishing reels and tangled line. He got out some.

"Those are deep-sea reels," said the clerk. "The fishing concession at Smith Mountain Lake went broke. They don't work."

"Fishing?" said Heller.

"Catch fish. Sport. Come on, kid, you're not that dumb. I ain't in any mood for jokes today. If you really want something, tell me, take it and get out! I ain't got any time to fool around."

Heller picked out several impressive reels, some broken rods and a hopeless tangle of line. He added some multihooked, steel-shafted bass plugs and a whole pile of weights that had steel hooks on the end. He put these on the counter.

He was staring at a tattered cardboard counter display for portable cassette recorders that were also AM/FM radios. "Give me one of these."

"You mean you're going to actually buy something?"

"Yes," said Heller and pulled out some money.

"Hell, I thought you was like the local kids: all eyes and no dough. You ain't from around here, then." He got a dusty recorder, even put some batteries in it and laid out a package of cassettes. He looked at the money Heller had in his hand and pretended to add something up. "That'll be a hundred and seventy-five dollars."

Heller paid him. They put the weird loot in sacks and Heller was on his way. And I, personally, thought he was as crazy as the clerk did. Obsolete cameras, broken fishing reels, tangled line. Idiocy.

Trotting along, Heller saw a sporting goods store. He right-angled in. He pointed at the window. A young, wild-haired clerk dived in and brought out a pair of baseball shoes.

Heller looked at them. They were black; they laced to the ankle; they had a long tongue that folded back over the laces. He turned them over. They had no heels, but they had two circles of cleats, one set under the ball of the foot, one set under the heel. The steel cleats were long, about half an inch high, and the plates which held them were solidly fixed in the leather sole.

"Let you have them cheap," said the clerk. "We got a ton of them. The coach over at Jackson High ordered full uniforms for the baseball team; first, he said they came in too big and wouldn't take them. Then, he ran off with the English teacher and the athletic fund."

"Baseball?" said Heller.

The clerk pointed to a pile of baseballs before he caught himself. "Quit it, kid."

Heller had evidently gotten smart. He said, "Do you have them for sale?"

The clerk just looked at him. Heller walked over to the display of baseballs. They were a trifle bigger and they were a little harder than a bullet ball.

There was an archery target standing up at the back of the store. Heller said, "Do you mind?"

He hefted the baseball. He flexed his wrist and then he threw the baseball at the archery target! I could hear the sizzle of the ball going through the air. It hit the bull's-eye! It plowed right on through, broke the back stand and went splat against the wall.

"Jesus!" said the clerk. "A pitcher! A real pitcher!"

Heller went over and recovered the ball. The hide had come off. He pulled curiously at the insides. "Well," he said to himself, "not so good, but it will have to do."

"Jesus," said the clerk. "You're a natural! Look, do you mind if I sort of put that target away and when the New York Yankees sign you, I can maybe put it on display?"

Heller was looking for a bag. He found one you could carry over your shoulder. He was counting baseballs into it. The clerk was trying to pump him as to what college team he was on and what were his plans on going Big League and apologizing because Heller looked so young nobody would think he was a veteran. Heller wasn't giving him much encouragement. He was shopping around the shelves. He found a book, *The Fine Art of Baseball for Beginners,* and mystified the clerk by putting it on the purchases pile. Then he added another book, *The Fine Art of Angling for Beginners.* Was he going fishing?

But the clerk was busy now. "Look, we got full uniforms. And let's see what shoe size you take. Look, can we kind of put out we outfitted you?"

I thought, that's all we need. Local publicity this very morning!

Heller had to turn down a lot more than he bought: three pairs of shoes, six white, long-sleeved undershirts, twelve pairs of baseball socks with red-striped tops, two white exercise suits, a dozen support underpants, two unlettered uniforms that were white with red stripes, a red anorak with captain's stripes, a black belt and a red batting helmet.

And then Heller saw the caps. They were red baseball caps, not as nice or as stylish as his habitual racing cap, but similar. The bill was longer: it would never crush properly under a racing helmet to act as padding. But Heller was enraptured. He made a sort of cooing sound. He pushed the pile around until he found one his size and put it on. He went over to the mirror.

I flinched. From the neck up, there was Jettero Heller, space-racing champion of the Academy! It had been easy to forget his amused blue eyes, his flowing blond hair and that go-to-Hells-who-cares smile! It was like being shot suddenly back to Voltar! But even then I'd missed it.

"What did you say the initials stood for?" he said.

"Jackson High," said the clerk.

I had been slow, possibly because of the intricate intertwine of the white team letters on the cap. J.H.! THAT was why he was grinning!

"I'll take half a dozen," said Heller, laughing now.

Heller ceremoniously made the clerk a present of the purple shirt and the orange suede shoes and the Panama hat.

They packed the gear up in a sports carry-all. Heller paid him three hundred dollars and took the card.

Heller was going out the door when the clerk yelled, "Hey! You forgot to tell me your name!"

"You'll hear," Heller yelled back and was gone.

Ah, well, there was hope. If he'd given the name he was supposed to use, that (bleeped) clerk would have been all over town with a megaphone. I was thankful Heller was modest. He certainly wasn't smart. He was trotting up the street now in a scarlet baseball cap with his own initials on it and wearing a long-sleeved baseball undershirt. He had retained the blue-striped pants and red-checked jacket. He stood out like a beacon! And worse than that, the spikes he was wearing were clickety-clacking on the pavement even louder than his old-time hull shoes!

It was Lombar's fault, really: he had ordered that Heller not be trained in espionage; any self-respecting spy would know you must remain unnoticeable. A trained agent would have looked at the population around him and dressed like that. He sure did not resemble anyone else in that quiet southern town! Looking at him now, to paraphrase the clerk: Jesus!

Heller glanced at his watch. It was getting on toward nine. But he had another stop. It was a candy store!

I groaned. I was dealing with an idiot, not a special agent. Special agents don't eat candy! They smoke cigarettes!

Some little twelve-year-old kids were in there haggling with the clerk over the price of gumdrops which seemed to have gone up. Two of them were wearing baseball caps, the way little kids do in America. And I realized that Heller, now wearing one, would mind-associate in people that he was even younger!

Heller went down the counter, apparently looking for one particular type of candy. He found it: it was individually wrapped in transparent paper; it was red and white in a spiral, just like it's advertised in magazines sometimes.

The kids bought their dime's worth and Heller promptly over-whelmed the aged lady clerk by purchasing ten pounds of candy! Not only did he buy the white and red kind, but also other kinds, and he wanted them all mixed up which brought about the problem of putting them in different bags, all mixed up, and then there not being a big enough bag to contain all the other bags. He sure ruined the day for the old lady clerk.

Laden, Heller got back on the street. There was a cop car parked at the corner. Now any trained agent would have gone the other way. But not Heller. He trotted right past the cop car!

I saw, in peripheral vision, the cops look at him.

It was time to go back and fortify myself with cold *sira*. And take time off for a small prayer. If they had special Hells for Apparatus case handlers, the one they would send me to would specialize in forcing totally untrained agents on me! Neither the *sira* nor the prayer helped!

If anything happened to Heller before I got that platen, I was done for!

PART FIFTEEN

Chapter 1

In the room, Mary Schmeck was still restlessly asleep. Heller threw his loot down on his bed. He lifted his two suitcases up on a long bureau, side by side, and unfastened the straps.

I was going to get a look at their contents! Maybe the platen was right on top!

Foolish hope. There were no rocks but there sure was a wild medley of little tubes and boxes and coils of wire. What a junk heap!

Heller got out a small tool case and two small vials. He picked up the two obsolete Nikon cameras and put them on a table. He inspected the edge of a label, then put some drops under the edge and the gold and black *NIKON* lifted right off! He did the other one.

Then he took two small cases from the grips and opened them. The time-sights! Both of them! Indeed, the tug *was* planet bound! I knew the Apparatus could never pry another one out of the Fleet!

From the second vial he took a bit of what must be glue and put it on the label backs and in a moment, glaring on the side of each time-sight was *NIKON*.

They looked now like two Super 8 motion-picture cameras!

He put them back in their small cases and back into the grip. He threw in the two obsolete ones as well.

Then he got out the candy he had made on the ship. The wrappers were a bit different but not remarkably so. He had what must be three pounds of it! He mixed it into the other candy sacks and then started packing the bags all through the other grip. Very unneatly, too.

Then he packed the broken fishing rods and reels hit or miss through everything. He added the tangles of line in snarls and coils in and over the other contents. Then he took the bass plugs and the weights and began to jam them in anywhere and everywhere.

What a MESS!

And I thought Fleet guys were always so neat!

He had to let the suitcase straps out to accommodate all the extra. He neated up the athletic carry-all and he was ready.

He had picked up a sweet roll, a container of milk and another of coffee while I was in my other room praying. He gently tried to wake up Mary Schmeck. She fought him off, trying to go back to sleep. I could see her pupils were contracted. She wanted nothing to do with the roll or the milk or coffee.

"We've got to leave," said Heller.

This got to her. "Washington," she said.

"Yes, we'll be going through Washington, D.C.," Heller replied.

She muttered, "There's sure to be some junk in Washington. There always is. It's full of it. Get me there, for Christ's sakes." She tried to get up. Then she screamed, "Oh, my God! My legs!" They were drawing up in knots. She fell back whimpering.

He picked up all the luggage, went out and put it in the back seat. Then he returned and carried Mary Schmeck out and put her in the front seat. He laid her shoes on the floorboards. He put the milk, coffee and the roll in the drink tray.

He had the key in his hand and didn't know what to do with it, didn't realize you just left it in the door and slipped away. There was a cleaning woman, an old black woman, coming out of the room next-door.

Oh, my Gods! He walked up to her and handed her the key! Drawing attention to himself. You NEVER do that! And then he compounded the felony. He said, "You know what road to take to Washington?"

She had not only *seen* him now, she knew where he was going! And the first thing police do when they're searching for a criminal is check the motels! She said, "You jus' follah Yew S. 29. Charlottesville, Culpeper, Arlington and cross the Potomac and there you is.

Mah sister, she lives in Washington and I don't know what the hell I'm doin' down heah in Virginia wheah we is still slaves!" I thought to myself, I doubt she'd dare say that to an adult Virginian. Slavery has its points! I almost drifted off thinking about Utanc and then something else happened that recalled me firmly and nervously to duty.

Heller backed out the car, leaned out the window and said, "Thank you, miss, foh a very nahce stay." And the woman smiled, stood there leaning on the broom and in a moment I could see, in the rearview mirror, that she was staring after the car. And more. I saw the newspaper which hid the license plate blowing off in the car's wake. For sure she would remember that car. (Bleep) Heller!

No, no, I mustn't (bleep) him! I must pray he would get through!

He had no trouble whatever in finding U.S. 29 to Charlottesville. He tooled along the four-lane through the lovely Virginia morning, admiring the view. The Cadillac was purring, surprisingly smooth, especially on this smooth road.

It was promising to be a very hot August day and he began to fool with the air conditioning. He set it at seventy-three degrees on the dial, got it functioning on automatic and after a bit, when apparently the hot air had blown out of the car, closed the windows. It was amazingly quiet!

A white board fence fled by. A big sign:

JACKSON HORSE RANCH

Beyond it were some animals in the field, leaping and prancing about. Apparently he added something up. He laughed. "So those are horses!" Then for some idiotic reason, he patted the Cadillac panel ledge. He said, "Never mind, you chemical-engine Cadillac Brougham Coupe d'Elegance. I like you even if you don't have any of those things under your hood."

I will never understand Fleet guys. Compared to a Voltar airbus, an Earth vehicle is a farce. And he knew it! Then I had it. Toys. Anything was a toy to Fleet officers, from landing craft to battleships to planets. They just have no respect for force! No.

Then I really had it: fetish worship.

He found he could drive with one knee and leaned back, arms spread out along the top of the seat. It made me nervous until I realized I was 105 degrees of longitude away.

But another shock was in store. He glanced at the speedometer and it was doing SIXTY-FIVE! The speed limit is fifty-five and all those roads have signs that say they are radar patrolled!

I saw he was not driving by the speedometer: he was running with the traffic—some big trucks and passenger cars—and by and large was doing sixty-five. But cops love to pick one car out of such a clump and arrest it. I went and got some more *sira*.

He got through Charlottesville all right. And then Mary Schmeck, who had been in a twitchy, comatose state, woke up.

"Oh, I feel awful!" she moaned. "My legs are killing me! I ache in every joint!" She was thrashing about, obviously in a bad state. "How far are we from Washington?"

"We're almost to Culpeper," he said.

"Oh," she moaned. "It's still a long way yet!"

"Only about an hour," said Heller.

"Jesus, I hurt! Turn on some music. Maybe it will redirect my focus intensity."

Heller fiddled with the radio and finally got some jazz. A song came on:

> *As I passed by the Saint James infirmary,*
> *I saw my sweetheart there.*
> *Stretched out on a long white table,*
> *So pale, so cold, so bare.*

Mary moaned, "Oh, my legs!"

> *Went up to see the doctor.*
> *"She's very low," he said.*
> *Went back to see my woman.*
> *Good God, she's lying there dead!*
> ***SHE'S DEAD!***

"Oh, my God," said Mary.

Sixteen coal-black horses,
All hitched to a rubber-tired hack,
Carried seven girls to the graveyard.
Only six of them comin' back!

"Turn that off!" Mary shrieked.

Heller turned it off. I was very sorry he did so. It was the first pleasant thing I had heard for days!

Mary was covered with goose pimples. "I'm freezing!" she cried out, writhing.

Heller quickly turned the thermostat up to eighty.

Long before it could have warmed up, Mary said, "I'm roasting hot!"

Heller turned the thermostat down again.

She kept it up, thrashing about. It was obvious to me what was wrong with her. She was in the third stage of withdrawal symptoms. People sure do complain about them.

"I can't get my breath," she was panting now. Well, that's normal, too, for somebody who has a bad heart. But still, respiratory failure is the usual cause of death in morphine addiction and it would be no different for its derivative, heroin. The lung muscles cease to function. And in her case, since she'd been complaining of a bad heart, I wondered idly whether she would die in the car or in the next motel.

Then it was I who almost had respiratory failure. What if Heller had a dead prostitute dope addict on his hands! With *his* assumed name!

Oh, Gods! He'd be front page in every tabloid dirt sheet in America! And what Rockecenter would do was *awful!*

I couldn't count on Heller to do the right thing. In espionage, he simply would have known enough to haul up out of sight and dump her in a ditch and leave her quick. But no, here he was, doing the wrong things as usual! He was trying to help her!

They were through Culpeper. Suddenly, the girl said, "You got to find a toilet! Look, that service station ahead! Stop there! Quick!"

Fourth stage. The diarrhea had hit her!

Heller zoomed into an unfrequented service station and Mary was out of the car like a shot, racing to the women's room. I prayed they wouldn't stay there long, exposed to view from traffic.

Heller told the gawky country boy attendant to "fill up the chemical repository" and the lonely boy made out that Heller meant gas. The usually idle boy then figured out for himself that Heller's early education had been neglected.

With careful instruction, Heller got taught to service the car: steering fluid, brake fluid, transmission fluid, correct radiator coolant, windshield wiper water with Windex in it, oil and the right and wrong kinds of oil, gas and the right and wrong kinds of gas. Apparently nobody in his whole life had ever listened to this country boy before and he really went flat out to educate a "younger Virginia kid," even though he seemed disappointed to find that Heller hadn't stolen the car.

The kid exhausted the subject of tires and then got bright. He said the car needed a grease job and the differential checked. He said it would only take a short while to grease it up. And onto the rack he drove it and up into the air the car went. Sure enough, the differential was half empty. And sure enough it needed grease and the airhose and greasegun pumped away. Heller marked where all the fittings were. And then he got worried about the girl and went to find her.

Mary was crumpled up on a toilet seat, passed out. Somehow, Heller roused her and got her to straighten herself up.

Then voices outside. Heller peeked through a window.

A cop car! Virginia State Police!

I turned up the gain. The cop was saying, ". . . man and a woman. They went up this road someplace last night."

"What kind of a car?" said the gawky country boy.

The officer consulted his sheet. "Cadillac. Same color as that one you got on the rack."

I went white. There went Heller and no platen!

"Could be that they passed when I was off shift," said the country boy.

"Well, you let me know iff'n you do see'm, Bedford," said the state policeman. "They're wanted awful bad!"

"Always willin' to oblige, Nathan," said the gawky country boy. And when the cop drove off, going back down the road toward Culpeper, the boy added, "You cocky son of a (bleepch)."

He got the Cadillac down off the hoist and Heller came out, carrying Mary. He put her in the front seat.

The gawky country boy was all smiles. "I *knew* you stole it!" He looked Heller up and down admiringly. Then he said, "I was going to remove and grease the wheels but that can wait. I got an idea you better be goin'."

The Cadillac had only taken ten gallons of gas. I was amazed. Then I realized it had just been a clever psychological ploy on the part of the girl to call it a gas hog.

The bill, in fact, was not all that great. And Heller paid it with a twenty-dollar tip. Count on Heller! He'd be broke soon which was another hurdle I'd have to cross. I couldn't just have Raht or Terb walk up to him and hand him money. They must be somewhere on this road but I couldn't contact them when they were moving.

Mary had to go to the can again and the boy instructed Heller how to wash windows: Never use a grease rag, only paper. Never use a wax glass cleaner. Amazing, he'd already been tipped!

Heller got the girl straightened out and back in the car once more.

"Next tahm you come by," said the gawky country boy, "stop off and I'll show you how to tune the engine."

Heller really thanked him and when they drove away, there was the boy by the pump, waving. Heller blew the horn twice and they were on their way to Washington.

And Washington, I groaned to myself, was just about the most over-policed city in the world!

I wondered if I should start writing a will. I had several things: the gold coming, the hospital kickback due and Utanc. Trouble was, I'd nobody to leave them to.

I never felt more alone and prey to the winds of fate than I did as I watched the road through Heller's eyes to Washington.

Chapter 2

Following the complex signs, Heller negotiated the various confusions the traffic departments of that area planned in order to prevent Americans from ever getting to their seat of government. He refused invitations to use State Highway 236, to go over to U.S. 66, to take State 123 and wind up in the Potomac River. He ignored directions to take U.S. 495—which is really U.S. 95 and bypasses Washington entirely. He even defeated the conspiracy to confuse the public on U.S. 29 to believe they were on U.S. 50. He steadfastly rolled along on U.S. 29, even untangled the parkways alongside the Potomac River without winding up at the Pentagon—as most unsuspecting public do—and presently was rolling over the Memorial Bridge. A masterpiece of navigation that he shouldn't be doing any part of!

The Potomac River was a beautiful blue. The bridge a beautiful white. The Lincoln Memorial at its end, an impressive piece of Greek architecture glowing white in the afternoon sun.

And Heller had trouble. Mary was flailing about to a point where it was almost impossible to drive. She was bending over with cramps. She was letting out small screams. She was striking out with her arms. And she was saying over and over, "Oh, God, my heart!" alternated with "Oh, Jesus, I've got to have a fix!" And neither prayer was getting any attention whatever from the deities of that planet.

Heller was watching her and trying to hold her down more than he was watching traffic. The giddy and foolhardy spin of cars and trucks around the Memorial circle may not disturb the calm majesty of Lincoln's huge statue inside, but it is designed to shatter less immortal nerves.

It was evidently plain to him that the combination of Mary and the traffic was a lot too much to cope with just now. He spotted a turnoff into the park which lies to the southeast of the Lincoln Memorial itself.

It is a very beautiful park: an unfrequented road and a pleasant pedestrian walk stretch out beside the Potomac River, separated from it by a wide expanse of lawn. It is one of the most quiet and lovely spots in Washington. The only trouble with it is the CIA uses it to try out their agent recruits in hidden sleuthing!

I freaked! Heller was stopping! I mourned my fate to be handling somebody without the slightest training in espionage. He should have known that Voltar agents have orders never to go near that park!

He had seen the drinking fountains which are paced every few hundred feet along the walk. He had probably sensed the false peace imparted by the beautiful willow-like trees between the path and water's edge. He may have been attracted by the abundance of parking places. It must have been a hot day in Washington but the lawns were deserted here.

He stopped. Mary was in a momentary coma. He got out and went to the drinking fountain. He had an empty paper coffee cup. He managed to figure out how you turned on the fountain and rinsed and filled the cup.

At the car, he said, "Maybe drinking some water would help." And, indeed, he was right. Withdrawal brings on heavy dehydration. He wouldn't know that but he could probably tell from her dry and swollen lips.

She managed to drink a little bit of the water. Then suddenly she turned sideways, got her feet on the ground and, still sitting on the car seat, began to vomit.

He held her head, speaking in a low, concerned voice, trying to soothe her.

In his peripheral vision I saw the side and saddle of a horse moving up the road.

Heller looked up. A mounted National Parks policeman went about fifty feet back of the car, stopped and turned his horse around. He sat there looking at Heller and the car.

I thought, well, Gris, you should have made out your will because here we go! Heller has had it!

The park policeman was fishing a hand radio out. He began to speak into it.

I hastily turned up the gain. ". . . I *know* I'm supposed to use numbers to report." Someone on the other end, his traffic controller, must be giving him a hard time.

Mary was trying to vomit some more but didn't have anything to throw up.

The park policeman was saying, "But there ain't any code number for a bullet hole in a license plate! . . . All right! All right! So it's 201, suspicious car!"

Mary couldn't sit there anymore. Heller opened the back door and pushed some baggage around. Then he got Mary and moved her to the back seat.

". . . Yeah," the mounted cop was saying. "Kid and a woman in it. No, I don't know who was driving. I didn't see them until after they'd parked. . . . No, *hell!* I'm not going to . . . I'm ALONE here! I'm just Park Police, not James Bond! They could be a CIA plant or something. . . . No! Shots would scare my horse. . . . Well, send the God (bleeped) squad car then!"

I prayed Heller would get the Hells out of there. But he was bathing her forehead with bits of cool water on his redstar engineer's cloth. I was so agitated I didn't even write it down as a possible Code break.

In no time at all, a D.C. squad car slinked up near the horse. Two D.C. cops got out and talked in whispers to the mounted patrolman. I could barely pick it up. All I caught was ". . . those are Virginia plates so phone them in for a check."

One of the cops was on his radio. Then the two of them, wide apart, walked toward the Cadillac.

Twenty feet away, the nearest cop drew his gun. "You, there! Freeze!"

Heller stood up straight. I prayed, no, no, Heller. Don't do something crazy! At that range they can kill you! And I don't have the platen!

The nearest cop was motioning with his gun. "All right, kid, move over there and lie down on the grass, belly to ground."

Heller moved to the spot and laid down. He kept his head turned toward the cop.

"All right," said the cop. "Where's your driver's license?"

There was a scream from the car. Mary had come to with sudden energy. "It's in my purse! That kid is just a hitchhiker. This is my car!" It was nearly too much for her. She sank back panting, holding her chest.

I realized now she was not a true psychologist. The whole purpose of the subject is to throw suspicion and responsibility on others either to get them in trouble or to protect yourself—which amounts to the same thing. But even though it was a violation of psychology behavior rules, I gratefully accepted the help.

The first cop detoured over toward the car and dug around to find her purse. He found it and looked at her license.

"Oh, God," moaned Mary. "Please, please get me a fix!"

The effect was electric. "A hop head!" said the first cop. He made a signal to the other cop to cover Heller and then began yanking the suitcases out of the car. He was going to look for dope!

He opened the sports carry-all, rummaged in it and then threw it aside. He grabbed one of Heller's cases, unstrapped it and flopped the back up.

"That's the kid's baggage," moaned Mary.

The cop reached in. He said, "Ouch, God (bleep) it!" He pried a multihooked bass plug off his hand and sucked his finger. Gingerly, then, he held up an old fishing reel and stirred at the mess of line. He said, "Cameras and fishing gear. Jesus Christ, kid, you sure do an awful job of packing. You could ruin some of this stuff." He slammed the case closed.

The other cop was well back with a gun on Heller.

The first cop opened Heller's second case.

"Jesus!" screamed Mary. "Get me a fix! Can't anybody hear

me?" And then she leaned out of the backseat and began to dry vomit.

"Candy!" cried the first cop. "Dope concealed in candy!" He turned to the other cop. "You see, I knew there'd be dope here. They hide it in candy!"

He gingerly evaded more fishhooks and untangled a candy bag from fishing line. He opened the bag and took out a piece. He got a jackknife from his pocket and cut the sweet in half. He touched one of the halves to his tongue.

Disappointed, he threw the cut pieces and the paper in the general direction of a *Don't Litter!* sign. He got another bag open and did the same thing.

"Ah, hell," he said. "It's just candy-type candy."

The second cop said, "Joe, I figure if there was any dope in that baggage, this dame wouldn't be going through withdrawal."

The first cop closed Heller's grip and then hauled out Mary's suitcase and got it open. "Hurray!" he shouted. "I knew it! Here's a dope kit complete!" And he held it up so his partner and the park patrolman could see it. "This is illegal as hell even if there is no dope! I knew I could catch them out!"

Oh, Heller, I prayed. Just keep on lying there. Don't do anything.

Mary had come out of a spasm of dry retching. She tried to get to the first cop, "That's my kit! I'm a doctor! My diploma is right in that bag!"

The first cop didn't even bother to push her back into the car and she collapsed, dangling half out of it.

The first cop disgustedly found it. "She's right." He dropped the suitcase shut and stood up. "Aw, (bleep), there's no smack here."

The second cop gestured with his gun to Heller. "You can get up, kid. You're clean."

I sagged with relief. I knew exactly what the prisoner felt when they told him he had been reprieved.

Heller got to his feet. He went over and tried to get Mary back into the car.

Heller suddenly saw a plain, green sedan quietly roll up and stop.

The first cop said, "Oh, (bleep). It's the FBI."

Two very tough looking characters got out. They wore box coats. Their hats were gangster-type hats.

As one, they drew and flashed their I.D. folders.

The first one had a puffy face and a sagging lower lip. "I'm Special Agent Stupewitz, FBI."

The second one said, "Special Agent Maulin, FBI." He was a huge, hulking brute of a man.

Stupewitz walked up to the park patrolman and the two D.C. cops. "This is out-of-state business—Federal! Move aside!"

Maulin went around to the back of the car and read the license. "This is the car, all right. Look at that bullet hole!"

Stupewitz gestured a Colt .457 revolver at Heller. It looked like a cannon. "Stand up and face that car, kid. Put your hands on the roof and spread-eagle, legs apart."

Heller did as he was told. That artillery could have blown him apart!

The first D.C. cop said, "He's just a hitchhiker. This is the woman's car."

Maulin said, "Filled with bags of dope."

The second D.C. cop said, "There's nothing in the bags but cameras and fishing gear. There ain't even any dope in the candy."

Stupewitz said, "You've got it all wrong, brother. That's why you locals have to have the support of the FBI. Without us, you'd just breeze along in total peace!"

Maulin said, "We got the whole story from Virginia."

I thought, well, Gris, it's too late to make a will now! Heller will be finished so quick, there won't be time.

Stupewitz had his gun trained on Heller. "What's your name, kid?"

Mary came to, threshing about. "Don't talk to them kid!"

Heller didn't answer Stupewitz.

Stupewitz said, "Kid, do you realize it's a felony not to give your name to a Federal officer?"

Heller didn't answer.

Stupewitz made a signal to Maulin. Maulin drew his gun

from his back belt, trained it on Heller from a distance. Stupewitz stepped up to Heller and began to frisk him.

I was certain I knew what was coming now. It was too late even to pray.

Stupewitz got to the papers in Heller's jacket. He yanked them out. He looked at them.

Suddenly Stupewitz drew off to the side, away from the other cops and Heller. He made a frantic beckon to Maulin. Maulin kept his gun on Heller but sidled around to get close to Stupewitz.

I frantically turned up more gain. I got wind in the trees. I got some birds. I got the far-off siren of an ambulance getting louder. But I couldn't make out anything Stupewitz or Maulin were saying as they examined the papers. I could see them whispering but as they were using their lips the way criminals do, talking from the side of the mouth, I couldn't even read the words.

An ambulance came up. It was marked *GEORGETOWN HOSPITAL*.

The attendants offloaded in a flash of white and stretchers. They opened the opposite door of the car, looked in at Mary and then grabbed her. She was so far gone, she didn't even fight. She did manage a faint, "So long, kid."

Heller, despite FBI orders, ducked down his head and yelled, "NO! Don't kill her!"

An attendant glanced up from trying to get Mary straight so they could get her out of the car and onto the stretcher. "Kill her? You're dead wrong, sonny. She needs our help. We'll take good care of her."

Heller said, "You promise not to kill her?"

"Sure, kid," said the attendant. And they had Mary on the stretcher. Stupewitz sidled to the attendant, whispered something, showed his badge. The attendant shrugged.

Heller looked toward Maulin. "Can I put her bag in that ambulance?"

Maulin made a tight wave with his gun. Heller got her purse and bag, walked over to the ambulance and put them in. The ambulance rolled away with Heller staring after it.

Stupewitz came back. He was pointing to the government car. "Get in there, kid."

Heller didn't. He walked over and closed his bags and put them in the trunk of the Cadillac and locked it, pocketing the separate key. Stupewitz then urged him into the front passenger seat of the government car.

Maulin got under the wheel of the Cadillac. He drove off.

Heller said, "NO! Our car!"

Stupewitz said, "Stop worrying. It's going to the FBI garage."

The D.C. cops and park patrolman were muttering and shaking their heads.

So was I!

Stupewitz started the government car and they sped away.

The jaws of the Federal Bureau of Investigation had closed on Jettero Heller. And the worst of it was, typically, they didn't even realize they had the fate of the planet between their vicious teeth! Stupid (bleepards)!

Chapter 3

They got out at the FBI building on Pennsylvania Avenue and someone whisked the car away.

Stupewitz said, "Don't try to run. You could get shot."

But Heller was not running. He was looking up at the gray-green marble façade and spelling out the HUGE, raised, gold-lettered sign that said

J. EDGAR HOOVER

The letters were feet high and it spread so wide he had to turn his head to read it.

"Are we going to call on J. Edgar Hoover?" said Heller.

"Don't be a smart (bleep), kid."

Heller said, "But I really never heard of him."

That got to Stupewitz. "Jesus! They sure don't teach history anymore!" He came very close to Heller and thrust his puffy face forward. "Look, you heard of George Washington." He pointed a quivering finger at the huge sign. "Well, J. Edgar Hoover was ten times what Washington ever was! The REAL savior of this country was HOOVER! Without *him*, the real rulers of this country couldn't run it at all!" He gave Heller a hard shove toward the entrance and muttered to himself, "Jesus, they don't teach kids *anything* these days."

Via elevators and stairs, pushing from time to time, Stupewitz got Heller into the first of a small pair of offices that adjoined. Stupewitz pushed Heller into a chair with an unnecessary "Sit there!"

Maulin came in. Stupewitz glared at Heller. "You're in serious trouble. You better not get any ideas of trying to run out of here because there are guards and guns all over the place. Be quiet and be good!"

They went into the second office but the door was ajar. They were whispering so I turned up the gain. I couldn't get what they were saying because, in some adjacent office, someone was being beaten and screamed now and then.

Heller had a partial view of Stupewitz through the slightly open door. The agent was at a desk, working with a phone. Maulin's huge bulk was attentively leaning over behind him.

"I want to talk to Delbert John Rockecenter, personally," said Stupewitz into the phone. "This is the FBI. . . . Then put me on to his confidential secretary." He covered the phone and said to Maulin, "Rockecenter is in Russia arranging some loans to keep them going." Then to the phone, "This is the FBI in Washington. We have a matter here . . ." The screams in the adjacent office drowned the next words. Then he covered the phone and said to Maulin, "They're putting me on to Mr. Bury, one of the attorneys from their firm, Swindle and Crouch. Bury handles all such matters."

They waited. Then Stupewitz got his connection. "Hello, Mr. Bury? I got one hell of a surprise for you. Is this a totally secure, confidential line? Oh, bug tested just this morning. Good. Now listen. We are Special Agents Stupewitz," and he rattled off a whole series of identification and addresses, "and Maulin," and he rattled off Maulin's. "Now, have you got all that for sure?"

Apparently Mr. Bury had. So Stupewitz spread out Heller's papers in front of him and began to read. He read the birth certificate, the diploma, the grades. "Got all that? I just wanted you to know there's no mistake. . . . Yes, we have the boy right here. To prove it, here's his description," and he rattled if off. ". . . no, he hasn't talked to anybody. We made sure of that."

Stupewitz now shot a gleeful grin back at Maulin. Then he said into the phone, "Now, don't be upset, Mr. Bury. But he's wanted in Fair Oakes, Virginia, for assault and battery of two police officers, both hospitalized . . . yes, he apparently did it with an iron bar when they weren't looking . . . yes, amounts to attempted murder. Also suspicion of car theft, speeding, refusal to halt. Fugitive . . . Right. And apparent possession of narcotics . . . Right. And the Federal offense of seeking to smuggle them across state lines . . . Right. And, as a minor, cohabitation with a known prostitute . . . Right. Also the Mann Act—crossing state lines for immoral purposes . . . Right. And refusal to divulge identity to a Federal officer."

I realized Heller could get life, the exact original thing planned for him.

Apparently some smoke was coming out of the phone. After a moment, Stupewitz went on. "Wait now, Mr. Bury. I'm just telling *you* this. The woman won't talk. We have the records, we have the car, we have the boy. . . . No, no reporters know anything about this. The name was not even known in Fair Oakes. . . . No. We're the only ones who know."

Stupewitz was now the one listening. Mr. Bury must be talking hard and fast. ". . . Yes, Mr. Bury," said Stupewitz. ". . . Yes, Mr. Bury. . . . Yes, Mr. Bury. . . . Yes, Mr. Bury." Then there must have been a long speech. Stupewitz gave Maulin an evil grin and nodded to him. Then he said into the phone, "No. No records or copies of anything here. The local police know nothing and we won't even report it to the Director." He nodded as though Bury could see him. And then, all over again, he gave all the identifying details and home addresses of himself and Maulin.

Stupewitz ended off with, "Yes, Mr. Bury. And you can be very assured that D.J.R.'s son is perfectly safe here in our hands; there won't be a whisper to the press or anyone. We are, as always, completely at the service of Delbert John Rockecenter. You got the idea, Mr. Bury. Goodbye."

He rose beaming from the phone. He and Maulin did a war dance round and round, laughing.

Maulin said, "And we were going to retire in a few years with nothing but our pensions!"

And Stupewitz said, "He'll hire us for sure. No other option!"

I was flabbergasted. These two crooked agents were using this case to forward their own advancement! They were blackmailing Delbert John Rockecenter! And what made it all the more criminal was that D. J. Rockecenter practically owns the FBI anyway!

And what made it even more stupid was that they actually thought they really had Delbert John Rockecenter's son.

Lombar's planning had taken a new twist!

But wait. This didn't get Heller off the hook. I hadn't worked it out yet just how, but there was real death in Heller's future now.

Chapter 4

The phone rang and the two crooked agents stopped their war dance and Stupewitz answered it, said something back and hung up.

The two came into the room with Heller. He had been sitting there quietly, his eyes occasionally straying to a bloodstain on the wall. I doubted he could have heard the phone conversation in anything like the clarity I had, if at all, and he must be wondering what they were going to do with him.

Stupewitz said to him, "Listen, Junior, that was your old man's personal family attorney, Mr. Bury, of Swindle and Crouch, New York. Your dad is over in Russia, bein' wined and dined and he won't be home for a couple of weeks."

Maulin said, "You just sit tight, Junior. There's a little delay before you can go." Maulin sat down at his desk and looked into a basketful of reports. I understood now that this was his office and the other one was Stupewitz's. They must be pretty highly placed in the FBI to have private offices.

Stupewitz went to the door to leave. "I'll handle the rest of this," he said to Maulin. "You keep your eye on the kid." He started to leave again and then stopped. He called back to Heller, "You can stop worrying about that hooker. She's dead."

My viewscreen seemed to jolt. Heller said, "Why did you have to kill her?"

"Kill her?" said Stupewitz. "She was D.O.A. at Georgetown Hospital. Heart attack." Then, innocence itself, he said, "You're lucky it was in the ambulance or you could have been charged with conspiracy to murder."

Maulin said, "Big H killed her, Junior."

Heller said, "I been meaning to ask somebody. What's a 'fix'?"

Stupewitz started for the door again. "Oh, this kid is too much for me! You grab it, Maulin. I'll get the rest done." He was gone.

With a weary shove at his basket of papers, Maulin leaned back and looked even more wearily at Heller. "No (bleep), kid. You don't know what a fix is? What the hell did they teach you at . . ." He had Heller's certificates on his desk and looked, ". . . Saint Lee's Military Academy? How to tat and knit?" He glanced at his watch and then shoved his basket further away with a detesting hand. "We got lots of time to kill, and as you'll be giving orders to this place yourself someday, I might as well begin the education of an All American Boy! Come along."

Pushing Heller ahead of him, Maulin plowed along down stairs and through halls. "Don't talk to people," he warned, "I'll answer any questions they ask."

Evidently, the building was huge. It was a long way down one corridor. Heller was clickety-clacking along.

"For chrissakes, Junior," said Maulin, annoyed by the noise. "Why are you wearing baseball spikes?"

"Comfortable," said Heller. "I got blisters."

"Oh, I get it. I got corns myself. Here we are." And he halted Heller at a door marked *Drug Lab* and shoved him through.

They were faced with yards and yards of wall racks on which assorted glass jars rested. A technician was crunched over a table, heating some water in a spoon, needles lying about.

"Now the Drug Enforcement Agency handles drugs," tutored Maulin in a gravelly voice, "but we still got our own drug lab. We're really in charge of the government and sometimes we even have to shake down the DEA. There's practically every known kind of drug in these jars."

"Do you sell them?" said Heller.

The technician looked up in alarm. He said, "Shh!" Then he looked closer at Heller and said to Maulin, "What are you doing bringing a smart (bleep) kid in here, Maulin? This isn't part of the public tour."

"Shut up, Sweeney."

The technician bent back over his Bunsen burner grumbling. Maulin said, "Now, kid, the trick is to know all these drugs by sight and smell and taste. Just start at this bottom row and go along in, jar by jar, noting the labels. But for chrissakes, if you do any tasting, spit it out! I ain't going to be accused of turning you into a drug freak."

Heller went down the rows, doing as he was told. A couple of times, Maulin made him rinse his mouth out at the sink, holding him by the back of the neck the way you do a willful child.

Heller, being Heller, was making very rapid progress. But I was worrying. It was obvious they were detaining him and, knowing the FBI, it had skulduggery in it—stupid skulduggery but skulduggery just the same.

"Hello, hello, hello!" said Heller. He had a big can with brown powder in it and was examining it. "What's this?"

"Oh, the label's off it. That's opium, kid. Asiatic . . ." Maulin looked at it closer. "No, Turkish."

Now, at any other time, I would have freaked out at Heller being shown just that. But I was sort of dulled by the shock of events.

"What does *Afyonkarahisar* mean?" said Heller, startling me out of my wits.

"(Bleep), I don't know," said Maulin. "Where's it say that?"

"Here on the side," said Heller. "It's kind of dim."

"I didn't bring my glasses," said Maulin. "Sweeney, what does *Afyonkarahisar* mean?"

"Black opium castle," said Sweeney. "Western Turkey. Why?"

"It's on this can," said Maulin.

Sweeney said, "It is? There's some black balls of it in the next jar from the same place. And that white jar down the line contains some of their heroin. (Bleep), now you got me lecturing." And he went back to work.

"You see," said Maulin learnedly, "there is a flower called a poppy and it has a black center and they scrape it and get a gum. They boil that and they get opium. They chemically process it and they get morphine. Then they chemically process that and they get heroin. The white heroin is Turkish and Asiatic. The brown heroin is Mexican . . . Sweeney, where's some of that drug literature? No sense me wearing my lungs out."

Sweeney pointed to a cabinet and Maulin opened it. "(Bleep)," he said, "they been using it for toilet paper again." He seemed baffled. Then he had a bright idea. He was reaching in his pocket. "Sweeney, go on out to the newsstand and get me one of those paperbacks on drugs." Then he suddenly stopped fishing in his pocket. "Hell, what am I doing? Here I am standing next to the U.S. Mint and was about to spend my own dough. You got any money, kid?"

Heller reached in his pocket and drew out his roll. The way he did it was the first indication I had had that he was rattled. He had tripped into a preconditioned habit pattern. Voltar gamblers—and Heller sure was one, as I knew to my grief—have a mannerism in handling money. They insert a finger in the center of the roll and let the *two* ends of the bills come up through their fingers and it looks for all the world as though they are presenting exactly *twice* as much money as they are actually holding.

Maulin looked at it. "Jesus," he said. Then, "I suppose this is your weekly allowance for candy." He plucked at the presented fistful. "Let's see. The book is about three bucks. Add two for Sweeney for his trouble. I'll take this fiver. No, on the other hand, you are probably hungry, so Sweeney can bring back some food: I'll take this sawbuck. No, come to think of it, Sweeney and me are also hungry, so I'll take this pair of double sawbucks." He apparently couldn't think of anything else, so he threw the money at Sweeney whose former hostility seemed to have evaporated.

"What do you want to eat, kid?" said Sweeney.

"Beer and a hamburger," said Heller, apparently recalling Crobe's diet advice.

"Aw, kid," said Maulin, "you are a con man. You know God (bleeped) good and well we can't buy beer for a kid your age. Tryin' to edge us into a felony? Bring him milk and a hamburger, Sweeney. I'll take a steak sandwich and beer."

Sweeney was gone and Heller went back to learning the more than two hundred different types of drugs on the shelves.

I had resigned myself to Heller knowing now what we did in Afyon. What I was worrying about was why they were delaying Heller. The FBI was totally out of character, so it was some kind of a ploy. They had something else going.

Sweeney came back with the required items and shortly Maulin and Heller were back in the former's office. Maulin ate his steak sandwich in one large bite and washed it down with beer.

Heller sat nibbling his and looking at the book. It was titled *Recreational Drugs* and it said it contained "everything you need to know about drugs." It said it was recommended by *Psychology Today,* so I knew it must be totally authoritative. There was everything in it from aspirin to wood alcohol.

So Heller, being Heller and a long way from knowing enough to put on a show the way a real spy would do, simply started "reading" it which, for him, was ingesting a page the way Earth people ingest a word. He still had a sip of milk left when he came to the end of two hundred and forty-five pages. He put the book in his pocket and finished his milk.

Maulin said, "What the hell? Oh, I guess you're just too nervous to read. I can understand that." He looked at his watch and seemed worried. Then he had a bright idea. "Tell you what, Junior. They have public tours through this building every hour or so. But we won't wait for one of those. I'll take you on one."

Why were they delaying him? They were using the approach "Detain subject without arousing his suspicions."

Maulin took him down to the exhibit of gangster guns and weapons. I was interested myself, thinking I could pick up some pointers. Maulin even took some out of their cases.

"Are all these weapons chemical?" said Heller.

"Chemical?" blinked Maulin.

"I mean, none of them electrical?"

"Oh, you dumb kids. Reading a bunch of Buck Rogers comic

books! If you mean do gangsters have any laser weapons, no. We caught somebody trying to sell us some a few years back and I think he's still doing time. They ain't legal, kid. Besides, powder is best. Now, you take this sawed-off shotgun: it'll blow a man in half! Completely in half, kid! Ain't that great?" He picked up a burp gun. "Now, you take this: point it down a crowded street and it mows down dozens of innocent bystanders. Totally effective."

They moved on to some views of modern bank robberies and Heller inspected them. Maulin showed where the bank security cameras were placed, told him about marked money packs, alarm buttons, alarm systems, police techniques and how the FBI always, without fail, caught each and every bank robber that had even tried to shortchange a teller. And Heller was so interested that Maulin even got an alarm system and showed him how it was rigged and could be disabled. "Your old man, being your old man," he said, "has a vested interest in all this, so I hope you got it."

Heller had gotten it, no doubt of that!

Maulin showed Heller, next, the FBI laboratory and all the most modern scientific investigative techniques including those on the drawing board. I didn't like that as it was edging over into things Lombar had forbidden us to teach Heller. And I was relieved when they came off of it.

The erratic "tour" was certainly not the scheduled public tour, even to the point of Maulin shouldering through a couple of small mobs of sightseers to show Heller something of special interest.

They finally came to the "Ten Most Wanted Fugitives" and Heller got an education on how people were spotted and traced. And how the FBI never, never failed to find them every time.

Shortly, Maulin had him back for an out-of-sequence look at the gangsters of the 1930s. "Now," he said, "here were the real gangsters. They weren't the cream puffs you find around today. They were really, really gangsters. And you got no idea how hard it was to catch them. But Hoover solved all that."

Maulin pointed at a death mask and a display of photos. "Now, take Dillinger there. He never had any record at all. Just one minor charge. But Hoover made him a famous man."

He got around in front of Heller and wagged a huge finger at him. "Hoover had the greatest imagination in history. He used to dream up," said Maulin proudly, "the God (bleepest) dossiers for people. Total inventions! Right off the top of his head. Pure genius! And then he could go out and shoot them down! In a blaze of glorious gunfire! A master craftsman! He taught us how and we are left with the heavy responsibility of carrying on this magnificent tradition!"

Heller waved his hand to include all of the most advertised criminals in history. "He got all these the same way?"

"Every one," said Maulin proudly. "And he included the general public, too, so don't think this is complete."

"Hey," said Heller. "There's a really vicious one!" He was pointing.

Maulin blew up. "God (bleep) it, kid, that's HOOVER!"

He was so upset that he simply stalked off. Heller clickety-clacked along behind him. Then, fitting his mood, Maulin went down some stairs and shoved Heller through another door. It was a firing range!

I was apprehensive. I knew they were up to something. I hoped it wouldn't include shooting Heller on the premises!

There were targets at the other end of the room and guns and ear protectors on the counter. I held my breath. I prayed to Heller not to get any notion of grabbing a gun and shooting his way out of the building.

"Where's the agent that does the public demonstrations?" demanded Maulin of an old man that was cleaning some guns.

"Hey? Oh, there ain't any more public demonstrations today."

Maulin socked some ear clamps on Heller and picked up a gun. He fired a round at the targets and it seemed to make him feel better. He turned to Heller. "You've classified on revolvers, of course."

"I've never shot one of those," said Heller.

"Military school!" snorted Maulin. "I knew all they taught was to tat and knit." But he proceeded to instruct Heller. "This is a Colt .457 Magnum revolver. A shot from it will go through a motor block and then some." And he showed Heller how to swing its cylinder, inspect it, load and unload it, and even how to carry it. Then he picked up a Colt U.S. Army .45 and showed Heller all about that.

Maulin looked at his watch and frowned. Obviously he had to delay Heller longer. "Tell you what, Junior. I'll give you a little demonstration of real marksmanship. Now, first, I take a look at a wanted poster here. And then several targets jump up and I have to select which one is the wanted man and put a bullet in his heart. If I shoot the wrong man, I get another chance."

He picked up a poster, glanced at it. He drew his own gun. He had the technician push some buttons. Face after face popped up. Maulin fired. He shot the wrong man.

"I told you to see an eye doctor, Maulin," said the old man.

"Shut up," said Maulin. "Hit the buttons again." He gripped the butt of the gun with both hands. He sighted carefully. He shot the right man.

"Here, Junior. You try it. You'll see it ain't so easy."

Gods, all Heller had to do was shoot the two of them and walk out. In the spot he was in, it was the textbook solution.

Heller looked at a wanted poster and put it down. The targets popped up. Heller fired and hit the right man, dead center. Nothing marvelous for a Fleet blastgun expert.

"No, no, no," said Maulin. "Jesus. Don't ever pull a trigger before you raise the gun to eye level. But I don't blame you for being nervous. And don't get cocky about accidental hits. They don't happen in real battles. Now hold the gun in *both* hands, spread your feet apart to get steadiness. Now sight carefully down the barrel. Good. Now we'll give you another chance. Hit the buttons, Murphy."

Heller with great pains did exactly as he was told. He hit the right target dead center.

"There, you see?" said Maulin. "That's what happens when you get good instruction. Now you want to try this Army Colt?"

Heller fired an assortment of weapons and finally, with a sigh of relief, Maulin, looking at his watch, said, "It's time we went back to my office." They left but Maulin used the whole long route to lecture Heller about the power and majesty and total world dominance of the FBI. It was just an act to cover up what they really intended. For I knew that, by now, whatever trap they were party to had been arranged.

Chapter 5

Maulin, puffing a bit from his exhaustive lecture on the glories of the FBI, had no more than entered his office when Stupewitz's phone rang. Maulin pointed to a chair and used the hand signal with which they order dogs to sit down and rushed to answer.

I didn't need to turn up the gain. "Maulin here," he bawled. Then, in an extremely polite tone of voice, he said, "It's all right to tell me. I am Agent Stupewitz's partner. I think he gave you my name." Then he grabbed a pad and started to write. Finally he said, "Yes, Mr. Bury. It's all under control here. . . . Oh, he's fine, Mr. Bury . . . No, he hasn't talked to anybody else . . . Yes, Mr. Bury . . . Yes, Mr. Bury. Thank you, Mr. Bury." And he hung up.

Stupewitz came in and he and Maulin whispered briefly together. Then they put Heller in a chair with two chairs facing him and Stupewitz turned on a bright light in Heller's eyes. The two agents sat down.

"Me first," said Stupewitz. "Junior, we reported to Virginia that a wrecked Cadillac with your license plates was discovered in Maryland. We also said it had a body in it answering your description that was burned beyond recognition. The people concerned did not have your name; the hooker is dead. So *you* are in the clear. So don't never mention that incident again and make liars of us. You understand?" he added severely.

The light was blinding Heller. But I suddenly realized with relief they were not interrogating him. They were briefing him! They just didn't know how to talk to anybody any other way.

"Now, here," continued Stupewitz, "is your car registration. It now has District of Columbia plates. The motor and body serial numbers have been changed. It is in your name now. We know you were the one who originally paid the dealer for that car, so don't get the idea we're doing anything illegal. Got it?"

Heller took the registration. It had a little slip fastened across the top of it that said

> All or any police: In case of contact, call Agents
> Stupewitz or Maulin only, FBI, D.C.

"We won't bother with insurance," continued Stupewitz. "But if you're in any accidents, with your name you could be sued for your shirt. So drive carefully. No more crazy hundred-mile-an-hour chases. Got it?"

Heller got it.

"Now, here," said Stupewitz, "is your driver's license."

Heller took it and, against the glaring light, saw that it had another little slip on it.

> All or any police: In case of contact, call Agents
> Stupewitz or Maulin only, FBI, D.C.

I suddenly realized what they had done: they had put "tail plates" on the Cadillac. In the computers used by all police departments, if those "tail plates" came up, the reply would read: "This car is under surveillance by the FBI. If spotted, report it to Agents Stupewitz or Maulin, FBI, D.C." It amounted to the FBI having a continuous tail on him!

"Now, here," said Stupewitz, "are all your papers back." And he gave him the birth certificate, diploma and grades. Heller put them in his pocket.

Maulin got up and hauled an old, tattered Octopus Oil Company road map out of a cluttered desk drawer. He sat back down.

"All right," said Maulin, opening the map and putting his phone notes on it. "Mr. Bury wanted to be sure you had money and

I said you did. Mr. Bury says you will probably be tired—he's quite concerned for your welfare. So you are to go to Howard Johnson's Motel in Silver Spring, Maryland. You leave here, go up Sixteenth Avenue, over the District line and the motel is right here. See it?"

Heller was studying the map. And I suddenly knew the why of the delay. It was not the FBI. It was Mr. Bury. Somewhere up that route, he had arranged a hit! I tried frantically to figure out how he would do it.

Heller had it. Actually, he probably had every road and byway on the east coast now.

"Good," said Maulin. "Now, he said some reporters had gotten wind of your refusing to come home this summer. Some crazy tale that you wanted to live your own life. Maybe join a baseball team or something. So he said that under no circumstances were you to register in a motel or hotel under your right name as he wanted no news release until you were reconciled with your family and you had talked with your father who is out of the country now. Got it?"

"Don't use my own name," said Heller. "Got it."

Oh, that Bury. He knew (bleeped) well there was no Delbert John Rockecenter, Junior! He was going to avoid any crazy newspaper stories by simply murdering the imposter. Rockecenter certainly had the resources and was not slow to use them. But how was he going to do it? And where?

"All right," said Maulin. "Now, tomorrow morning, you drive up to U.S. 495, the circle highway around D.C., and you turn off to the left onto U.S. 95. You go on that highway straight across Maryland, then across Delaware to this point where you go to the right on U.S. 295 across the Delaware River and then you're on the New Jersey Turnpike. You just follow along—actually you can't get off it. Now, you see here, just north of Newark, the turnpike splits? Well, there's a Howard Johnson's Motel right here," and he put an X on the map. "You're supposed to be there by about 4:30 in the afternoon. It's only a four-hour trip. No speeding! Don't register. Just go in the dining room, sit down and have an early supper. An old family retainer will be waiting there for you and will guide you home. Got that?"

Heller said he had.

"Now, Mr. Bury said to tell you you were in no danger whatever, so not to do anything silly. In fact, he said to tell you that Slinkerton will be tailing you all the way so you won't get scared."

"Slinkerton?" said Heller.

"That's the Slinkerton Detective Agency, the one your dad uses. They're the biggest in the country," said Maulin. "You won't see them but they'll be there." He laughed suddenly. "I think he's making sure you won't run off again, no matter how many hookers you meet!"

Stupewitz said, "Shall we go down to the car now?"

They went down to the FBI garage and there was the car. Heller checked the trunk: his gear was undisturbed. He glanced at the new D.C. plates, front and back. Then he got in.

Stupewitz said, "So it's goodbye, Junior."

"Thank you," said Heller (was that an emotional tremor in his voice?), "for making it possible for me to go straight."

Maulin laughed, "Save your thanks until you get your hands on your old man's money, Junior."

The agents both laughed and then, the way Americans do—talking in front of children as though the child isn't there—Stupewitz said to Maulin, "He's a good kid, Maulin. A little wild but okay."

"Yeah," said Maulin, "you can see his family's stuff in him. But all these kids is tamer than we used to be."

They both guffawed and waved to Heller as he drove off.

I didn't wait to watch Heller wrestle with the evening rush hour of Washington. I went plunging down the side tunnel that led to Faht's office. It's a long way and I was totally out of breath when I burst through the secret side door.

"I've got to contact Terb!" I shouted.

Faht opened a drawer and handed me a report. It was their daily radio transmission. It had come through at the rate of five thousand words a second, using hyperband. It contained, however, no five thousand words. It was very terse. Heller had gotten his birth certificate, beaten up two cops, was found by Terb again through bugs in Lynchburg, had gone to Washington, been arrested by the FBI and now was safely in their hands, probably about to be imprisoned as intended.

The Hells he was! I knew a lot more than Terb or Raht!

"I've got to contact our people!" I blared at Faht.

Heller was going to be killed! Within the next day or two. And I didn't have the platen! I had to get word to Terb to get into those motel rooms quick and ransack that baggage!

Faht shrugged. "They don't have a receiver-typer. They're bulky and you didn't order them to take one."

Oh, my Gods! I slumped in a chair. The worst of it was, I couldn't even talk to Faht or anybody. They must not know how I knew or they could get in on the lines and maybe do something wild!

"I might get word to them in New York," said Faht helpfully. "They'll probably report in there at the end of the week if they're out of money."

They weren't ever out of money. They had it by the bucket load!

I only knew three things for sure. One: Bury was going to have Heller killed, whatever else Bury was up to. Two: Soltan Gris was going to be executed if Heller was. Three: Earth population was going to be slaughtered if they interrupted Heller's communication line and I, right now, was part of that population!

I started to ask Faht if there was a good mortuary in Afyon. At least I could have a decent funeral. But I didn't even dare say that.

I slogged through the long, long tunnel to my room. My future looked even darker than the tunnel, and no room at the end of it—just a tomb, even an "unknown grave."

Chapter 6

Without hope, I watched my viewscreen as Heller entered the Silver Spring, Maryland, Howard Johnson Motel. I should have been relieved, for it meant that, with luck, I myself could end, for a few hours, the marathon of sleepless vigil he had been putting me through.

He wasn't looking behind him as he should have been. He didn't scan the desk or waiting area for suspicious figures. He was taking no precautions any normal agent would take.

He simply clickety-clacked up to the desk, told them he wanted a room for the night, laid down thirty bucks and wrote his new car license number, plain as day, on the registration form—he didn't falsify it or even make it illegible. And then he spurred me into near fury.

With a flourish, he signed the register, "JOHN DILLINGER!" He even put the exclamation point on it! A fat lot he'd learned at FBI headquarters: John Dillinger was one of the most famous gangsters of the 1930s. Pure sacrilege!

He threw his bags carelessly in his room as though he hadn't a care in the world. He washed up and soon clickety-clacked outside —not even looking into the many shadows—walked around the building and came into their restaurant.

Heller sat down. An elderly waitress promptly came over and told him he was in the wrong seat. She made him move to another booth in the corner with a flat white wall behind him. She fiddled with the lights until he was totally illuminated. And he didn't even register that she was putting the finger on him! He just busily puzzled away at the menu. And a Howard Johnson menu has nothing on it to puzzle about: they're all the same, numbers and pictures, from coast to coast!

The elderly waitress had gone off but now she returned. She took his baseball cap off his head and put it in the seat beside him, saying, "Young gentlemen don't eat with their hats on."

"I'll have a chocolate sundae," said Heller.

She stood there and she said, "You will have a Number 3. That's green salad, fried chicken, sweet potatoes and biscuits. And if you eat all that, *then* we will talk about a chocolate sundae." She imagined Heller was going to protest. She said, "I have boys of my own and you are all alike. You don't realize you have to eat good food to grow!"

She didn't fool me. She had for sure put the finger on Heller for someone. Helplessly I wondered if it would be a bullet or knife or arsenic in the chicken. Maybe, I thought, with a faint stir of hope, it was just a finger to identify. But she had certainly done a workmanlike job and a beautiful cover-up. One comes to learn the hallmarks of a real agent.

The food came. Heller peered about at other plates to see what others were eating. Then he seemed reconciled and fell to, even doing a creditable job of handling his utensils. He even picked the pieces of chicken up and ate them with his fingers, a thing he would never have dreamed of doing on Voltar! But although he was absorbing culture, he was also making mistakes. I realized that in D.C.; and here, he was talking in an Ivy League accent. He thought, apparently, that he was out of the South and this wasn't so. Maryland is as south as the fried chicken he was eating. He wouldn't be in New England unless he went just north of New York City. He was too crude and rough in his nonexistent command of tradecraft.

He had finished his meal, wiped the grease off his mouth and fingers when his attention was attracted by a movement on the other side of the room. It was hard to see as the lights were so strong in his eyes. Just a shadowy figure.

Then I froze. The figure had something held before its face. Was it a gun?

There was a bright blue flash! It was extremely brief.

My viewscreen went white with overload!

Then there were black spots dancing on it and I could not see even what Heller saw, if he saw anything.

The scene cleared. The black spots faded. And Heller was just sitting there, looking into the room. There was no figure there now.

The waitress came to him. "My, my. You ate it all. You have been a good boy, so you can order your chocolate sundae."

"What was the flash?" said Heller.

"Oh, the cashier's desk lamp just blew out. Did it hurt your eyes?" And with motherly concern she rearranged the lights near him so they would not shine in his face. Sure enough, the cashier was fiddling with her desk lamp.

Heller got and finished his sundae, paid his check with a generous tip and went clickety-clacking off around the building to his room, once more not even looking in the shadows. I was dealing with an idiot!

In his room, which he had entered without a fast door-swing-back and sudden spring, he did not check his baggage to see if it had been tampered with. He simply adjusted the air conditioning—no inspection for a gas capsule—and sat down in an easy chair and read the drug book again.

He did something then which put me into an idea conflict. On the one hand, he must NOT be killed until I had the platen. On the other hand, he would HAVE to be killed if he really penetrated what our Apparatus Earth base was all about.

Heller got up and found two ashtrays. He turned out the right-hand pocket of his jacket into the first and the left-hand pocket into the second. He was carrying DRUGS!

I couldn't understand it. Then I realized he simply had taken a small handful out of each of two jars at the FBI drug lab!

He opened up his suitcase and took out a little vial. It only had a tiny amount in it, a few specks of powder. Then he took out another vial and it, too, had a tiny amount in it.

There actually had been drugs in his suitcases when the D.C. policeman searched them! Microscopic amounts but drugs all the same! Where had they come from?

He inspected the vials. Then he put the contents of vial one into the ashtray over at the edge. He put the contents of vial two into the second ashtray over at the edge.

He went over to the light and held ashtray one to his eye.

The granules were suddenly HUGE!

It was Turkish opium!

He did the same with ashtray two.

It was Turkish heroin!

Then he went over to the long French doors to a porch which served as the motel room window and with a bit of fiddling got them open.

He took a book of matches and lit one. He dropped it in the ashtray. And, of course, the opium began to burn and smoke like mad.

He coughed and put a plastic table mat over it.

He lit the heroin the same way.

He coughed some more and put a mat over the ashtray to put it out.

The room went sort of wobbly for a moment on my screen. Naturally. He had had a whiff of opium smoke followed with a whiff of heroin smoke.

Heller went outside on the balcony and took a lot of rapid breaths of fresh air. Then he ran in place a bit, breathing noisily. Of course, the wobble in the view cleared up.

He went back and dumped both ashtrays in the toilet, washed them, washed out the vials, thoroughly dusted out his coat pockets and put everything away.

He satisfied himself that there was no trace of either one left anywhere.

But, all in all, it was a pretty amateur performance. No dope addict would ever waste drugs that way. And although you *can* burn heroin, it is too expensive a way to imbibe it. One has to shoot it into the blood to get the maximum good out of it.

Even though it was probably a hot night, he left the window

open. Looking for something to do, he found and read *The Fine Art of Angling for Beginners.* Finishing that, he tackled *The Fine Art of Baseball for Beginners.*

It was not yet eight. He got interested in the TV set. He got it on. He got a picture. And then he kept pummeling and picking at its switches. He got it all out of kilter and finally got it back in again. I couldn't figure out what he found wrong with it. It was working, sound and picture.

Somewhat impatiently, he went through the whole routine again. There was a sign that said if the TV didn't work to call the desk and he approached the phone. Then he apparently thought better of it and slumped in a chair. He addressed the set: "All right. You're the first viewer I ever met I couldn't fix. So just go on hiding your 3-D control. I'll look at you anyway!"

A movie was just coming on. The title was *THE FBI IS WATCHING YOU!*

He sat through all manner of shootings and car chases and wrecks. The FBI wiped out all the red agents in America. It then wiped out all the Mafia in America. It then wiped out the U.S. Congress. I could tell Heller was impressed. He kept yawning and, psychologically, that is a sure sign of tension building up and releasing.

The Washington, D.C., local late news followed. Whites had been mugged. Blacks had been mugged. Whites had been raped. Blacks had been raped. Whites had been murdered. Blacks had been murdered.

There is a law in America that TV must cover everything impartially without showing bias and they had racially balanced the program up pretty well.

There had been no slightest mention of any incident in Potomac Park. There hadn't even been a line about a Mary Schmeck, a junkie, dying on the way to a hospital—such deaths are too common to even get notice.

Heller sighed and shut off the TV.

He went to bed.

It was just past six in the morning in Turkey. I, too, turned in.

But I couldn't sleep. He had not even put a chain on his room door or locked the French doors to the balcony. He had not even placed any sort of a weapon under his pillow!

He was going to be hit. That was for certain. Somewhere on the path he was taking, Bury had it all arranged. There was no IF about it. There was only WHEN?

An idiot had me on a chain and was leading me straight to my death! Maybe I would go as anonymously and unremarked as Mary Schmeck. The thought saddened me.

Chapter 7

For a man about to be hit, Heller certainly was relaxed the next morning.

There was a small buzzer on my viewer which sounded when reception intensified, if you remembered to set it and I certainly had! At 2:00 P.M. Turkish time I was blasted out of bed by it. It was 7:00 A.M. in Maryland and Heller was up and taking a shower. At least he was still alive, though I was unconfident that it would be for long.

He was splashing around in the shower. His Fleet passion for cleanliness grated on my nerves. It had been just as hot in Turkey as it had been around Washington I was sure. I didn't have air conditioning and I was certainly more sweaty and dirty and rumpled than he had been, yet I didn't have to take any shower! The man was clearly mad.

I went out and got a small boy by the ear and hurled him in the direction of the cookhouse and, shortly, I was back hanging over the viewer, wolfing *kavun*, or melon, and washing it down with *kahve*, the Turkish name for coffee, which is a cousin to hot jolt. I was so intent that I was gulping it down with *sade* and omitting mineral water swallows between sips the way you are supposed to do. The fact was forcefully called to my attention when my already raw nerves began to leap peculiarly. I dumped in the sugar and drank about a quart of water very quick. But my nerves were still jumping.

It was absolutely horrifying to watch what Heller was doing—

or, more correctly, what he was *not* doing!

He made no baggage inspection—he simply got out a clean set of underclothes and socks from the carry-all and put them on, thus denying me any real inspection of his suitcases.

Dressed, he did not look up and down the hall before he stepped into it. He gave not the slightest glance around corners before he rounded them. He did not inspect the parking lot as he passed it for new, strange cars. And he did not even look over the restaurant when he entered but, with indecent carelessness, walked over to a booth and sat down.

A teen-age girl with a ponytail came to wait on him. He said, "Where's that elderly woman that was here last night?" Evidently the stupid idiot had formed some attachment—mother fixation no doubt!

The dumb girl went off to ask the manager of all things! She came back. "She was just temporary. You got no idea how the help shifts around in these motel chains. What'll y'have?"

"A chocolate sundae," said Heller. "That's to start. Then . . . what's these?" He was pointing at a picture.

"Waffles?" said the girl. "They're just waffles."

"Give me five," said Heller. "And three cups of hot jo—— coffee."

I made a hurried note. Although I realized it was quite plain that he was imitating the accents of the people he talked to, he had almost strayed into a Code break. When I had the platen, those could be used to hang him high!

She came with a big, gooey chocolate sundae and he demolished it. Then she came with five separate plates of waffles and spread them around and he demolished those. Then she came with three separate cups of coffee. He emptied the sugar bowl of cubes into them and demolished those.

She was hanging around, not giving him his check. "You're cute," she said. "It'll be fall semester soon. You going to sign up with a local high school?"

"I'm just passing through," said Heller.

"(Bleep)," said the girl and stalked off. She came back with his check. She had put all the items on it. She was very frosty and uppity. Even the dollar tip didn't seem to matter. She must have been looking at his back as she left the table but her voice came through clearly. "I never get the breaks."

Heller said to the cashier, "I understand your lamp blew out last night."

"Which one?"

"This one," said Heller, tapping it.

The cashier asked the manager who was fiddling around with the cigarette display. He said, "Oh, yeah. Outside fuse. But it didn't blow. The fuse got pulled somehow."

He bought a whole bale of daily papers and went back to his room. A golden opportunity had been missed, I realized suddenly. I cursed Raht and Terb. They were somewhere within two hundred miles of him or I wouldn't be getting a picture. They were depending on the fact that his clothes and suitcases were bugged to keep him ranged. I could have kicked them for not demanding a receiver-typer. Yes, I knew it was illegal for them to pack around more than a small transmitter that looked like an alarm clock. But they should have said, "(Bleep) the regulations, Gris must be served!" They hadn't. A pair of (bleepards), both of them. A golden chance to ransack his baggage had been missed! If I had that platen, I wouldn't be going through all this!

He got out a spin brush, filled its fluid container and washed his teeth and I was so bitter about the suitcases that I almost passed over a *real* Code break. That spin brush might even have a Voltarian manufacturing plate on it! Not that anybody on this planet could read it, but it was still a Code break. His obsession with cleanliness was going to ruin him yet. I didn't even own a spin brush: they cost three credits.

With suitcases dragging from each hand and the carry-all under one arm and the mass of newspapers under the other, he went down to his car.

And did he carefully inspect it to see if it had been set up with bombs? No! He just put his baggage in the back, the newspapers in the front seat, started up and started off. I had turned the volume down in case there was an explosion.

He went up to U.S. 495 and, tooling along comfortably, got onto U.S. 95 and, at a leisurely fifty-five, rolled across the beautiful leafy green of Maryland, admiring the trees and fields and not even glancing into the rearview mirror to see if he was tailed. That beauty he was impressed by was deceptive. I knew there was death waiting on that road!

He got into Delaware, admiring it down to the last huge barn. I didn't know why he was looking so thoroughly at all these chicken factories with their huge signs. Snipers wouldn't be concealed in them. Then suddenly a truck—glaringly labeled *Delaware Chickens Corp.*—swerved around to get ahead of him (he was dawdling), and he drove up so close to it he almost rammed it and then hung hard on its tailgate. It was a truck full of live chickens and he was looking them all over.

"So," he muttered, "*that's* what a *chicken* is!"

Hopeless! Absolutely hopeless!

Past Greater Wilmington Airport, he turned to the right onto the huge Delaware River Bridge. But was his mind on his business? No!

He stopped his car! Halfway across the span, disregarding traffic and horns and brake squeals, he stepped on his brakes!

A trailer-truck slued sideways frantically and blocked all lanes!

He got out. He left his car right there in the right lane, motor running, and got out! He gave only the slightest glance to the pandemonium he had abruptly caused.

He went over to the bridge rail and looked down at the Delaware River.

"Holy, jumping blastguns!" he said in Voltarian. Just like that!

And what was he looking at? He was looking down at the brown, roiling water. And what was there to see? Nothing but oil slicks and old floating tires and dead cats. Of course, I will admit the Delaware River is pretty big as rivers go and it looks bigger as at this point it becomes Delaware Bay and then part of the Atlantic.

The huge truck driver that had almost rammed the Cadillac now couldn't get out because of the stacked up traffic. He came roaring at Heller, shaking his fists. I only saw him on peripheral vision. Heller wasn't looking at him. He was looking northeast, up the river. The noise was absolutely deafening. Honking horns and angry yells and this truck driver. I had to turn down the gain.

Heller ignored the raised fists and profanity coming at him. Right into the middle of a tirade about "you (bleeped) kid," Heller said, "Is there a city up there?"

"Jesus!" exploded the truck driver. "Where the hell are you from?"

And Heller was so intent on whatever he was thinking about, he said, "Manco."

Then, into the middle of an "I don't care if you're from hell" sort of thing, Heller said, "I asked you, is there a city up this river?" Yikes! It was his piercing, high-pitched Fleet voice! I hastily lowered the gain some more.

The truck driver said, "Philadelphia, you (bleeped), ignorant . . ."

And into the middle of that, Heller pierced, "Is this their *sewer?*"

"Of course it's their God (bleeped) sewer!" screamed the enraged truck driver.

"Jesus," said Heller in English. And he just ignored the man and the crowd and the fists and went back and got in his car and drove on.

Heller was shaking his head. "Must be a hundred million people in that town and no sewer system. POH-LLU-*SHUN!* Jesus!"

As I say, he wasn't tending to business. Any passing sniper could have shot him.

But I had him now. He had actually told an Earthman where he was actually from! I started to write it down and then thought I had better reread Code Number a-36-544 M Section B. I dimly remembered it could be interpreted as "making an alien *aware* that a landing had taken place on his planet." I couldn't be sure. Had the truck driver been *aware* of Heller's definitive answer? I couldn't find the book.

When I sat down to watch again, Heller was on the New Jersey

Turnpike, tooling along at fifty-five. He was relaxed once more. He had all his windows up and the air conditioning on, so it must be a hot day.

The traffic was very jammy. This turnpike is one of the most overloaded highways in the world, carrying almost triple what it was designed for and despite the high price of gasoline and cars and consequent traffic reduction, the trucks were clogging its dozen lanes. Oranges from Florida seemed to be the biggest part of what Heller was trying to flow along with.

He drove for some time and then, possibly because he thought oranges might have an odor—a trailer had evidently been strewing the road with them after a collision—he opened his window.

He sniffed.

Suddenly he shook his head as though to clear it.

He sniffed again.

Then he sneezed!

Well, of course he sneezed. The state of New Jersey, particularly along the turnpike, has one of the highest air pollution concentrations in the world. I could have told him that. Everybody knows it.

Trucks or no trucks, he fished out a notebook and wrote some percentages of sulphur dioxide and some other symbols I don't know, but probably all noxious.

He closed his window. And then he said to the planet in general, "You're going to have to use hacksaws pretty soon even to get a plane to move through this stuff! How can you manage to do it so fast? This area is .06 percent up even since my survey."

He drove for a while and then he said, "I better get busy."

But it was miles later before he acted. And what he did made no sense at all.

He went through the lousiest tail-shaking procedure I have ever seen!

Somehow he had gotten ahead of the mobs of Florida oranges. Before him lay miles of two lanes, totally empty. It was completely flat—there is no scenery on this turnpike—it was without turns.

Despite the solemn warnings of Stupewitz and Maulin, he

suddenly tramped on the accelerator and zipped the car up to ninety miles an hour! I thought, at last he's gotten some sense! He's trying to get away!

It wasn't as fast as he could go. If he was trying to escape, he really should have stamped on it!

He sailed along, looking in his rearview mirror.

He was in plain view! This was no way to escape!

He clocked off three miles.

Then, still in full view, almost as if he wanted to be seen, he paid a toll and drove out through an exit gate.

He stopped. He backed the car over to the side where it could not be seen. And he just sat and watched the gate.

After a bit, he got one of the newspapers and began to read, looking up from time to time at the gate.

He found one story that fascinated him. It was in the *New York Daily Scum*.

REVERED REPORTER RUBBED

MUCKY HACK DOES HIS LAST SPREAD

Mucky Hack, veteran investigative reporter and crime exposer of the *Daily Libel,* was splattered all over 34th Street last night when his specially built Mercedes-Benz Phaeton was rigged for a blitz that went BOOM!

The car was worth $89,000 according to Boyd's, the only underwriters who would touch it. It was alleged to be a gift from I. G. Barben Pharmaceutical Corp. Car fans will miss its presence in the Annual Special Car Parade at Atlantic City.

Five shops were also destroyed in the blast. Police Inspector Bulldog Grafferty, who

---

investigated the car bombing, issued a carefully prepared statement today: "It was a valuable vehicle. The bomb rigging was extremely expert, the work of a master. Boyd's had required the car to be guarded by Tilt and five other independent alarm systems.

"The only possible person who could have set up the blast is Bang-Bang Rimbombo.

"Bang-Bang is an ex-marine demolitions expert left over from the last war.

"Many car bombings have been attributed to him in the past although no arrests were ever made.

"Bang-Bang is a trusted member of the notorious Corleone mob which Mucky Hack has always been exposing in his tireless reporting.

"The New York/New Jersey mob is run by the able and charming Babe Corleone, the ex of the late 'Holy Joe' Corleone.

"It is well known that Corleone received his gang cognomen of 'Holy Joe' because he would not push drugs and that Faustino 'The Noose' Narcotici has been making steady inroads on the former Corleone territories in Manhattan.

"Thus, the motive for the rigging of the bombs by Bang-Bang exists. The expertise bears the unmistakable Bang-Bang trademark.

"Bang-Bang has not been arrested solely because he doesn't complete his current sentence in Sing Sing until tomorrow and was still in jail at the time of the bombing.

"Several shopkeepers were arrested for permitting the car to park in that spot.

"The case, therefore, can be considered closed."

Mucky Hack is survived by his managing editor and an old Ford.

For the life of me I could not see what he could find of interest in this story. He could read so fast that to see him sit there looking at one news item for ten minutes was baffling.

Possibly my annoyance, however, to be honest, came from the fact that he was holding the paper folded. There was a Bugs Bunny strip that was thus only half-revealed: Bugs had Elmer Fudd in a bath of carrot juice, and not being able to see the beginning of the strip, I could not fathom how Elmer had gotten there or why. Possibly Elmer had been ill? Possibly the bath had been prepared by Elmer as a trap into which he himself had then fallen? But there was no way for me to tell Heller to open up the page so I could see. It was frustrating!

Finally Heller looked at his watch. My Gods, he was wearing a combat engineer's watch! In plain sight! I certainly put *that* down as a Code break. Then I was given pause: it looks like just a flat disc with a small hole in the center. Earthmen would mistake it for an identification bracelet or something like that.

He rotated his wrist, turning the watch downward and touched it. I had noticed before that he had this as a sort of nervous habit. But this is the first time I had really remarked it. It showed that he did have nerves after all.

He yawned—another nervous symptom. He looked at the toll gate area. Not one car had come through it in all the time he had been sitting there!

"So," he said, "no Slinkerton!"

Then it came to me in a flash what he had been up to. The Fleet must have battle tactics and he was practicing one of them. He had invited pursuit to lay an ambush. But he had no weapon, so he had probably done it because of training conditioning triggered by mounting nervous tension.

That must have been it, for he now started up the Cadillac, doubtlessly disappointed that his ruse had not worked, drove through the complexity of exits and entrances to the turnpike, got another fare ticket and was shortly on his way, rolling once more northeastward.

The traffic was quite heavy, and with all those trucks weaving in and out trying to pass each other, any normal driver would have felt he had his hands full. But Heller was taking time out now and then to read a story about "Economic Chaos Just Down the Road According to Financial Experts of Merrill Bull, Inc."

This expert watching him knew that the chaos which was down *his* road was not only economic! The lamb to slaughter had a better chance, in my opinion, than this idiot!

Chapter 8

At 4:20 that afternoon, Heller arrived at the rendezvous. He had dawdled along, stopping often, but he was still ten minutes early.

He parked the Cadillac carelessly in the higgledy-piggledy lot and made his way through the turmoil of tired kids and savage fathers and mothers that usually populate such temporary stop areas on a turnpike.

He made his way into the restaurant and was shortly seated at a table. He looked around.

I froze! Directly across the room from him was a dimly familiar face. Heller's glance passed over it but not mine! I mastered my nerves and, using the second screen, got back to that view, stilled.

The face was very Sicilian in bone structure. It was deeply pockmarked. A knife scar ran from the corner of the mouth straight back to the bottom of the left ear. The eyes were reptilian. My memory for faces is unsurpassed. But I could not place him.

Hastily, I yanked a camera from a shelf and, excluding the edges of the screen, got a close-up of that face! Rapidly, I stripped out the finished picture and, working very fast, blew it down onto Earth-type paper.

Keeping an eye on the current screen, I saw a tall, gray-haired man walk up to the Sicilian. The Sicilian showed the gray-haired man something he held cupped in his palm. A photo? Then he nodded almost imperceptibly toward Heller.

The Sicilian was acting as the finger man!

The gray-haired man drew back and idled against the wall. He was wearing a bowler. He was impeccably dressed, a three-piece suit, the vest of which was gray. He was wearing pince-nez glasses connected to his lapel with a black ribbon. He was also carrying an umbrella.

Heller ordered, got and ate a hamburger and washed it down with Seven Up. He was picking up his check when the gray-haired man approached him.

With a touch of a finger to his bowler, the gray-haired man said, "I am Buttlesby, young master. Mr. Bury wanted to be sure you were safely met. I am to show you where to go. If you are ready, may we go?" Very courteous English accent, the perfect fake family retainer.

Heller simply got up, paid his check and followed Buttlesby out.

The Sicilian passed them and, when they reached the parking lot, was getting into another car.

Buttlesby opened the door of the Cadillac for Heller and helped him get under the wheel. Then Buttlesby went around and got into the passenger seat.

"If you please," said Buttlesby, "proceed on up the turnpike. I will show you the turns."

Behind them, Heller saw the Sicilian's car was following them but after that he seemed to give it no heed.

"We will be leaving your car in a garage in Weehawken," said Buttlesby.

"Why?" said Heller.

"Oh, dear," said Buttlesby. "Absolutely no one ever drives across the river into New York! Heaven forbid! The Manhattan traffic positively devours cars, bangs them all up, ruins them. Anyone who is sensible leaves his car on the New Jersey side of the river and takes a taxi into New York. And in New York one uses taxis." He laughed slightly. "Let the taxis take the buffeting. Your car will be perfectly safe in the New Jersey garage."

Heller drove along in silence.

Buttlesby began to talk again. "Mr. Bury is dreadfully sorry, but he is detained in town. He has arranged for the young gentleman to stay at the Brewster Hotel on 22nd Street. Here is the hotel card." And he tucked it into Heller's outside breast pocket.

"Mr. Bury was very specific. The young gentleman is expected. He is not to register under his own name but, like any young gentleman, is to register incognito. It's what all the young bloods do when they go for a fling in town.

"Mr. Bury will call on you in person at precisely eight o'clock tomorrow morning at your hotel. He asked me to reassure you that you are perfectly safe, that no one is the least bit cross with you and that everyone has your best interests at heart. So, you will wait for him at the hotel?"

"Sure," said Heller.

The idiot! That would be the site of the hit! Or would it be even sooner?

Buttlesby directing, they left the turnpike and went with signs pointing to the Lincoln Tunnel. But at a sign, *J. F. Kennedy Blvd*, they turned off and were soon in the New Jersey town of Weehawken, a very shabby place. They rolled along to 34th Street and the fake family retainer gave more directions and shortly they were on the ramp of a large but dingy building, a garage.

The escort got out, rapped on the door three times and then twice with the handle of his umbrella and in a moment the huge mechanical door swung up, revealing a vast, dark interior.

A rather overweight young man with huge, somewhat scared eyes, dressed in paint-spattered khaki coveralls, was standing there, pointing.

Heller drove in the direction of the point.

The floor was paint-spattered. There were some battered machines evidently used in body work. But there were no other cars there.

Way back at the end there was an area cleaner than the rest and no paint spatters. Heller stopped the car.

He got out and opened up the back. Buttlesby was there

helping with the baggage—he couldn't manage all of it and Heller carried one suitcase.

The plump young man had his hand out. "The keys," he said. "We maybe got to move it."

Heller separated the keys and for the first time I noticed there were two sets on the ring. And then the idiot handed one set over to the young man.

They went outside and there was a taxi waiting! The driver had his cap down, possibly to hide his face. Buttlesby got the baggage into the cab and stood back, holding the door open for Heller to enter. Heller got in but Buttlesby didn't.

"Aren't you going with me?" said Heller.

"Oh, dear no. Cross into Manhattan when I don't have to? Dreadful place. They ruin cars. Someone will be by to pick me up directly. Driver, take this young gentleman to the Brewster Hotel on 22nd Street. And no accidents, mind you."

The cab drew away and behind them the Sicilian drove up and Buttlesby got in the Sicilian's battered old car.

Shortly they were in the Lincoln Tunnel and Heller seemed more interested in the tile work that was flying by than he was in being en route to the hit spot.

As they exited from under the river, his eyes were all over the place, taking in New York. He seemed to be remarking about the fenders. And it is true that New York City fenders are the most bashed fenders in the world. He looked at dents rolling beside them and dents parked at curbs and possibly he was satisfied with Buttlesby's explanation. I wasn't. Bury had successfully separated the alleged Delbert John Rockecenter, Junior, from a car link that would lead back to the FBI.

They came at length to 22nd Street, which is narrow. And shortly they were drawn up before the Brewster Hotel, which is squat.

The buildings in that shabby section are only a few stories high. The garbage cans abounded.

While the Brewster may not be the worst hotel in New York, it is where the winos probably stop when they have money.

Heller removed his baggage and paid the driver—who probably already had been paid—and was shortly at the desk in the narrow excuse for a lobby.

The clerk, a man whose complexion was totally gray, looked at him with sunken eyes and then reached for a key. It must be all set up, even the exact room!

A card was pushed at him and Heller registered with a flourish. *Al Capone.* Address: *Sing Sing.*

The clerk gave him a key, not even bothering to read the registration card.

Heller squeezed his baggage into the elevator, worked out it must be the fourth floor and was shortly in his room.

What a shabby room! A double bed against the far wall. One easy chair. One straight back. A side table by the easy chair, an 1890 bathroom and a TV.

Heller put his baggage on the bed and went over to the double window. Directly across the street, the building there was exactly the same height: it had a flat roof and parapet—the exact requirements for a sniper post.

But Heller gave it no special heed. He tried to turn on the TV. The picture and sound came on but it was a black and white TV.

Heller tapped it on the side. Then he fiddled with the settings and got it all out of kilter. Then he opened a panel and found some more settings and twisted those with a tool from his tool kit.

I couldn't comprehend what he was up to. Rigging a bomb? Doing something equally sensible?

And then it came to me. No stereo picture, no color. He thought it was broken!

He finally got the interior settings straight again and then the exterior knobs and got the picture and sound back.

He pulled the TV, which was on casters, slightly into the room and adjusted the easy chair. He had the back of that chair to the windows! My Gods, didn't he realize that's where the shot would come from?

And then this utter simpleton sat and watched the evening news in all its gory details.

Then he found a motion picture on the channels and sat yawning while the Mafia won World War II for America in Italy.

I did not wait for the end of that. Gripping my paper picture, I sped through the tunnel to Faht's office.

I slammed the picture in front of Faht's face. "Who is this man?" I demanded.

He shrugged and indicated the cabinets marked *Student Files*. They contain, amongst other things, a rogues gallery of customers so that we do not go adrift and sell to the wrong people.

It took me half an hour of digging—and how I longed for a proper computer system, illegal though it might be to install one on this planet.

I found him!

Unmistakable!

He had visited Turkey on two occasions to inspect the work of buyers for their mob.

It was Razza Louseini! *Consigliere* of the mob of Faustino "The Noose" Narcotici. The New York Mafia lot that is the outlet for I. G. Barben Pharmaceutical!

Important people.

The direct-line connection to Rockecenter's disguised control of the drug industry!

And the *consigliere*, the advisor and administrative head of the most powerful mob in New York, had personally gone down to act as the finger man on Heller!

One of our best customers had been given the job of knocking off Heller!

It was just, of course, but none of these people would know any part of this connection to Heller. Lombar had known. He had quite understood the fury that would boil in the Rockecenter camp when an imposter showed up. The Rockecenter name is sacred!

I felt an awe of Lombar. He had fed Heller straight into the fire. For a moment, at the FBI in Washington, I had thought Lombar had gone wrong. But no! The power of the Apparatus chief was reaching straight through, handled unwittingly by puppets!

And then the awe turned into sickness. Heller had a contact in the Grand Council we had not known about. And I did not have the code!

There was no possible way to get Heller's baggage ransacked in time.

This planet was a goner!

But who cared about the planet? It was I, Soltan Gris, who would be dead in the echo of a fatal rifle shot through that window!

Chapter 9

At 7:10 New York time, there was a knock on Heller's hotel room door. A sloppy delivery boy with *Gulpinkle's Delicatessen* on his coat was handing Heller a bag.

Heller took it!

"That'll be two bucks and a four-bit tip," said the boy.

Heller made out that this was two dollars and fifty cents, paid him and closed the door. He opened the bag and found a plastic container of coffee and two jelly rolls.

No hotel like that ever had service like this! Was the stuff poisoned? Drugged?

Heller sniffed the coffee. He broke open a roll and sniffed it. Then the (bleeped) fool proceeded to consume them. He didn't pass out or drop dead, so I realized they had just been making sure he didn't leave his room or walk about to be seen.

He put on a clean baseball pullover. He finished dressing and combed his hair. He spin brushed his teeth.

He arranged the room. He put the easy chair with its back to the window, put the side table against it to the left hand. He put the straight-back chair in front of it, facing it. Then he took the two glass ashtrays and put them on the side table near the easy chair.

Then, possibly finding waiting heavy, he seemed to discover that the inside doorknob of the hall door was loose and he got a tool from his kit and worked at it. Then he unlocked the door completely.

He went over to the bed, made it and then opened both his suitcases on it, wide open!

He emptied the carry-all and made a neat pile of the contents at the bed top.

The portable radio he had bought attracted his attention and he fiddled with it, getting a station or two. It seemed to amuse him that the music was not stereo. How could it be, with Earth electronics! The whole thing was made just to dangle from the wrist by a strap. He took it back to the easy chair and sat down. He listened to the morning news. Toys! All Fleet guys are crazy with toys. Here he was about to be hit and he was amusing himself with a toy. The muggings and murders and political corruption of New York aren't news.

It was getting close to eight. He got up and went to the window. He was looking down into the street, maybe watching for his caller to arrive.

But I saw something else! By peripheral vision, I saw a man come out of a door on that other roof! A man carrying a violin case!

Heller went back and sat down. The radio came to the end of the news.

The elevator door down the hall opened. Heller, possibly because his toy was new, had to do a lot of fiddling to get the radio off. He dropped it into the top of an open suitcase, stepped backwards and dropped into the easy chair.

There was a knock on the door. Heller called, "Come in. It's open."

In walked the perfectly groomed Wall Street lawyer. The type is legendary. Three-piece suit in a somber gray. No hat. Impeccably neat. Dried up like a prune from holding in all the sins they commit. He was carrying a fat briefcase.

"I am Mr. Bury of Swindle and Crouch," he said. Very Ivy League accent.

Heller gestured to the straight-backed chair. Bury sat down on it and put his briefcase beside him. He wasted no time. "Where did you get this idea?" he said.

"Well, most people get ideas," said Heller.

"Did somebody talk you into this?"

"Don't know anybody much around here," said Heller.

"How many times have you used the name Delbert John Rockecenter, Junior?"

"I haven't!" said Heller.

"Did you use it to the men who met you?"

Aha! Razza Louseini and Buttlesby weren't in on it! They were just there to escort an anonymous somebody. Mr. Bury had kept this pretty tight!

"No," said Heller. "No one has used it to me and I haven't used it to anybody."

Bury seemed to relax. "Ah, I see I am dealing with a very discreet young man."

"That you are," said Heller.

"Do you have the papers?"

"They're there in my coat."

Bury got them. He also looked in the pockets. He sat back down.

"Now," said Bury, "did the FBI copy them?"

"They used them at the phone and they lay on a desk the rest of the time, turned over."

Bury was becoming more and more pleased. He was almost smiling, if a Wall Street lawyer can ever be said to smile beyond a tiny twitch of the mouth corners. "And you have no more copies?"

"Search the place," said Heller. "There's my jacket and there are my baseball clothes and there are my grips."

Bury got up again and looked through the sports clothes. He was looking for labels! I had more than an inkling of what was intended now.

The lawyer got to the grips. He got tangled up in fish line and then snagged a finger on a bass plug. He drew back cautiously and peeked at the contents.

The sides of his mouth actually twitching, he came back and sat down, facing Heller. "I have a deal for you," he said. "You give me these papers and in exchange I will give you another, completely bona fide identity and twenty-five thousand dollars."

"Let's see it," said Heller.

Bury opened one side of his case. He pulled out a birth certificate, Bibb County, Georgia. It said that JEROME TERRANCE

WISTER had been born in Macon General Hospital on a date seventeen years before. The parents were Agnes and Gerald Curtis Wister and the baby was white, blond and male.

"That is totally valid," said Bury. "Also, the parents are both dead, there are no brothers or sisters or other kin."

Heller made a gesture for more. Bury pulled out a Saint Lee Military Academy certified record of grades. The grades were all D's!

"No junior college certificate here," said Heller.

"Ah, you have missed something. This credits you with one more year than your other certificate. That gives you only one more year and you will have your full college degree of Bachelor. You will probably finish college, yes?"

"People don't listen to you unless you have a diploma," said Heller.

"How true that is," said Bury. "I couldn't have stated it better myself. So you see, you are the gainer. One more year of college and you will have your diploma."

Hastily I shuffled through my wits to recall what the catch must be here. Then I had it. With all D's he'd have trouble getting admittance into another college and with a missing year—and Bury had no way of knowing all Heller's Earth education was missing—Heller would fail. But this was just gratuitous sadism on Bury's part. He knew that grade sheet would never be presented. It told me something else about the man. He was devious. He planned against failures of his plans even when success seemed certain!

"It gives you more than you had," urged Bury. "I am being completely fair with you."

Wall Street lawyer fair, I told myself.

Heller was beckoning for more.

"Now, here," said Bury, "is your driver's license. It is for New Jersey, quite valid in New York. And notice it is for all vehicles including motorcycles. This is in exchange for the D.C. one you have handed me. See how generous I am being?"

Heller inspected it.

"Now, here is the registration for your car in exchange for the

D.C. one I hold now. And these are the plates. Note they are New Jersey plates, quite valid for New York. But I will take these along and have them put on your car. You will be picking up your car, won't you?"

Heller nodded and Bury seemed relieved. But Heller was still beckoning.

"Here is a social security card," said Bury. "It is brand-new as you have never before had a job. You'll find it vital for identity."

The identity of a corpse, I told myself.

Heller was beckoning for more. The corners of Bury's mouth twitched and he handed Heller a U.S. passport. Heller opened it and stared at the picture of himself. "Where did you get this?"

"Last night," said Bury. "That's why you had to stop in Silver Spring."

"The flash at dinner," said Heller.

"You don't miss much. As a matter of fact, you can have the rest of the copies. I won't be needing them now." And he handed Heller a dozen more passport photos.

"How do I know this identity is all valid?" said Heller. "How did you get it?"

"My dear fellow," said Bury, "the government has to provide full verifiable identification all the time. They have witnesses they have to hide, people who have risked their lives to give testimony. The State Department does it continually. And we, you might say, own the State Department. You were quite imaginative to take us on this way. But we are nothing else than kind."

Rockecenter, kind? Oh, my Gods!

"Don't you worry about the validity of any of this," said Bury. "Indeed, it would be very bad for me if it were false."

Indeed, it would be, Mr. Bury, I gritted. The identity found on a corpse gets very close scrutiny!

"Now for the money," said Mr. Bury. And he hauled out wads of it from the left side of his briefcase. "Twenty-five thousand dollars, all in old bills, unmarked and untagged."

Heller laid it on the side table, back of the ashtrays.

"Just one thing more," said Bury. "It's illegal in New York to register in a hotel under a false name. A felony, in fact." (Oh, what a LIE!) "So I just brought up a registration blank. Sign it with your new name and put Macon, Georgia, down as the address and we'll be finished."

Heller took it and balanced it on his knee. "One more thing," said Heller.

"Yes?" said Bury.

"The rest of the money in your briefcase," said Heller.

"Oh!" said Bury, like he'd been punched in the solar plexus.

Aha, the man was also crooked. He probably had intended to keep the rest of it for himself!

"You drive a hard bargain, young man," said Bury.

But Heller just had his palm up. Bury pulled a wad of money out of the right side of the briefcase. "It's another twenty-five thousand," said Bury.

Heller put it with the rest of the money, quite a pile! And then, sure as if it were his death warrant, he signed the hotel registration blank, *Jerome Terrance Wister, Macon, Georgia.*

Bury said, "You drive a hard bargain. But that's not bad. You'll really get along in the world, I can tell."

For about ten minutes more, I said to myself. As soon as you get clear of this room, Mr. Bury, and have yourself an alibi, a bullet is going to come through that window and that will be the end of Heller! And *me!*

Bury stood up, "Have I got everything?" He chuckled as he showed Heller the briefcase was empty and then he put all the re-claimed I.D. and the new license plates in it, probably gloating. He carefully looked around the room. He moved over toward the door.

"One more thing," said Heller. "Pick up that telephone and tell the clerk to go out in the street and tell that sniper on the roof to come over to this room."

Bury went rigid. Then he grabbed for the doorknob.

It came off in his hand!

He stared at it for an instant.

Then as he dropped it, his hand darted to the inside of his coat.

He was going to pull a gun!

Heller reached sideways.

He picked up a glass ashtray so fast his hand blurred.

The ashtray sizzled across the room, hit Bury a glancing blow on the arm, caromed off and shattered into a shower of glass against the door, spattering Bury.

The lawyer stepped back, arm numb. He stared at Heller.

The second ashtray was in Heller's hand. "This one," said Heller, "takes the top of your head off!"

Bury was shaking, he was holding his arm. He moved over to the phone. He told the clerk to go out in the street and call up to the roof across the way and tell the man there to come over quickly.

Except by the window, the room was too dark and curtained to see deeply into. Heller moved over in a leisurely fashion and took Bury's gun.

"Just sit down there on the bed in plain view of the door. And look more relaxed."

"I think you broke my arm."

"Better than your head. Now, when he knocks, tell him in a normal voice to come in."

They waited, Heller against the wall by the door.

In about five minutes there was a knock.

"Come in," said Bury.

The door opened and a man stepped in.

Heller slammed the side of his hand against the back of the man's neck. It catapulted him forward into Bury!

The violin case dropped.

As the man had gone by him, Heller had extracted a Cobra Colt from his waistband.

Holding two guns, Heller put the Cobra in his pocket. He stepped out, flopped the squirming sniper onto his back. The man was a thin weasel, penitentiary stamped all over his face. Heller plucked a wad of bills from his inside pocket. He riffled them.

The sniper glared at Bury. "I thought you said he was just a kid!" He was starting to get furious.

Heller stepped forward. He made a cuffing motion and the assassin flinched. And Heller had his wallet and I.D.

With his foot, Heller pulled the briefcase to him and then opened it. He took out only the car plates. "I keep my bargains, Mr. Bury. You bought some papers and you can have them. I received some in exchange and I will keep them. A deal is a deal."

Heller moved them over off the bed and against the wall away from it. "However, Mr. Bury, I somehow doubted you were strictly a man of honor. So . . ."

He took the radio/cassette player out of the top of the suitcase. He hit the rewind. He pushed play. Heller's voice came out the tiny speaker, "Come in. It's open." And then Mr. Bury's voice, "I am Mr. Bury of Swindle and Crouch." Heller spot-checked it. It was all there on the cassette.

"So," continued Heller, "we will just put this in a safe place in case anything odd happens to me."

"Tapes aren't court evidence," sneered Mr. Bury.

"So, one more thing," said Heller.

"I'm sick of your 'one more things'!" said Bury.

Heller opened the hood's wallet. He took a notebook and, in a blur of fast writing, took down all the particulars in it. Then he read the criminal's name aloud: "Torpedo Fiaccola" and added his home address and social security number.

Heller took the money he had removed from the assassin. "This is about five thousand, I should judge." He put it in the wallet, making it bulge. "It is probably half the contract price."

He gave the wallet to the gangster. "I would not want to be accused of taking the daily bread out of anyone's mouth. So I am buying a contract on Mr. Bury's life."

Bury and the gangster looked at each other and back at Heller.

"But I don't want it executed yet," said Heller. "If any of this I.D. turns out to be funny or if I hear any Bury bullets going past my ears, I will phone you and you can execute the contract on him. You will be paid another five thousand cash if you then execute it." He must have smiled at the hood. The fellow didn't know what to think.

"Oh, I can reach you," said Heller. "I have your mother's address and phone number here."

The gangster flinched. I actually don't think Heller understood that the gangster now thought Heller was saying that if the hood didn't comply, his mother would be executed. But the gangster, I could see, took it that way.

Bury was another matter. As Heller studied him, I could see that Mr. Bury had another trick up his sleeve.

"You have nothing to fear from me, Mr. Bury," said Heller. "You have your papers. I will keep the deal as long as you do. So let's leave it that way."

Heller took the shells out of the revolvers. I freaked! He didn't have a gun on them now!

Heller opened up the violin case and inspected the dismantled sniper rifle. Then he took its supply of shells. He gave the guns and case and briefcase to them. With a screwdriver, he got a grip on the knob shaft socket and opened the door.

With a courtly bow, he signalled they could leave.

"May we never have occasion to meet again," said Heller.

The look Bury gave him would have disfigured a brass statue. They left.

Heller was a fool! His grand heroics might serve in another time and place but not New York, New York, Planet Earth— Blito-P3!

He should have quietly killed them both. That would have been the tradecraft thing to do!

He had humbled one of the most influential attorneys on the planet and gotten the better of Rockecenter, a thing that man never tolerates.

Then, just as if he had not made mortal enemies, Heller neatly put the doorknob back on, packed, made everything tidy. Then, as he put his baseball cap on the back of his head in front of the mirror, he said, "There's nothing like FBI training to see you through." And he laughed.

But they hadn't taught him enough. Bury already had realized that any threat to Heller from anyone could be interpreted by Jerome Terrance Wister as coming from Bury. It left Bury with no other choice than, one way or another—if not at once, then at some convenient future time—to use much more adroit methods to eradicate Jerome Terrance Wister. Top Wall Street lawyers don't ever really lose. They only postpone.

At his fingertips, Bury had at his command not only government agencies but whole governments. He could sic any of them on Heller. Money meant nothing to him. Very possibly, right this minute he was offering Torpedo Fiaccola three times what Heller had offered to give it another try. And Fiaccola, frantic at that foolish threat to his mother, as well as his disgrace today, would now listen to anything.

Heller really was dealing in a subject he knew too little about. And he was a lot too cocky! Spies are deadly things, like scorpions in hiding. They don't walk out the door singing after they have set in motion the most powerful and vengeful machine on the planet— the Rockecenter power.

I sat and gloomed. I could think of no way to get that platen before Heller was killed. No wonder the life expectancy of combat engineers was only a couple of years of service. The life expectancy of anyone handling one, such as me, might even be much shorter!

And as I sat there glooming, a special messenger from Faht's office rushed in with the day's report from Raht and Terb. It said, "He registered at the Brewster Hotel and just checked out." My Gods, I didn't even get backup from my own men! Hells had no future like the one that waited for me!

PART SIXTEEN

Chapter 1

Heller couldn't find anybody in the Brewster lobby, so he went behind the desk, put the thirty-dollar room price under the counter where it could be seen, put his Al Capone registration card on top of it and wrote himself a receipt on their invoice machine, signing it *Brinks*. The FBI had not taught him very well: Capone had never once robbed a Brinks armored car. I know my American history!

Working on deciphering the scribbled numbers around the lobby public phone—some of them girls, some of them pimps and some of them gays—he found a taxi company and phoned it.

After getting his baggage into the cab, he said to the German-looking driver, "I'm looking for a place to live. A better hotel than this one. Something with some class."

With Heller noting bashed fenders of cars and darting amongst collision-fixated cars, they were soon over on Madison Avenue, roaring uptown.

At 59th Street and Fifth Avenue, the cabby dumped Heller in a driveway. Heller unloaded his baggage and offered a twenty-dollar bill. The cabby simply took the bill and drove rapidly away, though the fare had been much less. Heller was learning about New York.

He looked up. The Snob Palace Hotel soared above him. Although there were uniformed doormen and bellboys racing about, nobody took his baggage. He gathered it up and went in. A vast, glittering lobby stretched about him, almost a hangar. Sparkling but decorous light fixtures illuminated the subdued and decorous furnishings. An expensive and decorous throng eddied around him as he made his way to the Room Desk.

There were numerous clerks, all busy. Heller waited. Nobody looked up. Finally, he said to one clerk, "I'd like a room."

"Do you have a reservation?" said the clerk. "No? Then see the assistant manager. Over there, please."

The assistant manager was busy. He was answering a complaint on the phone in a suitably decorous voice. Something about a poodle not having been aired. Finally he looked up. He did not much care for what he saw. By a mirror that covered the back wall behind him, I could see it, too.

Here was somebody in a loud, too-small, red-checked jacket and a pair of blue-striped pants that didn't reach his baseball shoes and who had, of all things, a red baseball cap on the back of his head. "Yes?" said the assistant manager.

Heller chipped the ice off it. "I'd like a nice room, maybe two rooms."

"Are you with your parents?"

"No, they're not on Earth."

"Suites start at four hundred dollars a day and go up. I shouldn't think you would be interested. Good day." And he got on the phone to scold the help for not decorously airing somebody's poodle.

I knew what was wrong. Heller was thinking in credits. A credit was worth several dollars. He picked up his baggage, walked out and walked into a cab which had just discharged a Pekingese that had been getting aired.

"I am looking for a room. I want something less expensive than they have in this place."

The driver promptly dashed downtown, switched over to Lexington Avenue, avoided numerous smashups and dumped Heller at 21st Street. Heller offered a twenty-dollar bill. The driver was very surprised when it didn't come out from between Heller's fingers. He grumblingly got change and in a swift movement, they swapped monies. Heller gave him a fifty-cent tip. He was learning.

Heller looked up at a ramshackle building. The canopy over the sidewalk said:

The Casa de Flop

He picked up his bags and walked in. A sodden group of winos sagged on sodden furniture. A sodden clerk slumped over a sodden desk. It was a very sodden lobby.

An odd sound hit my ears. Then I identified it. It was Heller sniffing. "Oof!" he said to nobody. "You'd think this place was run by the Apparatus!"

Code break! Code break! *And* unpatriotic! I made a hasty note and marked the recording strip. Nobody can accuse me of not doing my duty!

He hefted his bags, turned around and left.

Outside he stopped and looked back at the building. "You hotels can go sink yourselves! A house would cost less and be cleaner!"

It was two blocks before he could find another cab. It was sitting at the curb and Heller hailed it before it could drive off.

The driver looked like he had been up every night for the past year. He also didn't have any space between his eyes and hairline. A Neanderthal type.

Heller loaded his baggage. He leaned forward to speak through the glass and wire New York cabbies hope will protect them from muggers.

"Do you know of a house?"

The driver turned around to look at him. He thought. He said, "Do you have any money?"

"Of course I have money," said Heller.

"You're awfully young."

"Look," said Heller, "do you know of a house or don't you?"

The driver looked at him doubtfully but then nodded.

"All right," said Heller, "take me there!"

They bashed their way up into the Forties and headed over toward the East River. The black, tall slab of the United Nations pointed skyward in the near distance. They were drawing into a quieter, more elegant neighborhood full of imposing, high-rise buildings.

They pulled up at the curb before one. It was a building of gleaming stone and opaque glass, a beautiful modern structure many stories high. A patch of greenery and a brief curved drive set it back slightly from the sidewalk. An elegant, decorous sign, lettered in gold on black stone, was part of the wall to the left of the imposing entrance. The sign said

The Gracious Palms

The cab had not pulled into the drive because a squat, low, black limousine was sitting there, chauffeur at the wheel. Heller got his bags out of the cab and put them on the walk. He was fishing in his pockets for the fare.

And then a remarkable thing happened!

The cabby, who had shortly before been so dopey, stared at the limousine and front entrance. His eyes suddenly shot wide with fear!

With a screech of tires, the cabby got his hack the Hells out of there!

Without being paid!

Heller gazed after the fleeing cab. He put the money back in his pocket. He hefted his bags and walked toward the entrance.

The limousine had its engine running.

There was a tough-looking young man lounging outside the door to the right of it. He was dressed in a double-breasted suit and he had a hat pulled down over his eyes. He pried himself off the wall as Heller approached.

The young man's right hand came up. Something in it!

It was a miniature walkie-talkie radio. He said something into it, eyeing Heller.

Something was going on! Something dangerous!

And Heller, the idiot, wasn't taking alarm! He walked on in through the entrance.

The lobby was small but dignified. Iron spiral staircases went up to a balcony on the far wall. Gold elevator doors were set into the polished tan stone. Designs in gold colored metal wandered gracefully on the walls. There were some upholstered chairs of beautiful design, in groups of two, half-hidden by lovely green plants. A long, gold-colored counter was the obvious reception place.

There was nobody in sight! Not a soul!

Heller clickety-clacked across the polished, multicolored stone terrazzo floor, going toward the counter.

A small door in the wall to the left of the counter, marked with a sign: *Host,* opened about six inches. There was a man's face there. A tough one. A hand came out and beckoned silently to Heller.

Heller put down his baggage and walked over to the door. It swung open.

It was a large, ornate office. At the far end there was a carved desk. At it sat a man, small, well-dressed, black hair, narrow face. The sign on his desk said

Vantagio Meretrici, Manager

Sitting to the desk's right were two men, hats on, right hands out of sight. The three were all looking toward Heller.

Behind Heller the door closed.

Suddenly he was seized from behind!

His arms were pinned with a lock grip!

He was wrestled to a straight-back chair in the corner beside the door!

He was forced to sit down in the chair, his captor behind him, still holding him.

One of the men beside the desk gestured at Heller and addressed the manager. "So this is one of your fancy boys."

"No! No!" cried the man behind the desk. "We don't use young men here!"

The other gangster near the desk laughed in disbelief. "Aw, quit the (bleep), Vantagio. What do you charge for a boy with a pretty face like his?"

"Let's get back to business, Vantagio. Faustino says you are going to push drugs here and you push drugs here. We supply, you sell."

"Never!" said Vantagio. "We'd lose all our clientele! They'd be sure to think we were trying to bleed them for information!"

"Aw, what the hell do the niggers and chinks at the U.N. know about information!" sneered the gangster nearest Vantagio. "You got to learn new lessons. Faustino calls the shots now and you know it! So where do we start? Before we waste *you*, that is. Wrecking furniture? Disabling a few whores?"

The other gangster said, "How about the pretty new boy?"

The two hoods looked at each other and grinned. The one who had just made the suggestion lit up a cigarette and got it burning brightly. "For starts, we'll just put a few deep holes in his face and cost you some fees!"

Holding the glowing cigarette, the gangster got up and started across the room. The man gripping Heller from behind tightened his lock on Heller's arms.

Abruptly Heller brought his feet off the floor!

He did a sitting back flip!

His toes struck the man behind him on the head!

Heller's hands caught the sides of the chair seat. He catapulted himself backwards, straight over the head of the one who had been holding him! He landed behind him!

He had the man's gun out of its shoulder holster!

The gangster halfway across the room had stopped, staring!

The one still near the desk swung up a gun. "Get out of the way!" he screamed at the fellow in the middle of the room. That one promptly dropped to the floor!

The hood near the desk fired!

Heller was behind the one who had held him. The bullet struck the gangster's chest!

Using his former captor as a shield, Heller was trying to get off a shot.

The hood near the desk fired again. Twice!

Both shots struck Heller's former captor.

The hood at the desk realized he was shooting his own man! He flinched.

Heller slammed a shot straight into his heart!

The one crouched in the middle of the floor had his gun out. He was trying to get a shot.

Heller got a glimpse of him, momentarily putting himself in view. The man on the floor fired!

Another shot slammed into Heller's former captor.

Heller ducked to floor level.

He drove a shot straight into the skull of the man who had been crouching on the floor.

Two dead men! The third still flopping about in his death agonies.

"Jesus!" said Vantagio Meretrici at the desk.

Running feet outside approaching.

Heller jumped back away from the door.

The hood who had been at the entrance got half his face and an arm in. He saw Heller.

He was raising a gun!

Heller slammed a shot into his upper shoulder.

The man was hurled back out the door, spinning around. But he did not go down. The door banged shut. Running feet were racing away.

With a roar, the car outside revved up. A car door slammed and the limousine could be heard racing away on screeching tires.

"Jesus!" said Vantagio. Then he seemed to come to life. "Kid, give me a hand, quick!"

The body closest to the desk had fallen on a throw rug. Vantagio grabbed a corner of it and, using it as a kind of sled, sped to the door. He blocked the door open with a chair. Then he grabbed the rug again and skidded it and its burden out into the lobby.

The manager pointed at the man Heller had used for a shield and then out into the lobby. Heller lugged the body out and dumped it in the lobby.

The chortle of distant cop cars sounded.

Together, the manager and Heller dragged the third body out.

An old woman had appeared in the lobby, a neatly uniformed cleaning woman. "Get the blood off the floor in the office!" the manager yelled at her. "Be quick!"

The cop cars were nearer.

The manager dived behind the desk. The clerk was there on the floor, tied up and gagged. Heller took the clerk and cut the bonds off.

The manager arranged the bodies in the lobby. He took the gun Heller had used and wiped it off and put it in the hand of the one who had been Heller's captor.

The cop cars were drawing up. "The (bleepards)," said the manager. "They had the fuzz tipped to rush in and grab me if there was any shooting!"

The manager surveyed the scene, said something fast in Italian to the clerk and was about to tell Heller something, probably to beat it, when a stentorian voice called out from the entrance, "Everybody freeze!" The everybody was the manager, Heller and the clerk.

A police inspector, fronted with two cops holding riot shotguns, was there. He was a huge man, middle-aged, flabby. "All right, Meretrici, you're under arrest!"

"For what?" said Vantagio.

The police inspector was looking at the bodies. He glared at the clerk. "What happened?"

"Just like you see," said the clerk. "That one," and he pointed to the body that was furthest from the entrance, the one Heller had used for a shield, "was evidently trying to get away from the others. And they came busting in the door after him and they all started shooting each other."

The police inspector examined each of the bodies and the guns.

"They should be arrested," said Vantagio. "We don't allow shooting in here!"

"Wise (bleep)," said the inspector. He came over to Heller. "Who the hell are you?"

"He's a delivery boy," said Vantagio. "He came in from the back after the shooting."

"(Bleep)," said the inspector.

"I wish you'd do your civic duty," said Vantagio, "the ones the taxpayers pay you for and get these bodies the hell out of here. They already ruined one rug!"

"Don't you touch nothing," said the inspector. "The stiff team will be here in a few minutes and they'll want pictures of all this. And you two," he pointed at the manager and clerk, "don't fail to show up at the coroner's inquest! I oughta jail you as material witnesses!"

"We'll be glad to perform *our* civic duties," said Vantagio. "You just make sure you give honest businessmen better protection hereafter!" He glared at the bodies. "Hoodlums running all over the streets!"

The inspector left. A patrolman stood guard over the bodies so no one could corrupt the evidence.

"I'll take that baggage in my office," Vantagio said to Heller and beckoned.

Heller picked up his suitcases and the carry-all and followed him in.

Chapter 2

The cleaning woman had finished mopping up the blood. Vantagio turned the air conditioner on to "vent," probably to clear out the drifting cordite smoke. He seated Heller in a chair and then sat back down at his ornate desk.

"Kid," said Vantagio, "you saved my life! I never before *seen* such terrific shooting!" He regarded Heller for a bit. "How did you come to get here, anyway?"

Heller told him he had been looking for a place to live and then quoted his conversation with the taxi driver in which he had asked for a house.

Vantagio laughed. "Oh, kid, you are a greenhorn. Strictly from the backwoods. Listen, kid. In the vernacular of our fair city, the word 'house' means a brothel, a bordello, a bagnio, a crib, a sporting house, a cathouse, a whorehouse or, in short, a house of prostitution. And here you are. This is the pleasure palace of the United Nations, the top 'house' in all Manhattan!"

He started to laugh again and then he sobered. "But I can thank *La Santissima Vergine* that you arrived. I was sure my number was up!"

He sat back, looking at Heller, and thought for a moment. "You're kind of handy to have around. Kid, could I offer you a job? Something respectable like a bouncer?"

"No," said Heller. "Thank you. I've got to get a diploma. People don't listen to you unless you have a diploma."

"Oh, so true! I'm a great believer in education! I have my

master's degree in political science from Empire University," he said proudly, "and here I am at the top of my profession, head of the UN whorehouse!"

At that moment there was a commotion at the door and two very disheveled men rushed in. Although their clothes were expensive looking, they were very crumpled.

"Where you been?" Vantagio shouted at them.

"We got here as fast as we could," said one. "At dawn that God (bleeped) Inspector Grafferty busted into our apartment and arrested us for vagrancy and littering. It took until just now for the shyster to bail us out!"

"It was a setup," said Vantagio. "Police Inspector Bulldog Grafferty," and he spat sideways on the carpet. "He was right up the street waiting! He got you two gunsels out of the way so the Faustino mob could come in here and put the pressure on. If I'd refused and they'd have killed me, Grafferty was right on hand to prove they wasted me in self-defense. If this kid hadn't crashed the party, I'd be dead!" And he told them exactly what had happened and what Heller had done.

"Jesus!" said the two men in unison, looking at Heller.

"Now go down to the dry-cleaning room and get yourselves pressed up and get on duty. We can't have you looking like a couple of bums! This is a high-class joint!"

"Yes, Mr. Meretrici," they both said and rushed out.

"This really is a high-class joint," Vantagio repeated to Heller. "The UN crowd is funny. If they thought we pushed drugs, they'd be sure we were trying to bleed information out of them. No, sir. We stay with tradition. We serve bootleg booze. And booze and drugs don't mix, kid."

"Lethal," said Heller, doubtless remembering his book.

"Eh? Oh, right. You sure said it, kid. No gang wars in booze at all these days. And there's just as much money to be made in bootleg booze as there ever was in Prohibition. Did you know Federal taxes was ten bucks a fifth now? And it's more respectable. More traditional.

"Now, there are those that will tell you you can't have

prostitution without having drugs. But that's baloney. The whores go silly. They get all dried up. They don't last two years. And they're an expensive investment! We have to train them, send them to Towers Modeling School and hygiene clinics as doctors' assistants and postgraduate them to an ex–Hong Kong whore. That's expensive. You can't amortize it fast enough. Internal Revenue Service won't let you write off the investment that quick. So, no drugs, kid."

"No drugs," said Heller, probably thinking of Mary Schmeck.

"Right," said Vantagio. "The UN clientele would simply evaporate. And we'd have to pay off the DEA. We'd go bankrupt!"

"Well," said Heller. "I'm sorry I made a mistake. I'll be going now."

"No, no!" said Vantagio in alarm. "You saved my life. And even Clint Eastwood couldn't have beaten that gun play! You're handy to have around! Listen, business is slack—the UN isn't in session and it's summer and nobody's in town. You came for a room. There's two hundred rooms and suites in this building! I got a little room—it was once a maid's room—up on the second floor you can have."

"Well," said Heller, "if you'll let me pay for it."

"Pay? Well, how about you just sitting around the lobby now and then, two or three times a week maybe. For just an hour or two. I'll see you get some decent clothes."

I thought, no, no, Heller. He knows the Faustino mob saw you! He's just going to use you to scare them off!

He must have seen Heller was reluctant. "Look, kid. You're going to college. If you go to Empire, I can give you some steers and pointers. We don't have a restaurant but we have a kitchen that serves great food to rooms and you can get sandwiches. We can't serve you any booze because it's obvious you're a minor and it would be illegal. But you could have all the soft drinks you wanted. Listen. We'll even keep you from being embarrassed by the UN people thinking you're part of the help. We'll cook up some story about you being the son of a dictator or something incognito and living here to go to college."

It wasn't the danger I was worried about. I couldn't see how I could sneak Raht in there to rifle his baggage! Whorehouses go crazy when you try to rifle baggage. They think you're trying to roll the customers and get them in trouble with the police! And those gunsels had looked formidable! It would be like trying to reach Heller in jail!

I knew what was wrong with Vantagio. He was still in shock and overreacting with gratitude. Heller wasn't all that prepossessing!

"Now, this place is full of good-looking women," said Vantagio, "and a good-looking kid with muscles like yours will have them swarming at you. But you can always call one of the madames if they bother you. What say, kid? Is it a deal?"

"Do you have boys here?" said Heller.

"Cripes no!" exploded Vantagio. "That was just that dumb hood's idea. He's . . . was . . . gay. So how about it, kid?"

Heller barely started to nod when Vantagio was out of his seat and racing to the door. He peeked into the lobby. The stiff team and bodies were gone. The cleaning lady was mopping up the floor.

Vantagio said to the clerk, "Hit the buzzers." And shortly numerous staff began to drift in and then the elevators started going and numerous beautiful women in various stages of dishabille began to drift into the lobby. They were of all colors from all parts of the world, though white predominated. The lobby got pretty full of half-bare legs and half-exposed breasts.

Vantagio grabbed off Heller's cap and told him to stand up on a marble ledge. The sea of upturned lovely faces looked like the color plates of the porno and movie magazines had all gone into a mad shuffle. A montage of alluring beauties!

In a very commanding voice, Vantagio said, pointing at Heller, "This kid just saved my life. I want you to treat him decent."

A whoosh of pent-up breath sounded in the room and a concerted "Ooooo!" I couldn't understand it. What could they see in Heller? Then I realized it was off-season for them. Man-starved.

"He's going to live here," said Vantagio.

If the "Ooooo" was loud before, it doubled now, interspersed with some pants!

Oh, my Gods, I thought. If the Countess Krak could only see this!

"Now, listen," said Vantagio, raising his voice to be heard, "he's underage as you can plainly see. He's jail bait! And if he complains about anybody bothering him, out that (bleepch) goes!"

Mutters.

Vantagio shouted up to the balcony, "Mama Sesso! You hear that?"

A big, heavy-breasted woman, black-haired, muscular, mustached, shouted, "I'm here, Signore Meretrici!" And she came forward to the rail and looked down.

"As Chief Madame," shouted Vantagio, "you're going to see that enforced and that all the other madames enforce it!"

"I got it, Signore Meretrici. If they don't do what the young boy tells them, out they go."

"No, no, no!" cried Vantagio. "You're to keep them off him! He's a kid. Jail bait! They could get us on a morals charge!"

Mama Sesso nodded severely. "I a-got it, Signore Meretrici. I a-seen what the boy do on-a the close circuit TV. He save-a you life. He's-a faster than a-Cesare Borgia! He's a-good to have around. Maybe he save-a all-a our lives next. *La Santissima Vergine* send-a him. If they don' do right by the young boy, out-a they go!"

"Right!" said Vantagio.

Some madames swatted their palms together and the assemblage began to disperse, several sets of lovely eyes remaining reluctantly on Heller. Did they suppose, I thought disgustedly, that he was something to eat? He was far too young for their general taste!

A uniformed attendant came up and struggled with Heller's baggage. Heller helped him, and because the elevator was jammed, they walked up to the second floor on thickly carpeted stairs.

Vantagio led the way down a long hall and they came to a small room. It was plain but it was clean—almost sanitary. The iron bedstead was white and so was the chest of drawers. The bathroom was small but modern. All strictly utility.

"How's this?" said Vantagio.

"Fine," said Heller.

Some of the women had followed down the hall. But Vantagio peremptorily ordered them away. He got out some old cards and a ball point. Using the back of one, he wrote an address on it.

"Now, this," he said to Heller, "is a tall man's shop. You go out and buy yourself a summer suit you haven't grown out of. And get something besides baseball shoes! You got dough?"

"Lots," said Heller.

"Good. But you wash up and when you come down, bring any excess dough and I'll give you a small personal safe with your own combination. We want to keep this an honest house!" He left.

Heller stowed his things, washed up, checked the lock on his door and then went down with the fifty thousand in the paper sack his breakfast had come in.

Vantagio showed him the battery of private safes and how to open one. It seemed UN people carried documents and things around they wanted stowed for the few hours they might be there.

Heller mastered how to change the combination and then changed it so fast I couldn't read it off! But it would be impossible to get near it or even get to his baggage. My interest in stealing it was purely academic. It punched through how protected he was now!

He left the Gracious Palms on foot, happy I suppose to have some exercise. I wasn't happy. He had more guns pointing at him now than I could easily count. The Faustino mob knew his face and he had killed three of their men, one of them maybe a lieutenant of the mob! And add in Police Inspector Grafferty. He had seen Heller face to face and cops remember things—that's their trade: mentally cataloguing who to shoot down next!

Shortly it did not help my morale a bit to receive the day's report of Raht and Terb. It read:

> Went to whorehouse and got (bleeped) and they stole his baggage. He's probably broke but seems safe.

I could have killed them!

Chapter 3

Miles from the U.N. area, and now in the garment district, Heller was clickety-clacking along, on his way to I knew not where but, if I knew Heller, up to no good.

It was evidently a hot midday in New York and people were slouching along, mopping their faces and carrying their coats over their arms. One would have thought that they would have glanced at Heller but New York is a peculiar place: practically nobody ever looks at anybody no matter what they are doing—including rape and murder. Even dead bodies can lie on the street until the sanitation department gets a complaint—and answers it if they happen to have any appropriation that month. So Heller was attracting no attention.

Wait! I was wrong!

Heller glanced back and I saw someone quickly turn. Was it Raht or Terb? I got the other screen working and stilled it. No, it wasn't Raht or Terb. It was too brief a glimpse to make it out. But someone had noted his departure.

They push delivery carts of racked clothes through the streets of the garment district at a mad pace and Heller was dodging these. He had come to a shop. The sign said:

TALL AND BIG MEN

Heller was shortly involved in trying to purchase something that fit. It was off-season—too late for summer clothes to be in demand, too soon for winter clothes—and because business was bad, the shop was dedicated to making it worse.

He found a dark blue suit of summer weight. He couldn't find a normal shirt—they all had collars of twenty-five or so inches and girths of sixty. Finally he located three drip-dry cotton ones. They had Eton collars! These are the kind the undergraduates wear in England!

The real tailor that did adjustments was on vacation and the helper he had left behind botched the suit alteration. He adjusted the coat sleeves and pants cuffs too short again!

But Heller dressed anyway. He was now in dark blue with an Eton collar and he looked younger than ever!

He presented the store with the red-checked jacket and the blue-striped pants. And because those clothes were bugged, I bitterly surmised that Raht and Terb, who were depending on those bugs, would now stake out the tall man's shop!

He couldn't find any shoes he liked so he kept the baseball spikes on, popped his red baseball cap on the back of his head and was shortly engaged again in what seemed his favorite pastime: examining fenders of parked cars.

In peripheral vision, I saw the figure again. He was being tailed!

But Heller? Did he take evasive tactics? Run through a large store with two entrances? Dash into a crowd? Not Heller! He didn't even inspect the street behind him! Amateur!

He knelt down by the fender of a very modern car and bent it with his fingers—an easy thing for anybody to do. Then he looked around quickly to see if the unintentional act of vandalism had been noticed. Apparently to make sure he covered it up, he stood, turned, folded his arms and sort of lounged back against the fender. It really buckled!

He walked off. And then, abruptly, began the craziest series of actions I had yet seen him engage upon.

He caught a cab. Breathlessly, he said to the driver, "Quick! Take me to the bus terminal! Five-dollar tip!"

They went westward. No especially hurried ride. Heller got out at the Port Authority Bus Terminal and paid the driver.

Immediately, he got another cab. He leaped in and said urgently, "Quick! Take me to the Manhattan Air Terminal! I'm late! Five-dollar tip!"

Aha! I thought I understood at last! He had noticed the tail and was shaking it!

Cross-town rides are slow and it was very uneventful.

At the Manhattan Air Terminal, he paid the driver and got out.

Then Heller walked along a line of cabs, looking at their fenders. He found one with some bashes. It was a Really Red Cab Company hack.

Heller leaped in. "Quick! I have to be at Broadway and 52nd Street in two minutes and nineteen seconds. There's a five-dollar tip!"

Disregarding other drivers' protests that it was not his turn to go, the cabby zipped out of line, screamed into high gear. He cut a corner, bashed a car out of his way, ran a red light, sent a works-in-progress sign skyrocketing and stopped at Broadway and 52nd Street. Heller looked at his watch. It was two minutes!

Heller paid him the fare and the five-dollar tip.

AND THEN HELLER JUST SAT THERE IN THE CAB!

The driver, expecting Heller to rush out, looked at him in amazement.

"How would you like to teach me to drive in New York?" said Heller.

Oh, my Gods! Heller was not shaking a tail. He was trying to find a reckless cab driver! Heller was a hopeless idiot!

"I ain't got the time, buddy," said the driver.

"For a hundred bucks would you have the time?"

Silence.

"For two hundred bucks would you have the time?"

Silence.

Heller opened the cab door to get out.

The driver said, "I'm almost off shift! I'll race up to the barn, turn in and come back. You wait here. No. You come with me. I'll turn this wreck in and get a decent hack."

Promptly, driving rapidly, the cabby started for the Really Red Cab barn. "What's your name?" he shot back through the open glass partition.

"Clyde Barrow," said Heller.

I snorted. That was a famous gangster! Nothing was sacred to Heller!

"I see on the card here," said Heller, "that you're called Mortie Massacurovitch. Been driving cabs long?"

"Me?" said the cabby, glancing back at Heller without regard to a near collision. He was a very tough-looking oldster. "My old man was a hacker in this town and I learned how from him. In the last war, on the strength of it, they made me a tank driver."

"Get any medals?" said Heller.

"No. They sent me home—said I was too brutal to the enemy!"

Heller waited outside while the hacker turned his cab and receipts in. And suddenly it dawned on me what he was up to. He had believed that tale about it being too hard to drive in New York! He was going to bring the Cadillac into town!

Oh! No, no, no! There was no way to warn this naive simpleton! One of the things Bury would surely have done was to have that Cadillac rigged to explode! Bury had not wanted it to be near the planned murder of the bogus Rockecenter, Junior. But aside from that, it was strictly textbook that he would have it set to explode, particularly now that he had missed. Bury was the sort of man who did multiple planning and handled eventualities.

So I sat there helplessly while Heller, in a forthright fashion, industriously planned his own suicide!

Chapter 4

Shortly, Mortie Massacurovitch came out of the huge garage they called a barn. He beckoned and Heller went inside.

Way back in the corner, covered with dust, sat the remains of a cab. Most of the paint was off by reason of dents and scrapes. It still had its meter and its top taxi lights but it was a long way from a modern cab. It was sort of square, with no smooth gentle curves.

"Here," said Mortie, "is a *real* cab! It has real steel fenders, quarter of an inch thick. It has real bumpers with side bars and hooks. It has real bulletproof, nonshatter glass." He looked at it proudly. "They really used to build them! Not plaster and paper like today."

A passenger could ride with the driver in this one and Mortie wiped off the seat and got Heller in. Then the cabby got in. "Gives you the edge," he said. "My favorite cab!"

He got its oil and gas checked and off they went, back to town. And, in truth, there was nothing wrong with its motor. It seemed to have more acceleration than modern cabs in that it got away from lights way ahead of everybody. "Geared down for fast darts," said Mortie.

Heller learned how to handle the gear shift and clutch on a quiet street and Mortie, satisfied now on that score, took over. "Now, let's see, where is the traffic thickest this time of day?" He looked at his watch. "Ah, yeah. Grand Central Station." And off they roared.

It was creeping up to afternoon going-home time when they

neared the area. The traffic was THICK! And fast!

"Now," said Mortie, "this is going to require your close attention because it is a very high art. People are basically yellow. They always give up before you do. So that leaves you a very wide scope."

Chattering along, naming each maneuver as he went, Mortie Massacurovitch performed.

It was horrifying!

They dashed between two cars to make the cars split each way! They squealed brakes to startle people "because honking was frowned upon." They swerved to make a car dodge away from its intended parking place and then stole it. They dove in ahead of another hailed cab and when the passenger tried to get in, told him the cab was engaged. They bashed backwards to widen a place to park. They bashed forward to get a place to park. They did a skid "to alarm a motorist, who then stamps on his brakes and you grab his place in line." They followed an ambulance to get somewhere quick. They followed a fire engine to really run the meter up fast, "but setting a fire ahead to get the engines to run is frowned on."

Heller then got under the wheel. He did all those things Mortie had done, with a few embellishments.

With bent fenders, raw voices and screams of anguish and terror strewn behind them, Mortie now guided Heller to a cabby bar on Eighth Avenue. It was a time of traffic lull and one had better have a sandwich.

Heller tried to order a beer and got scolded both by Mortie and the proprietor: "Trying to make the place lose its license?" So Heller had milk with his steak instead. "You got to have respect for the law, kid," Mortie told him. "Learn to grow up to be a good, peaceful, orderly, law-abiding citizen. That's the only way to get ahead.

"Got to get going!" said Mortie. "Time for theater traffic around Times Square."

En route, Mortie told him, "Now you got to learn how to handle police. When a cop stops you for speeding, you stop, see. You wait until he comes up and then you whisper, 'Run for your life.

This fare is holding a gun on me.' And the cop will beat it every time!"

Heller thanked him.

"You got to know these things, kid." But something else had attracted Mortie's attention. "You got any enemies, kid? Your parents looking for you or something?"

"Why?"

"Well, it'd have to be you. I never made an enemy in my life. A cab started up behind us when we left the eatery and it's still back there."

Mortie did a right-angle turn, went down an alley, went wrong way on a one-way street. Looked back. "Don't see him now. I think we shook him. So we can get busy."

They were into the theater district. It was well before the evening start of the shows but the traffic was THICK!

"Now, you see that line of cars, kid? Watch!"

Mortie came up alongside of a cab in the line. He stopped. He screamed an insult at the driver. Mortie made a motion to get out of his cab. The other driver, in a rage, leaped out of his. Mortie didn't leave his cab. The line moved ahead. Mortie slid the cab into it, taking the place of the immobilized cab. "See, kid? Art!"

Mortie got to an intersection near a big hotel. There were several cabs and few customers. Mortie sailed in, skidding to block the exit of the driveway, and killed his engine. Other cabbies screamed at him. He screamed back, "I'm stalled!" As he was now first in line, an elderly, well-dressed man and woman tried to get into Mortie's cab. "Sorry," said Mortie, "I'm going to the barn." He drove off. "See, kid, I could have had my pick of fares. You got to know what you're doing and think, think, think all the time."

He raced down a line of traffic. A car looked like it was going to turn out and block him. He sideswiped it with a scream of metal. The car pulled hastily back. "Don't try it with limousines, kid. They're really yellow. Scared for their paint. You don't have to sideswipe. You just gesture, like this." He veered toward a limousine and it promptly climbed the curb.

The bright lights of theater marquees, the flashing advertising signs, the throngs and ticket lines. A lively, blazing night.

"Now, you see that car ahead there that's stopping. I'll show you how to take off doors."

The street side door swung open. The old cab was there before anyone could get out. There was a rending crash and off came the door.

"It's timing, kid. All timing. Now, you see that guy up the street waving for a fare? Over there on the wrong side for us?"

Mortie zoomed ahead to forty miles an hour, stamped on the brakes, did a hundred-and-eighty-degree turn and skidded sideways to the curb. The hopeful fare started to get in. "Sorry, we're heading for the barn," said Mortie.

He found a one-way street. They backed down it at forty miles an hour. "You see, we're pointed the right direction so it ain't illegal.

"See that red light? Now we're going to rush it. If you listen you can hear the switch in the box and you can claim it was yellow.

"Now here is a curb bounce. That's a nice curb. If you hit it right, you can bounce back into the street and the guy that was about to pass you, thinking you was parking, gets sideswiped! Watch."

They bounced. There was a rending scream of metal. Headlight glass tinkled to the pavement.

"All right, kid. Now let's see you do it."

Heller took the wheel. He started up. He went through the routine. But just as he was about to rush a red light, the sound of a heavy thud shook the cab.

"What was that?" said Mortie. Then he pointed. The side window had a star. "Jesus, that's a bullet!"

Another thud!

"Get the hell out of here, kid! Somebody is breaking the firearms law!"

Heller was on his way!

He went down 42nd Street, headed west. He was not going very fast.

"Step on it, kid! A cab just came around the corner behind us!"

"You sure?" said Heller.

"Hell, yes! He's gaining!"

But Heller was loafing.

He was watching in the rearview mirror. Sure enough, there was a cab behind them, gaining!

A bullet hit the rear window!

"Now we can go!" said Heller.

He fled down 42nd Street.

He passed the Sheraton Motor Inn.

I grabbed a New York map to see if he was leaving the country.

The old cab negotiated the approaches to the West Side Elevated Highway. Traffic was light. Below them over the rail, the ground level street was dim. To their left lay the North River and the passenger steamship docks. Yes, on this route he could escape to Connecticut!

Heller checked the rearview mirror. The pursuing cab was still coming.

Below the elevated highway, to their right, the De Witt Clinton Park fled by and was gone.

Heller wasn't moving fast. The other was close behind!

A sign ahead and a split in the elevated highway: 55th Street!

Suddenly, with a yank of the wheel, Heller sent the cab into a ninety-degree right turn! He stamped on the brakes! The rail was right in front of him! The lower street was fifty feet down!

He was stopped!

The other cab was coming on.

Heller suddenly backed up!

There was room for the other cab to pass in front of his radiator. It started through the hole.

Heller sent his cab ahead!

The bumper hit the other cab's front wheels.

The other cab was punched over toward the rail!

With a shattering crash, it went through the guard!

It catapulted into space!

Chapter 5

Even before it hit the street below, Heller shouted to Mortie, "Take over!"

There was a crash below!

Heller was out. The rail was torn into jagged pickets where the cab had disappeared.

He peered down. There were girders and supports.

He went through the hole in the rail. He swarmed down a girder. He slid down a pillar and hit the lower street.

The other cab had landed on its wheels, shot ahead and struck a stanchion.

Gas was flooding the street!

A traffic light was nearby. Heller looked at the control box.

He raced over to the cab.

The doors were buckled.

He yanked a small jimmy out of his pocket and went to work on the rear door. The metal bent around the jammed lock. He inserted the jimmy higher and pried. He got his fingers in and, with a heave, got the door open.

He glanced at the spreading gasoline and then at the traffic light. Suddenly I knew why. Fumes, rising, would explode when they hit those control box switches! Like a bomb! I know bombs!

Heller had the driver out. Then he reached in and grabbed the man in the back.

Lugging two bodies, he sped over to the curb.

He looked back. He evidently decided he was not far enough. He went another fifty feet.

On the pavement, in the protection of a big concrete abutment, he laid the bodies out.

With a shattering blue crash, the wreck exploded!

The "cabby" was dead. But even though the top of his head was half off, he was obviously a Sicilian.

Heller turned to the other one.

The weird hue of the street light shone down upon the face of Torpedo Fiaccola!

The hit man's eyelids fluttered. He was still alive!

A squad car chortled in the distance. Nobody could have missed that blast for a mile!

Torpedo opened his eyes. He saw Heller. He recognized him.

Torpedo said, "You ain't going to kill my mother?"

Heller looked down at him. "I'll think about it."

"No!"

Heller reached into Torpedo's coat and took his wallet. The money was only the five thousand that Heller had given him back. But there was a slip of paper. It said

Valid with the evidence. Hand package to bearer.

Heller shook the paper at Torpedo. "Hand to who?"

Torpedo said, "You going to kill my mother?"

"I was thinking about it. Give me the name and address for this slip and I might reconsider."

The hood was blinking hard. Then he said, "Mamie. Apartment 18F. Two thirty-one Binetta Lane. Downtown."

"And the evidence?" said Heller.

"Look," moaned Torpedo, "Bury is going to kill me!"

Heller said, "Mothers should be cherished."

Torpedo shuddered. "Your baseball cap with blood on it and a lock of your hair."

Heller took off his cap, turned it wrong side out and swabbed it through the mess that had been the driver's head.

He said, "I hear an ambulance coming. Get yourself patched up in the hospital and then I'd advise you to take up residence at the North Pole." He bent over him and put the wallet and five thousand back in his pocket. "I keep trying to give you this. Now take it and learn to speak polar-bear. I'm not a mother killer but I sure enjoy exploding torpedoes!"

The squad car had been drifting slowly closer, cautiously. The flames flickering from the wreck made a shifting patchwork on it. The cops got out.

"How come you drug the bodies from the wreck, kid?" said the first cop, threateningly.

"He just missed me," said Heller. "I wanted to give him some advice."

"Oh," said the cop in sudden comprehension. "But I'll have to give the driver a ticket all the same." He got out his book and called to his partner. "What would you say the charge was, Pete?"

"Littering," said the other cop.

"It's that one that was driving," said Heller. "He's dead."

"Gets the ticket all the same," said the cop, writing.

The ambulance was whining up, probably called by the cops earlier.

Mortie Massacurovitch had brought the old cab down to the lower level. Heller got in. "Take me to 231 Binetta Lane."

"That's Little Italy," said Mortie. "Wrong time of night. You got a gun?"

"I got another hundred," said Heller.

They zipped downtown. They went from Eleventh Avenue to Tenth, shifted over on 14th Street, went down Greenwich Avenue, worked their way around Washington Square and were soon in Little Italy. They stopped across the street from the address. It was awfully dark.

Heller took out a knife, cut off a small lock of his own hair and pasted it into the baseball cap with the blood. Then he put the note in it.

He turned to Mortie. "Go to Apartment 18F and ask for Mamie. Give her this and she'll give you a package."

"In there?" said Mortie, looking at the ominously dark building.

"And when you return," said Heller, "I'll give you another hundred."

Mortie grabbed the cap and contents, leaped out, raced up the steps.

Three minutes later, he raced down the steps carrying a package. He threw it at Heller, started the car up and got out of there.

"Mamie was a man with a gun," said Mortie. "But he took it with no questions."

Heller told him to take him to the corner of First Avenue and 42nd Street. He shook the pack, listened to it and then sniffed it. Well, at last he was getting cautious for it well could have been a bomb. He pried up a corner and pulled something out.

"What's a first class ticket to . . . Buenos Aires, Argentina, worth?" he asked Mortie.

"I dunno," said Mortie. "Maybe three grand."

"Can you cash one in?"

"Oh, sure," said Mortie. "Just take it to the air terminal. What's the matter, ain't you going?"

Oh, if Heller only were!

Mortie let him out at First and 42nd. Heller said, "Now, do you think I really passed, or do I need more lessons?"

Mortie appeared to be thinking it over carefully. Then he said, "Well, kid, with experience you could become a top New York cabby. There's more I could teach you about short-changing customers and running up extra meterage but, otherwise, that's about it. You pass. Yes, I'd say you pass."

Heller counted him out six one-hundred-dollar bills. He instantly stuffed the money in his shirt and drove away at high speed.

Heller trotted along, clickety-clack, and soon arrived at the Gracious Palms.

In his room he opened the pack. Money in small old bills!

He counted it. ONE HUNDRED THOUSAND DOLLARS!

I shuddered. My Gods, Bury must be angry to offer such a price!

Heller put it in the paper sack his breakfast had come in. He went down to the personal safes and put it in.

Vantagio was in his office and saw Heller through the open door. He called to him, "Getting out some money, kid? You'll need dough for school! Don't blow all you got on night life. This is an expensive town!"

"It sure is," said Heller, adding the hundred grand to his fifty thousand already in the safe. "Prices just keep going up!"

He went to bed and was shortly peacefully asleep.

I wasn't! Bury had unlimited funds and I didn't even have a clue on how to get that platen!

Some hours later, the next report of Raht and Terb didn't help. It said

> He went to a place called the Tall Man's Shop and they must have given him a job and a place to sleep. He's still there! But we have our eyes on him.

The Hells they did! They were still spotting in on the bug we had sewn in his coat!

I was getting frightened that I might have to go to America myself to handle this. And I didn't have the least idea what I could do even if I did.

Chapter 6

Heller was up bright and early the following day, the viewer alarm blasting me out of a sodden sleep.

He was being very industrious and purposeful. He brushed his new suit where it had been messed up on the girders, put on a clean white shirt with an Eton collar, put a new baseball cap on the back of his head and then packed a shoulder-strap satchel which looked, for all the world, like one of these kiddy schoolbook bags.

In the bag he put a spool of fish line, a multihooked bass plug, a tool kit, a dozen baseballs, a roll of tape and the New Jersey license plates. Was he going fishing?

Down to the lobby he went. It was early for a whorehouse: the desk clerk was asleep, a guard in a tuxedo was reading the *Daily Racing Form*, ball point in hand, and an Arab sheik was wandering drunkenly around, apparently trying to choose amongst several throw rugs as to which would be best to use for morning prayer.

Heller counted ten thousand out of his personal safe and put it in his pockets. The Arab gave him a deep obeisance, Heller repeated the bow and hand motion exactly and presently was trotting down the street, clickety-clack.

He stopped at a deli and got breakfast in a sack, went out and found a cab.

"Weehawken, New Jersey," said Heller. "One way." And he gave the address of the garage where the Cadillac was!

"Double fare as you won' be comin' back," said the cabby.

I suddenly chilled. Up to then I had not grasped what Heller was going to do! He was on his way to get his car! Bury knew where that car was. It would be rigged! That "won't be coming back" was all too prophetic!

"Double fare," agreed Heller.

He had his sweet rolls and coffee as he rode along. They were soon across town. They dove into the Lincoln Tunnel and roared along under the Hudson River. They soon were in New Jersey and turned north on the J. F. Kennedy Boulevard.

They turned out of the roaring traffic to approach the garage. But one block away from it, Heller told the cab to stop and wait. The cabby looked at the decayed, semi-industrial neighborhood. "You mean wait *here?*" he asked.

Heller took a fifty-dollar bill, tore it in half and gave the driver half.

"I'll wait," said the cabby.

Heller got out and trotted around a corner en route to the garage. He stopped.

Trucks! Trucks! Trucks! The whole area in front of the huge, low building was jammed with trucks! Crews of men were unloading stacks of cartons onto handcarts and taking them into the building.

Heller went closer. He stood at the garage door and looked in. The place was being filled up with stacks of cartons higher than a man's head and in separate islands.

He moved a bit to see deeper in. The Cadillac was there. The license plates were missing.

There was something else going on. Voices. Heller shifted. He saw the plump young man and a burly monster dressed like a trucker. They were having a flaming argument.

"I don't care! I don't care!" the plump young man was shouting. "You can't store that stuff in here. I don't care whose orders it is! You don't understand!" He half gestured toward the Cadillac and then didn't.

Abruptly I knew his dilemma. The crews were putting valuable stuff in a garage/warehouse with a car which was rigged! And the young man couldn't say why.

"We ain't clearing nothing back out!" said the burly man. "If you'd been here on time, we mighta listened. But it's too late now! This stuff stays! Besides, we get our orders just like you. I am not going to let some punk like you work my men's (bleeps) off just . . ."

The plump young man had seen Heller at the door. He stiffened. He turned and raced off to an exit in the back wall like the devil was after him. He vanished.

Heller quietly withdrew. He walked through the boil of men and handtrucks, turned the corner and got back in the cab.

"You got further to go," said Heller. "Take me to 136 Crystal Parkway, Bayonne."

The New York cabby had to look at a map. "This is foreign country," he explained. "It ain't as if you were still in civilization. This is New Jersey. And you can't ask directions. The natives lie!"

But soon they were headed south on J. F. Kennedy Boulevard, got through Union City, went under the Pulaski Skyway, passed St. Peter's College and roared along through the increased traffic of Jersey City. Docks and glimpses of the New York skyline could be seen.

"Is that a statue way over there in the water?" asked Heller pointing east.

"Jesus," said the cabby, "don't you recognize the Statue of Liberty? You should know your country, kid."

They went past the Jersey City State College and were soon in Bayonne. The New York cabby was shortly all tangled up. They got turned back from the Military Ocean Terminal, got trapped into going to Staten Island, came back over the Bayonne Bridge—paying a toll both ways—and finally asked a native.

Ten minutes later they were in an isolated area of new high-rises and on a quiet street. Here was 136 Crystal Parkway, a very splendid building. A new condo.

Heller repaired the torn fifty and paid the driver off. "I don't know if I will ever find my way home," mourned the cabby.

Heller added a twenty. "Hire a native guide," he said.

The driver drove off.

All this time, I had been cudgeling my brains to remember where I had heard that address.

Heller walked in through a plush entrance. There were several elevators. One of them said:

Penthouse

He pushed the call button.

Expecting an automatic elevator, I was a bit surprised to see the door opened by a man. He was not an elevator operator. He wore a double-breasted coat and a hat pulled down. I could see the bulge of a shoulder-holstered gun. He was very dark, very Sicilian.

"Yeah?" he said noncommittally.

"I would like to see Mrs. Corleone," said Heller.

I freaked! He was calling on the head of the New Jersey Mafia! "Yeah?"

"I saw Jimmy 'The Gutter' Tavilnasty recently," said Heller.

Then it all came to me with a flash. That meeting in Afyon when Jimmy, in the dark, had mistaken him for a DEA man! Well, they'd soon see through *that!* And I didn't have the platen!

"I.D.," demanded the gangster and Heller showed it to him.

The hood was on the elevator telephone. It was in a felt-lined box. You couldn't hear what was being said.

With a slit-eyed look at Heller, the hood frisked him lightly, inspected his bag and then gestured for him to get in.

They rode up to the top. It was a one-stop elevator, penthouse only. The hood opened the door and pushed Heller out ahead of him. With little punches from behind he directed him down a beautifully decorated hallway. He opened a door at the end and shoved Heller in.

It was a gorgeous room, all done in modern gold and beige. A vast picture window looked out over a vast park and a bay.

A woman was seated comfortably on a couch. She was wearing beige lounging pajamas of silk. She was blond with blue eyes. Her corn silk hair was in coiled braids that wound around the top of her head to make a sort of crown. She was about forty.

She laid down a glossy style magazine she had been reading and stood up.

My Gods, she was tall!

She looked at Heller and then walked across the room to him. She was at least four inches taller than Heller! An Amazon!

She was smiling. "And so you are a friend of dear Jimmy's," she said. "Don't be shy. He has often spoken of his friends in the younger street gangs. But you don't look like one of those." She had a sort of cooing, affected voice and a fake Park Avenue accent.

"I'm going to college," said Heller.

"Oh," she said in sudden understanding. "That is the smart thing to do these days. Do sit down. Jimmy's friends are always welcome here. Would you like something to drink?"

"It's a hot day," said Heller. "How about some beer?"

She wagged a finger at him, kittenishly. "Naughty. Really naughty. You realize that would be against the law." Then she raised her head and bellowed, "Gregorio!"

Almost instantly, a white-coated, very dark Italian popped in.

"Get the young gentleman some milk and bring me some seltzer water."

Gregorio was taken aback. "Milk? We ain't got any milk, Babe."

"Well, get out and get some God (bleeped) milk!" roared Babe Corleone. Then she ensconced herself again on the couch. In her sweet, cooing, affected Park Avenue voice she said, "And how is dear Jimmy?"

Heller only sat down when she did. He now had his cap on his knee. The courteous Fleet officer!

"He was just fine a few days ago," said Heller. "Seemed to be right on the job."

"Oh, that is so nice to hear," cooed Babe. "And nice of him to send word."

"And how is the family?" said Heller.

Ouch, I thought. The (bleeped) fool thought a "family" was a real family. In that country, on this planet, it means a Mafia mob!

She looked sad. "Not too well, I'm afraid. You see, dear 'Holy Joe'—how I miss him—was a man of tradition. He used to say, 'What was good enough for my father is good enough for me.' And he stuck with good, honest bootlegging and smuggling and such. And, of course, we have to respect that. And drugs are no good anyway."

"They sure aren't!" said Heller with conviction.

She looked at him with approval. Then she continued. "Since Faustino 'The Noose' Narcotici has gotten so much backing from upstairs, there's no holding him. He has been muscling in on our New York interests and is even trying to push his way into New Jersey. When they wasted dear 'Holy Joe,' that was just the beginning of it. But," she looked up with sad bravery, "we are trying to carry on."

"Oh, I'm sure you'll succeed," said Heller politely.

"That's very nice of you to say so, Jerome. I can call you Jerome, can't I? Everyone calls me Babe."

"Certainly, Mrs. Corleone," said Heller. Fleet manners. And then, for a moment, I thought he'd blown it. "Mrs. Corleone, do you mind if I ask you a personal question?"

"Go ahead," she said. Was she a trifle wary?

"Are you a Caucasian?"

Oh, my Gods! Here he went on that (bleeped) fool Prince Caucalsia kick! She had blond hair, she was as tall as some women around Atalanta, Manco.

"What makes you ask?"

"It's your head," said Heller. "It is very beautiful and it has a long skull structure."

"Oh!" she said. "Are you interested in genealogy?"

"I've studied it a bit."

"Ah! College, of course!" And she rushed over to an ornate desk, opened it and got out a large chart and some papers. She pulled up a chair beside Heller and spread the papers out. "These," she said impressively, "were specially drawn up for me by Professor Stringer! He is the world's foremost expert on genealogy and family trees!"

Aha! I knew already about the fixation American women have on family trees! And this Stringer was probably making a fortune out of the racket.

She gestured at Heller. She had the Italian habit of talking with her hands, head and body. "You have no idea how prejudiced some people are! I was a famous actress at the Roxy theater when dear Joe married me." The memory broke her train of thought for a moment and her eyes went moist.

Oho! I spotted her now. One of the Roxy chorus girls! A chorus line is composed of girls that are six feet six.

She recovered. "A *capo* is supposed to marry a Sicilian girl and the old cats carped and meowed and criticized. Particularly the mayor's wife. So dear Joe had this drawn up. And did it put them in their places! I keep it around to make the (bleepches) stay there!"

She spread out the chart. It was all scrolls and swirls and illuminated with little pictures. It was in the shape of a tree.

"Now," lectured Babe impressively, "as a student you are undoubtedly aware of all this but I will go over it anyway. Reviewing one's studies is a good thing. Now, the Nordic race is composed of the Caspian, Mediterranean and Proto-Negroid types. . . ."

"Caspian?" said Heller. "That's the sea over by the Caucasus."

"Oh, right," she said vaguely and then plunged on with energy. "Now, you can see here how the Germanic races came out of Asia and migrated. The Goths, via Germany, came down into Northern Italy in the fifth century and the Lombards in the sixth century. These are the dolichocephalic—means long-headed, which is to say, smart—elements in the Italian population. They are blond and tall." My Gods, had somebody rehearsed *her!* She was probably quoting Professor Stringer, word for word!

"Trace this line here. These are the Franks. From Germany, they came down and took over France, which is named after them. That was in the fifth century. Now, one branch—trace this—the Salians, took over northern Italy. One of the Salians, in the ninth century, was emperor of all the Franks and Holy Roman Emperor besides. He was named, you see here, Carolus Magnus, which, in American, means Charles the Great. In history books he is called Charlemagne. He was the emperor of the whole God (bleeped) world!"

She stopped and looked impressively at Heller. He nodded. She went on. "Now, Charlemagne had quite a few marriages. And he married—that's this line here—the daughter of the Duke d'Aosta. That means 'of' Aosta and that's a province in northwest Italy just south of Lake Geneva.

"There are blond and tall Italians clear across northern Italy but they are *thick* in the Valle d'Aosta.

"Now, follow this line here. From the Duke d'Aosta we come right down to Biella, which was my father's name. You still with me, kid?"

"Oh, yes, indeed," said Heller in a fascinated voice.

"All right. Now, at the start of World War II, my parents fled to Sicily. They stayed in Sicily four whole years! At the end of the war, they emigrated to America and that's where I was born. So," and she drew up in triumph, "I'm just as Sicilian as any of them! What do you think of that?"

"Complete proof!" said Heller.

Babe flipped a finger at the chart. "And, furthermore, I am a direct descendant of Charlemagne! Oh," she gloated, "the mayor's wife went absolutely *green* with envy!"

"I can see why she would!" said Heller. "But wait. There's something that's not here. That maybe you don't know. You ever hear of Atalanta?"

"I never been to Atlanta."

"No, Atalanta," said Heller. "Now, at the beginning of this tree, a lot earlier than it starts here, there was a prince."

This had her attention. And it sure had mine! Code break! He was about to be carried away with his stupid enthusiasm for Folk Legend 894M. I reached for my pen.

"His name," said Heller, "was Prince Caucalsia. He . . ."

From the door came a piercing, *"Pssst!"*

Babe and Heller turned toward it.

There was a Sicilian there. He was holding a large money sack. He had come halfway through the door and was bending over, beckoning urgently to Babe Corleone. His face. I had seen his face! I was trying to place it!

Babe went over and bent down. The Sicilian stood on tiptoe to reach her ear. He was urgently pointing toward Heller. I could not hear what he was whispering. She shook her head, negatively, a bit puzzled. Then he whispered and seemed triumphant.

The woman's eyes shot open. She stood up. She turned and stamped across the room to Heller. She seized him!

Then she pushed him off, holding him by the shoulders. She stared at him as though memorizing his face. Then she whirled. In a voice that could have knocked the walls down, she said, "Where the hell is that Geovani?"

Geovani was right there. The hood that had brought Heller up in the elevator.

"Why the hell didn't you tell me this was *that* kid?" she thundered.

There were other faces in the door. Scared!

"Here I been treating him like dirt!" She turned. She pushed Heller down into an easy chair. "Why," she pleaded, "didn't you tell me you were the one that saved our Gracious Palms?"

I could hear Heller swallow. "I . . . I didn't know it was yours."

"Hell, yes, kid! We own and control the fanciest cat houses in New York and New Jersey! Who else?"

Gregorio, glasses shaking, belatedly walked in with the milk and seltzer.

"To hell with that," said Babe. "This kid wants beer, he can have beer! To hell with the illegality!"

"No, no," said Heller. "I've really got to be going." He thought for a moment. "You can tell me where to find Bang-Bang Rimbombo. I think I've got car trouble."

So *that* was why he had walked in on the Corleone mob!

Suddenly, it all added up. He had read of Bang-Bang in the papers, knew he was part of the Corleone mob. He had Babe's address from Jimmy "The Gutter" Tavilnasty. To find himself an expert car bomber, he had simply gone to Babe's. Very, very smart detective work at locating somebody.

But wait! He had shown himself at that garage! They would be waiting for him when he came back there. Very, very dumb!

Heller was going to drive me crazy yet! He was too brightly stupid to live!

Babe turned to the people inside the door. They were whispering to each other and pointing at Heller and trying to get a better look at him. "Geovani, get out the limo and run this young gentleman over to Bang-Bang's. Tell him I said to do what the kid wants."

She turned back to Heller. "Look, kid, anything you want, you let Babe know, see?" She turned to the staff. "You hear that? And you, Consalvo, I want a word with you." She was pointing at the one who had identified Heller.

I suddenly remembered who the Sicilian with the money sack was. He was the clerk at the Gracious Palms! Trying to keep up with Heller was exhausting me, spoiling my recall for faces even.

Heller took his leave. Babe bent down and gave him a big kiss on the cheek. "Come back any time, you dear boy. You dear, dear boy!"

Chapter 7

Heller sat in the front seat of the limousine with the hood, Geovani, driving.

"You really wasted them punks just like that!" said Geovani in a voice of awe. "Did you know one of them was Faustino's nephew?" He drove for a while and then, taking his hand off the steering wheel, he made a gun out of his fingers and, pointing at the road, made the motions of firing and said, "Blowie! Blowie! Blowie! Just like that! Wow!"

They drew up in front of a down-at-the-heels apartment house. Geovani led Heller up to the second floor and knocked on a door, a code signal. A girl's face came out through the door crack. "Oh, it's you." She opened it wider. "For you, Bang-Bang."

Bang-Bang Rimbombo was in bed with another girl.

"Come on," said Geovani.

"Hell, I just got sprung!" protested Bang-Bang. "I ain't had any for six months!"

"Babe says you go."

Bang-Bang was out of bed in a flash. He struggled into his clothes.

"Car job," said Geovani. "This kid will show you."

"I'll get my things," said Bang-Bang.

Geovani used the phone and called a cab. Waiting, he covered the phone. "We never use the limo for wet jobs," he said apologetically. "And we control the cab companies. They don't talk."

Shortly, Geovani shook Heller's hand and left. Halfway down

the hall he turned and made a pistol out of his fingers again. "Blowie! Blowie! Blowie!" he said. "Just like that!" He was gone.

The cab arrived and Bang-Bang, dragging a big bag, got in. Heller followed him. Heller gave an address a block away from the garage.

He was learning, but he was not really up on this tradecraft. They would be alerted. I knew he was going into a battle. And I didn't have that platen. Short of sleep, haggard, I hung on the viewscreen. He had my life in his hands!

Heller paid the cab off and walked around the corner toward the garage.

"Wait," said Bang-Bang. He was a very narrow-faced little Sicilian. He looked pretty smart. Maybe he had sense enough, I hoped, to keep them out of trouble. "If that's the place," he said, "I know it. It's a garage Faustino uses to repaint stolen cars and other things. You sure you know what you're doing, kid?" He shook his head. "Sneaking in there to rig a car for a blitz is a little bit steep."

"It's my car and I want you to unrig it," said Heller.

"Oh, that's different," said Bang-Bang. He hefted his heavy shoulder bag and approached the garage.

The door was locked on the outside with a big padlock. Heller put his ear to the wall and listened. Then he shook his head. He went around the building and checked the back door. It, too, was locked with a padlock. He returned to the front. He stood back and saw that there was a window beside the front door, about six feet from ground level.

He took out a tiny tool, inserted it in the padlock, fished it, and almost at once had it open.

Heller was moving very fast, very efficiently. It was so much in contrast with his sloppy disregard for routine espionage that I had forgotten for some time what he actually was. I was looking at a combat engineer. Getting into an enemy fort was something they did with a yawn. He was in the field of his own tradecraft!

He opened the entry port of the front door, swished his hand around to make sure, probably, there were no trip wires and then stepped inside, placing his feet to avoid where feet would normally step—probably to avoid mines.

He got a box and put it under the window, stood on it and undid the latch.

He returned to the door, beckoned to Bang-Bang to enter. Then Heller went outside. He carefully relocked the padlock, just as it had been.

Heller went to the outside of the window, lifted it and entered the building. He closed the window carefully. Now, to all intents and purposes, anyone approaching from the outside would have no sign that anyone was inside. Clever. I would have to remember how to do that.

The whole interior was stacked with islands of cartons, leaving only aisles and room to drive a car down the center. And it was these cartons which were getting Bang-Bang's attention.

"Well, I'll be a son of a (bleepch)," said Bang-Bang. "Will you look at this!" He had pried a carton open and was holding a bottle. "Johnnie Walker Gold Label! Look, kid. I heard of it but I never seen any." In the dimness he must have seen that Heller wasn't tracking. "Y'see, there's Red Label and there's Black Label and you can get that easy. But Gold Label, they keep only for Scotland or sometimes export it to Hong Kong. It's worth forty bucks a bottle!"

He looked at the cap. "No revenue seals! Smuggled!" He got the cap off adroitly to hide signs of opening. He touched his tongue to the top and tilted it.

Heller's hand tilted the bottle back, vertical.

"No, no," said Bang-Bang. "I never drink on duty." He rolled the drop around on his tongue. "It ain't fake! Smooth!" He put the top back on and restored it to the carton. Then he began to make an estimate of the number of cases, walking about. The islands were piled nearly to the ceiling and the garage/warehouse was big.

"Jesus!" said Bang-Bang, "there's close to two thousand cases in here. That's . . ." he was trying to add it up. "Twelve to the case and forty dollars . . ."

"Million dollars," said Heller.

"A million dollars," said Bang-Bang, abstractedly. He went

deeper into the building. "Hey! Look at this." He had his hand on some differently shaped cases. He expertly pried up a lid with a knife and hauled out a small box. "Miniature wrist recorders from Taiwan! Must be . . ." he was counting, ". . . five thousand of them here. Two hundred dollars apiece wholesale . . ."

"A million dollars," said Heller.

"A million dollars," said Bang-Bang. Then he planted his feet and glared down the widest aisle. "Well, God (bleep) me! You know what that son of a (bleepch) Faustino is trying to do? He's trying to cut in on our smuggling! The (bleepard)! He's trying to muscle in on us! He's going to flood the market and drive us out of business! God (bleep)! Oh, when Babe hears about this, she is going to be livid!"

He stood and thought. "It's that crook Oozopopolis!"

"Can we get on with this car?" said Heller.

Bang-Bang was promptly all business. "Don't touch it!"

The Cadillac was sitting apparently where Heller had parked it. The license plates had been removed. The light was very bad there.

Bang-Bang got out a torch. Keeping his hands off the car, he gingerly slid under it. He was looking at the springs. "They sometimes put it under the leaves so when the car tilts, off it goes. Nope. Now for the . . . oh, for Christ's sakes!"

Heller was kneeling down watching Bang-Bang under the car. Bang-Bang seemed to be working on the inside of a wheel. His hand emerged and he tossed something to Heller who caught it. A stick of dynamite!

Bang-Bang was working on another wheel. He tossed up another stick of dynamite. Heller caught it. Bang-Bang, scrambling around, shortly tossed a third and then a fourth stick to Heller. After playing his light around further underneath, Bang-Bang emerged.

"Cut-rate job," said Bang-Bang. "There was a stick taped vertically to the inside of each wheel. Dynamite of this type is just sawdust and soup. The soup is usually spread all through the sawdust and is safe to handle unless concentrated."

"Soup?" asked Heller.

"Nitroglycerine," said Bang-Bang. "It explodes when you jar it. This car was rigged to blow up miles from here! As the wheels spun, the centrifugal force would make the soup move from the stick as a whole and concentrate at just one end. Then an extra bump on the road and BOOM! Cut-rate. They saved the expense of detonators! Cheap-o!" he added with scorn.

"But maybe these were placed just to be found," said Heller, "and the real charge is still in there somewhere."

"So these could have been decoys and the real charge is still in there somewhere," said Bang-Bang.

He passed a very thin blade down through the window slit to make sure there was no trip wire and then opened the door. He looked under the panel. Nothing. He opened the hood. He looked back of the motor.

"Aha!" said Bang-Bang. "A cable job!" In a gingerly fashion he slid a matchbook cover between two contact points. Then he snipped some wires. Shortly he fished up a revolution counter.

"A second odometer!" he said. "The speedometer cable was taken off the back and put to this thing." He was spinning its gears. It suddenly went click. He read the numbers. "Five miles! It was set to go five miles from here." He peered back down behind the motor. "Jesus! Ten pounds of gelignite! Wow, did they blow dough on setting this up! Somebody is big bucks mad at you, kid! That's enough to blow up ten——"

"Shh!" said Heller.

A car was coming!

Hurriedly, Bang-Bang closed the hood and door. Heller dragged him to a point about fifteen feet from the main entrance and back between two stacks of boxes.

The car stopped.

Bang-Bang whispered, "You got a gun?"

Heller shook his head.

"Me neither! It's illegal to carry a gun on parole." He shifted his heavy sack of explosives. "I don't dare throw a bomb in all this whiskey. We'd go up like a torch!"

"Shh!" said Heller.

A car door closed. "I'll put the car around back," somebody said. Silence.

A car door slammed in the back of the building. Footsteps going around. Then, in front, "The door's still locked back there."

"I told you," said a new voice. "There ain't nobody here."

A rattle of keys. "You just got the jumps, Chumpy. He's probably still running."

"Anybody could have come in the time it took you!" It was the plump young man. He backed in. The door opened inward more widely.

Two men in expensive-looking clothes followed him through. "We came as fast as we could. Jesus, you don't get from Queens to here in five minutes. Not in this traffic! See, there's nobody here! Waste of time."

"He'll be back!" said Chumpy. "He's a mean (bleepard)! If you don't do nothing, I'm going to call Faustino!"

The other man said, "Look, Dum-Dum, it won't do any harm to wait around for a while. Jesus, after all that drive. Tell you what. Leave the door unlocked and a tiny bit ajar, kind of inviting, and then we'll go over and sit down behind those boxes opposite and wait. Jesus, I got to catch my breath. All those God (bleeped) trucks!"

He left the door ajar. Chumpy, getting out a burp gun, went over and sat down on the floor back of an island of boxes, in profile and in full view of Heller. I went cold. Then I realized Heller was looking through a slit between two cartons.

The other two disappeared behind the island opposite the door.

"Don't shoot toward that old car in the back!" said Chumpy. "It's a walking boom factory!"

"Shut up, Chumpy," said one of the men. "We'll give it an hour. So you just shut up."

Heller looked down and slipped out of his shoes. He moved sideways until he could see the door. It was very dark right near it, the effect heightened by the slit of light coming through the ajar door.

He was fishing in his satchel. He got out the fish line. He got out the multihooked bass plug. He tied the line to the eye of the plug.

My hair felt like it was going to leave my head! This (bleeping) fool was going to try something! Bullets flying into that whiskey or near that car would turn the place into an inferno! All he had to do was wait for an hour and they'd leave! The idiot!

He was coiling the fish line in big, loose loops around his left hand. He took the end he had fastened the bass plug to. He began to swing the plug back and forth.

With a toss he sent the plug sailing through the dimness toward the door! At an exact instant, he tugged it back.

There was a tiny thunk.

There was a rustle from behind the island of boxes where the men were hidden.

Heller slowly began to take in the slack. The line was nearly invisible. I could not make it out.

He shifted the sack on his shoulder and opened it. He shifted the line to his left hand.

He yanked the line!

The door came open with a crash!

There was a sizzling sound and a thud!

Heller had heaved a baseball at Chumpy!

Through the slit, I could see Chumpy fold up, motionless.

Silence.

Minutes.

"(Bleep)," said one of the men. "It was just the wind."

"Go close it!" said the other.

Through a slit, Heller was watching. A man, gun in hand, crossed the open place toward the door.

There was a sizzle and crack!

Heller had thrown another baseball!

The man jarred sideways. He fell and lay still.

"What the hell? . . ."

Heller threw again. The baseball hit the far wall and rebounded. He was throwing at the sound! With a bank shot!

Heller threw again!

There was a scramble. The man raced out the rear opening in the island and raced toward the back door! Stupid. It was locked!

The man raised his gun to blow off the lock.

Heller threw!

The man was hurled against the door. He slumped.

Heller casually walked to the front door and closed it.

Bang-Bang, more practical, raced to the last man and grabbed the gun. Then he raced from one to the other. He came back to Heller. "Jesus Christ! Their skulls is smashed in. They're dead!"

"Get the rest of the explosives out of that Cadillac," said Heller. "We got to get to work now."

Chapter 8

Heller fished the car keys out of a dead man's pocket, opened the full building door wide open, found the hood's car in the back. It was an old Buick sedan.

He drove it in and closed the full doors again. Then he inched it down the narrow aisle between the islands of cartons and brought it to a halt beside the Cadillac.

Bang-Bang was just finishing. He was sniffing at the oil dipstick. "No additives in the crankcase." He put the dipstick back. "There was no sugar in the gas—no other tricks. And there's the gelignite." He pointed to where it was perched on a window ledge rather precariously.

He went into the Cadillac rear interior, probing the seats. Then he said, "Oh, look! Draw curtains!" He promptly pulled them all down.

Bang-Bang went to a pile of cartons, got one and lugged it to the Cadillac and put it in the back. Then he went and got another one. As he worked, he began to sing softly:

> There once was a con who was awful, awful dry.
> Sing, sing them Sing Sing blues.
> He tried from the guard a little drink to buy.
> Sing, sing them Sing Sing blues.
> He tried from the warden saying thirst will make me cry.
> Sing, sing them Sing Sing blues.
> He even wrote the governor his thirst to satisfy.

Sing, sing them Sing Sing blues.
He even begged the president, I will not tell a lie.
Sing, sing them Sing Sing blues.
But none of them would tell him how he could qualify.
Sing, sing them Sing Sing blues.

He sang on and on. He was absolutely jamming the back of the Cadillac with whisky cases. Then he got Heller to open the trunk and he piled it full of boxes of miniature wrist recorders. He went back and looked into the rear seat area of the Cadillac again. He juggled it around so there would be more room. He went and got two more whisky cartons.

So he prays each night unto the Lord his thirst to gratify.
Sing, sing them Sing Sing blues.
And drown him in a tub of gin, if he has to die!
Sing, sing them Sing Sing blues!

With one last shove, he managed to get the rear door closed.

Heller had been working industriously. He had put the Buick's plates on the Cadillac. Then he had the hood of the Buick open. He piled the gelignite on top of the Buick's motor. He went and got a dead man's revolver and made sure that there was a live cartridge under the pin when it was cocked. He took some of his tape and then taped the weapon, pointed at the gelignite, to the Buick's cowling.

Heller got in the Cadillac and drove it to the main door, opened it and then drove outside. "Wait in the car," he said to Bang-Bang. And Bang-Bang went out and got in, petting the whisky cartons.

Heller went back in. He closed the main door and its entry port. He found the bass plug and hooked it into the top inside edge of the door. He ran the fish line over a nail and then unreeled it all the way back to the Buick. Then, very gingerly, he tightened the fish line and tied it to the cocked trigger of the revolver.

Then he did something very odd. He took two blank pieces of paper and laid them on the seat of the Buick.

He looked around the garage. He found a heavy iron jimmy.

Starting near the Buick, he raced down the rows of cartons; smash right, smash left. The crash of glass and the gurgle of whisky followed in his wake.

Heller climbed out the window, made it secure so it didn't look like it had been touched. Then he gently closed the padlock on its hasp.

He got in the Cadillac.

"You booby-trapped it, didn't you," said Bang-Bang.

Heller didn't answer.

Heller drove up the street six blocks. There was a hamburger stand there and an outside pay phone. He got out. He went into the phone booth. From his pocket he took a handful of change. Then from another pocket, he took a card.

Swindle and Crouch!

He deposited coins and dialed.

A telephonist at the other end simply repeated the number for an answer.

In a high-pitched voice, Heller said, "I got to speak to Mr. Bury."

The telephonist said, "I am SOR-ree. Mr. Bury left for Moscow this morning to join Mr. Rockecenter. WHOM shall I say CAlled?"

Heller hung up. "Blast!" he said in Voltarian.

Bang-Bang was near the phone booth. "You look like the sky fell in."

"It did," said Heller. "There was a guy made a bargain. This is twice he didn't keep it. He doesn't have any sense of honor or decency at all! Won't keep his word."

"So that's who the booby trap was for," said Bang-Bang.

"Yes. I was going to tell him some papers had been left in a car. He would have been over here by airbus in ten blinks of an eye." He sighed. Then he said, "Well, I guess I better go back and undo the booby trap."

"Why?" demanded Bang-Bang.

"Some innocent person could come along and get killed," said Heller.

Bang-Bang was looking at him in round-eyed astonishment. "What's that got to do with it?"

And I could certainly agree with Bang-Bang. Heller with his scruples. Far too nice. I scoffed aloud at the viewscreen.

"I don't just run around killing people, you know," said Heller. "We're not at war!"

Code break! He'd be telling this gangster about the threatened invasion next.

"Oh, the hell we aren't!" said Bang-Bang. "It's war flat-out! That Faustino is pushing our backs straight against the wall. Don't go wasting a booby trap!"

"I suppose you mean we should phone Faustino," said Heller.

"No, no, no. He'd never cross the river to Jersey. But I got a real candidate! A turncoat!"

"Somebody who is dishonorable?" said Heller. "Somebody who double-deals?"

"You said it! I got somebody who really deserves it! A filthy, boozing, two-timing crooked crook!"

"You sure?" said Heller.

"Of course I'm sure. There's no crookeder rummy drunk on the whole planet."

"Ah, a 'drunk,' " said Heller. "What's his name?"

"Oozopopolis!"

Heller shrugged, Bang-Bang took it as assent. He got his satchel from the car and sped into the booth closing it.

Through the glass door, Heller watched Bang-Bang wad a rag around the mouthpiece. Then he took a rubber glove out of his satchel and put the cuff over the rag and mouthpiece. Then he took a small tape recorder out of his satchel and turned it on. Faintly, the sound came out of the telephone booth. It was planes taking off.

At least this Bang-Bang knew some tradecraft. He was messing up his voice pattern and, with the planes, was mislocating the source of the call to some airport.

Bang-Bang spoke briefly into the phone and then hung up. Yes, he did know some tradecraft. His call had been too short to trace.

He recovered his gear and went back to the car window. "Like a hamburger?" he said.

Heller shook his head. Bang-Bang dove into the joint and the girl there began to fry a hamburger in a leisurely fashion.

My toes curled! Tradecraft be (bleeped)! After you make a sensitive call, you don't hang around the phone booth!

Then I reviewed the rest of it. The car they'd left in there had motor numbers. It was a different make even! If it blew up, nobody would be fooled!

Heller's tradecraft might be good in its place—getting into forts and blowing them up. But shortly after, in his profession, he would be out in space and not on the planet!

They were howling amateurs!

Six blocks down the street, the garage was in full view!

Heller said, "There'll be concussion." He turned the Cadillac around so that it faced the blast more squarely.

Bang-Bang came out with a hamburger and a beer. "You sure you don't want one?" said Bang-Bang. But again, Heller shook his head.

Bang-Bang settled down and began to eat. "He lapped it up," he said. "I told him in Greek—I was raised in old Hell's Kitchen and that's gone Greek. Otherwise he wouldn't have believed me."

"What was his name again?" said Heller.

"Oozopopolis. About a year ago, he stopped taking bribes from us, changed his coat and started taking them from Faustino. And he's been hitting at us ever since." He took another bite of hamburger. "I told him a couple of the Atlantic City mob had been seen looting Faustino's liquor right down at that address and they were inside stealing the place blind with the outside door locked. Wouldn't do to get the name Corleone mixed up in it. He sure leaped at it."

Bang-Bang finished his hamburger and washed it down with beer. He then passed the time by filling Heller in on mob politics.

After a while there was a roar of cars.

Three sedans went streaking by. The seats were full. "You can tell they're government men, all right," said Bang-Bang. "The way they carry those riot shotguns. Did you see Oozopopolis? He was the big fat slob in the front seat of the second car."

The three cars raced the last six blocks and drew to a skidding halt in front of the garage, a reeking bomb of gelignite and alcohol fumes.

Men bailed out, guns ready and threatening.

"Come on out of there! We got you covered!" drifted faintly up the street.

Then a very fat figure raced forward and slammed the flat of his foot against the door.

There was a tremendous flash!

Blue flame and red battered the street!

A fireball bloomed!

The concussion and sound hit the Cadillac! It recoiled and then rocked!

Through the smoke and falling debris six blocks away one could see the strewn bodies.

Heller turned the Cadillac around. "Who was this Oozopopolis?"

"He was the New Jersey district head of BAFT. That's the U.S. Treasury Department Bureau of Alcohol, Firearms and Tobacco. The Revenooers. The dirty turncoats. Aside from changing sides on us, it was Oozopopolis that planted a machine gun on me and got me sent up."

Bang-Bang was smiling happily. "Oh, my! Babe certainly will be pleased. Not only did we cost Faustino two million bucks, but we also got rid of the Feds! And it's about time she got some breaks, let me tell you!"

They wended their way through the fire engines now charging toward the sky-leaping conflagration.

PART SEVENTEEN

Chapter 1

Heller drove north. He patted the car's windshield ledge. He said, "Well, you chemical-engined Cadillac Brougham Coupe d'Elegance, we got you out of that free and clear."

I sneered, Fleet officers and their toys. Fetish worship!

Bang-Bang Rimbombo said, "Hey, kid. While in this moment of glory I don't want to spoil things, I got to point out you are driving on stolen plates and that's illegal!"

"I've got another set of plates, registration card and everything," said Heller.

"Where'd you get them?"

"Why, from that guy I was going to call."

"The one you wanted to bump? Listen, kid, there's a lot you got to learn. The fuzz runs on car plates. If they didn't have plates, they couldn't trace nobody. They'd be lost. Their whole system is founded on license numbers. So, if you got dough, I'd advise you to buy a new car. I know a guy . . ."

"No, I want this one," said Heller.

"But it's a gas hog!" said Bang-Bang.

"I know," said Heller. "I need it."

Bang-Bang sighed. "All right, I know another guy that can change its motor numbers and get a new license. I owe you. I don't wanta see you get pinched! Turn left right up ahead onto Tonnelle Avenue. We're going to Newark!"

They were soon amongst the roar of trucks and gas fumes and, with Bang-Bang's direction, came to Newark, drove down numerous side streets amongst numerous light and heavy industries but only in heavy polluted air and came at length to the Jiffy-Spiffy Garage. They threaded their way amongst numerous vehicles in various stages of repair and painting.

Bang-Bang leaped out and shortly came back with a portly, greasy Italian in a white foreman's coat. Heller got out.

"Kid," said Bang-Bang, "this is Mike Mutazione, the owner, proprietor and big noise of this joint. I told him you was a friend of the family. So, tell him what you want."

Heller and the man shook hands. "Maybe he better tell me," said Heller.

Mike looked over the Cadillac. "Well," he said, "the first thing I would do is run it into the river."

"Oh, no!" said Heller. "It's a good car!"

"It's a gas hog," said Mike. "A 1968 Cadillac only gets about ten miles to the gallon."

"That's what I like about it," said Heller.

Mike turned to Bang-Bang. "Is this kid crazy?"

"No, no!" said Bang-Bang. "He's a college kid."

"Oh, that explains it," said Mike.

Bang-Bang was hastily tearing something inside the car. He came out with a bottle of Scotch.

"What the hell is this?" said Mike. "Gold Label? I never seen none of this before."

Bang-Bang wrestled off the top. "It's so good the Scots guzzle the whole supply of it themselves. Have a gulp."

"You sure it ain't poison?" He cautiously took a little. He rolled it around on his tongue. "My God, that's smooth! I ain't never tasted anything like that."

"Just off the boat," said Bang-Bang. "We brung you a whole case of it."

"Now, as I was saying, kid," said Mike, "let's look over this beautiful car." Gripping the bottle tenaciously, he raised the hood with the other hand. He got out a flashlight. He was looking at the engine block. Then, he shook his head sadly. "Kid, I got bad news. That engine number has been changed too often. And the last ones that did it scored it too deep. It can't be done again."

He stood there. "Aw, don't look so downcast, kid. You must have sentimental attachments for this car. First one you ever stole or something?" He took another sip of Scotch and leaned against the radiator. He was deep in thought. Then he brightened. "Hey, I just remembered. You can buy brand-new engines for a 1968 Cadillac, this model. They been in stock ever since at General Motors. You got money?"

"I got money," said Heller.

"I'll check." Mike went into his office and got on the phone. He came back beaming. "They still got them! You in a hurry or can this job take a few weeks?"

"I'm in no hurry," said Heller. "That will fit into my plans just fine."

Suddenly, I was all adrift. I had been so certain he just wanted the car to bash around in New York with, so certain that this was just more Fleet officer fixation on toys that I had not examined the possibility that he had some diabolical plot in mind. I hastily reviewed his actions so far. He was NOT idly drifting as I had thought! He was working! The (bleepard) was plowing straight ahead on his mission! The horrible idea that he might succeed rose over me like Lombar's specter. What the Devils was he up to?

"All right," said Mike. "But what do you want out of this car, really? Speed? If it's speed, I could put new aluminum alloy pistons in the new engine: they get rid of the heat quicker and the engine is less likely to blow up. And you could get a lot more revs out of it."

"Would that increase or decrease the gas consumption?" said Heller.

"Oh, possibly increase it."

"Good," said Heller. "Do it."

"All right. I could put special carburetors on it," said Mike.

"Good," said Heller.

"But if she is going to go faster, she better have a new radiator core and maybe an oil radiator for cooling."

"Good," said Heller.

"There may be some worn parts like axle spindles and such that would have to be replaced."

"Good," said Heller.

"She better have some new tires. Racing ones that'll do a hundred and fifty without blowing out."

"Good," said Heller.

"Lighter magnesium wheels?" said Mike.

"Would it make her look different?"

"I should say so. Much more modern."

"No," said Heller.

Mike had received his first no. He stood back, had a drink, thinking fast.

Bang-Bang interrupted him. "Ain't that a Corleone pickup truck?" he said, pointing to a newly repainted and now black Ford.

"Ready to go," said Mike.

"I'll take it along when I go," said Bang-Bang and promptly began to remove his cartons from the Cadillac and load the pickup.

Mike, refreshed, returned to the fray. He picked at a fender. "There are some small dents that need body beating. She could use a sandblast and a new coat of paint. Hey, listen kid, we got some original Cadillac paint: we can never use it because it is too showy! I'll get a card." He rushed to the office and came back. "Here you are. It's called 'Flameglow Scarlet.' It makes the car shine even in the dark! Real flashy!"

"Good," said Heller.

I couldn't track with him. He had originally chosen gray because it was more invisible. Now he was choosing paint that practically burned my viewscreen! What *was* he up to?

"But," said Mike, moving to the front seat and picking at it, "this upholstery—yes, and them back curtains—has had it. Now, it just so happens we have some upholstery that was bought and never used. It's called 'Snow Leopard,' white with black spots. Sparkles! It'll really show up wild against that red body! We can even get it thick enough for floor rugs, too."

"Great," said Heller.

Mike couldn't think of anything else. "Now, was there something special *you* wanted in addition?"

"Yes," said Heller. "I want you to fix the hood so it can be locked down all around with keys. And under the car, I want a very light sheet of metal that will seal the engine absolutely."

"Oh, you're talking about bomb jobs and armor," said Mike. "Now, the reason they built these cars with so much horsepower was so they could carry the weight of armor. I can put you in bulletproof windows, armor plate in the side walls . . ."

At last, I understood. He was afraid his car would be rigged for a blitz again!

"No," said Heller. "Just a light sheet underneath and locks on the hood so nobody can get to the engine."

"Burglar alarms?" said Mike hopefully.

"No," said Heller.

I gave up. The only explanation was that Heller was crazy!

"That's all?" said Mike.

"That's about it," said Heller.

"Well," said Mike, appearing to be a little apprehensive, "that whole lot we been over will add up to about twenty G's."

Bang-Bang had been removing the last of the recorders. He dropped the box. "Jesus!" He came over. "Look, kid, I can steal and get converted fifteen up-to-date Cadillacs for that!"

"I'll throw in the new license," said Mike. "And honest, Bang-Bang, it will cost that to tailor rebuild this car."

"I'll take it," said Heller. He reached into his pockets and pulled out a roll. He counted and held out ten thousand.

"This kid just knock off Brinks?" Mike demanded of Bang-Bang.

"It's honest hit money," said Heller.

"Oh, well, in that case," said Mike, "I'll take it on account." And he went to his office to write out a receipt. "What name?" he called back. "Not that it matters."

"Jerome Terrance Wister," said Heller.

Now I knew he was crazy. Bury could find out he was alive and could trace him! And with a flashy, different car like that . . .

Bang-Bang had finished loading the pickup. He presented a grateful Mike with the case of Johnnie Walker Gold Label. "Get in, kid. Where do I drop you?"

"I'm going over to Manhattan," said Heller.

"In that event, I'll take you to the train station. It's quicker."

He did so and when Heller got out, Bang-Bang said, "Is that your real name, kid? Jerome Terrance Wister?"

"No," said Heller. "I'm really Pretty Boy Floyd."

Bang-Bang laughed uproariously and so did Heller. I was offended. Pretty Boy Floyd was a very famous gangster, too famous to be joked about. Sacred.

"What do I owe you?" said Heller.

"Owe me, kid?" said Bang-Bang. He pointed through the back window at his cargo. "For six months up the river, I been dreaming of a drink of Scotch! Now I'm going to swim in it!" And he drove off singing.

I wasn't singing. I was in new trouble just when I thought it couldn't get worse. Heller was going to pull Bury straight back in on him by using that name and I didn't have the platen. But at the same time, Heller was sailing ahead on his job. I could feel it! He might make it!

The whole thing had me spinny. On the one hand, Heller must NOT get himself killed before I had the means of forging his reports to Captain Tars Roke. On the other hand, a very great danger loomed that he was up to some dastardly plot to succeed in his mission and definitely had to be put away or killed.

I went out and laid down in the yard and buried my face in my hands. I had to be calm. I had to think logically. This was no time to go off my rocker just because I had to keep a man from being killed that would have to be killed. I had to think of something, something to do!

And that (bleeped) wild canary kept trilling at me from a tree. Mockery. Sheer mockery!

Chapter 2

Heller clickety-clacked across the drive at the Gracious Palms and trotted into the lobby. It was still afternoon, and in the hot off-season of late summer the place was deserted.

He was about to mount the steps to the second floor when one of the tuxedoed guards stepped into view and stopped him. "Wait a minute. You don't have your room anymore, kid."

Heller had stopped dead.

"The manager wants to see you," said the hood. "He's pretty upset."

Heller turned to go to the manager's office.

"No," said the guard. "Get in here. He's waiting for you." He pushed Heller toward an elevator. They got in and the hood pushed the top floor button.

They got out into a padded, soundproofed hallway. The hood walked behind Heller, shoving him along with little pushes that made my screen jolt.

From an open door at the end of the long, long hall, the manager's voice could now be heard. He was cursing at people in Italian. He sounded absolutely livid!

There were others in the room, throwing things about, rushing around.

The hood shoved Heller into the hubbub. "Here he is, boss."

Vantagio Meretrici gave a cleaning woman a shove out of his way and came stamping up to Heller.

"You're trying to get me in trouble!" he shouted. "You're trying to cost me my job!" His hands, Italian-like, were flying about. He made a gesture across his own throat as though to cut it. "You could have cost me my life!"

He stopped to scream something in Italian at two cleaning women and they rushed into each other, one dropping a stack of sheets.

Italians. They are so excitable. So theatrical. I turned down my sound volume.

Sure enough, he came nearer and was louder!

"That was not a nice thing to do!" cried Vantagio. "To sneak in here like that!"

"If you could tell me what you think I did . . ." began Heller.

"I don't think! I know!" cried Vantagio.

"If I did something . . ." Heller tried.

"Yes, you did something!" shouted Vantagio. "You let me put you in that old second-floor maid's room! You didn't say a word! She was absolutely livid! She practically burned out my phone!"

He put his hands on Heller's shoulders and looked up at him. His voice was suddenly pleading. "Why didn't you tell me you were a friend of Babe's?"

Heller drew a long breath. "I actually didn't know she owned this place. I do apologize."

"Now, look, kid. In the future, speak up. Now, will this do?"

Heller looked around. It was a two-room suite. The huge living room had walls of black onyx tile adorned with paintings. The rug, wall to wall, was beige, covered with scatter rugs of expensive weave and patterns of gold. The furniture was light beige modern with seductive curves. The lamps were statues of golden girls completely naked. A garden balcony was outside and wide glass doors showed a view of the United Nations Building, its park and the river beyond.

Vantagio turned Heller in the other direction. There was a beige, leather-covered bar and gold shelves and scrollwork behind it. A barman was hastily emptying it of hard liquor and putting the bottles in cartons.

"I'm sorry, I can't leave the liquor here. It would cost us our license, you being a minor. But," he rushed on hastily, "we'll fill the fridge with soft drinks of every kind you can imagine. And we'll leave the jumbo glasses and you can fill them from the ice machine there. And we'll put fresh milk here every day. And ice cream?" he pleaded.

Then Vantagio was showing Heller the various hidden closets and drawers around the bar. He stopped and came close to him. "Listen, I was only kidding about sandwiches. We don't have a dining room because it's all room service. But we got the fanciest chefs and kitchen in New York. You can order anything you like. You want anything now? Pheasant under glass?"

He didn't wait for an answer. He yelled into the bedroom and the cleaning people came hurrying out. He escorted Heller in, throwing his hands to indicate the place. "I hope this is all right," he pleaded.

It was a vast bedroom. The entire ceiling was mirrors. The walls were all mirrors, set in black onyx edging. The enormous bed was circular. It occupied the center of the room. It was covered with a black silk spread that had gold hibiscus worked into it in patterns. There were red, low footstools all around the bed. The carpet was wall-to-wall scarlet.

There was an inset of sound speakers, quad, around which curled naked girls in a golden frieze. Vantagio rushed to the wall and showed Heller buttons and selections: Drinking Music, Sensual, Passionate, Frenzy, Cool Off.

Vantagio rushed Heller into the bathroom. It was rug-covered. It had a huge Roman bathtub, big enough for half a dozen people. It had separate massage showers. It had lots of cabinets with things to be explored. And it had a toilet and two bidets surrounded with various douche devices. Heller was looking at *Automatic Hot Towel* and pushed it. A steaming hot towel came out in his hand and he wiped his face.

Vantagio led him back to the sitting room. "Now, is it all right? This was the suite that was made up for the Secretary General, the old one, before he got assassinated. I know it's a little plain but it's more spacious. We almost never use it, so you won't be moved around. It hasn't been used for so long, we had to clean it up quick.

The others are fancier but I thought, for a kid, this would be better for you. Do you think it will do?"

"Gods, yes," said Heller.

Vantagio whistled with relief. Then he said, "Look, kid, all will be forgiven and we can be friends if you get on that phone and call Babe. She's been waiting to hear all afternoon!"

Heller almost got run into by a houseman who was responding to a signal from Vantagio and rushing a cart with Heller's baggage into the room.

He picked up the phone. The switchboard immediately connected him to Bayonne, evidently on a lease-line.

"This is me, Mrs. Corleone."

"Oh, you dear boy. You dear, dear boy!"

"Vantagio told me to call and tell you that the new suite was okay, Mrs. Corleone. And it is."

"Is it the Secretary General's suite? The one with the original paintings of Polynesian girls on the walls?"

"Oh, yes, it's quite beautiful. A lovely view."

"Hold on a minute, dear. Someone is at the door."

The sound of voices in the room, dimly heard through a covering palm. A sort of squeaking, "He *what?*" Then very rapid Italian, which was also too muffled to be heard clearly.

But then Babe was back on the line. "That was Bang-Bang! He just arrived here! I can't BELIEVE it! Oh, you dear, dear, dear boy! Oh, you dear, dear, dear, dear boy! Thank you, thank you! I can't discuss it on an open line. But, oh, you dear boy, THANK YOU!" The sound of a torrent of kisses being shot along the wire! Then a sudden roar, "Put that Vantagio back on!"

I suddenly figured it out. She had just learned of the destruction of two million dollars' worth of her rival's booze, etc., and the demise of Oozopopolis, her nemesis!

Vantagio had evidently not liked what he could hear from his end. He timidly took the phone. "... *si* ... *gia* ... *si*, Babe." He looked a bit haggard. "... *no* ... *non* ... *si* ... *Grazie, mia capa!*" He hung up.

He took the hot towel out of Heller's hand and wiped his own face. "That was Babe." Then he looked at Heller, "Kid, I don't know what you did now but it must have been *something!* She said I could keep my job, but, kid, I don't think I'll really hear the last of putting you in a maid's back room." He braced up. "But she's right. I wasn't grateful enough and you did save the place and my life. I didn't show respect. So, I apologize. All right, kid?"

They shook hands.

"Now," said Vantagio, "about this other thing. This is the best suite we can offer you but she says you haven't got a car. So, you're to go out and buy any car you want. We have a basement garage, you know. And I told her you didn't have many clothes. So, we have a great tailor and I'll get him in and you're to be measured up for a full wardrobe. Real tailored clothes of the best fabrics. Will that be all right?"

"I really shouldn't accept . . ."

"You better accept, kid. We're friends. Don't get me in more trouble! Now, is there anything else you can think of that you want?"

"Well," said Heller, "I don't see any TV."

Vantagio said, "Jesus, I'm glad you didn't tell her I'd forgotten that! Nobody looks at TV in a whorehouse, kid. It just never occurred to me. I'll send out somebody to buy one. All right, kid?"

Heller nodded. Vantagio went to the door and then came back. "Kid, I know what you did here. You saved the joint. But you must have done something else. But even that . . . She treats you so different. Could you let me in on what you and she talk about?"

"Genealogy," said Heller.

"And that's the whole thing?"

"Absolutely," said Heller. "That's all that happened today."

Vantagio looked at him very seriously. Then he burst out laughing. "You almost took me in for a minute. Well, never mind, I'm lucky to have you for a friend."

He started toward the door again but once more stopped. "Oh, yes. She said you could have any of the girls you wanted and to hell with the legality. See you later, kid."

Chapter 3

My concentration on the viewscreen was jarred by a knock on the secret passage door that led to the distant office. I had raised so much pure Hells with Faht that he had finally gotten it through his lard-padded skull that he must send an Apparatus messenger with any reports that came in from America. And here was one! I removed it from the door slit. I opened it with trembling fingers. Possibly Raht and Terb had gotten smart. Perhaps they would be of help!

I read

> We think he is done for. We traced him to the city
> garbage scows and he's now somewhere on the
> bottom of the Atlantic. Be assured we're on the job.

The idiots! That shop had simply thrown away those bugged clothes!

But the surge of anger hardened my resolve to act. I would carefully survey the Gracious Palms area and his rooms, note exactly where he put things, exactly what his routine was. Then I would disguise myself as a Turkish officer assigned to the UN, penetrate the place, pick his room locks, get the platen out of his baggage, plant a bomb and escape. It was a brilliant plan. It came to me in a flash. If I could do that, Heller would be dead, dead, dead and I would be alive!

Sternly, I went back to the viewscreen. He would unpack

shortly, of that I was sure, for the houseman had left the baggage on the cart.

Heller was still walking around his suite. While it might not be up to his rooms at the Voltar Officers' Club, it had its own peculiar charm: girls! Each lamp stand was a naked torso, each throw rug had a golden girl in its pattern.

He walked up to one of several paintings on the wall and stopped and stared at it and said something in Voltarian I didn't get. It was a beautiful painting. A brown-skinned girl, dressed mainly in red flowers, was posed against palm trees and the sea. It was, if you know painting, a conceptual representation, which tends to dominate the modern school.

He bent close to look at the signature. It was *Gauguin.*

I know painting values: one does when he is interested largely in cash. If that painting was an original, it was worth a fortune!

I hastily played back what he had first said. I knew my own reaction would have been to steal it. Maybe I would include that in my planning. I must know what his own intentions were with regard to it.

He had said, "The boat people!" Ah. One of the Atalanta races he and Krak had talked about.

He had moved on to a second Gauguin.

A new voice penetrated the room. "No, no, no!" It was Chief Madame Sesso. Her mustache was bristling. She was wagging a finger at him, very disapproving. "No! Young-a boys should-a not-a look at-a dirty pictures! You not-a goin' to do-a nasty things-a here! If-a the young-a signore, he's-a want to look at-a the naked women, he's-a goin' to-a do-a it right!"

She fixed him in place with a finger, grabbed the phone and spoke an avalanche of Italian into it. She slammed it down. "Right away, you gonna get me-a in-a bad trouble if-a it ever gotta out I taught-a you to look at-a dirty pictures! *Mama mia!* What would-a the customers theenk!"

There was a running patter of footsteps. A small woman burst into the room in a near panic!

She had a short nose, beautiful teeth, raven black hair, high, firm breasts. She was a golden brown. She had European stockings and a chemise on and was holding a silk robe about her. She was obviously a Polynesian!

Luscious!

"Wot ees eet?"

"I catch-a this-a young signore, he's-a look at the dirty pictures on th' wall. Now, Minette, you go right-a now and you jump in-a his bed. Quick-quick!"

"No, no," said Heller. "I just want to look!"

"Aha!" said Minette. "A voyeur."

"No, no," said Heller. "There are some people in . . . in my native land that look exactly like you. I just wanted to look. . . ."

"Aha, you zee, Madame Sesso," said Minette. "A voyeur! He get hees keeks by the look, so!"

Madame Sesso walked sternly up to her. "So you-a let-a the young signore look!" And she snatched at the robe. It came half off, baring Minette's firm, uplifted breast. Like a golden melon!

But Minette stepped back. "Madame Sesso. You air crooel! Zee business she is nothing, nothing. For t'ree week, I have no man. Zee bed ees empty. I go half mad. All zee girls, zey talk about thees boy. Eef I do zee strip, I go wil' for heem, Madame Sesso."

Madame Sesso was upon her. Her hand seized the shoulder of the silk robe and gave it a yank. It flew up to block Heller's vision. "You-a will do-a the strip right-a now!" bawled Madame Sesso.

Heller was trying to get the silk robe off his face.

"Aw right!" shrieked Minette. "I go get zee grass skirt, I go get zee flowerz een my hair. Zen I do zee strip. But only on zee one condeetion zat afterwards he . . ."

The picture went into streaks! The sound became a roar!

I could not see what was going on! I could hear only that roar!

What a shock!

Interference of some sort!

It was the first interference I had seen on this system.

The equipment had failed!

I checked power. All fine. I turned up gain. I only got more roar. It was not the quiet blackness when he was asleep.

I wondered for a moment if it was an emotional overload in the subject.

I tried to think of everything I could, made all the guesses of which I was capable. Finally, I dug out the instruction book. I had never read all of it.

Finally, on the next to the last page, I found an entry:

WARNING

As the equipment is used in a carbon-oxygen body, it must, of necessity, be hypersensitive to the carbon atom and molecule wave configuration.

The only known disturbance of the double-wave pattern employed can come from carbon spectrum emitters. These are extremely rare devices but the spy should be warned to stay at least a hundred feet from such an energy emission source if present in the culture where the spy is being employed.

And that was all it said. And as Heller did not know he was being employed, one could not, of course, warn him.

But warn him of what? What in Hells was a carbon spectrum emitter? It was one of the few times I was sorry I had not done something to stay awake in Academy classes. There must be one now within a hundred feet of Heller! But on an electronically primitive planet like Earth?

Whatever it was, it had me boxed! I turned down the gain. I looked at the jagged mess on the screen. Haggardly, I slumped over the equipment, helpless.

It was midnight where I was. The days of strain were telling on me.

I went through the secret door into my bedroom. I made the cook get up and fix me some hot soup. At length, I dropped into a restless sleep.

Suddenly, I woke up. It was the silent hours of the night. Silence! The small ragged roar from my secret room was missing.

I sprang through the back of the closet.

And there was a picture as nice as you please!

Heller was sitting there in his suite, watching TV! I looked at my watch. It must be about seven in the evening there. The news was on.

What had happened to or with Minette?

Had she gotten her way?

Had Heller let her do a striptease and then taken her to bed as she had demanded?

I did not know. I could not tell.

A Hispanic-looking newscaster was going on and on about murders, and then he said, "New York motorists exiting from the Jersey side of the Lincoln Tunnel, today were entertained by a massive fireball, rising into the sky. The telephone company was besieged by callers wanting to know if World War III had begun." He laughed lightly. "They were reassured to find that it was only the Acme Car Painting Company blowing up. Inventories showed thousands of gallons of stored paint were on the premises. The origin of the blaze was labelled arson by the insurance underwriters, as a hundred-thousand-dollar policy had recently been taken out. Eleven bodies, none of whom have been identified, were found in the vicinity." The newscaster smiled. "But that is life on the Jersey side." I surmised this must be a Manhattan channel!

Wait, what was that? A shadow? No, a black hand and arm close to Heller's face! Coming in from Heller's left! He wasn't focused on it. It held some sort of implement!

A fork!

Somebody was feeding him something as he watched TV!

The hand vanished and my sound was blurred by crunchy chewing.

There was somebody with him! Minette?

Had she won after all?

The newscaster was droning on about some celebrities that had been mugged. It was quite a list.

Heller turned his head slightly to the right. Wait! What was that? Something white over to the *right* of the TV!

In his peripheral vision, I managed to make it out. *Two* pairs of white feet! One in slippers with lace puffs, the other set bare!

And there was a low murmur over to his right. I had missed it in amongst the news. I hastily replayed the auxiliary screen, turning up its gain. Two girls' voices! Was one Minette?

I made one out amongst the news overplay. A middle-western accent. ". . . and honey, let me tell you, he was very, very good! I think he was the best . . ."

Then the other girl's murmur. Was this Minette? I turned the gain higher and changed the tone controls. ". . . well, I really thought it was quite impossible to have that many orgasms in one . . ." An English accent! These were two entirely different girls!

The newscaster was continuing. He went through some stock-exchange data. Then he said, "A Treasury Department spokesman stated this afternoon that the New Jersey BAFT chief, Oozopopolis, and several other revenooers are missing. Shortages in their accounts were denied although it is well known that Oozopopolis had extensive banking connections in the Bahamas. Airports on this side of the river are being watched." He chuckled again. "But that's life in Jersey, isn't it, folks."

Heller leaned forward and pushed a button to turn it off. The automatic gain control made my screen go more normal. He turned to his left. Sitting across the side table from him was a gorgeous, slinky, high-yellow girl! She had on next to nothing! A flimsy scarf was draped over her shoulders, her breasts clearly visible through it.

Where was Minette?

What was this girl doing here?

She was laughing, her beautiful teeth flashing. "And so, honey, you better believe him. Stay away from that Jersey side. Just cuddle around here." She made a sensuous movement with her breasts. She pushed a fork into a huge Caesar salad in a crystal bowl. She brushed the mouthful against her lips and then pushed it seductively across the table to him. "When you is done eating, pretty boy, would you like me to demonstrate how it's done in Harlem?" She laughed a low, seductive laugh. Utterly tantalizing! Then her eyes went hot. "In fac', I think that's enough supper." She put down the fork and began to stand up.

She only had on that flimsy scarf.

She was wearing nothing else!

She reached out her hand. . . .

The interference hit again!

I moaned. I waited for it to die down.

It didn't.

After a couple of minutes, very upset, I went back to my sleeping room and lay down in my bed.

Flesh can only stand so much!

After a little, I got hold of my spinning wits and emotions.

One thing was very plain. There was interference. It came on and off.

He had probably unpacked his baggage and put it in several of the many cubicles and closets. If I were patient, no matter how long it took, I could piece out exactly where he must have put the platen.

I would still carry out my plan!

Chapter 4

In the other room, the equipment stopped buzzing. Led by a dreadful fascination, I tottered back in to see what was going on now.

Heller was just stepping out of the elevator into the lobby.

I looked at my watch. It must be wrong. I have trouble with time conversion from one part of a planet to another but I couldn't be *that* wrong. Only ten minutes ago, I had seen the slinky high-yellow girl standing up in invitation. Yet here was Heller in the lobby.

Let's see. It would have taken him a few minutes to dress. Say a minute to come down in the elevator . . .

Well, let's say he was awfully fast.

It was early evening in New York. There were quite a few people in the lobby, mostly in Western business suits but with the multihued faces of many lands. Prosperous looking, debonair men about town from deserts and mountains and villages on stilts—the typical UN crowd. They were piled up a bit at the desk, making appointments, sitting about until they heard their number called or sauntering around trying to work up a new appetite.

I realized Heller was putting in the agreed-upon lobby appearance to discourage certain visitors. I could see in a reflecting mirror that he did not yet have his new clothes—he was wearing his plain blue suit. At least he didn't have his baseball cap on. But when he walked on bare floor, I could tell he still wore those baseball shoes.

He sat down in a chair where he could be seen from the door and where he could see the office entrance of the "Host." Almost at once, a houseman entered the lobby from the street. He was carrying a pile of magazines and newspapers. He walked straight to Heller, gave him the pile. Heller handed him a twenty-dollar bill and waved away the change.

Wait! Heller must have called him from his suite! So subtract that, too, from the ten minutes! What *had* happened with that slinky high-yellow girl?

Casting an eye now and then on the street entrance and the manager's door, Heller settled down to read. Ah, I would have a clue as to what his plans were by analyzing what he was reading.

Racing magazines!

The American Hot Rod, Racing Today, The Blowout, Hot Stock Cars. He leafed through them but, knowing Heller, he was reading every page. Sneaky. But I had learned his habits. When he was really interested, he would pause and stare at a page and think about it.

He halted his leafing. The magazine had a picture of an old Pontiac sedan. The article was "Out of the Pit to Glory."

Of course! Heller the speedophile! Heller the stopwatch-oriented lunatic. Heller, an obvious case of velocity dementia in its last stages of progressive terminalization!

But wait. As he paused, his eye was on a figure and stayed on the figure. The last sentence of the article read:

> "And so, for the pittance of $225,000 in expenses, we were able to cover the entire stock-car circuit for one whole season and wound up with all bills paid, which is glory enough for anybody!"

His eyes kept straying back to that "$225,000."

He watched the crowd for a while. Not much of a throng as the UN wasn't in session. One of the tuxedoed security guards drifted over beside his chair and said, out of the corner of his mouth, "Watch out for that deputy delegate from Maysabongo. He just came in, there. The one with the opera cloak and top hat. He carries a kris up his sleeve. Must be two feet long. Runs amok now and then." The guard drifted away.

Heller yawned, a sure sign of tension. He opened a newspaper, the *Wall Street Journal*. He wandered through it. He paused on a page of box ads featuring real estate offerings. He examined the "ex-urban" ones—those way past the suburbs and out of town entirely. They had them for Bucks County, Pennsylvania, for Vermont and for various counties in Connecticut. All ideal for the executive weekend. He began to stare at one. It said:

> OWN YOUR OWN FEUDAL FIEFDOM
> BE A MONARCH OF ALL YOU SURVEY
> Vast estate going for peanuts
> FIVE WHOLE ACRES, NO BUILDINGS
> UNTOUCHED WILDERNESS OF CONNECTICUT
> ONLY $300,000

His eye was stuck on the $300,000.

He opened the paper to other sections. He looked over "Commodity Markets" with all their vast rows of figures for the various futures for the day. He inspected the stock market with all its tangles of incomprehensible abbreviations.

A movement over at the "Host" door. A huge, dark-complected man in a turban came out with Vantagio. They stood on the lobby side of the door, completing their discussion. I hastily turned up my gain.

It was in English. The turbaned one was thanking Vantagio for straightening out the bill. Then, he looked around and saw Heller.

"New face," said the turbaned giant.

"Oh, that youngster," said Vantagio. "It's in confidence. His father is a very important man, a Moslem. Married an American movie actress. That's the son. He's going to go to college and his father insisted he live here. We couldn't say no. Would have caused endless diplomatic repercussions had we refused."

"Ah," said the turbaned one. "I can clear up that puzzle for you. You have to understand the Mohammedan religion. You see," he continued learnedly, "in the Middle East, it is tradition that the children, including boys, are raised in, and have to live in, the harem. And this whorehouse is probably as close as his father could come to a harem in the United States. Quite natural, really."

"Well, thank you for clearing up my confusion," said Vantagio, the master of political science.

"I'll just go over and greet him in his native tongue," said the turbaned giant. "Make him feel at home."

Here he came! He stopped in front of Heller. He went through the elaborate hand ritual of the Arab greeting. He said something that sounded like *"Aliekoom sala'am."* And then a long rigamarole. Arabic!

Yikes! Heller didn't speak Arabic!

Heller rose. With elaborate politeness, he copied the hand motions and bow exactly. Then he said, "I am dreadfully sorry but I am forbidden to speak my native tongue while I am in the United States. But I am doing fine and I truly hope you have a nice evening."

They both bowed.

The turbaned giant went back to Vantagio. "A well-brought-up youth, obviously raised in a harem like I said. I can tell by his accent. But I will keep your secret, Vantagio, especially since he is the son of the Aga Khan."

Leaving Vantagio, the huge turbaned man went promptly over to a little group by the door and whispered to them. Their eyes flicked covertly toward Heller. The secret was being well kept. By everybody.

A half an hour passed and Heller's perusal of the papers had exhausted them. He was sitting there quietly when the deputy delegate from Maysabongo came out of the elevator and rushed over to the desk. He slammed his top hat down on the counter.

"Where is that pig Stuffumo?" he demanded of the clerk.

The clerk looked anxiously around. There were no security guards in the lobby at the moment.

"I demand it! I demand you tell me!" The deputy delegate was gripping the clerk's coat.

Heller stood up. The fool. He had been told the man had a kris in his sleeve! A *kris* is the wickedest short sword there is! And I didn't have that platen!

"Harlotta was not there!" snarled the deputy delegate. "She is with Stuffumo! I know it!"

The elevator door opened and a thin man in a business suit carrying an umbrella walked out.

"Stuffumo!" screamed the deputy delegate. "Enemy of the people! Capitalistic warmonger! Death to aggressors!"

He raced across the room. The clerk was madly pushing buzzers. Stuffumo flinched, tried to get back into the elevator.

The deputy delegate whipped the kris out of his sleeve, two feet of wavy steel!

He made a slash through the air. The blade whistled!

The top of Stuffumo's waistcoat gapped!

The deputy delegate drew back the blade to strike again.

Suddenly, Heller was in front of him!

The blade swished as it began the second slash.

Heller caught the man's wrist!

He pushed his thumb into the back of the man's hand. The blade fell.

Heller caught it by the handle before it hit the floor.

Two security guards were there. Heller waved them back. Heller gently pushed the deputy delegate and Stuffumo into a corner of the elevator.

"What room is Harlotta in?" said Heller, hand poised over the elevator buttons.

Both Stuffumo and the deputy delegate stared at him. Heller was hefting the kris. "Come, come," he said. "At least tell me what floor. We can find her."

"What do you mean to do?" said the deputy delegate.

"Why," said Heller, "she has caused two important men embarrassment. She'll have to be killed, of course." And he hefted the kris.

"No!" cried Stuffumo. "Not Harlotta!"

"NO!" cried the deputy delegate. "Not my darling Harlotta!"

"But I am sure it is house rules," said Heller. "She could have caused you both to kill each other. It isn't permitted!"

"Please," said Stuffumo.

"Please don't," said the deputy delegate.

"I'm afraid there's no other way," said Heller.

"Oh, yes, there is!" cried the deputy delegate, triumphantly. "We can have a conference about it!"

"Correct!" said Stuffumo. "The proper solution to all international disputes!"

The two promptly sat down in the corner of the elevator, facing each other.

"First, the agenda!" said the deputy delegate firmly.

Heller pushed the out-of-operation button and walked out, leaving them in the elevator.

One of the Italian security guards said, "Thank you, kid. That was good knife work. But you should pay attention when I tip you off. They have diplomatic immunity, you know, and can't be arrested for anything, no matter what they do. But law-abiding Americans like you and me can be. We usually don't stick around when that one arrives. Maybe he'll be good now."

Vantagio came out. Heller handed him the kris.

The two ex-combatants walked out of the elevator. "We have come to an accord," said Stuffumo. "Bilateral occupation of territory."

"I will have Harlotta Mondays, Wednesdays and Fridays. He will have her Tuesdays, Thursdays and Saturdays," said the deputy delegate.

"We have to spend Sunday with our wives," added Stuffumo.

"Vantagio," said the deputy delegate, "may we borrow your office for the formal ratification and signing of the treaty?"

Heller watched them until they vanished into Vantagio's office. He yawned. He gathered up his papers, entered the elevator and exited at the top floor.

As he passed down the hall to his room, a nearby door opened and a girl rushed out. She had on a silk robe but it wasn't tied and her forward motion blew it back and exposed everything she had. She was a beautiful brunette!

"Oh, there you are, pretty boy. Business is too slack tonight. Some of the girls say you have something beautifully new." She looked at him seductively, stroking his arm. "Please, pretty please, can I come in with you and we . . ."

My screen flashed out. The interference roared.

But I had a lot of other things to puzzle over. He was interested in his usual hobby, speed. He was interested in an executive retreat in the wilderness. I felt I should be able to piece it together.

But even though I labored into the Turkish dawn, I could not figure out how you would run a racing car in a tree-infested wilderness. Or why.

Chapter 5

It was three in the afternoon in Turkey when I arose. Not really thinking, still numb with sleep, I walked into my secret office and, like a fool, looked into the viewscreen.

I nearly fainted!

I was staring twenty stories straight down!

I felt like I was going to fall!

The people were small spots in the street below; the cars were toys!

The strain I had been under was telling. The shock was too much. I pulled my eyes away and shuddered into a chair. After a few minutes, I got control of my stomach and dared take another look.

What in *Hells* was he up to?

He was on a cupola that crowned the Gracious Palms. Fifteen feet below him, firmly on the asphalt roof, a whore in a green jump suit was steadying a line up to him.

He was rigging a TV antenna kit! That's what it read on the top of the box he was steadying on his knees:

HANDY JIM-DANDY FULLY-AUTOMATIC INSTALL-IT-YOURSELF RADIO-CONTROLLED REMOTE TV ANTENNA WITH SIGNAL BOOSTER.

He had inset the feet into the concrete top of the cupola. He was now adjusting the booster. He glanced around and it was visible that several nearby buildings had them. He must have had it sent out for the day before.

Oho! So he was having signal trouble, too! But wait, this must mean that the TV wasn't working when my equipment wasn't working, so those girls in his room weren't there to watch TV!

He completed the upper installation and then, box under his arm, he started down a line.

I had him. Code break! It was a spacer safety line! He was carrying Voltarian gear in his suitcases!

He was working with a stapler, fastening the TV cable to the stone as he descended.

He got to the bottom and turned toward the woman. There she was, a New York whore, holding a spacer safety line manufactured in Industrial City, Voltar! I watched like a hawk. Did she realize it? Everything depended on that! I could simply order him off the mission and court-martialed!

"Here's your clothesline, honey," she said. "Now, what do I do?"

He took it, gave it the snap that causes it to come loose at the top and caught it in coils around his wrist as it fell—a typical show-off spacer gesture: I don't know how they do it.

"You just uncoil this reel, Martha. Just walk along and I'll fasten it down as we go."

"Okay, dearie," she said. And along they went. She had a stick through the reel and Heller was snubbing it under the parapet with the stapler.

Then, I realized something else. Heller must know where the interference was coming from. The roof he was laying the cable on was about three hundred and fifty feet long, perhaps double the building width. The antenna was outside the interference zone. I tried to plot from this where and what the interference might be, for I was not only very curious about what he *did* in that suite, I also had to know where he could have hidden the platen. I got all tangled up.

The girl had come to the far end of the roof. "Now what do I do, pretty boy?"

"You go down to my room and open the double doors and stand on the balcony and steady the safety line again."

She ran off. Heller tied the reel to the safety line and then paid it out so that it landed on his balcony below. The girl came out on the balcony and got the reel.

He pegged the upper end of the safety line into the stone parapet, stepped over the edge . . .

I turned my face away. This guy was driving me mad! He had no sense. He didn't give a (bleep) about height or his neck. I heard the staples going into the vertical wall but I wouldn't look. I knew I would see the tiny people and cars far too far below!

The sound of a disintegrator drill. I dared look. He had snapped the spacer safety line loose and was putting a cable hole in the wall. With a Voltarian disintegrator drill!

I watched intently to see if I got a reaction from the whore. There she was watching a tiny palm-sized gadget, with nothing spinning, bite the exact sized hole through the wall. No chips or sparks. A miracle on this planet. All she had to say was "Hey, man, look at that gimmick eat up stone!" and I had him!

She said, "I'll go call room service to send you some breakfast, dearie." And she went inside the living room. It depressed me.

Heller went inside, put the base plate together and shortly had it all connected with the TV. He turned the set on. He fiddled with the radio antenna rotator. The difference in reception showed it was turning.

"Hey, great picture," said the whore. "We done it! They'll send breakfast up right away."

Heller neated up his kit. Aha, now I would see where he stowed his gear. He certainly would hide a safety line and disintegrator drill! And I had no interference!

He was fastening the tool kit up. OH! Right on the face of the kit, big as life, it said:

JETTERO HELLER
FLEET CORPS OF COMBAT ENGINEERS

It said it in Voltarian script but it said it, just like that!
He tossed the kit on the sofa. It landed face up!

He went into the bathroom and kicked off his tennis shoes and the baseball exercise suit. He stepped into the massage shower.

The massage drops were hammering at him but I could hear somebody banging cabinets in the bathroom. All that woman, Martha, had to do was notice that kit and come in and say "Hey, what's this writing? It looks like something not of this planet," and he would be open to being shot!

The shower door opened. Her hand was in view. She didn't have her jump suit on. She was holding a cake of soap. She said, "Honey, let me wash your back before we . . ."

The interference came on!

I railed around. The screen simply flashed in jagged lines and the sound roared. It was actively preventing me from getting enough data on that suite and where he stowed his gear and thus blocking me from embarking on my raid for the platen and the end of Heller. The minutes stretched agonizingly into half an hour.

Then, it was off!

Heller was sitting on the couch drinking coffee. He was all alone in the suite.

There was a knock on the door and Heller said, in that penetrating Fleet voice, "Come in, it isn't locked."

In came a mob of tailors!

They started displaying bolts of fine fabrics, summer silk and mohair, tweeds, gabardine, shirt silk, passing each one under Heller's nose.

The lead tailor, with Heller's permission, sat down on the couch with a book of styles. He found he was sitting on something, reached under him and picked up the tool kit. All he had to do was inspect the inscription and some of those odd tools and he would know he was talking to an extraterrestrial!

"Now, we've brought a throwaway suit you can wear today, young sir. But we must choose both a society wardrobe and a college wardrobe. Now, it so happens that the styles this autumn will be ever so slightly gauche. Neat but gauche. In this Ives St. Giles book, we can see that the collar . . ."

Sickening. Who cared about all these fancy styles and the

pant width in the mode. There was a gabardine trench coat with innumerable straps and a gun pocket that I liked, however. It looked very like one Humphrey Bogart used to wear. But the rest of it . . . Then I realized the true source of my antipathy. It wasn't the styles, it was the tailor. He was a homo. If there is anything I can't stand, it's a gay!

"Now, could you please stand up, young sir?"

And he was kneeling in front of Heller, measuring him for trousers. He seemed to be having trouble with his tape. He kept stretching it.

"Oh," said the lead tailor, giggling, "you're really built!"

"What's the matter?" said Heller. "Hips too narrow?"

"Oh, no, young sir. I wasn't talking about hips."

On went the interference!

Off went my patience!

I stood up. I was being personally and vindictively harassed! Harassed? If I did not get that platen, I was dead!

There was a knock on the tunnel door to Faht's office. Another Raht and Terb message slid under. I snatched it up.

It said

> Have our eye on that spot offshore. We're standing
> by in case he surfaces.

That did it!

I bolted out of the house and walked agitatedly around the garden.

That (bleeped) screaming canary! Trilling and whistling gaily in the tree! A party to all this!

I went inside and got a twelve-gauge shotgun. I loaded it. I saw a flutter of yellow on a limb.

I fired both barrels!

The roar was deafening.

A hole had been blown through an ornamental tree.

One solitary feather came floating slowly down in the utter silence.

It made me feel immensely better.

A guard car came dashing up, of course, but I laughed and sent it away.

I felt better. I could think. I sat down on a bench.

What did I actually know? Aha, I had learned one vital thing so far today. The whore had not had the slightest recognition that she was handling a Voltarian safety line. The tailor had even sat on a Fleet tool kit, plainly labelled, and had simply tossed it aside. The people around Heller's place of residence were totally incapable of observation! Perhaps it would be different when he got into a college. But nobody would notice anything at all anywhere around the Gracious Palms!

I went to my desk. I wrote a brutal communication to be transmitted at once to the New York office. I said

> RAHT AND TERB ARE SOMEWHERE IN THE NEW YORK AREA. FIND THEM AND FORCE THEM TO REPORT IN. IF THIS ORDER IS NOT PROMPTLY EXECUTED THE ENTIRE PERSONNEL OF YOUR OFFICE WILL BE.
> SULTAN BEY.

When they reported in, I would direct them to get all plans of that building and pave the way.

With that backup, I would get this handled once and for all. And before I myself started to show signs of a nervous breakdown.

I phoned for a messenger and got the message on its way.

I got a pitcher of *sira* and went back to the viewer.

The interference was off. Heller was on his way downstairs in an elevator.

Chapter 6

Heller was wearing the new "throwaway" suit, I saw in an elevator mirror by peripheral vision. It was a light blue summer weight and it fitted for a change, but its pockets were bulging. He had on a blue shirt with a wide collar spread over the jacket lapels, the gauche look, I suppose, but it still made him look awfully young. However, whatever the tailor was trying to achieve was spoiled utterly by the fact that he still wore his red baseball cap on the back of his blond head and when he went across the lobby, I could hear that he still wore baseball spikes! He might be clean and neat, some might think him very handsome, but he still didn't have a clue about espionage and looking the part! The baseball cap was easy to explain—he considered himself to be working. The spikes, just because he didn't have comfortable shoes. An idiot!

But I could be tolerant. He was a marked man.

He went to the safes and halted before his personal one. I noted the combination.

He spread out his money inside the safe.

I became aware of other voices, an undertone in the otherwise quiet area. I turned up the gain. Somebody on a speaker-phone! I could hear both sides! They were speaking Italian.

". . . so that is no excuse to let him sleep late!" It was Babe Corleone's voice!

"But, Babe," said Vantagio, "it didn't have anything to do with the girls. Those two UN bigwigs spend half their countries' UN appropriations in this place and it's a good thing he didn't let them kill each other."

"Vantagio, are you trying to pretend I didn't appreciate that?"

"No, no, *mia capa!*"

"Vantagio, are you trying to stand in the way of this boy's career?"

Heller was counting out his money, bill by bill. He seemed to think a few of the bills were counterfeit.

Vantagio had apparently been struck speechless. Finally, gasping he said, "Oh, *mia capa,* how could you say such an awful thing!"

"You know an education is important. You are jealous and you want him to wind up like some of these bums?"

"Oh, no!" wept Vantagio.

"Then please explain to me. I will listen. I will not yell at you. I will listen with patience. Answer this one question: I see in the Sunday paper two days ago, Vantagio, that Empire University began registering yesterday. And when I ask you, patiently and quietly, Vantagio, the simple question, 'Is the boy properly registered now and starting school?' I get a stupid answer that he slept late."

Vantagio tried to talk. *"Mia capa . . ."*

"Now, you know and I know and the good God himself knows that boys hate to go to school," continued Babe. "You know that they have to be driven, Vantagio. You know they have to be forced. My brothers, God rest their souls, had to be beaten so there is no reason to explain that to me."

"Mia capa, I swear . . ."

"So the one question I want answered, Vantagio, if you will only let me speak, is why haven't you asserted your authority and control over this boy? Why is he not obeying your orders? Now, do not bother to argue. Just phone me up in exactly one half an hour and tell me he has started to school." There was a sharp click. She had hung up.

Heller had decided that just because some bills had Benjamin Franklin on them, they were not counterfeit. He had packaged the money up neatly. But he was not happy with what he had counted. He was shaking his head.

He put fifteen thousand in his pocket, already bulging with Gods knew what. He closed and locked his safe and was about to leave the Gracious Palms when Vantagio's voice arrested him, calling from the office.

"Can I see you a minute, kid?"

Heller went in. Vantagio's brows were lowered. He looked very down. He gestured to a chair. But like any Italian, he did not come right to the point. They think it impolite.

"Well, kid, how are you getting along with the girls?" He said it very glumly.

Heller laughed. "Oh, it's fairly easy to handle women."

"You wouldn't think so if you had my job," said Vantagio.

Aha, I was on the trail of something here. Vantagio was jealous of Heller. He was afraid Heller was going to get his job!

"Say," said Heller. "You may be the very one I should be seeing about this."

"What?" he said, very guarded, very defensive. Yes, something was biting Vantagio.

"Well, actually," said Heller, "I've got quite a bit of money but I think I will need much more."

"For what?"

"Well, I've got to do something about the planet."

"You mean you're planning to take over the whole planet? Look, kid, you'll never do that without a diploma."

"Oh, that's true," said Heller. "But also, things like that take money. And I wanted to ask you if you could tell me where the gambling is in this area."

Vantagio blew up. "Gambling! You must be crazy! We run the numbers racket and let me tell you, kid, you'd lose your shirt! They're crooked!"

Oho, Vantagio was antagonistic! Was he jealous of Heller?

"All right, then," said Heller. And he took out a copy of the *Wall Street Journal* and opened it. It was the Commodity Futures Market page. "I make out that you buy and sell these as they go up and down, day by day."

Vantagio brushed it aside. "That's a good way to lose an awful lot of money, kid!" He was glowering.

It occurred to me right that moment that maybe I had an ally in Vantagio. He was obviously hostile to Heller. I began to work out why.

Heller was unfolding another spread of paper. "Then how about these? They apparently change in price, day to day."

"That's the stock market!" said Vantagio. "That's a great way to go bankrupt!"

"Well, how do you buy and sell them?" said Heller.

"You need a broker. A stockbroker."

"Well, could you recommend one?"

"Those crooks," said Vantagio. Quite obviously, he did not want Heller to get ahead. He was nervous, edgy. I became more convinced there was something here—that maybe I could cultivate an ally.

"You know of one?" said Heller.

"Aw, look in the phone book classified. But I don't want anything to do with it. And listen, kid, you don't either. Listen, kid, you told me you were going to go to college."

"Yes," said Heller. "Nobody will listen to you if you don't have a diploma."

"Right," said Vantagio. But he was edgy. "That's why I called you in here, kid. You know what day this is?" And to Heller's head shake, "It's the second day of registration week at Empire College. You got your papers?"

"Right here," said Heller, tapping his pocket. "But if it's a whole week . . ."

"You," said Vantagio harshly, "have got to go up there right now and register!"

"But if I have a whole week . . ."

"Be quiet!" said Vantagio. He reached into a drawer and got out a book, *Curriculum, Empire College, Fall Term*. "Geovani Meretrici" was on the catalogue. I thought his name was Vantagio. "What subject is your major?"

"Well, engineering, I suppose," said Heller.

"What kind?" demanded Vantagio.

"Well, if you give me the book there, I can study it over and maybc in a couple of days . . ."

Vantagio was really cross now. What was this temper all about? He was reading from the book, " 'Aerospace Science and Engineering'? 'Bioengineering'? 'Civil Engineering and Engineering Mechanics'? 'Electrical Engineering and Computer Science'? 'Mineral Engineering'? 'Nuclear Science and Engineering'? Just plain 'Engineering'?"

"Nuclear Science and Engineering," said Heller. "That sounds about right. But . . ."

Vantagio raised his voice. "They have a Bachelor, Master, Doctorate and other degrees in it. So, that's it! Nuclear Science and Engineering! Sounds impressive."

"However," said Heller, "I would like to look . . ."

"All right!" said Vantagio. "Now, here is a map of Empire University. See, here is the library and all that. But this is the administration building and this is the entrance. And here is a map of subways. You walk over to this station near here. Then, you go across town. And you transfer at Times Square to Number 1 and you get off at Empire University at 116th Street and you walk along here and right into that administration building and you sign up! You got it?"

"Well, yes. And I appreciate your help. But if there is a whole week . . ." He trailed off because Vantagio was sitting there looking at him in a strange way.

Vantagio started up again. "Kid, have you lived around New York before?"

"No," said Heller.

Vantagio assumed a confidential air. "Then you don't know the customs. Now, kid, when you're in a strange place, it is absolutely fatal not to follow the customs."

"That is true," said Heller.

"Now, kid," said this master of political science, "it so happens that there is a mandatory, American Indian custom regarding saving a man's life. And Indian law remains in full force by prior sovereignty. Did you know that when you save a man's life that man is responsible for you from there on out?"

I boggled! Vantagio was telling Heller an Earth *Chinese* custom! And he was telling Heller absolutely backwards! In old China, according to our Apparatus surveys, when you saved a man's life you were then and there responsible for that man forevermore! So we warned operatives never to save anyone's life in China! Vantagio was using his learning with a twist and he must know very well he was lying!

"Are you sure?" said Heller.

Vantagio looked at him, smug and superior. "Of course, I am sure. I am a master of political science, ain't I?"

"Yes," said Heller doubtfully.

"And you saved my life, didn't you?" said Vantagio.

"Well, it seems so," said Heller.

I suddenly got it! Vantagio! He was a tiny man, only five feet two inches tall. Right next door to Sicily lies Corsica, same people. And a small man in Corsica named Napoleon also felt inferior to everyone. Vantagio was suffering from an inferiority complex in the face of Heller's deeds and acclaim! The things Heller had done had the Sicilian writhing with insecurity. And then I really got it: Vantagio was not his given name—it was his nickname! It means "Whiphand" in Italian!

Vantagio rose to his full five feet two and looked sternly at the seated Heller almost at eye level. And then this master of political science said, "You saved my life, so therefore you have to do absolutely everything I tell you! And that's the way it is now from here on out!"

Heller must have looked contrite. "I see that that's the way it seems."

Suddenly, Vantagio was all smiles and cheer. "So, we have settled that! Have a cigar. No, I forgot, you mustn't smoke. Here, have some mints." And he shoved a box at Heller.

Heller took one and Vantagio came around and patted him on the back. "So, now we know where we stand. Right?"

"Right," said Heller.

"So, you go straight down to the subway and go register

right now!" But he said it with cheer.

Heller got up and walked to the door with Vantagio, who opened it for him and gave him another pat.

When Heller glanced back, Vantagio was all beaming and waving goodbye.

Well, it is very hard to understand Sicilians. This Vantagio appeared pretty treacherous, changeable. I had reservations about trusting him and including him in my plans. Still, there was a chance I could turn that burning jealousy and inferiority to account.

Chapter 7

Expecting, of course, that Heller would now do everything Vantagio had told him to do, I was not paying much attention. Heller went down into a subway station and looked into a phone book. I thought he might be calling the college.

He got on a subway and roared along. He seemed to be interested in the people. It was a hot New York day and in such weather the subways are very, very hot. The people were sweaty, soggy.

I was not being any more alert than they were. I suddenly saw a station sign flash by that said

23rd St.

Then one went by which said

14th St. Union Square

Hey, he was on the wrong subway. He was going DOWNtown, not UPtown! And he wasn't on the proper line! He was on the Lexington Avenue subway!

Hastily, I backtracked on the second screen. He had changed, not at Times Square, but before that, at Grand Central! I backtracked further. I got to the phone book he had looked at. He had found *Stocks and Bonds Brokers* in the yellow pages. Then his finger had halted at *Short, Skidder and Long Associates, 81½ Wall St.*

He was playing hooky!

Oho, maybe all that with Vantagio was not in vain. Maybe I

could gather data and show Vantagio that Heller was not obeying him and Vantagio would let me into Heller's room. A beautiful daydream of a smiling Vantagio, waving an arm to bid me go in and saying, "Yes, Officer Gris. Feel free! Ransack the place! I'll even call housemen to help you find the platen! And it serves this disobedient young kid right, doesn't it, Officer Gris." A beautiful dream!

But back to reality.

Heller, red baseball cap on the back of his head, trotting along on baseball spikes, found 81½ Wall Street and by means of elevators was very shortly breasting a counter at Short, Skidder and Long Associates. There were big blackboards with current prices on them. Ticker tapes were chattering.

A gum-chewing girl said, "Yeah?"

"I want to see somebody about buying stocks," said Heller.

"New account? See Mr. Arbitrage in the third cubicle."

Mr. Arbitrage was immaculately groomed and all dried up. He remained seated at the cubicle desk. He looked Heller up and down as though somebody had thrown a fish into the room, a fish that smelled bad.

"I want to see somebody about buying stocks," said Heller.

"Identification, please," said Mr. Arbitrage, going through the motions out of habit.

Heller, unbidden, sat down across from him. He pulled out the Wister driver's license and social security card.

Mr. Arbitrage looked at them and then at Heller. "There is probably no need to ask for credit references."

"What are those?" said Heller.

"My dear young man, if this is some kind of a school assignment, I am afraid I have no time to teach the young. That is what we pay taxes for. The exit is the same door you came in."

"Wait," said Heller. "I have money."

"My dear young man, please do not trifle with me. My time is valuable and I have a luncheon appointment with the head of J. P. Morgan. The exit door . . ."

"But why?" demanded Heller. "Why can't I buy stocks?"

Mr. Arbitrage sighed noisily. "My dear young man, to deal in stocks, you must open an account. You must be of age to do so. Over twenty-one in our firm. To open an account, you must have credit references. You obviously have none. Could I suggest that you get your parents to accompany you the next time you call? Good day."

"My parents aren't on Earth," said Heller.

"My condolences. Please hear me when I say you have to have a person, over twenty-one, who is responsible for you before you can deal with this firm. Now, good day, please."

"Do all firms have this restriction?"

"My dear young sir, you will find all firms will slam their doors in your face even harder than I am doing! Now, good day, young sir. Good day, good day, good day!" And he reached up and got his bowler and left for lunch.

Heller went down to the street. The luncheon mobs were beginning to boil out of the buildings—luncheon on Wall Street looks like a full-fledged riot in progress.

Thoughtfully, Heller bought a hot dog from a pushcart and drank some orange pop on the sidewalk. He noticed that Mr. Arbitrage was doing the same thing further along.

Heller looked at the towering, cold buildings, the hot and sweating throngs. He checked the pollution dirt on the building sides. He seemed to find it of great interest. He took some pages from a notebook, wrote an address on one and wiped it against a building. Of course it came out black. He trotted through the throngs and took a similar sample on another building. Then he went back down into the subway station and reached over the platform edge and did the same thing. He put the carefully folded and labelled papers away.

He studied the subway map, apparently decided you couldn't get from Wall Street over to Chambers by subway, caught a train to Grand Central, shuttled over to Times Square, transferred to a Number 1 and was soon roaring north.

At 116th Street he debarked and was shortly trotting along College Walk through mobs of students of every color and hue, a throng that was going here and coming from there or standing about. It was a drably somber crowd.

A young man walked up to Heller and said, "What should I take this term?"

"Milk," said Heller. "Highly recommended."

Like someone who knew where he was going amongst a lot of people who didn't know where they were going, Heller went up steps and found himself in a hall where registration was being administered to long lines. Registrars sat at temporary desks, barricaded in paper. He looked at his watch and it winked the time at him. He looked at the long lines.

A young man, apparently clerical help and a student at the same time, entered, carrying a huge stack of computer printouts of class assignments. Heller walked over to him and said with the ring of Fleet authority, "Where are you taking these?"

"Miss Simmons," said the young man, timidly, nodding toward one of the registrars at a temporary desk.

"You should be on time," said Heller. "I'll take these. Go back and get some more."

"Yes, sir," said the young man and left.

Heller stood back until the girl Miss Simmons was interviewing and registering began to gather up her things to depart. Heller went over and put the stapled computer printout booklets down on Miss Simmons' desk and sat down in the chair, bypassing the unattentive waiting line. He took out his own papers and handed them to Miss Simmons.

Miss Simmons did not look up. She was a severe-looking young woman, her brown hair pulled into a tight bun. She had thick glasses and began to paw about the desk in front of her. Then she said, "You haven't made out your application form."

"I didn't know how," said Heller.

"Oh, dear," said Miss Simmons, wearily. "Another one that can't read or write." She got a blank and started to fill it in from Heller's papers. She wrote and wrote. Then she said, "Local address, Wister."

"Gracious Palms," said Heller and gave her the street and house number.

Miss Simmons gave him an invoice. "You can pay the cashier.

But I don't think it will do any good. Payment of fees does not guarantee enrollment."

"Is something wrong?"

"Is something wrong?" mimicked Miss Simmons. "There is always something wrong. But that's beside the point. It's these grades, Wister. It's these grades—a D average? They clearly show that your only A was for sleeping in class. And in a practically unknown school. Now, what major are you demanding?"

"Nuclear Science and Engineering," said Heller.

Miss Simmons gave a shocked gasp like a bullet had hit her. She glared. She ground her teeth. When she had recovered enough to continue, she said in a level, deadly voice, "Wister, some of the prerequisites are missing for that. I do not see them on your transcript of grades. I am afraid all this is irregular. It does not conform. You are seeking to enroll here for your senior year. It does not conform, Wister."

"All I want is a diploma," said Heller.

"Ah, yes," said Miss Simmons. "Wister, you are demanding that at commencement next May, Empire University certify on a diploma that you are a Bachelor of Nuclear Science and Engineering, lend you its prestige and send you out, a totally uneducated savage, to blow up the world. Isn't that what you are demanding, Wister? I thought as much."

"No, no," said Heller. "I'm supposed to fix it up, not blow it up!"

"Wister, the only thing I can do is take this application under advisement. There must be other opinions gotten, Wister. So be back here tomorrow morning at nine o'clock. I can offer no hope, Wister. NEXT!"

It was a bright moment for me. Heller always had such a marvelous opinion of himself, always bragging. And here was a sensible person who saw through him completely. And Bury was a very clever fellow to lay such an adroit trap. I drank a whole glass of *sira* straight down in a toast to Bury.

Heller was slowed to a crawl!

PART EIGHTEEN

Chapter 1

Heller slowly paid the fees at the temporary cashier's desk and then, hands in pockets, wandered about, not looking at very much, apparently immersed in thought.

After a while, he studied the posted building layout.

He began to read bulletin boards. Students were looking for rooms and rooms were looking for students and Mazie Anne had lost trace of Mack and Mack had lost touch with Charlotte and Professor Umpchuddle's classes were transferred to the left wing. Then his eyes clamped on to a formally printed plastic sign. It said

THOSE DESIRING TO HIRE GRADUATES ARE NOT PERMITTED TO RECRUIT ON THE CAMPUS DIRECTLY. THEY MUST SEE THE ASSISTANT DEAN OF STUDENTS IN THE JUMP BUILDING.

Promptly Heller was out on College Walk again, trotting through the throng of milling students, clickety-clacking on a zigzag course and presently clickety-clacked into the office labelled

Mr. Twaddle, Assistant Dean of Students

Mr. Twaddle was sitting at his desk in shirt sleeves filling out stacks of forms. He was a small, bald-headed man. He pointed at a chair, sat back and began to pack an enormous briar pipe.

"I want to hire a graduate," said Heller.

Mr. Twaddle stopped packing his pipe. Then he stopped staring. "Your name?"

Heller showed him the invoice.

"Possibly you mean your family wants to hire a graduate?"

"Do you have any?" said Heller.

"A graduate in what, Wister?"

"Stocks and bonds," said Heller.

"Ah. A Doctor of Business Administration." Mr. Twaddle got the pipe going.

"He'd have to be over twenty-one," said Heller.

Mr. Twaddle laughed indulgently. "A Doctor of Business Administration would certainly be over twenty-one, Wister. There are so many changes in the rules each year, it practically takes them forever. But I am afraid this is the wrong season of the year. You should have been here last May. They all get snapped up, you know. There won't be another crop until the October degrees are awarded almost two months from now and it just so happens there aren't going to be any in that October crop." He smoked complacently.

"Haven't you got any leftovers? Please look."

Mr. Twaddle, being a good fellow, opened a drawer and got out a tattered list. He dropped it on the desk before him and made the motions of going over it. "No. They've been snapped up."

Heller inched his chair forward to the desk. He pointed a finger halfway down the list. I hadn't known he could read upside down. But he couldn't read very well because the name had a lot of marks and cross-outs after it.

"There's one that isn't marked assigned," said Heller.

Mr. Twaddle laughed. "That's Israel Epstein. He didn't graduate. Thesis not accepted. I'm acquainted with this one. Oh, too well acquainted. You know what he tried to hand in? Despite all cautions and warnings? A thesis called *Is Government Necessary?* But that isn't why they refused to re-enroll him."

"But he's over twenty-one," said Heller.

"I should say he is. He has been flunked out on his doctorate for three consecutive years. Wister, this young fellow is an activist! A deviant. A revolutionary of the most disturbing sort. He simply will not conform. He even boycotted the Young Communist League! He's a roaring, ranting tiger! A wild-eyed, howling anarchist, of all things! Quite out of fashion. But that wasn't why they refused to re-enroll him. The government cut off his student loans and demanded immediate repayment."

"Why would they do that?" said Heller.

"Why, he was doing all the income tax forms for students and the faculty and he was costing the Internal Revenue Service a fortune!"

"Is that his address?" said Heller. "That number on 125th Street?"

Mr. Twaddle said, "It probably was up to a few minutes ago. Ten IRS agents were just here demanding that address. So he will soon be beyond reach entirely."

"Thank you for your help, Mr. Twaddle," said Heller.

"Always glad to assist, Wister. Drop in any time."

Heller closed the door behind him. Then he started to run.

Chapter 2

Heller was down 116th Street and up Broadway like a quarter horse. If anyone noticed he was going faster than was usual, he wasn't looking at them—but New Yorkers never notice anything. And, factually, I don't think he was moving at any exceptional speed: some cars were going faster than he was. I was glad to note that gravity differences had not given him any phenomenal powers. Things to him weighed only a sixth less than usual.

Judging by the scenery flow, he was probably only doing twenty.

I was, of course, a little bit puzzled by his obvious antagonism to an anarchist. Or did he fear for the IRS agents, faced by a maniacal wild man of huge powers? Perhaps his contact with the FBI had inclined him to defect to the Earth government. I know that in his place, I would have been seeking political asylum.

He came to 125th Street and raced along, looking for the address. But he found it because of three double-parked government cars. There was no one in them.

Heller checked the building. The street number was almost decipherable. It was one of those innumerable abandoned apart-nt houses with which New York is strewn. The taxes are high, enants destructive. If the owner tries to repair the building, the tes go up and the tenants tear it down again. So owners abandon them to rot. And this one was so bad off that not ants had to wreck it. Obviously no one in his right mind to live there. The front entrance looked like it had been target.

He circumvented fallen debris and went in. He stopped was coming from the second floor—ripping sounds.

Heller went up what was left of a stairs.

A government agent was standing outside a door, picking his teeth.

Heller walked up to the agent. "I'm looking for Israel Epstein," he said.

The agent found a particularly succulent morsel in his teeth, ate it and said, "Yeah? We ain't got a warrant out for him yet, so that don't make you an accomplice. But as soon as they get through planting the evidence in there, we'll be able to get one."

"Where is he?" demanded Heller.

"Oh, him. Well, if we let him escape first, then he becomes a fugitive and we can send him up for that if for nothing else."

"Where did he go?" demanded Heller.

"Oh, he ran off down 125th Street," said the IRS agent, pointing west. "Said he was going to drown himself in the Hudson River."

Heller turned to leave. Two IRS agents stood squarely behind with drawn guns.

"Sucker," said the tooth-picking one. "Hey, McGuire!" he yelled into the apartment, "Here's one of his friends!"

The two agents in the hall pushed Heller ahead of them with their guns. They shoved him well into the apartment.

The place might have been a wreck before. It was an emergency disaster now. It was torn to splinters!

IRS agents were using jimmies to pry up boards, hammers to smash furniture.

A huge hulking brute out of a horror film stood, hands on hips, glaring at Heller. "So, an accomplice! Sit down in that chair!"

It was pretty broken up but Heller managed it.

"Say SIR when you're spoken to!" said McGuire.

"Sir?" said Heller. "You a nobleman or something?"

"We're a hell of a lot more important than that, kid. We're Internal Revenue Service agents. We run this country and don't you forget it!"

?" said Heller.

Now, where are the books you and Epstein cooked? Where are
, hidden?" demanded McGuire.

"Sir?" said Heller.

"We know God (bleeped) well that you had actual IRS manuals! Copies of the real law and everything. Where are they hidden?"

"Sir?" said Heller.

"Do you realize," said McGuire, "if they got into public hands
it would ruin us? Do you realize this is treason? Do you know
what the penalty for treason is? Death! It says so right in the
Constitution!"

"Sir?" said Heller.

"I don't think he'll talk," said another agent.

McGuire said, "I'll handle this, Malone."

"There ain't any manuals here," said still another agent.

McGuire said, "Shut up, O'Brien. I'll handle this. This kid is a
red-hot suspect. I got to read him his rights. Now listen carefully.
You have to testify to whatever IRS wants you to testify to. You
have to swear to anything IRS tells you to swear to and sign
anything you are told by IRS to sign. If you fail to do so you will be
charged with conspiring to conspire with conspirators regardless of
race, color or creed. Sign here."

Heller had a slip of paper under his nose. "What's this?"

"By the Miranda Rule," said McGuire, "the prisoner must be
informed of his rights. I have just informed you of yours. The IRS
is totally legal, always. This attests you have been warned. So sign
here."

Heller signed, "J. Edgar Hoover."

"Good," said McGuire. "Now, where are the God (bleeped)
cooked account books and where are the God (bleeped) IRS manuals and regulations?"

"Sir?" said Heller.

"He ain't going to talk," said Malone.

"I better just plant this Commie literature and these bags of
heroin and we can get going," said O'Brien.

"You know what's going to happen to you, kid?" said McGuire

with obvious satisfaction. "We're going to force you to report down-town to the Federal Building. We're going to cross-examine you, kid. We're going to put you under the hot lights and we're going to find out all about you. Everything. When we get through with you, there won't be a thing about you we don't know. Take this."

McGuire had been scribbling a name on a legal document. He handed it to Heller. It said:

SUBPOENA! THE PEOPLE VERSUS EPSTEIN. J. Edgar Hoover is hereby summoned to appear at 0900 hours at the Federal Building, Room 22222, Permanent Federal Grand Jury, Internal Revenue Courts.

"Cross-examination?" said Heller.

"Correct."

"You find out everything there is to know about me?"

"Correct."

"Actually, I think," said Heller, "that under that board over there is a good hiding place."

"That's better," said McGuire. "Which board?"

Heller got up. He went over. He knelt down.

And out of his pocket, his action hidden from them by his body, he took a red-and-white piece of candy. I recognized it. It was the candy he had been making aboard the tug! It had a wrapper that looked like paper. With a thumbnail and a twist, he pushed the paper down into the candy. He put it under a board.

He stood up. "There are no manuals there now."

"Shows the right spirit. You can go now but you show up! Federal Building, nine hundred hours!"

Heller walked out.

He walked down the remains of the steps.

Outside, he walked up to one of the government cars. He bent over.

He had four sticks of dynamite strapped to his leg!

He undid the tape.

He laid the dynamite into the back seat of the car. No cap, no means to explode it. He just laid it there.

Then he walked very rapidly west on 125th Street.

The buildings on either side of him shook in concussion!

A gigantic flash whipped at the sky!

A roaring blast of sound struck a sledgehammer blow!

Heller looked back. As the smoke soared, I saw that the whole front of the abandoned apartment house was falling into the street in slow motion. Pieces of the roof were still sailing in the air!

The government cars, showered with rubble, did not explode. So he wasn't that good with explosives after all.

Pieces of apartment house were falling out of the sky. Torrents of flame began to leap up.

It was the candy!

I knew what the stuff was now. It was a binary concussion-flame grenade. It didn't operate until the wrapper, the needful element, was shoved down into the explosive. It had activated on a forty-second dissolve. The Apparatus never used them. They were too risky to carry!

"What the hell was that?" said an old man near Heller.

"There were ten terrorists in that building," said Heller.

"Oh," said the old man. "Vandals again."

Heller went along 125th Street, first at a casual walk and then at a distance-increasing run.

Behind him, fire sirens were screaming.

Heller didn't look back again. He was headed, apparently, for the river.

Chapter 3

Speeding along, Heller could catch glimpses of the river ahead. His view was impeded with underpasses and overpasses of major roads.

He veered slightly to his left. The river lay just on the other side of some trunk highways along which traffic blurred.

Heller negotiated the obstacles.

Before him stretched a long dock, reaching west into the water.

He slowed, alert. He jumped up to see over some obstacles. Then he went speeding ahead.

On the end of the dock lay a tangle of something. Heller raced to it.

Right at the dock end lay a jacket. A pair of horn-rimmed spectacles was sitting on it.

The Jersey shore, opposite, was a yellow haze of polluted air. The Hudson was blue with sky reflection despite the scum and filth in it.

Heller was looking up and down the river. Apparently an incoming tide from the ocean was slacking the current for the bits of dunnage and trash were going neither upstream nor down.

A hat!

A soggy, dark blue, snap-brim hat, still afloat with the air trapped in it.

Heller threw off his jacket. He pulled off his shoes. He zipped out of his pants. He threw his cap to the dock.

In a long dive he went into the water, debris and oil!

Down he went! Hands grabbing out and back, he was pulling himself toward the bottom.

The light went from brown to dim gray.

Yikes! How deep was this river?

Down, down, down, his eyes sweeping left to right through the murk!

Ooze!

He had hit bottom!

Up he went like a streak.

He blew to the surface. He treaded water, jumping his head up to look around.

He inverted.

Down he went again. Down, down, down, looking left and right.

Black ooze!

Around in a circle on the bottom. Old tires and cans.

Up, up, up! He blew to the surface again.

More treading water. More jumps to lift his head out.

A faint sound!

Heller made a bigger jump, lifting himself out of the water.

A faint voice, "I'm over here."

Heller treaded water and looked toward the dock.

There in the water, clinging to an old ring sunk in concrete, was somebody, just a hand and head showing.

Heller struck out in that direction.

In a minute or two he was beside a very small young man, covered with oil, mostly eyes.

"I'm a failure," moaned the pitiful figure. Then he coughed. "I lost my nerve. I couldn't keep my head under long enough to drown."

"Are you Israel Epstein?" said Heller.

"Yes, I'm sorry I can't shake hands. I'd lose my grip."

Heller was surveying the fellow's plight. The dock end was sheer above him and had no handholds.

A passing ship engulfed them in waves. Epstein lost his grip on the ring and got banged against the concrete. Heller put

Epstein's hand back on the ring. "Hold on!"

"I can't climb up. I was a failure at drowning myself and now I'm a failure at saving myself. You better go off and leave me. I'm not worth rescuing."

Heller swam along the dock and found an iron ladder that reached down into the water. He climbed up.

He went to his jacket and took out a coil of fish line. He went back to the dock edge above Epstein. "Just hold on," he called down. A passing tug's wash engulfed Epstein.

Heller's hands were moving rapidly in a strange repeating rhythmic pattern. He was plaiting the fish line into a thin rope!

He made a nonslip loop in the end of his product. He lowered it down to Epstein. "Put your legs through it and sit on it."

Epstein couldn't do it.

Heller secured the top end to an old rusty ring and dived back into the water. He paddled over to Epstein, found a piece of driftwood, broke it and forced it into the loop to make a seat and got him onto it and showed him how to hold the upper strands.

"You shouldn't go to all this trouble," said Epstein. "I'll only come to another bad end."

Heller splashed at the water to get oil scum to float away and when he had a clear patch, he used it to get some of the oil off Epstein's head and shoulders.

"Now, don't go away," said Heller. He swam back to the ladder, got up on the dock and shortly had Epstein up beside him, safely on the concrete.

Chapter 4

A pair of cops wandered up. "What are you doing?"

"Fishing," said Heller.

"You sure you're not swimming?" said one cop.

"Just fishing," said Heller.

"Well, see that you don't swim," said the cop and he and his partner wandered away, idly swinging their nightsticks.

"You didn't turn me over to them," said Epstein. "But you might as well. They'll get me anyway."

Heller had recovered his redstar engineer's rag. He was wiping the oil off Epstein. Then he got Epstein's shoes off and got him out of his pants and put the articles in the sun, which seemed to be quite hot.

He took a few more swipes at Epstein's face and then put the young man's horn-rimmed glasses on him.

I wondered if Heller had made a mistake in identity. According to Mr. Twaddle, this Epstein was a roaring anarchist, a terror and a threat to civilization. But he was quite small, had a narrow face, a beaked nose, weak eyes and was shivering.

"You cold?" said Heller.

"No, it is just what I have been through," said Epstein.

"What do they want you for, really?" said Heller.

Epstein looked like he was going to cry. "It all started when I realized that the usual Internal Revenue Service agent just made up regulations as he went along. But one fatal day I was in the law library and found the actual Congressional law and the IRS manual of regulations. I xeroxed them. I started to do the income tax returns for the faculty and some students with all the correct deductions." He sighed and was silent a bit. "Oh, the way of the revolutionary is hard! I'm not up to it."

"So what happened?" said Heller.

"The local IRS office lost about two million dollars in illegal collections they'd been getting. And the bonuses of agents McGuire, O'Brien and Malone shrank to nothing."

He sighed a long, shuddering sigh. "They will never forgive me. They will persecute me all my days. You shouldn't have rescued me. I am a lost cause."

Heller had gotten some of the oil off of himself. He went over to his jacket and fished out the subpoena. He brought it back and handed it to Epstein. As he sat back down, he said, "What is this?"

Epstein looked at it, turned it over. "It's just a subpoena. It tells you to appear before a grand jury and testify."

"And what does that consist of?" said Heller.

"Oh, very simple. You just take the Fifth Amendment—which is to say, refuse in case it incriminates you—and they put you in jail and bring you out every few weeks and you just take the Fifth Amendment again."

"Then they really don't examine you and make you tell all you know?"

"No, it's just a method of keeping innocent people in jail."

Heller was looking at the water. "Oh, those poor fellows," he said.

"What poor fellows?" said Epstein.

"McGuire, Malone and O'Brien and seven other agents. They're all dead. I thought I was facing a Code break, you see."

"Dead?"

"Yes, your apartment blew up. Killed them all."

"If those three are dead, then the case is ended. They didn't have any evidence, only their own testimony. It means I am not being hunted. The thing is all over!"

"Good," said Heller. "Then you're free and clear!"

Epstein sat for a short time, looking at the water. Then

suddenly his teeth began to chatter and from this he went into a torrent of tears.

"If you're free and clear," said Heller, "what's wrong now?"

After a bit Epstein was able to talk. But he still kept on crying. "I know something awful is going to happen in the next few minutes!"

"Why?" said Heller in astonishment.

"Oh," wept Epstein, "I wouldn't be permitted to have this much good news."

"What?" said Heller.

"The news is too wonderful! I don't deserve it! A world record catastrophe is going to strike any moment now to make up for it! I know it!"

"Look," said Heller patiently, "your troubles are over. And there's more good news. I have a job for you."

"Oh?" said Epstein. "You mean I've got a chance to pay back my student loans and re-enroll for my doctorate again?"

"I think so," said Heller.

"What is your name?"

"Jet."

Oh, my Gods! This *was* a Code break. Heller was going to tell him his real name.

"That isn't all of it," said Epstein.

"Well, no," said Heller. "The full name on my papers is Jerome Terrance Wister. That makes my initials 'J. T.' My real friends call me Jet."

Oh, that slippery dog. He'd just squeaked by on that one.

"Oh, J. T. Wister. Jet. I get it. The name on the subpoena was J. Edgar Hoover and I was sure you wanted me to murder somebody. I am not the type, you know. I can't even kill cockroaches."

"Nothing drastic like that," said Heller. "You're over twenty-one, aren't you?"

"Yes, I'm twenty-three and an aged wreck."

"Well, all I want you to do is open a broker account for me."

"Do you have credit?"

"Well, no," said Heller. "But all I want you to do is open an account so I can buy and sell stocks—some firm like Short, Skidder and Long Associates."

Epstein drew a shuddering sigh. "It isn't that simple. You have to have an address so you can have a bank account. Then you have to arrange credit and open a brokerage account. Do you have any money?"

"Yes. I have a hundred thousand to use in such gambling."

"Do you have any heavy debts or liabilities like me?"

"No."

"I know everybody has enemies. But do you have any special enemies that would like to get at you?"

Heller thought a bit. "Well, there's a Mr. Bury, an attorney I've run into."

"Bury? Bury of Swindle and Crouch?"

"Yes, the same."

"He's Delbert John Rockecenter's personal family attorney. He's one of the most powerful lawyers on Wall Street. And he's an enemy?"

"I would say so," said Heller. "He keeps working at it."

"Oh," said Epstein. He was silent for a bit and they sat in the hot sun drying off. Then he said, "This thing you're asking is pretty big. It's going to take an awful lot of work. You would need somebody on it full time, not just to start it but to run it for you."

"Well, how much do you earn a week?"

"Oh, I don't earn much of anything," said Epstein. "I'm not really an accountant—that's just one of the things a business administrator has to know. They wouldn't take my last thesis for my doctorate. It was a good thesis, too. It was all about corporate feudalism—industrial anarchy, you know—how the corporations could and should run everything. Its title was *Is Government Necessary?* But I think I could get them to accept my new title. It's *Anarchy is Vital if We Are Ever Going to Establish Industrial Feudalism.*"

"Well," said Heller, "you could have time to work on that."

"You see," said Epstein, "they argue with me that it isn't in the field of business administration. They say it is a political science subject. But it isn't. No! About eighty percent of a corporation's resources are absorbed in trying to file government reports and escort inspectors around. If they would listen, I could get the Gross National Product up eighty percent, just like that!" He brooded a bit. "Maybe I ought to change my thesis title to *Corporations Would Find Revolution Cheaper Than Paying Taxes.* "

"I would pay you five hundred dollars a week," said Heller.

"No. If I did it, it would be for one percent of the gross income with a drawing account not to exceed two hundred dollars a week. I'm not worth much."

Heller went over to his jacket and fished out two one hundred dollar bills. He tried to hand them to Epstein.

"No," said Epstein. "You don't know enough about me. The offer is probably very good. But I can't accept it."

"Right now, do you have any money? Any place to live? Your apartment isn't there anymore."

"It's no more than I deserve. I didn't have any other clothes and I can sleep in the park tonight. It's warm weather."

"You've got to eat."

"I am used to starving."

"Look," said Heller, "you've got to take this job."

"It's too good an offer. You do not know me, Mr. Hoover—I mean, Mr. Wister. You are probably a kind, honest, patient man. But your efforts of philanthropy are being directed at a lost cause. I cannot possibly accept your employment."

They sat for a while, dangling their legs off the dock edge, drying out in the warm sun. The Hudson had begun to flow again as the tide ebbed.

Suddenly Heller said, "Is ethnology included in business administration studies?"

"No."

"How about the customs of people?"

"No. You're talking about social anthropology, I guess. I've never studied that."

"Good," said Heller. "Then you would not realize that the laws of the American Indian were still binding on Manhattan, due to prior sovereignty."

"They are?" said Epstein.

"There was an Indian law that when you saved a man's life, that man was thereafter responsible for you from there on out."

"Where did you hear that?"

"I was told by a master of political science from your own university."

"So it must be true," brooded Epstein.

"Good," said Heller. "I just saved your life, didn't I?"

"Yes, you did. I'm afraid there's no doubt about that."

"All right," said Heller. "Then you are responsible for me from here on out."

Silence.

"You have to take the job and look after my affairs," said Heller. "It's prior Indian law. There's no way out of it."

Epstein stared at him. Then suddenly his head dropped. He broke into a torrent of tears. When he could talk, he blubbered, "You see, I knew when I heard all that good news, some new catastrophe was lurking just ahead! And it's arrived! It's been horrible enough, in the face of malignant fate, trying to bear up and take responsibility for myself. And now," a fresh torrent of tears, "I have to take responsibility for you, too!"

Heller laid the two one-hundred-dollar bills in his hand. Epstein looked at them forlornly. He got up and went over to his jacket. He put them in his empty wallet.

He sadly looked at Heller. "Meet me on the steps of High Library on the campus tomorrow at noon and I will have the plan of what we have to do."

"Good," said Heller.

Epstein picked up his coat and walked a little ways. Then he turned. "I am sure that, with my awful fate, you will live to regret the kind things you have done. I am sorry."

Head down, he trudged away.

Chapter 5

That evening, in the Gracious Palms lobby, Heller sat reading the *Evening Libel*. He was wearing his old, blue, too-short suit. The "throwaway" suit had really been thrown away after Heller's swim in the polluted river water. And evidently the tailors had not delivered any new clothes.

The story he was reading said:

> In a strongly worded statement today, Mayor Don Hernandez O'Toole censured the New York District Office of the Internal Revenue Service.
>
> "The IRS practice of blowing up perfectly good tax-deductible property must cease," said Mayor O'Toole. "It places all New York at risk."
>
> The censure came on the heels of an explosion this afternoon on West 125th Street where an IRS squad was visiting a tax-deductible apartment house.
>
> Dynamite found in the government cars was clear proof of intent to dynamite, according to New York Fire Commissioner Flame Jackson.
>
> Premature dynamission was the stated cause of the blast.
>
> A U.S. Government spokesman said, "IRS has a perfect right to do what it pleases,

> when it pleases and to whom it pleases and New York better get the word, see?" This was generally accepted as an evidence of cover-up as usual.
>
> There were no lives of any importance lost in the blast.

Heller had just turned the paper over and half a strip of Bugs Bunny became visible and I was much annoyed when he was interrupted.

Heller looked up. Vantagio was standing right beside his chair.

"Did you get registered?" His voice was edgy. Hostile? "If you did, why didn't you call me?"

"Well," said Heller, "it's sort of up in the air. It's my grades: D average and I'm asking to be accepted as a senior. It's possible I won't make it."

Had Vantagio gone white? Hard to tell as he was shadowed by a lobby palm. "What did they say?"

"It's 'under advisement.' I am to go back at nine in the morning."

"*Sangue di Cristo!* You wait until eight o'clock at night to tell me this!" Vantagio rushed off. He slammed the door of his office. Oh, he was angry.

Yes, I felt I could make, possibly, use of this jealousy for Heller.

But I made a more important observation about nine, New York time. Heller disengaged himself from some African diplomat he was talking to, got in the elevator and went to his suite. I could see that, down the hall, his door was wide open!

And down close to the floor, as though she were lying on it, a beautiful brunette girl was extending her hand out into the hall. In a musical voice she called, "Come along, pretty boy. We're waiting!"

A torrent of giggles came out of the room.

The interference went on. But I had made my observation. Heller never locked his door! Those women simply walked in whenever they chose!

A wide-open invitation to rob the place!

I myself had a very happy afternoon nap, contemplating it.

I must have overslept but there was ample excuse for it. I had not dared sleep for days. But things were running my way now. When I awoke, Heller was already disembarking from the subway at 116th Street. I watched tolerantly. His fate would soon be sealed.

He went directly to the temporary reservation area. There were quite a few students about, milling, finishing off their sign-ups. I realized that it wasn't registration *week*, really. It had been registration day, per se, yesterday, judging from the crowd sizes.

I sat back to enjoy Heller getting his comeuppance. No way would this Miss Simmons let him into this school. Not with those grades. Heller's plans would be thrown into a cocked hat!

And there she was. She had just finished her last student. She ignored her short waiting line. She had a smile on her face but it was the kind you see on the female spider just before she has a meal of a male.

"Well, if it isn't the young Einstein," said Miss Simmons. "Sit down."

Heller sat down and Miss Simmons scrambled through her papers and then sat back with that horrible smile. "It appears," she said, "that they don't care who blows up the world these days."

"You called me 'Wister' yesterday."

"Well, times have changed, haven't they. Who do you know? God?"

"Has my enrollment received advisement?" asked Heller.

"That it has, young Einstein. Now, ordinarily we do not permit a transfer from another school into the senior class."

"I could make up——"

"Hush, hush. But in your case, it seems this is to be allowed. And into our competitive School of Engineering and Applied Science, too."

"I am very grate——"

"Oh, hush, young Einstein. You have not heard it all. Ordinarily we require a fresh American College Test that must average

28% or above. But you, young Einstein, seem to have had that waived."

"Well that's goo——"

"Oh, there's more," said Miss Simmons. "It has always been mandatory that a student entering engineering school receive a Scholastic Aptitude Test and that the grade for verbal and written be above 700. But you are not being required to do any SAT at all."

"That's truly marv——"

"And more, young Einstein. Our requirement for a B average for such enrollments has been waived. Now, isn't that nice?"

"Indeed," said Heller. "It is very ni——"

"It is far *too* nice, young Einstein. I have direct orders here to admit you. As a senior. In the School of Engineering and Applied Science. As a candidate for a Bachelor in Nuclear Science and Engineering, graduating next May. And the order is signed by the president of the university himself."

"Really, I'm overwhel——"

"You'll be overwhelmed shortly," said Miss Simmons and her smile vanished. "Either somebody has gone stark raving loony *or* the reduction of government subsidies and the lack of a post-war boom makes them slaver for your twenty-five hundred dollars *and* they have gone stark raving loony! You and they are NOT going to get away with it. I will not have my name on the form registering you and turning upon the world a nuclear scientist who is a complete imbecile. Do I make myself clear, young Einstein?"

"I'm very sorry if——"

"Oh, don't waste energy on getting upset at this point," said Miss Simmons. "You are going to be upset enough later to need every calorie! Oh, I have no choice but to enroll you, young Mr. God Junior. But there are ways of enrolling and ways of enrolling. Now, shall we begin?"

"I really——"

"Now, to start with," said Miss Simmons, "you do not have all the requisite credits in former schooling for this degree. There are four subjects here which are omitted and I am signing you up to take them IN ADDITION to the heavy engineering subjects you will be required to take for the semester."

"I am sure I——"

"Oh, don't thank me yet! There's more! Now, I very much doubt that with those D grades, you were firmly founded in the subjects in which you received them. So I am making your acceptance conditional upon special tutoring to bring those subjects up to the mark along with your regular class work."

"I think I——"

"I know you are grateful," said Miss Simmons. "So I will add another favor. Your Saint Lee's was a military school. And I adjudicate that your military science and study credits given there are not valid unless you continue on with and complete your entire ROTC—Reserve Officers Training Corps—schedule in this, your senior year. You can really get a bellyful of how nasty war is! And the Army can be persuaded it is unpatriotic not to complete them. I intend to write them a little note. That means three additional class periods and one drill period a week. All on top of the extra subjects and tutoring. Now, isn't that nice, God Junior?"

Heller was just looking at her by now. Stunned, no doubt.

She had turned to her accordion-folded computer printouts of class timings and assignments already made. "But here is where you are really going to thank me, God Himself. When I received this order at breakfast, I worked it all out. There is no way to assign all these hours in such a way that the classes are consecutive. Several of them occur at the same exact hours. You have to be in two, and in one case three places at the same time. And that is the way you have been assigned. You will be absent, one class or another, any way you want to look at it. The professors will rant. You will find yourself in front of deans. And it is they, not I, who will tell you that you cannot graduate and get your diploma next May. If they come back on me, I will say you just demanded it all, and you did, didn't you, Jehovah?"

Miss Simmons sat back and tapped a pencil against her teeth. Then after a bit she said, "Oh, I don't blame you for being over-awed in appreciation. You see, Master of All He Surveys and Creator Himself, I do not like INFLUENCE. Also, I am a member of the Anti-Nuclear Protest Marchers, its secretary in fact. And though the organization may be old and it may be suppressed and it may be that the New York Tactical Police Force is just waiting to bash in our heads again, the thought of letting a nuclear scientist as unqualified as you loose upon the world turns my blood to leukemia. Do we understand each other, Wister?"

"Really, Miss Simmons——"

"Oh, I almost forgot. Just in case you find time heavy on your hands—loafing about with this schedule—I have added another course to make up for a missing optional. It is Nature Appreciation 101 and 104. One goes out every Sunday, all day, and admires the birds and trees and learns, perhaps, what a nasty thing it is to make those world-destroying bombs! I teach this class myself, so I can keep an eye on your vicious proclivities. Now you can thank me, Wister."

"Really, Miss S——"

"And as they are so interested in money, all this adds another fifteen hundred and thirty-three dollars to your bill. I hope you don't have it. Pay the cashier. Good day, Wister. NEXT!"

Heller took the papers she had already made out. He took the invoice.

He went over and paid the cashier.

Aha! My heart had gone out to Miss Simmons more and more. What a sterling character! I toyed with the idea of sending her some candy "From an Unknown Admirer." No, on the other hand, a pair of brass knuckles would be more in her line. With maybe a Knife Section knife to keep on her desk. But really, did she need it?

Chapter 6

Just before noon, Heller came to the High Library. It was a very imposing building with a Roman look—ten huge columns stretched across the front, an enormous rotunda, a very noble façade. It was fronted with a vast expanse of steps almost as wide as the building itself.

He passed a fountain and then a statue with the words *Alma Mater* on it. He went halfway up the upper steps and slumped down on the stone.

And well he might slump. I had been kept laughing for the last two hours following his zigzag course around the enormous campus. He trotted here and he trotted there. He was locating every single one of the large number of classrooms, halls, armories and drill fields he would have to attend. He had constantly checked a copy of a computer printout and he had found that he had a schedule which went two classes at the same time, followed by no class for the next hour and then, in one case, three classes at the same time! I was kept in stitches. Not even the great Heller could cope with that schedule. And it went seven days a week!

As he sat there in the hot noonday sun, he must be realizing that there was no way on Earth he could get a diploma and carry out the silly plans he had undoubtedly made to carry his mission through just to spite me. And get me killed.

Students were drifting up and down the steps, no vast throng. Young men and women, not too well dressed. Heller must look younger than some of them, despite being, in fact, several years older in time and, in all honesty, decades older in experience. How silly he must feel, a Royal officer of the Fleet, sitting there amongst these naive creatures. Another joke on him and on them, too. I idly speculated what they would think if they knew a Voltar combat engineer was sitting right there, in plain view, a Mancoian from Atalanta more than a score of light years away, a holder of the fifty-volunteer star, that could blow their planet to bits as easy as he could spit or could prevent an invasion that would slaughter every one of them. What a joke on them. How stupid they were!

A couple of girls and a young man drifted by. One of the girls said, "Ooo! Are you on the baseball team?"

"I didn't know they were still turned out," said the boy. "Why, you're wearing spikes!"

Heller looked at one of the girls. "You can't get to first base if you don't."

They all of them burst into screams of laughter. I tried and tried to figure out what they were laughing about. (Bleep) that Heller, anyway. Always so *obscure*. And he had no right to start currying popularity. He was an extraterrestrial, an interloper! Besides, they were pretty girls.

"Name's Muggins," said the boy. "This is Christine and Coral —they're from Barnyard College: that's part of Empire but all women, oh boy!"

"My name's Jet," said Heller.

"C'm up'n see us s'm'time," said Christine.

They all laughed again, waved and walked on down the broad steps.

And here came Epstein!

He was dragging an enormously long roll of something behind him. It was about a foot in diameter and certainly over twelve feet long! He passed the fountain and then the statue. He stopped a couple steps below Heller. He was dressed in a shabby gray suit and a shabby gray hat and, in addition to the roll, he was carrying a very scuffed up, cheap attaché case. He sank down on a step, puffing.

"And how is Mr. Epstein?" said Heller cheerfully.

"Oh, don't call me that," said Epstein. "It makes me uncomfortable. Please call me Izzy. That's what everybody does."

"Good. If you'll call me Jet."

"No. You are really my superior as you have the capital. I should call you Mr. Wister."

"You have forgotten," said Heller, "that you are responsible for me now. And that includes my morale." Then he said very firmly, "Call me Jet."

Izzy Epstein looked unhappy. Then he said, "All right, Mr. Jet."

Heller must have given it up. "I see you found some clothes. I was worried that they'd all been destroyed."

"Oh, yes. I took a bath in the gym and I got two suits, this hat and this briefcase from the Salvation Army Good Will. They wouldn't do for you, of course, but if I dressed too well, I would attract attention and invite bad luck. One must never appear to be doing too well—the lightning will strike."

This Izzy Epstein was turning my stomach. It was quite obvious that he was a neurotic depressive with persecution complexes and had overtones of religio-mania, evident in his fixations on fate. A fine mess he would make for Heller. Neurotics are never competent. But on the other hand, it was really a break for me that Heller had run into him. The fellow couldn't even manage his own affairs, much less Heller's.

"Well, you look better, anyway," said Heller.

"Oh, I'm exhausted! I have been working flat out all night to prepare a proposal for you. The only building I could find open was the Art College, so I had to use their materials."

"Is that what that is?"

"This roll? Yes. All they had left out was studio paper—the kind they use behind models, twelve feet wide, a hundred feet long. And they didn't leave out any scissors. So I used that."

He tried to unroll it. But he didn't have enough arm reach. Heller started to help him but Izzy said, "No, no. You're the investor. You there!" he called out suddenly.

A couple of new students had come out of the library. Izzy

stopped them at the top of the huge, wide stairway. "You hold this end," he said to one. "And you this end," he said to the other. "Now, hold it tight." The two stood there, twelve feet apart, holding the top of the roll.

Heller had followed Izzy up. Izzy took the roll and backed down two steps, unreeling it. At the top, in wild, garish ink, all along it, it said: *Confidential Draft.*

"You will probably find it too colorful," said Izzy, understating it like mad, for it was blazing in the sunlight, "but they had only left around old dried-up pots of poster paint and I had to mix it with water. And there were only some discarded brushes. But, it will give you the idea."

He backed down two more steps. Revealed to view were some odd lines and symbols. It looked like three wooden hay forks raking apples—and all of different colors, all bright.

"Now, that first row is what we call the mask corporations. We incorporate those separately in New York, New Jersey, Nevada and Delaware. They all have different, noninterlocking boards of directors."

He backed down another step unrolling the roll further. But there was a bit of wind. Two more students, eating sandwiches, were paused nearby. Izzy sent one to the far side and one to the right side and told them to hold it steady and they did.

Izzy pointed to the newly displayed mad thunder of color, lines and symbols. "Now, those are the bank accounts for those corporations."

He backed down another step, got two more students to hold the sides and two more to hold the extreme top which was buckling. "Now there, and notice the arrows as they intertwine, are the various brokerage firms which will handle orders placed with the mask corporations."

Izzy backed another step, unrolling the roll further.

"What is this?" one student, wandering up, asked another.

"Psychedelic art," said one already holding.

"Now, here we are getting to the more important stages," said Izzy. "The corporation on the right is in Canada. The one on the left is in Mexico. And these two corporations invisibly control the center one which is in Singapore. Get it?"

Izzy backed further. He needed more students and got them. Several were now up on a big stone parapet, looking down on it.

"Now, this series of arrows—the green series is the most important although the purple ones there are useful—transfer the funds of the above corporations in such a way as to bypass all reporting to governments."

"Is it a poster?" asked a student.

"Poster for some new riots, I heard them say," said another.

Izzy stepped down another broad step and unrolled it further. He got more holders. "Now, this is the Swiss-Liechtenstein consortium of corporations. You may wonder why these seem so independent. Well, actually they are not."

He unrolled more chart, got some newcomers to hold it. "The Swiss-Liechtenstein fund flow goes underground to West Germany and thence to Hong Kong. Do you get it? No?"

More of the chart was unrolled and held, "You can see why, now. The Hong Kong funds—see the purple arrow there—flow to Singapore, come back to Tahiti and . . ."

He unrolled more chart, ". . . arrive right in our own backyard in the Bahamas. Clever, eh? But look at London."

He unrolled more chart. One whole width was devoted to three corporations, three stockbrokers and three bank accounts, all in London. Orange lines radiated out and came back to Hong Kong. "And that is how we get the funds into the Bahamas from the City as they call it. But you will be interested in this."

He unrolled more chart and got more holders. There was an interlocking series of lines which stretched out to every bank account and brokerage house, a spider web of royal blue. "That is the arbitrage network. By means of a centrally controlled system, we can take advantage of the differences of currency prices throughout the whole network and every time we transfer any funds, we also make a mint! It requires telexes and lease lines from RCA, of course. But it will pay for itself every week."

He unrolled more chart, got more holders. The steps were pretty thronged by now.

"What was the artist thinking when he drew it?" asked a girl.

"Soul music," said a learned boy.

"I think it's quite lovely," said another girl. "It certainly makes one tranquil."

"And now," Izzy said to Heller, "I'll bet you've been holding your breath waiting until I got around to this." He waved his arm in a grand gesture at a single corporation marked with a circle and red arrows. "That," said Izzy, "is MULTINATIONAL! By reason of nominee shares, noninterlocking controlled boards, it orchestrates the entire conduct of the entire remaining chart. And listen, here is the best part: it calls itself a MANAGEMENT company! It isn't visibly liable for a single thing any other company does! Isn't that great?"

"But why," said Heller, "why all these different corporations and brokerage houses and bank accounts?"

"Now, I am responsible for you. Right?"

"Right," said Heller.

"If any one of those corporations goes broke, it folds all by itself and it doesn't do a thing to any other part of the entire consortium. You get it? You can go bankrupt to your heart's content! You can also sell them for tax losses, buy other corporations with them. You can also hide and vanish profits. Everything."

"But," said Heller doubtfully, "I don't see that so many——"

"Well, I will admit I haven't told you the real reason." He leaned over to Heller's ear. "You told me you had an enemy. Mr. Bury of Swindle and Crouch. He is the most vicious, unprincipled lawyer on Wall Street. With this setup, he will never be able to touch you."

"Why not?" said Heller.

Izzy leaned much closer and whispered much more quietly, hard to hear above the chatter of the crowd. "Because in every record, neither you nor your name will ever appear in any of this. And anything you are publicly connected with will not feed back into any of this. They are all private companies, all for profit, all controlled by actual stock shares. It is impenetrable!"

He stood back. "There is just one thing more I need your approval on. I didn't put it on this chart. An art student did it for me at breakfast."

Tucked in the bottom of the roll was another roll. It opened to a picture about two feet by three. It was a round, black globe. It had a little piece of rope or something sticking out of the top of it. Sparks were flying from the tip.

"What is it?" said Heller.

"It is my proposal for the evolving logo of Multinational! Actually, it is the old symbol of anarchy, a bomb! See the lit fuse?"

"A chemical powder bomb," said Heller.

"Now, we turn the poster over and we simply see a dark sphere with a wisp of cloud at the top. And that's what we will put out as the logo but you and I will know what it really is. Now do you approve?"

"Well, yes," said Heller.

"The chart and the logo?"

"Well, yes," said Heller.

"I know it is crude and hastily done. I haven't even filled in many of the names. I think it is very tolerant of you to approve it."

"What is this?" a newcomer asked Heller. "A work of art?"

"Yes," said Heller. "A work of art!"

"Well now, let's roll it up," said Izzy.

"No," said several of the crowd at once. One said, "A lot of people haven't been able to see it. We'll spread it out on the steps here and people can go up on the parapet there or climb the statue and get a real look."

Overruled, Heller and Izzy drew back and let them have their way.

"Did you get re-enrolled?" said Heller.

"Oh, yes," said Izzy. "That's why I was a little late. While I was doing all this, I got a brand-new idea for a doctorate thesis. And I saw them about it. It's 'The Use of Corporations in Undermining Totally the Existing World Order.'"

"And they agree to let you re-enroll and write it?"

"You see, the mistake I was making was getting off into political science and they kept telling me so. My doctorate is in business administration. But this new idea is perfect. It doesn't contain the word *government,* it does contain the word *corporations.* And *world order* can be interpreted to mean 'capitalistic finance.' So unless some horrible, malignant fate overtakes me from some other quarter, I can get my doctor's degree at the end of this October."

"Then you paid your bill," said Heller.

"Oh, yes. You can have your two hundred advance back."

"But how . . . ?"

"Right after I left you yesterday, I went to the Bank of America. I showed them the two hundred which proves I had a job and borrowed five thousand dollars without collateral. I paid off the government loan and have far more left than I really need. I won't have to sleep in the park—I'm always afraid of being mugged. I can stay in a dorm a couple of nights until we get our offices. And, if you don't mind, I'll sleep there when we do."

I was speechless. How could this ragtag, mucked-up mess of a timid little man walk into a bank and borrow five thousand just by showing them a couple of hundred-dollar bills?

"Now wait a minute," said Heller, obviously having afterthoughts. "It will take a long, long time to set up all those corporations in Hong Kong and Tahiti and wherever. What do you have in mind as a time schedule?"

"Oh, that is my fault," said Izzy. "I have been under such a nervous strain lately. I didn't want to tell you because I was afraid you would balk."

"So, how long? Two months? A year?"

"Oh, heavens, no! I was shooting for next Tuesday! I thought you would want it Friday but there's a weekend . . ."

"Next Tuesday," said Heller. Then he seemed to rally. "You're going to need money for all this. So here is ten thousand to start with. Will that be enough?"

"Oh, heavens, yes. Too much, actually. I'll put it in a locker at the bus station to keep it safe. And then put it in the first bank account. And then, when everything is set, you can put your capital in the various bank accounts and it will get transferred around and start to get to work. Is it too much to ask to meet you here on these steps 4:00 P.M. Tuesday?"

And then I thought I had it. This Izzy was a sly, clever crook. He was going to take all of Heller's money, deny him any control and leave him broke. I cancelled any idea of interfering with Izzy Epstein! He didn't even give Heller a receipt!

Izzy got his chart back from the congratulatory crowd. Several even helped him carry it as he went away.

I laughed. Maybe that was the last Heller would ever see of him!

Chapter 7

I was quite heartened by the number of potential allies I was picking up in case everything else went wrong with my plans for Heller. Vantagio, Miss Simmons, this Izzy Epstein. I began to keep a list. When Raht and Terb called in, possibly I could greatly embellish my planning.

Heller spent the afternoon doing some more checking on class locations, obviously still trying to figure out how to be in two or three places at once and get tutored at the same time. And then he went around to the other side of what was labelled "Journalism" and found the college bookstore on Broadway.

All day he had been running into people and sticking his nose into professors' offices and making up a list. He had been using the back side of a computer printout with the staples removed and now had this yard long sheet with titles and texts and manuals and authors scribbled all over it. He handed it to the girl behind the counter. She was obviously some graduate student doing part-time work to handle the current rush. Pretty, too.

"All this?" she said, adjusting her horn-rimmed glasses. "I can't read some of this writing. I wish they would teach kids to read and write these days."

Heller peered over at what she was pointing at. Yikes! He had annotated the list over on the edge with Voltarian short-hand!

My pen was really poised. Oh, I've seen Code breaks in my time. Maybe a whore and a tailor wouldn't know they were dealing with an extraterrestrial but he was in a college area and those people are smart.

"It's shorthand," said Heller. "The main titles and authors are in English."

They were, too. In very neat block print.

"What's this here?" said the girl, lifting her glasses above her eyes to see better. She was pointing at *The Fundamentals of Geometry* by Euclid. "We don't have any books by that author. Is it a new paperback?"

Heller told her she'd have to help him as he didn't know either. She went to her catalogues and looked up under "Authors." She couldn't find it. So she looked in a massive catalogue of alphabetical book titles. Then, cheered on by Heller, she looked up the author in the book titles. "Hey, here it is!" she said. *"Euclidian Geometry as Interpreted and Rewritten by Professor Twist from an Adaption by I. M. Tangled."* She went and found a copy. "You wrote here that his name was 'Euclid' when it was 'Euclidian.' You should learn how to spell."

They couldn't find anything by somebody named "Isaac Newton" and the girl decided he must be some revolutionary banned by the New York Tactical Police Force. But Heller persevered and they eventually came up with a book, *Laws of Motion I Have Rewritten and Adapted from a Text by Dr. Still as Translated from an Archaic English Newtonian Work by Elbert Mouldy* by Professor M. S. Pronounce, Doctor of Literature.

"You should have told me it would be in the literature section," said the girl. "You don't even know how to read a card catalogue."

"I'll try to find out," said Heller.

"Jesus," said the girl, "they teach card catalogues in the third grade! God, didn't anybody ever teach you anything? There's a staff at High Library devoted to showing students how to do it. You ask them over there. I'm here to sell books, not teach kindergarten! But let's get on, this is an awfully long list! You're keeping others waiting!"

They did make progress, however, and the pile of books grew and grew. Finally the girl, peering between the columns of books and lifting her glasses to see Heller, said, "You can't carry all these. And I'm not going to wrap them. So you go over to the college store and get about five rucksacks while I get an assistant to add up this bill."

Heller did as he was told.

When he returned, he packed the five rucksacks and paid the bill. Then he began to adjust straps and finally managed to get the sacks hung around him. Other students who had been waiting made room for him disinterestedly.

"Can you manage?" said the girl. "That must be about two hundred pounds. Books are heavy."

"Just barely," said Heller. "But we haven't got everything on this list."

"Oh, the rest of that stuff. Well, take that one about thirty from the top, *World History Rewritten by Competent Propagandists for Kiddies and Passed by the American Medical Association*, that's fourth grade grammar school. We don't carry that sort of thing. You'll have to get them at Stuffem and Glutz, the city's authorized school supplier. They're on Varick Street." And she gave him the number. "My God," she added, "how'd you ever get here not knowing those texts?"

Heller made his way through the backlog of student customers who stepped aside patiently. The girl said to the next student in line, "Jesus, what we get for freshmen these days."

"It says on your slip there he's a senior," said the student.

"I got it!" said the girl. I quickly and hopefully jacked up the audio. "He's here on an athletic scholarship! A weight lifter! Hey, call him back. I was awful impolite. I need a date for tonight's dance! Boy, am I dumb! He was cute, too."

Yes, she certainly was dumb! She had denied me opportunity after opportunity to file charges against Heller for Code breaks! And they had watched somebody heft two hundred pounds of rucksacks like they were air and I'm sure if they had looked out the door or window they would have seen Heller running along, clickety-clack, without a care in the world to the subway. My faith in the powers of observation of college students had suffered a heavy blow. Maybe they were all on drugs. That was the only possible explanation! An extraterrestrial right under their noses making all kinds of giveaways and they hadn't even blinked an eye!

Heller got right on down to Varick Street on the same subway. He got into the city authorized bookstore. And he was shortly showing a half-blind old man his list. In the subway he had ticked off missing titles with a red pen and now he handed it over, Voltarian shorthand and all, for the red checks to be filled.

The old man bustled off to a storeroom. "You want thirty copies of each?" he called back.

"One will do just fine."

"Oh, you're a tutor. All right." And he came back in about ten minutes, staggering under a stack of books. "I'll get the rest now." And he went back and came out staggering under a second stack.

Heller checked off the titles. He got almost to the end. "There's one missing: *Third Grade Arithmetic*."

"Oh, they don't teach that anymore. It's all 'new math' now."

"What's 'new math'?" said Heller.

"I dunno. They put out a new 'new math' every year. It's something about greater and lesser numbers without using any numbers this year. It was numerical subset integers last year but they were still teaching them to count. They stopped that."

"Well, I've got to have something about basic arithmetic," said Heller.

"Why?"

"You see," said Heller, "I do logarithms in my head and the only arithmetic I've ever seen done was by some primitive tribe on Flisten. They used charcoal sticks and slabs of white lime."

"No kidding?" said the old man.

"Yes, it was during a Fleet peace mission. They wouldn't believe we had that many ships and it was really funny to see them jumping about and counting and multiplying and writing it down. They were more advanced than others I've seen, however. One tribe had to use their fingers and toes to count their wives. They never had more than fifteen wives because that was all the fingers and toes they had."

The old man said, "A Fleet man, huh? I was in the Navy myself, war before last. You just wait there."

He went back and searched and searched and finally came out with a dusty, tattered text that had been lying around for ages. "Here's a book called *Basic Arithmetic Including Addition, Multiplication and Division With a Special Section on Commercial Arithmetic and Stage Acts*." He opened the yellowed pages, "It was published in Philadelphia in 1879. It's got all sorts of tricks in it like adding a ten digit column of thirty entries by inspection. Old-time bookkeeper stuff. Lot of stage tricks: they used to go on stage and write numbers and do complicated examples upside down leaning over a blackboard and get the answer in three seconds and the audience would flip out. Mr. Tatters said to throw it out but I sort of thought I should send it to a museum. Since they passed the law that kids had to use calculators in class, nobody is interested in it anymore. But as you're a navy man like myself you can have it."

Heller paid and the old man wrapped up the books into two more huge packages. Another two hundred pounds of books. I expected Heller to heft them up and walk off. It disappointed me when he found four hundred pounds too cumbersome. I'm sure he could have, with some strain, walked off with them. He had them call him a taxi. The old man even got a dolly and helped him load up. Heller thanked him.

"Don't throw that book away," said the old man at the curb. "I don't think there's a soul in this country knows how to do it anymore. I don't think they even remember it ever existed. When you're through with it, give it to a museum!"

"Thanks for piping the side!" said Heller and the taxi drove away leaving the old man waving at the curb.

Code break. "Piping the side!" It must be some Voltarian Fleet term. No, wait a minute. I had never heard the term on Voltar. But Heller wouldn't know Earth terms like that. Or would he? The Voltarian Fleet doesn't use pipes. A lot of them use puffsticks. Only Earth people smoke pipes. It was moving into the New York rush hour so I had a lot of time to work on this. I got as far as "Earth sailors as well as spacers have a lot to do with whores" when my concentration was interrupted.

A houseman was wheeling all that book tonnage across the lobby and Vantagio popped out of his office like some miniature jack-in-the-box.

He stared at the packages, tore a piece of paper off a corner and opened a rucksack to verify they were books. "They accepted you!" He let out a wheeze of relief and mopped his face with a silk handkerchief. He waved the houseman on and pushed Heller into his office.

"You did it!" said Vantagio.

"I think *you* did it," said Heller.

Vantagio looked at him with feigned blank innocence.

"Come on," said Heller. "They waived everything including having a head! How did you do it?"

Vantagio started laughing and sat down at his desk. "All right, kid, you got me. It was awfully late and I had an awful time getting hold of the university president last night but I did it. You see, at peak periods, we use some of the Barnyard College girls here. So I just told him that if you weren't enrolled in full by 9:30 this morning, we'd cut off our student aid program."

"I owe you," said Heller.

"Oh, no, no," said Vantagio. "You don't get off that easy. You still have to do what I tell you. Right?"

"Right," said Heller.

"Then get on that phone and call Babe and tell her you're enrolled!"

Heller turned the desk speaker phone around to face him and Vantagio pushed the lease line button. Geovani in Bayonne transferred the call to Babe in the dining room.

"This is Jerome, Mrs. Corleone. I just wanted to tell you what a great job Vantagio did in getting me enrolled."

"It's all complete?" said Babe.

"Absotively," said Heller. But I noted he did not tell her, as he had not told Vantagio, that Miss Simmons had really set him up to fail. Heller was sneaky.

"Oh, I'm so glad. You know, you dear boy, you don't want to grow up to be a bum like these other bums. Mama wants you to have class, kid, real class. Become president or something."

"Well, I certainly do thank you," said Heller.

"Now, there's one more thing, Jerome," said Babe, a little more severely. "You've got to promise me not to play hooky."

That stopped Heller. He knew very well he would be missing in as many as two or three classes a day! Bless Miss Simmons!

Heller found his voice, "Not even one class, Mrs. Corleone?"

"Now, Jerome," said Babe, her voice hardening, "I know it is a terrible job bringing up boys. I never did but I had brothers and I *know!* Let down your guard for one second and they're off and away, free as birds, skylarking and breaking neighbors' windows. So the answer is very plain. I give it to you absolutely straight. No hooky. Not even one class! Mama will be watching and Mama will spank! Now promise me, Jerome. And Vantagio, if you're listening to this, which you are—I am sure you are as I can tell it's the speaker phone on your desk—you look at his hands; no crossed fingers, no crossed feet. All right?"

Vantagio peered at Heller. "They aren't crossed, *mia capa.*"

Oh, what a spot Heller was in! With his nonsense Royal officer scruples about keeping his word, I knew he was suffering agonies. He couldn't keep that promise so he wouldn't make it. And I was sure that, to Babe Corleone, the phrase "Mama will spank" translated more truthfully into "concrete overcoat."

"Mrs. Corleone," said Heller. "I will be truthful with you." Ah, here it came! "I promise you faithfully that, unless I get rubbed out, or unless something happens that closes the university, I will complete college on time and get my diploma."

"Oh, you dear boy! That is even more than I asked! But nevertheless, Jerome, just remember, Mama will be watching. Bye-bye!"

Vantagio closed the circuit and sat there beaming at Heller.

"There's one more thing," said Heller. "Vantagio, could you get me the phone number of Bang-Bang Rimbombo. I want to call him from my suite."

"Celebrating, are you?" said Vantagio. "I don't blame you. As a matter of fact, he's right here in Manhattan and the parole officer is riding his (bleep) off." He wrote the number on a scrap of paper and handed it over. "Have fun, kid."

It left me blinking. Vantagio might be smart but he hadn't penetrated that one. Heller was full of surprises, (bleep) him. What was he going to pull? Blow up the university? That was the only way I could think of that would let him keep the promise he had just made to Babe Corleone.

Chapter 8

About an hour later, Heller came out of his room. The tailors must have delivered something, for in the elevator mirrors I could see that he was dressed in a charcoal gray casual suit—the cloth must be some kind of summer cloth that was very thin and airy but looked thick and substantial. He had a white silk shirt with what appeared to be diamond cuff links and a dark blue tie. For a change he wasn't wearing his baseball cap and in fact wore no hat at all. But when he crossed the lobby he was obviously still wearing spikes!

He clattered down the steps of a subway stop and caught a train. He got off at Times Square and was shortly clattering up Broadway past the porno shops. He turned into a cross street. I thought he must be going to a theater for he gave some attention to billboards of stage plays as he passed them.

Then he was looking up a flight of stairs. *K.O. ATHLETIC CLUB,* read the sign. He clattered on up and entered a room full of punching bags and helmeted boxers sparring around.

He was evidently expected. An attendant came over, "You Floyd?" and then beckoned. Heller followed him into a dressing room and the attendant pointed to a locker. Heller stripped and hung up his clothes. The attendant gave him a towel and shooed him through a door into a smoking haze of steam.

Heller groped around, fanned some steam out of the way and there was Bang-Bang Rimbombo, sitting on a ledge, streaming sweat and clutching a towel about him. The little Sicilian's narrow face was just a diffused patch in the fog.

"How are you?" said Heller.

"Just terrible, kid. Awful. I couldn't be worse. Sit down."

Heller sat down and dabbed at his own face with a towel. The sweat started to pour off him, too. It must be awfully hot.

They sat in utter silence, steam geysering around them. Now and then Bang-Bang would take a gulp of water from a pitcher and then Heller would take a gulp.

After nearly an hour, Bang-Bang said, "I'm starting to feel human again. My headache is gone."

"Did you take care of what I asked?" said Heller. "I hope it wasn't too much trouble."

"Oh, hell, that was easy. Hey, I can bend my neck. I haven't taken a sober breath since I saw you last." He was silent for a while and then apparently remembered what Heller had asked. "This time every week, Father Xavier goes down to Bayonne. He's Babe's confessor, knew her since she was a kid on the lower East Side. He has dinner with her and then hears her confession and then brings a load of hijacked birth control pills back to town. One of his stops is the Gracious Palms. So it wasn't any trouble. You'll have them later tonight. You don't owe me nothing. They wasn't no use."

"Thank you very much," said Heller.

"If all things was handled that easy," said Bang-Bang, "life would be worth living. But just now it ain't. You know, life can be pretty awful, kid."

"What's the matter? Maybe I can help."

"I'm afraid it's all beyond the help of God or man," said Bang-Bang. "Up the river I go next Wednesday."

"But why?" demanded Heller. "I thought you were out on parole."

"Yeah. But, kid, that arrest was very irregular. A machine gun is a Federal crime but the late Oozopopolis rigged it to be found by the New York Police and they got me on the Sullivan Law or whatever they call illegal possession. I didn't go to a Federal pen; they sent me up the river to Sing Sing."

"That's too bad," said Heller.

"Yeah. They're so crooked they can't even send you to the right jail! So when I was paroled, I of course went home to New Jersey. And right away, the parole officer dug me up and said I was out of jurisdiction, that I couldn't leave New York. So I come to New York and we don't control New York like we used to before 'Holy Joe' got wasted. So Police Inspector Bulldog Grafferty is leaning all over the parole officer to send me back to the pen to finish my time—they tell me now it's eight months, kid. Eight dry months!"

"Is it because you haven't any place to live? I could——"

"Naw, naw. I know a chick on Central Park West and I moved in with her and her five sisters."

"Well, if it's money, I could——"

"Naw, naw. Thanks, kid. I got tons of money. I get paid by the job and under the counter and that's the trouble. The parole officer made it a condition that I get a regular job. Imagine that, kid. A regular job, an artist like me! The job I do have nobody dares report and that leaves me bango right out in Times Square with no clothes on. Nobody will hire an ex-con. Babe said she'd arrange a regular pay social security job in one of the Corleone enterprises but that connects the family up to legit business—I'm too famous. I won't risk getting Babe in trouble, never. She's a great *capa*. So that's what I'm up against. They said, 'Regular job: social security, withholding tax or a charge of vagrancy and back you go this next Wednesday.' That's what the parole officer said."

"Gosh, I'm awful sorry," said Heller.

"Well, it made me feel better just getting it off my chest, kid. I feel tons better. Headache gone?" He shook his head experimentally. "Yep. Let's get a shower and get out of here and have some dinner!"

They were soon dressed. As they passed out through the training room, I suppose Heller just plain could not resist socking something—it's his vicious character. As he passed by a punching bag, he hit it. It flew off its springs.

"I'm sorry," said Heller to the attendant.

"Hey, boss!" the attendant yelled at somebody.

A very fat man with a huge cigar in his mouth came over.

"Look at what this kid did," said the attendant.

"I'll pay for it," said Heller.

"Hmm," said the fat man. "Punch this one over here, kid."

Heller went over to it and punched it. It simply vibrated back and forth—slam, slam, slam, slam.

"That other one just had a weak spring, Joe," said the fat man. "You ought to keep this equipment under repair."

I laughed. Heller couldn't punch so hard after all. He's always bragging and showing off. Good to see him come a cropper now and then.

The theater crowds had gone in. "Y'ever want to see the last end of a show," said Bang-Bang, "wait for intermission when the crowd comes out to smoke and then walk back in with them. You get to see the last acts but I always get to wondering how they got into all that trouble in the first acts, so I don't do it."

They came to a huge, glittering restaurant with a huge, glittering sign:

Sardine's

The maitre d' spotted Bang-Bang in the line and dragged him out. He led them to a small table in the back.

"Some of them diners," said Bang-Bang, "is celebrities. That's Johnny Matinee over there. And there's Jean Lologiggida. The theatrical stars all come here to eat. And after the opening night, when the stars come in, if it's a hit everybody claps and cheers. And if it's a bomb, they turn their backs."

The maitre d' put them at a small, secluded table and handed them menus. Heller looked at the prices. "Hey, this place isn't cheap. I didn't intend for you to invite me to dinner. I'll pick up the tab."

Bang-Bang laughed. "Kid, for all the glitter, this is an Italian restaurant. The Corleone family owns it. There ain't no tab. Besides, he'll just bring us antipasto, meatballs and spaghetti. Good, though."

Bang-Bang was hauling at his side. He brought out a full, unsealed fifth of Johnnie Walker Gold Label and set it on the table. "Don't look so surprised, kid. It's just going to sit there and be admired by me. I got cases of it left but I won't have any in Sing

Sing for eight months. I just want it to tell me I'm not in Sing Sing yet."

The antipasto came and they got busy on the crisp odds and ends.

A waiter drifted by, a different one, with huge spiked mustaches. *"Che c'e di nuovo, Bang-Bang?"*

"All bad," said Bang-Bang. "Meet the kid here. One of the family. Pretty Boy Floyd, this is Cherubino Gatano."

"Pleased," said Cherubino. "Can I get you anything, Floyd?"

"Some beer," said Heller.

"Hold it, hold it!" said Bang-Bang. "Don't let this bambino kid you, he's a minor and they'd have our (bleep). Got to keep it legal."

"Hold it, hold it yourself," said Cherubino. "If he's a minor, he can still have some beer."

"Since when?"

"Since now." Cherubino went off and came back shortly with a squat bottle and a tall Pilsener glass on a tray.

"You're breaking the law!" said Bang-Bang. "And me about to go back up the river. They'll add 'contributing to the delinquency of a minor' this time and never let me out!"

"Bang-Bang," said Cherubino. "I love you. I have loved you since you were a child. But you are stupid. You can't read. This is Swiss beer all right and the very best. But in this case they have taken all the alcohol out!" He pushed the bottle label at Bang-Bang. "Imported! Legal!" Then he poured the Pilsener glass full and gave it to Heller.

Heller tasted it. "Hello, hello! Delicious!"

"You see," said Cherubino, starting to take the bottle away. "You always were stupid, Bang-Bang."

"Leave the bottle," said Heller. "I want to copy the label. I'm so tired of soft cola I could burp!"

Cherubino said, "Bang-Bang and I used to stand off all the Greeks in Hell's Kitchen together, so don't get the idea we're not friends, kid. But he was always stupid and when he came back from the war they'd made him even stupider and that's impossible. See you around." He left.

Bang-Bang was laughing. "Cherubino was my captain in that same war, so he ought to know."

"What did you do in the war?" asked Heller.

"Me? I was a marine."

"Yes, but what did you *do?*" said Heller.

"Well, they say a marine is supposed to be able to do anything. They have to handle all kinds and types of weapons so they specialize less than the Army and get shot at with more variety."

"What training did you get?" said Heller.

"Well, it was pretty good. I started out real good. When I got out of boot camp, I went right to the top. They made me a gunship pilot."

"What's that?"

"Gunship, whirlybird, Green Giant, chopper. A helicopter, kid. Where you been? Don't you ever see old movies? Anyway, there I was dashing about shooting the hell out of anything that moved on the ground and suddenly they sent me to a specialist school."

"In what?"

"Demolitions." Their meatballs and spaghetti had arrived. "Oh, well, hell, kid. We're pals. I might as well tell you the truth. I crashed so many whirlybirds a colonel one day said, 'That God (bleeped) Rimbombo shows talent but he's in the wrong branch of the service. Send him to demolitions training school.' I tried to point out that choppers full of bullets don't fly well but there I went and here I am. Nobody else knows that, kid, so don't spread it around."

"Oh, I won't," said Heller. After a bit he said, "Bang-Bang, I want your opinion about something."

Ah, now we were getting to it. This Heller was sneaky. I knew all the time he was not there for nothing. I was alert. Maybe he would antagonize Bang-Bang. He sets people's nerves on edge. I know he does mine. Dangerous!

He was taking a form out of his pocket. It said:

RESERVE OFFICERS TRAINING CORPS

It was an enrollment form.

"Bang-Bang," said Heller, "look at this line here. It makes one promise to be faithful to the United States of America and support the Constitution. One is supposed to sign it. It looks like a pretty binding oath."

Bang-Bang looked at it. "Well, that's not the real oath. This next line here says you promise that when you graduate from the ROTC you will serve two years in the U.S. Army as a second lieutenant. Hmm. Yes. This is the junior or senior year form. Now, when you get out of the ROTC, they make you take the real oath. You stand up, hold up your right hand and repeat after them and get sworn in for real."

"Well, I can't sign this allegiance form," said Heller. "And later, when I graduate, I can't take any such oath."

"I understand completely," said Bang-Bang. "It's true they're just a bunch of crooks."

Heller laid the form aside and ate some spaghetti. Then he said, "Bang-Bang, I can get you a job driving a car."

Bang-Bang was alert. "With real social security, withholding tax and legit? That would satisfy the parole officer?"

"Absolutely," said Heller. "By Tuesday I'll have a corporation, all legal, and it can hire you as a driver. And that will beat your Wednesday deadline."

"Hey!" said Bang-Bang. "And I won't have to go back up the river!"

"There are a couple of conditions," said Heller.

Bang-Bang looked even more alert.

"The driving itself won't amount to much. But during the day you'll have to run some errands. It isn't really hard work and it's actually in your line."

Bang-Bang said, "Do I smell some catches in this?"

"No, no, I wouldn't ask you to do anything illegal," said Heller. "There are lots of girls around the place of work."

"Sounds interesting. But I still smell a catch."

"Well, actually, it isn't much of a catch," said Heller. "You've been a marine and know all about this sort of thing, so it's no strain. What I want you to do, in addition to these other duties, is sign this

ROTC form as J. Terrance Wister, report to three classes a week and do the drill period."

"NO!" said Bang-Bang, refusing utterly.

"They don't know me by sight and I realize we look different, but if I know such organizations, all they're interested in is somebody to yell 'Yo' when the roll is called and somebody to march around as part of the ranks."

"NO!" said Bang-Bang. And of course he was right. He was a small Sicilian, a foot shorter than Heller, brunette where Heller was blond.

"If you keep telling people your name is Terrance, and if I keep getting people to call me Jet or Jerome, other students will think we are two different people but the computers will think there's just one of us."

"NO!" said Bang-Bang.

"You could give me the material they teach and coach me in the drills. I'd be earning the credits honestly."

"NO!"

"I'll pay you whatever you ask a week to do these other things and this and you won't be sent back to prison."

"Kid. It isn't the pay. A couple hundred a week would be great. But it isn't the pay. There are just some things one can't bring himself to do!"

"Such as?" said Heller.

"Look, kid. I was a marine. Now, once a marine, always a marine. The Marines, kid, is the MARINES! Now, kid, the Army is a hell of a downstairs sort of organization. It is the Army, kid. Dogfaces. I don't think you realize that you're asking me to throw away all my principles. I couldn't even *pretend* to join the Army, kid. I'd feel so degraded I wouldn't be able to live with myself! And that's everything, kid. Pride!"

They ate some more spaghetti.

There was a change of noise level. Bang-Bang looked toward the distant door. "Hey, a new show must have just let out. I think that commotion at the door must be the stars. Now watch this, kid. If it's a great show, this whole crowd of diners here will applaud and if it was a flop, they'll turn their backs."

Heller looked. Johnny Matinee was half out of his chair, looking toward the door. Jean Lologiggida was craning her pretty neck. Three of the Sardine photographers, that had been running around taking flash pictures of diners for personal albums, got ready to shoot a big scene.

The buzz at the door increased. The crowd there parted.

In walked Police Inspector Grafferty, resplendent in full uniform!

The diners turned their backs on him with a groan.

"That's Grafferty," hissed Bang-Bang. "Got his nerve walking into a Corleone place. He's in Faustino's pay!"

Grafferty knew exactly where he was going. He was coming straight through to the back. To Bang-Bang's table!

He stopped with his right side to Heller. His interest was in Bang-Bang. "The undercover cops in the street spotted you coming in here, Rimbombo. I just wanted to get one last look at your face before they sent you back up the river."

But Heller was not looking at Grafferty. He had picked up the corner of the tablecloth and was tucking it into Grafferty's coat pocket with a fork! What a crazy thing to do! Clearly showed he had a trivial mind.

"What's this?" said Grafferty. He was reaching out for the bottle of Johnnie Walker Gold Label. "Hooch without a revenue seal on its cap! I thought I could find something if I just came . . ."

Heller's voice cut into the speech and into the room for that matter. The drone of diners' voices vanished. "Don't try to pinch my friend for contributing to the delinquency of a minor!"

Grafferty let go of the Scotch and turned to face Heller. "Who's this? Haven't I seen your face before somewhere, kid?"

In that penetrating Fleet voice of his, Heller said, "This beer is legal!"

"Beer?" said Grafferty. "A minor and beer? Oh, boy, Rimbombo, you are in for it now! And this is a licensing matter! I can get the Corleone license revoked for this whole place!"

"Look here!" said Heller. "It's nonalcoholic beer. Look at the label!"

Heller was fumblingly, hastily, pushing the empty beer bottle forward toward Grafferty. It seemed to slip. Grafferty grabbed for it.

The beer bottle hit the bottle of Scotch!

The Scotch went over the table edge!

Grafferty grabbed for the Scotch.

The Scotch hit the floor with a splintering crash!

Grafferty was still going down. He seemed to trip.

The whole tablecloth was pulled off!

Bowls of spaghetti, utensils, dirty plates and red tomato sauce hit Grafferty in an avalanche!

Jean Lologiggida was half out of her seat, looking white, hand pressed to her bosom.

Heller was up. "Oh, my goodness!" he cried and raced around the table to help Grafferty. His spikes stepped on the broken glass of the Scotch. He looked down and kicked the cap and label far away with a twitch of his foot.

He was assisting Grafferty up. From a nearby table he grabbed a red-checked cloth. He began to swab at Grafferty's face.

What a horribly bad job of cleaning! He was smearing spaghetti all over Grafferty's face, in his hair, on his tunic.

Jean Lologiggida was pressed back against the side of her booth.

Heller took Grafferty by the elbow and led him toward the star's table.

The photographers were batting out shot after shot!

Heller got Grafferty to her table. "Oh, Miss Lologiggida! Inspector Grafferty demanded the right to tell you how terribly sorry he was to disturb your dinner. The tablecloth caught in his belt. And you are sorry, aren't you, Inspector?"

Grafferty didn't know whether he was up or down. He stared at the star. He said, "Oh, my God, it's Lologiggida!" Then he saw he was still trailing the tablecloth and plates. He tore the corner of it off his belt, and while the flashguns flashed, rushed from the restaurant.

Suddenly Jean Lologiggida burst into gales of laughter! She was doubled up with it!

Johnny Matinee rushed over. "Ye gads, I wish I'd been part of that. It'll make the front page!"

Somebody, evidently Johnny Matinee's public relations man, was grabbing the photographers and having a hurried consultation with the proprietor.

The PR man said, "It's nothing to you, kid," to Heller. "Do you mind if Johnny takes your place on the front page? We'll overpaste the shots they took."

"Feel free," said Heller.

They put Johnny Matinee where Heller had stood in front of Lologiggida, got him to assume the same pose. The flashbulbs flashed.

Heller went back to the table. The restaurant was still rocking with laughter. Somebody belatedly started to applaud and Heller turned and took a bow but indicated, with his hand, Johnny Matinee. This seemed even funnier to people.

Bang-Bang was sitting there, doubled over with laughter. "Oh, *sangue di Cristo!* That Grafferty won't come near a Corleone place for a while. And you bought the joint a million in publicity!"

Heller said, soberly, "And Grafferty won't connect that bottle up with the warehouse job."

Bang-Bang looked at Heller as Heller sat back down. "Hey, I never thought of that!"

Cherubino came over. He had another nonalcoholic beer. He was grinning when he set it down. "This a good kid you got here, Bang-Bang. I'm glad he's part of our family and not some other mob! Maybe you ain't so stupid as I thought!" He went off.

Bang-Bang sat there, looking at Heller. "You know, kid, I'm going to take you up on that offer. I'll even swallow my scruples and join the Army for you." He thought for a bit. Then he said, "It's not because it'll save me from going back to jail. It's just because you're kind of fun to be around!"

But I was not as impressed as they were. Heller's tablecloth trick was something we used to do at the Academy to dumb recruits.

And any spacer has vast experience in handling barroom brawls. Heller was just taking advantage of the fact that Voltar technology was far higher than that of Earth's. Still, he was too tricky, too sneaky. And he was making too much progress!

Where the Hells was the communication from Raht and Terb? I couldn't abide the idea of seeing Heller fool all these people into thinking he amounted to something. All that (bleeping) applause!

PART NINETEEN

Chapter 1

Bright and early, Heller and Bang-Bang got off the subway at Empire Station. This morning Heller was wearing tailored gray flannel tennis slacks and a gray shirt with a white tennis sweater tied by its sleeves loosely around his neck. And he wore his inevitable red baseball cap and his spikes. He was carrying two heavy rucksacks evidently jammed with things I had no clue about.

Bang-Bang was something else. He had on some nondescript jeans and denim shirt. But on his head he wore an olive drab cap and across it in black was stenciled *USMC*.

They came up College Walk. Students were moving along, burdened with books, on their way to classes.

But Heller and Bang-Bang, much to my surprise, did not seem to be headed for a class. Heller striding along and Bang-Bang double-timing to catch up, they turned north past High Library and, threading their way around buildings, came almost to 120th Street. There was an expanse of lawn and a tree. Heller headed for the tree.

"All right, this is the command post. Synchronize your watch."

"Right," said Bang-Bang.

"Here is the schedule of plantings we took up last night in the suite."

"Right."

"Now, you've got to look at this from the viewpoint of timed fuses."

"Right!"

What in Hells were they up to? Was Heller trying to get out of his promise to Babe by blowing up the school?

"You put them in undetectably."

"Right."

"And what happens if you don't need an area mined anymore?"

"You pick them up undetectably," said Bang-Bang. "It's a secret operation. Run no risks of barrage."

"Right," said Heller. "Wait a minute. What does *USMC* mean?" Heller was looking at Bang-Bang's cap.

"Christ! 'United States Marine Corps' of course!"

"Give it to me."

"And leave myself under enemy fire with no morale support?"

Heller took it off his head. He removed his own baseball cap and put it on Bang-Bang. Of course, it was miles too big. Heller put the USMC cap on his own head. I couldn't see it but it must have looked very funny.

"I can't see," said Bang-Bang. "How am I going to plant a sensitive——"

"You're falling behind schedule," said Heller. He handed Bang-Bang one of the rucksacks. Bang-Bang sprinted away, lugging the filled bag and trying to keep the cap off his eyes.

Heller took out a ground sheet. Voltarian by the Gods—one of those inch square ones that open up to ten square feet! The kind that change color to match the ground!

It blended with the grass color. Leave it to him to keep himself neat! Bah, these Fleet guys!

He took out a gas inflatable backrest. Voltarian! It puffed up. He upended the rucksack over the ground cloth. Books spilled all over the place!

Heller sat down comfortably against the backrest, pawed the books over and found one. Aha! If Babe only could see this! He was not going to class! He was playing hooky!

The book he had was *English Literature for Advanced High-School Students as Passed by the American Medical Association. Book One. The Complete, Rewritten and Abridged Works of Charles Dickens.* It was a quarter of an inch thick and had large type. Heller, in his customary show-off way, demolished it, turning the pages faster than I could see what the page numbers were. It took him about one minute. He turned the book over, seemingly puzzled that there was no more book there. Then he took out an erasable Voltarian pen—he's always so NEAT, it really gets on your nerves! —and marked the date and the Voltarian mathematical symbol that means "equation completed pending next stage."

He put the book aside and got another one, book two of the same series, *The World's One Hundred Greatest Novels Complete, Rewritten and Abridged.* It was also a quarter of an inch thick with large type. It took him another whole minute. He marked the date and the Voltarian symbol.

There was no book three so he opened a notebook and wrote *High-School English Literature.* And then the Voltarian mathematical symbol for "operation complete."

This must have made him feel good for he looked around. Most of the students were in classes, apparently, for there were only a couple of girls loafing along, maybe graduate students. They waved, he waved.

He found another book. It was *English Literature I for First Year College as Passed by the American Medical Association. The Complete Significances You Should Get Out of Literature and What You Should Think About It.* He demolished that.

I was getting so dizzy watching the screen blur with turning pages that it was with some horror that I realized the worst. He was writing in his notebook, *First Three Years College English Literature* and the same Voltarian math symbol: "equation completed pending next stage."

I verified it twice on my watch. Only ten minutes had gone by!

Oh, I know disaster when I see it. (Bleep) him. When he went to get tutored on English literature he would just make a vulgar gesture with his thumb and say, "Yah, yah, yah!"

Bang-Bang came back. "I planted them."

"What took you so long?"

"I had to stop by the college store and get another hat. I couldn't work in your cap." And he had on a tasseled, black mortarboard. He gave Heller back his baseball cap, lay down on the

Voltarian ground sheet and promptly went to sleep.

Heller had started on journalism, an unlikely subject that had been on his grade sheet. The book was *College Journalism First Year. Essential Basic Fairy Tales of Many Lands.* I was glad to see that it was taking him longer. He wasn't reading so fast. He seemed to be enjoying something, so I split the screen and still-framed the other one so I could read it. My Gods, it was the story of the lost continent of Atalantis!

He dawdled along and it took him a half hour to finish College Journalism. Then he saw that he was supposed to have written a sort of end-of-course paper. He got out his bigger notebook, the one he doodled in. He wrote:

CONTINENT SINKS

MILLIONS LOST

Circulation today was boosted by the timely event of a continent vanishing. Publishers ecstatic.

The event was further heightened by a conflict of opinion by leading experts.

However, an unknown expert leaked to this paper—sources cannot be disclosed despite Supreme Court rulings—that all was not known about this event.

The unidentified expert, who shall be nameless, declared that this colony had been founded by an incursion from outer space under the command of that sterling revolutionary and nobleman of purpose and broad vision, none other than Prince Caucalsia from the province of Atalanta, planet of Manco.

Some of the survivors, who emigrated immediately to the Caucasus, which is behind the Iron Curtain and human beings can't usually go there, were incarcerated by the KGB. Deportation soon followed and they arrived maybe in New York.

The public will be kept informed.

Heller punched Bang-Bang. "Read this."

"Why me?" said Bang-Bang, groggy in what must have been a warm morning.

"Well, somebody has got to read it and pass it. It's the end-of-course paper in Journalism. If nobody reads it and passes it, I can't have the credit for it."

Bang-Bang sat up. He read it with lip movement. "What's this word *incarcerated*?"

"Put in the slammer," said Heller.

"Oh, yeah. Hey, that's a good word. 'Incarcerpated.'"

"Well, do I pass?"

"Oh, hell, yes. Anybody that knows that many big words is a genius. Hey, I got to get going. Time for another line of charges!" Bang-Bang raced off, tassel of his mortarboard streaming in the wind.

Heller wrote, *College Journalism. Passed with In-the-Field Citation.*

Two more girls drifted by. They stopped to pass the time of day. "What's your major?" one asked Heller.

"It was Journalism. But I just passed it with Battle Honors. What's yours?"

"Advanced Criticism," said one.

"See you around," said Heller.

After a while, Bang-Bang came back. "First charges picked up. Second series laid." He went back to sleep.

Frankly, they were driving me nuts! What were they doing? Why didn't I hear some explosions as buildings went up?

Heller demolished a couple more subjects and passed himself in his notebook. Bang-Bang had come back again and was once again fast asleep.

Now Heller had gotten into high-school chemistry. But this time he was really tangled. I could tell. He was yawning and yawning. Tension! In fact, it was evidently too much for him for he laid it aside and picked up a text on high-school physics. He read for a while, yawning. Then he picked up the chemistry text again and began looking from it to the physics text.

"Hey," he told the texts. "Agree amongst you on *something*, will you?"

A clear-cut case of animistic fixation, his habit of talking to things. No wonder he couldn't understand clear-cut texts.

He finished up the chemistry including the college texts on it and then got going once more on physics. He kept going back earlier and looking again.

And then, I couldn't believe it! He started to laugh. He always was sacrilegious. Little spurts of laughter kept erupting. And then he read some more and he laughed some more. And then he got to laughing harder and harder and rolled off the backrest and beat at the ground with his fists!

"What the hell is going on?" said Bang-Bang, waking up. "You reading comic books or something?"

Heller got control of himself and it was time he did! "It's a text on primitive superstitions," said Heller. "Look, it's almost noon. Pick up those last charges and we'll have some lunch."

Ah, they were threatening the school! Demanding ransom?

Heller had everything gathered up and they went off and bought sandwiches and pop from a mobile lunch wagon.

"Operation right on schedule," said Heller.

"We made our beachhead," said Bang-Bang.

They enjoyed the view of girls as they strolled around. Heller bought a couple of papers. Then, "Time!" said Heller sternly. And Bang-Bang raced off again. When he came back, Heller had the command post all set up and Bang-Bang went to sleep.

If they weren't blowing things up, and I had heard no explosions, this was about the strangest way to go to college I had ever seen. You're supposed to go and sit down and listen to lectures and take notes and hurry to another class. . . .

Heller was halfway through trigonometry when Bang-Bang said, "I'll pick up the last series and lay the next. But then I got to go report to the Army and you'll have to take over."

Heller finished trigonometry and told it, "You sure go the long way round." But he entered it in his notebook as passed.

Bang-Bang returned and dropped the rucksack he had been racing about with. "Well, here goes the pig into the mire. You got the watch now."

Heller had gotten tired of studying, apparently, for he packed his books up. His watch winked at him in Voltarian figures that it was a bit after two. He opened up one of the papers he had bought.

He looked all through it. He couldn't find a trace of what he was looking for: he kept muttering, "Grafferty? Grafferty?"

He opened up the second paper. He got clear back to the photo section before he found it. It was a picture of an indistinct fireman climbing down a ladder carrying an unrecognizable woman. The caption said:

Police Inspector Grafferty last night rescued Jean Matinee from a burning spaghetti parlor.

Heller told the paper, "Now that I am a passed-with-honors journalist, I can truly appreciate the grave responsibility of keeping the public informed."

I heard that with some amusement. It just showed one how superficial he was. He had the purpose of the media all wrong! Its purpose, of course, is to keep the public *mis*informed! Only in that way can governments, and the people who own and use them, keep the public confused and milked! They trained us in such principles very well in the Apparatus schools.

And then an irritation of worry tinged my amusement. All this data he was getting, right or wrong, could be dangerous to me. It might accidentally make him think.

There was one field he mustn't study. And that was the subject of espionage. I didn't think it was taught in American public schools, even though I knew it was a required subject in Russian kindergartens so the children could spy on their parents. I knew that America often copied what the Russians did. I crossed my fingers. I hoped it wasn't one of his required subjects. I tried to read some of the text titles that were spread around.

Heller went back to his studies. At 2:45 he packed up all his gear, hefted the two rucksacks and trotted off. He paused in a hall, watching a door.

Ah, now I was going to find out what they had been up to!

Students streamed out of the room. The professor came bustling out and went up the hall.

Heller walked into the empty classroom. He went straight to the lecture platform. He reached down into the wastebasket.

He pulled out a tape recorder!

He shut it off.

He put it in the rucksack.

Heller pulled out a small instant recording camera, stepped back and shot the diagrams on the blackboard.

He put the camera away.

He left the room.

He raced over to another building.

He stepped into an empty classroom. He went to the platform, took a different recorder out of the rucksack, verified that it was loaded with 120-minute tape, put it on "record," placed it in the bottom of the wastebasket and threw some paper over it and then walked out of the room just as a couple students were entering.

Outside, he leaned up against a building. He took the first recorder he had recovered, checked to make sure it had worked properly and removed the cassette. He marked the tape with date and subject, fastened the blackboard picture to it with a rubber band and put the package in a compartmented cassette box marked Advanced Chemistry. He checked the recorder battery charge, reloaded it with blank 120 tape and put it back in the rucksack.

Oh, the crook! He and Bang-Bang were simply recording all the lectures! He didn't intend to go to a single class in that college!

Oh, I knew what he would do. He would speed-rig a playback machine as he had done with languages and zip a lecture through it in a minute or so at his leisure! Maybe even save them up and do the whole three months' course in under an hour!

What dishonesty! Didn't he know that the FBI arrested people for doing unauthorized recording? Or was that for copying and selling copyrighted material? I couldn't remember. But anyway, it was an awful shock to me! He had a chance of getting through college in spite of Miss Simmons!

I had a momentary glimmer of hope. There might be quizzes. There might be lab periods. But then I sank into a deeper gloom. Heller had probably figured those out, too!

(Bleep) him, he was defeating the efforts to defeat him! My hand itched for a blastick! I had better quadruple any effort I was making to put an end to him!

Chapter 2

Rucksacks and all, Heller went for a run. He went west on 120th Street, south on Broadway, east on 114th Street, north on Amsterdam, circumnavigating the whole university. He was obviously trying to kill time. I hoped he would look out of place and maybe even get arrested for something, but there were lots of other joggers or people late for something.

At 3:45, he began to drift back to the job of picking up and planting recorders. Then he went back to the original "command post" and looked expectantly around for Bang-Bang. He muttered, "The marines should have disengaged by now. Where are you, Bang-Bang?" No Bang-Bang.

Heller went for a run on a path in Morningside Park and then came back and picked up what seemed to be the last recorder of the day.

He returned to the "command post." No Bang-Bang. His watch winked at him in Voltarian numbers that it was 5:10.

Heller found a shady place, spread his ground sheet again, reinflated his backrest and sat down. He didn't study. He just kept watching for Bang-Bang. The shadows grew longer and longer. He looked at his watch oftener and oftener. Finally it was 5:40.

And here came something!

It was approaching down a path. It looked more like a mound of baggage with two legs than a person.

Towering and unsteady, the mountain came near Heller. It tipped over and crashed on the lawn. It avalanched for a few seconds longer and then there was Bang-Bang, standing amongst the debris. He was out of breath from the effort. He moved over and collapsed on the ground sheet.

"Well," said Bang-Bang, "the engagement was bloody and prolonged. I will give you my battle report, Marines versus Army." He composed himself. "You presented yourself on time to the standard army confusion of ROTC induction. You signed the form as 'J. Terrance Wister.' You then presented yourself to the first obstacle of the obstacle course.

"As you were new to this ROTC, you had a physical examination. Now, you will be horrified to know that you have incipient cirrhosis of the liver from overindulgence in alcohol. I'm glad it wasn't my physical. I have sixteen cases of Scotch left. So you were passed, providing you stop drinking.

"You then proceeded to the next obstacle. Uniforms and equipment. Those are them," he indicated with a disdainful hand toward a pile of clothes. "The quartermaster insisted everything would be a perfect fit. But I'll have to get them to an alterations tailor right away, get them taken in and let out to really fit me. I refuse to have you looking so *sloppy!* Even if it *is* the Army, there is just so much a marine can take! So, you got over that obstacle.

"The next wasn't so easy. You know what those (bleepards) did? They tried to issue me a defective M-1 rifle! Now, you know and I know that a marine can be socked a whole month's pay if his piece is found defective. And (bleep) it, kid, its firing pin was sawed off! Yes! Sawed right off! They tried to argue with me and I bench stripped it right there down to the last screw! They said ROTC trainees weren't allowed to have a firing pin. They said somebody might put a live round in the chamber and when they did inspection arms it might go off. And, boy, I let them have it. The *dangerous* thing is to have an inoperational weapon! You get charged, you can't shoot! And I said, 'What if you want to shoot some colonel in the back? How about that?' And that stopped them. They couldn't put the weapon back together and I refused to as I said it ought to be sent to the gunnery sergeant and repaired, and finally a Regular Army captain said he'd put in a request to allow you to have a nondefective

M-1. So they'll issue the rifle later but you got by that. All right so far, kid?"

"Perfectly reasonable," said Heller. "Bad enough to have a chemical weapon already without its being defective. Must be an awful army."

"Oh, it is, it is," said Bang-Bang. "Dogfaces. Anyway, then you came to the swamp and no ropes to get over it so I had to make up your mind for you and I hope I did right.

"Some Regular Army lieutenant with glasses noticed it was your senior year and noticed in your prior military training at Saint Lee's that you'd never indicated preference for branch of service. Well, I hedged. But he said the classroom work in your senior year depended on it and you had to choose. And so he handed me a long list.

"Well, kid, I knew you didn't want to dig latrines, so the infantry is out. And I didn't want some dumb army jerk pulling a lanyard on a 155 when your head was in the barrel, so the artillery is out. And these days, all tanks is good for is to get burned up in, so that's out. I knew that you, like me, hated MPs, so that's out. When I finished the list, it left only one thing. I hope you will like it. G-2."

"What's that?"

"Intelligence. Spies! It seemed to sort of fit my job right now— a marine infiltrating the Army. So I knew it would make you feel good, too."

I didn't feel good. I reeled!

Bang-Bang got to the books and pamphlets in the mountain. They were marked *Restricted* and *Confidential* and *Secret.*

"Look at this one," said Bang-Bang. "*Codes, Ciphers and Cryptography. How to Talk Secret.* Look at these things. *How to Train Spies. How to Sneak Somebody Back of the Enemy Lines to Poison the Water. How to Seduce the Wife of the Enemy General and Get Her to Get You Tomorrow's Battle Plans.* Good, solid stuff! And look at the number of these manuals. Dozens! *How to Tail a Russian Agent. How to Select Sensitive Targets to Destroy Industrial Capacity.* Good, solid stuff, kid!"

"Let me see those." And he got hold of one about blowing up

trains. And then another about the art of infiltration. Heller started to laugh.

"Are you pleased, kid?"

"Fantastic," said Heller.

"Oh, I'm glad you're pleased, kid. I just thought I was being a little bit selfish. You see, it makes me feel less degraded."

Bang-Bang recovered his USMC fatigue cap and put it on. Then he got an army fatigue cap and put it on over it, hiding the marine one.

Then Bang-Bang got down on all fours and crept to the other side of the tree and peered out with exaggerated care. He was clowning!

"Spies," said Bang-Bang. "A marine spying on the Army! Get it, kid?"

Heller was laughing. He was laughing very hard. But I knew he wasn't laughing at the same thing Bang-Bang was.

Suddenly I knew how Izzy Epstein must have felt when the catastrophe he had dreaded struck. This Earth espionage technology was probably pretty crude. But it *was* espionage technology. It would make my job so much harder!

I hastily wrote another dispatch to the New York office repeating my earlier order to find Raht and Terb and promising torture along with extinction if they didn't comply! Heller had to be stopped!

Chapter 3

About the only thing different about Friday was that they had a different command post and iced soft drinks in a bucket!

What a way to go to college! Lying around on the lawn, watching the girls go by. Well, it was Bang-Bang who did most of the girl watching. Heller was getting caught up on grammar school and high school and college. But Bang-Bang did enough girl watching for both of them. Still, what an idyllic scene. How pastoral! Disgusting!

Saturday, however, was different. Bang-Bang had disappeared somewhere, some muttering about drilling. But Heller reported to some hall and began to take "counseling examinations" to determine which subjects and what part of them he should be tutored on.

I had slept late and when I did the scan through, I simply ignored his rapid pen movements on the exams he was doing. He is always showing off. I sped straight through to an interview he was having with some assistant dean.

"Agnes," the assistant dean was calling over his shoulder. "Are you sure that marking machine is in repair?"

A voice floated back. "Yes, Mr. Bosh. It has been flunking its quota all morning."

Mr. Bosh, an intense-eyed young man, fiddled with the big stack of completed exam papers he had and then looked at Heller. "There must be some mistake here. Your grade transcript said these were all D average and these exams are A average." A very severe glint came in his eye. "There is something unexplained here, Wister."

"Sometimes students have been known to date the wrong some-body's daughter," said Heller.

Mr. Bosh sat up straight and then beamed. "Of course, of course. I should have thought of that. Happens all the time!"

Chuckling to himself, he bundled the exam papers up and marked them *To be microfilmed for student's file.* "Well, Wister, all I can say is, you're off the hook. There are no weak spots here to be tutored, so we will simply mark that completed in your admission requirements. All right?"

"Thank you very much," said Heller.

Mr. Bosh leaned forward and said in a low voice, "Tell me, just off the record, you didn't knock her up, did you?"

Heller leaned over and whispered, "Well, I'm *here* for my senior year, aren't I?"

Mr. Bosh went into howls of laughter. "I knew it, I knew it! Oh, priceless!" And with great camaraderie, he shook Heller's hand and that was that.

There was something in Bosh's attitude that irritated me. Possibly the way he was beaming at Heller. There was nothing that remarkable about Heller's passing: he had had several days and several long evenings in the lobby to review those subjects and, to him, it must have been a sort of ethnological study of how some primitive might view these things. There was nothing remarkable at all about a postgraduate combat engineer of the Voltarian Fleet passing a few lousy kiddie subjects like perverted quantum mechanics. It made me quite cross, really. Spoiled my faith in these Earth people—not that I'd ever had any. Just riffraff.

I walked around the yard for a while. Two of the children were picking grapes and I accused them of eating more than they picked and after I'd gotten them crying real good, kicked them and felt better.

I called the taxi driver and wanted to know when the Hells he was going to complete delivery of Utanc and he told me it was all on schedule. That made me feel a lot better. Watching that (bleeper) Heller being whistled into his room every night by gorgeous women had been getting to me more than I had admitted. And that I never actually saw him doing anything with them made it even worse! One's imagination runs riot sometimes!

Only the possible early arrival of Utanc gave me morale enough to go back and watch what was happening around Heller. But all he was doing was trotting around a track in a running suit, not even making good time. He stopped and watched a football squad being mustered up, apparently lost interest and resumed his running. How can anybody just run for a couple of hours? What do they think about?

I went outside again, and after a long delay in locating him, talked on the phone to the hospital contractor who said the earth-moving was almost finished, the water, electrical and sewage ready to place and he'd be into pouring foundations tomorrow. So I couldn't find anything to rag him about beyond being at the building site working when I was trying to call him.

It was late evening, Turkish time, by now. There was a sort of fascination about watching Heller. I desperately longed for a time when I would see him curl up in a ball, preferably in agony, and die and yet, so long as I did not have the platen, he carried my life in his careless, brutal hands. So I hung on to the viewscreen and raced the strips forward to the present.

Heller was going down in the elevator. He was dressed in a casual dark suit but there was nothing casual about the way he was acting.

He rushed out of the elevator and burst into Vantagio's office. "It's here! It's here! The car I want is here!"

Vantagio was in a tuxedo, apparently all ready for a Saturday night rush not yet started. "Well, it's about time! Babe mentions it every day and ever since you spaghettied Grafferty she's been insisting it be the best. Where is it? Out front or down in the garage?"

"Garage," said Heller. "Come on!"

Vantagio needed no urging. He went rapidly out of his office, followed by Heller, and into the elevator they went and down to the garage.

"It better be a beauty," said Vantagio. "I got to get this action completed so I can have some peace. Been over a week since Babe told me to buy you a lovely car!"

At the garage elevator exit, there stood Mortie Massacurovitch. Heller introduced him to Vantagio. "I been workin' double shift," said Mortie. "I couldn't get here until this evening. But there she is!"

Standing in the middle of the vast pillared structure, surrounded by sleek limousines of the latest model, stood the old, shabby, paint-worn-off, cracked-window Really Red Cab of decades ago.

It looked like a piece of junk that had been shoveled in.

"Where's the car?" said Vantagio.

"That's the car," said Heller.

"Oh, come off it, kid. A joke's a joke but this is serious business. Babe will just about tear my head off if I don't get you one."

"Hey," said Heller, "this is a great car!"

"This was built when they really built cabs!" said Mortie.

"Kid, this isn't any joke? You mean you are really proposing I buy this piece of scrambled trash for you?"

"Hey," said Mortie, "the company ain't charging hardly anything!"

"I'm sure they wouldn't dare!" said Vantagio. "You ought to give the buyer twenty-five smackers to get it towed to a junkyard!"

"Oh, come on," said Mortie. "I'll admit she don't *look* like no limousine. But I had quite a time trying to get the company to agree to sell it. It's sort of a keepsake. Like old times. Tradition! Of course, you can't keep it red or run it as a Really Red Cab in competition and you can't have its taxi license—that's expensive and stays with the company. But it's a perfectly legal car and the title would be regular."

Vantagio had looked inside. He backed off holding his nose. "Oh, my God."

"It's just the leather," said Mortie. "They didn't have vinyl in them days so it's real leather. Of course, it's kind of rotted and saturated a bit. But it's real leather."

"Please," said Heller.

Vantagio said, "Babe would kill me. She would have me whipped for two or three hours and then kill me with her bare hands."

"I got orders that you can have it cheap," said Mortie. "One thousand dollars and that's rock bottom."

"Quit torturing me!" said Vantagio. "I got a tough night ahead. This is Saturday night and the UN is hotting up—in just two weeks it is reconvening! Kid, have you got any idea——"

"Five hundred," said Mortie. "And that's absolutely rock bottom."

Vantagio tried to walk away. Heller got him by the arm. "Look, real quarter-inch steel fenders and body. Look, Vantagio, real bulletproof windows! See those stars in them? They stopped real bullets just a while ago."

"Two hundred and fifty," said Mortie. "And that's rock rock bottom."

"Kid," said Vantagio, "please, for God's sake, let me go upstairs and call the MGB agency, let them send over a red sports car."

"This cab," said Heller, "is a real beauty!"

"Kid, let me call the Mercedes-Benz agency."

"No."

"Alfa Romeo?"

"No."

"Maserati. Now, there's a good car. A real good car," said Vantagio. "I can get one custom built. Custom built and bright red, kid. A convertible. I'll fill it full of girls."

"No," said Heller.

"Oh, *che il diavolo lo porti,* kid, you're going to get me killed! I wouldn't even dare put that in this garage! It's just an ancient wreck!"

"It's an antique!" cried Mortie. "It ain't no wreck! It's a bona fide antique!"

Vantagio stared at him. Then he went on pacing.

Mortie pressed on. "You put that cab in the Atlantic City Antique Auto Parade and it'll win a twenty-five-thousand-dollar prize. I guarantee it! Antique cars are the rage!"

Vantagio stopped pacing. "Wait. I've just had an idea. If we put that car in the Atlantic City Antique Auto Parade . . ."

"And filled it full of girls dressed in costumes of the 1920s," prompted Heller.

"And put guys on the running boards holding submachine guns," said Vantagio.

"And prohibition agents in 1920 costumes chasing it," said Heller.

"And painted 'The Corleone Cab Company' on the doors," cried Vantagio, "Babe would LOVE it! Tradition! And a million bucks' worth of advertising! Right?"

"Right," said Heller.

"Now, you have to do what I tell you, kid. Right?"

"Right."

"Choose this as the car."

"Like I was saying," said Mortie. "The price is one thousand smackers."

"Five hundred," said Vantagio, "providing you can get it to this address. And I'll buy its cab license later from your company." He was scribbling on the back of a card, *Jiffy-Spiffy Garage, Mike Mutazione, Newark, N.J.*

"Can I drive it and monkey with the motor?" said Heller.

"Oh, hell, yes, kid. It's your car. Just so long as you make it available for the parade and just as long as you let Mike Mutazione put it in new-car condition before you park it in here. You see, I can tell people it's for the parade and the UN diplomats will be happy on cultural grounds. They love to see tribal customs preserved."

A new voice was heard. "Hey, where'd this battle casualty come from?" It was Bang-Bang.

"That's the car you're going to drive," said Heller.

"Don't try to snow me under, kid," said Bang-Bang. "I've had a tough day trying to teach the Army the difference between their left feet and their (bleep)."

"Look, Bang-Bang," said Heller, pointing to a star in the glass.

"Hey, that's a 7.62 mm NATO round. See, it dropped down into the ledge outside. Belgian FN? Italian Beretta? Flattened the hell out of it. Bulletproof glass!"

"And fenders. Quarter-inch steel," said Heller.

Vantagio tapped Bang-Bang. "As long as you're working for the kid, go over to Newark with this cabby and tell Mike what to do. Use the same material but replace everything! New bulletproof glass, new upholstery, beat the body out, paint the whole car orange and put 'The Corleone Cab Company' on the doors. Make it all look brand-new. Even the motor. Tell him to do it in a hurry so the kid can have his car."

"I ain't supposed to leave New York," said Bang-Bang.

"It's Saturday night," said Vantagio.

"Oh, that's right," said Bang-Bang.

"I'll go, too!" said Heller.

"No, you won't," said Vantagio. "It's going to be a busy night and I want you in the lobby for a while. And I told two South American diplomats you'd be pleased to meet them. And there's something else you got to do."

Vantagio was signing papers that Mortie had been holding out. He counted five hundred into his palm.

Mortie and Bang-Bang jumped into the cab and with a roar, smoke and clatter were gone.

Vantagio and Heller got back into the elevator. "Now we got to go up," said Vantagio, "and phone Babe and tell her what a great idea I had. No, on the other hand, you phone her from your suite and tell her you thought it up. Tradition is the key to her character, kid. And when you mix tradition and sentiment, it's a winner every time. Old 'Holy Joe' got his start running hooch in cabs just like that!"

"You're a wonder," said Heller.

"Yes, you do what I tell you and you'll be in the money every time. Just remember that, kid."

I was baffled, utterly baffled. What was Heller doing with *two* cars? He already had that old Cadillac being specially rebuilt and didn't seem to be in any rush for it, yet here was this cab being rushed through. For once, some sixth sense—which you can't do without in the Apparatus—told me that this went beyond the Fleet toy fetish. I writhed. (Bleep) him, he was going too fast! Too fast! He could finish up and accomplish something and ruin me!

Chapter 4

Because I knew that on Sunday, coming right up, he was going to have his first Nature Appreciation class with Miss Simmons—who, I was sure, would do him in—I was not terribly interested in what happened to Heller the rest of that Saturday night and scanned him only lightly.

The two South American diplomats were completely unimportant. Vantagio brought them over to Heller and introduced them—they had names about a yard long. Heller was wearing a silk and mohair tuxedo with diamond cuff links and studs but these two South Americans put him to shame with black embroidery on their powder blue tuxedos and lace all over their chests: it heartened me to see Heller outdone.

They had an International Bank loan to build a lot of bridges and they'd heard Heller was a student engineer and they didn't think the bridges would stand up. So they showed him some drawings and he told them to float both ends of the bridges so the earthquakes couldn't affect them. He even drew them some little sketches to show their contracting firm. But I knew it was all silly—a bridge *crosses* water you don't stick its ends *in* the water. But South Americans are polite and they went away beaming. Riffraff.

The only other thing that happened was also disgusting. Stuffumo and the kris-wielding deputy delegate that Heller had unfairly disarmed sought him out where he sat behind some palm fronds—he sat there often as it half hid him from the door.

They had an ornate box and they were both holding on to it. Both speaking English in chorus, they stood in front of him and said, "Thank you for your mediation on the treaty subject of Harlotta. Our two countries have united to give you a token of appreciation. There has never been such peace."

They opened up the box and there, in purple velvet, lay a Llama .45 caliber, large-frame automatic pistol finished in gold damascene and gold butt plates, with the coats of arms of their two countries intertwined with a heart. Some engraver had been working overtime at vast expense! It had extra magazines and fifty shells. It also had a back belt holster with a white dove of peace and *Prince X* engraved on it. Aside from the fact that it was all chased with gold instead of being black, it looked just like a gangster gun, an Army Colt .45.

Heller thanked them and they went away beaming.

It absolutely ruined my dawn sleep! The idea of getting a beautiful weapon like that for some petty, trifling, cheap trick! And he had obtained it unfairly, too! Masquerading under a false identity. "Prince X" indeed! He was just a Fleet combat engineer with middle-class origins like mine. I even outranked him! What an awful waste of a fine handgun!

So, as I say, I was really looking forward to Miss Simmons!

Around nine in the morning, New York time, the interference went off in his suite. But was he bustling out to go to his Sunday class? No! He was certainly taking a perverted angle on Nature Appreciation!

The first thing that came on the screen was the back of a girl's neck. She was a brunette and she was evidently lying face down on the sofa, head to one side, arm trailing limply to the rug, the very picture of exhaustion.

Heller was stroking the back of her neck, sort of working at it with his thumbs. There was a silver pitcher on a nearby table and, in peripheral vision, I could see that he was wearing a white bathrobe and sitting on the edge of the couch above the half-naked girl.

"Oh," she was groaning, "I think I'm going to die!"

Heller was working at the back of her neck with his thumbs.

"There, there," he said soothingly. "You'll be all right, Myrtle."

She groaned again. "Seventeen times is too many!"

"Can you lift your head now?" said Heller.

She tried and groaned. "I feel like I've been raped by an elephant."

"I'm sorry," said Heller.

Suddenly I understood. This monster had really been abusing this poor girl! And she was a pretty girl, too, as I could see, now that she had turned on her side.

"It is better, honey," she said. "Jesus, I don't want another night like that!"

Aha, so he was not as popular with these girls as I had thought!

She got up unsteadily, got hold of her robe as an afterthought and half-heartedly covered her nakedness.

"You go get a bath," said Heller, "and a nice sleep and you'll be fine."

"Oh, Jesus, I hope so. Can I come back later?"

My Gods, I thought. He has effected a transference on this poor girl! Enslaved her into chronic masochism!

"I've got a Nature Appreciation class at one," said Heller.

"I've had all the nature I can appreciate for the moment," said Myrtle and stumbled, barefooted and half-clad from his room. The poor, abused creature.

Heller called down for some breakfast and while he was waiting, got on the phone. No wonder I couldn't keep track of him. He was transacting business under the cover of the interference. Sneaky!

A kid came on.

"Let me talk to Mike Mutazione," said Heller. And when the kid had put "papa" on the line, Heller said, "Sorry to bite into your Sunday, Mike. But did you get the cab?"

"Sure thing, kid. A beauty! Fix her up in no time!"

"Great. Now listen, Mike. I am sending you over a little bottle of stuff. I'll write the full directions. But I want you to put it in the paint as an additive. That's on the exterior body and in any of the signs you paint on it. It is easy. It just mixes into whatever paint you use. So when you get the motor and glass and body and upholstery work done, only use paint with this additive in it."

"Makes it shinier?" said Mike.

"Something like that," said Heller. "I'll send the little vial over. It'll be there by the time you're ready."

"Sure, kid, no trouble. The Caddy is doing fine. Bit of a holdup with the new engine but it's on its way. So are the new alloy pistons. She'll do 190 when we're done." Mike laughed. "You'll have to keep the brakes on to keep her from taking off for the moon."

"Take your time on it," said Heller. "The cab I'd like yesterday."

"You'll get it, kid. Want to come over and go to Mass with us?"

"Today is my day for Nature Appreciation. Thanks just the same, Mike. *Ciao.*"

Mass? These (bleeped) Sicilians would be converting him to Christianity next!

His breakfast came, starting with a huge chocolate sundae. The waiter had no more than gone out the door when a gorgeous, slinky blonde came in.

"Hiya, Semantha," said Heller. "Have some breakfast?"

She shook her head and sat down in a nearby chair. She indicated the door. "Myrtle was just in here, wasn't she? Pretty boy, you've got to watch that Myrtle."

Heller laughed.

"No, seriously, pretty boy. You've got to watch her. She's full of wiles and tricks. I know her. Now, look, when she came in, did she do this?" Semantha loosened her robe. She didn't have anything on under it! Was this Heller's idea of nature appreciation?

She drew her legs to Heller's right. "And then did she sit sideways like this?" She made sure no robe was covering her legs. "And then did she show you her naked thigh like this? And then trail her fingers along it and say that it was bruised and please look?

"Oh, you have to watch that Myrtle, pretty boy. After she'd done all that, did she stand up like this and let her robe fall off like so?

"And then did she say she had an ache in her left breast? And, typically Myrtle, hold it up like this and ask you to see if there was a bruise there?

"And then did she walk real close like this and ask you to really examine it to be sure?"

Heller was laughing. "Watch it, you'll get ice cream on you!"

"And then," said Semantha, "did she sort of walk around like this? Oh, you've got to watch her! And pick up her robe like this? And pretend she'd just noticed she was naked, like this, and trail her robe behind her like this and go into your bedroom, looking back at you like this? You watch that Myrtle, pretty boy!"

"The bed isn't made," said Heller.

He could see what she was doing now from the multiple reflecting mirrors in the bedroom. "Then," continued Semantha, "did she poke at your bed like this? And then wonder if it was softer than hers and could she please get in it like this?"

Semantha had gotten in, but not under the covers. She was stretched out stark naked on the bed, legs apart. "And then did she stroke her body like this? Did she, pretty boy? She takes some watching, that Myrtle does! And then did she raise her arms toward you like this and move her hips around like that and tell you that she was feeling sort of empty and needed . . ."

"Semantha," said Heller. "Get out of that bed and come in here."

"Oh, pretty boy," she pouted. "You're going to make me stand up and hold that position while you . . ."

The interference came on. Well, I didn't need to see any more. It was obvious that he was one of those weirdos that liked odd positions.

Why the Hells couldn't that (bleeped) taxi driver rush up Utanc? I went out petulantly to call him. He didn't know what he was putting me through. I tried for quite a while and couldn't get him. I kicked around the yard and then had dinner.

Actually, I was outraged at Heller's idea of preparing himself for a Nature Appreciation class. How he could go from his dark den of vice into the bright sunlit world without his conscience withering, I did not know. He was not fit to associate with the dear little children and the charming Miss Simmons in their coming outing. But I knew I could count on Miss Simmons! Heller would catch it! A firm character, Miss Simmons!

Chapter 5

The first Nature Appreciation class was apparently being held in the United Nations park between 42nd Street and 48th Street and bordering the East River—just a few blocks from where Heller lived.

It was a beautiful September afternoon: the grass and trees were green and the sky and water were blue. The enormous bulk of the Secretariat Building reared its white slab behind the General Assembly Building and the Conference Building.

Some of the class had already gathered, as scheduled, in front of the Statue of Peace. They were college kids, mostly in jeans and rough clothing; some wore glasses, some did not; some were fat and some were thin. Heller looked them over. None of them were talking to one another or to him: obviously, they were all mutual strangers.

Heller was wearing, I knew from the elevator mirrors, very tailored brushed jeans, his baseball cap and spikes. He must look a bit out of place—neater and more expensively dressed aside from those two items, cap and shoes. He was also taller than the rest. And he carried a little brushed denim haversack while the rest had satchels or just big purses. It must make him stand out for an occasional eye flicked in his direction, especially the girls.

More class drifted up and now there were about thirty.

And here came Miss Simmons! She was marching with a purpose! She was wearing heavy hiking shoes and, despite the heat of the day, a heavy tweed skirt and jacket. She was carrying a walking stick that looked more like a club. Her brown hair was tightly swept back and imprisoned under a man's shooting hat.

She came to a halt. She pushed her horn-rimmed glasses up on her forehead so she could see them. She looked them all over. When she came to Heller, she let go of the glasses and let them fall back on her nose. Ah, this was a good sign. I had confidence in Miss Simmons. If all else failed, this was the one who would stop Heller cold! And her opening words encouraged me greatly!

"Oh, there you are, Wister," she said in front of the whole class. "How is the young Einstein today? Suffering from a swelled head? I hear you used more INFLUENCE yesterday to get out of further tutoring. Well, have no fear, you are not through the barbed wire yet, Wister. The war you so ferociously favor is barely begun!"

She raised her glasses again so she could see the class and proceeded to address them. "Good afternoon, tomorrow's hope. I always start our Nature Appreciation itinerary here at the United Nations park. The United Nations was founded in 1945 to prevent the further escalation of WAR and atomic war in particular. This hope was then entombed here in these great white mausoleums.

"It is of historical significance that this part of Manhattan was once an area covered with slaughterhouses. It is a very apt and fitting fact.

"The UN, this dark grave of all man's greatest hopes, has money, authority and POWER! Yet, I must call to your attention that, despite that, these greedy, self-seeking and egotistical MEN sit in these tombs all day every day, all year every year and do nothing but plot ways and means of avoiding their true duties, duties to which they were pledged by the most sacred vows!

"If these craven, base scoundrels had their way, they would blow up the whole world with thermonuclear fission and fusion! Wister, pay attention." She lowered her glasses and scowled at him.

She raised her glasses and addressed the rest. "So, class, we start with a could-have-been, the United Nations. Everything you see alive throughout this course will soon be dead forever— destroyed by the vicious idleness, the indecision, the behind-the-scenes plotting and downright craven cowardice of the UN Wister, what are you looking at?"

Heller said, "This grass is standing up pretty good despite the foot traffic. If they didn't water it with chlorinated water, it would do better."

"Pay attention, Wister," said Miss Simmons, severely. "This is a class in nature appreciation, not the use of poison gas! Now, class, and I hope you are taking notes of the important data I am giving you. Do you see that group of men there? I want to call your attention to the smug, maddeningly blithe expressions on the faces of those UN people stalking about the park."

Heller said, helpfully, "It says on their blue and gold caps and badges 'American Legion Post 89, Des Moines, Iowa.' Is that a member country?"

Miss Simmons quite rightly ignored him. "So you must note, class, and note with horror and indignation, the attitude of irresponsibility which prevails here. If these men would only do their duty . . . Wister, what *are* you looking at?"

"These leaves," said Heller. "All in all, these trees are doing pretty good in all these oil fumes from the river. I think the soil is probably slightly demineralized, though."

"Pay attention to your classwork!" snapped Miss Simmons. "Now, class, if the UN would ever do its duty, we could end utterly and forever man's lemming fixation on self-destruction."

"What's a *lemming*?" said a girl.

"They are hordes of horrible rats that go plunging in masses into the sea annually, committing mass suicide," said Miss Simmons helpfully. "If it wished, in a single, soul-stirring surge, the UN could rise up with clarion voices and cry 'DEATH TO THE CAPITALIST WARMONGERS!' Wister, what in the name of God are you looking at NOW?"

There were three seagulls lying along the concrete parapet. Their feet were stuck into black blobs of oil, pinning them to the concrete. Two were dead. The third, his feet stuck and his feathers saturated with oil, was still making feeble efforts to get free.

"Those birds," said Wister. "They got into an oil slick."

"And I suppose that will make it easier for you to trap them and blow them up with an atomic bomb! Ignore his antics, class.

There is always some student who tries to get others to laugh." A helicopter was coming down the river very low and the sound blotted her voice out.

Heller was putting on a pair of gloves from his kit. He went over and verified that the two motionless ones were actually dead. Then he went to the third one. It feebly tried to defend itself with its beak.

Kneeling, Heller got a small spray out of his haversack. By Gods, he skirted on the edges of real Code breaks: it said *Solvent 564, Fleet Supply Base 14* right on it in Voltarian! I made a note of it. Somebody might notice!

He took out a redstar engineer's rag and protected the bird's eyes and air holes and rapidly sprayed its feathers. Of course, the oil vanished.

Then he unstuck its feet, wiped them off and sprayed them. He inspected the bird, found a couple of spots he had missed and handled those. He was always so maddeningly neat!

He took out a water bottle and filled the cap. The bird, head loose by now, started to strike, then thought better of it and took some water from the cap. The bird did it several times.

"You were dehydrated," said Heller. "It's the hot sun. Now take a few more sips." What a fool. He was talking to it in Voltarian and it was an Earth bird!

Then he took out half a sandwich and broke it up and laid it on the grass. The bird stretched its wings, doubtless with some surprise. It was going to fly away but saw the sandwich and decided to have lunch first.

"Now, that's a good bird," said Heller. "You stay away from that black stuff. It's oil, understand? Petroleum!"

The bird let out some kind of a squawk and went on eating the sandwich. I don't know why it squawked. It couldn't understand Voltarian.

Heller looked around. Of course, the Nature Appreciation class was gone. Heller listened intently. He heard nothing. He did a fast scout.

And then he was sniffing. What the Hells was he sniffing about?

He glanced back. The seagull was just taking off. It sailed by him and curved outward over the river and was gone.

Sniffing some more, Heller trotted ahead and was shortly in the reception center of the General Assembly Building, according to the signs. There was even an information sign but he didn't approach it.

He seemed to find the place very curious. The light was coming through the walls from outside in a translucent effect. He went over to a wall and examined it to find out why, probably.

He went over into the Assembly Hall and there was the class. Miss Simmons was lecturing. ". . . and here it is that the delegates could rise with one voice and in stentorian and noble tones denounce nuclear weapons forever. But alas, they do not. The men who occupy this place are silenced by their own fears. They cower. . . ."

Heller was examining some marble.

The class trailed out on Miss Simmons' heels and, with her still lecturing and totally ignoring the guide who seemed to have attached himself to the party, went into the Conference Building and were shortly in the gallery of a chamber labelled

The Security Council

They gazed across the two hundred or so empty public seats—for, of course, nothing was in session and would not be for another couple of weeks—and Miss Simmons continued her lecture. ". . . And so we come at last to the lair of the powerful few who, even if the General Assembly did act, this fifteen-nation body would veto any sensible ban proposed. The five permanent members—United States, France, United Kingdom, Russia and China—each have the right to turn down, individually, the anguished pleas of all the peoples of the Earth! They block any effort anyone makes to outlaw nuclear power and disarm the world! Greed, lust for power, megalomania and paranoia cause these self-annointed few to surge onward and onward, closer and closer to the brink."

Heller had been admiring the gold and blue hangings and a mural. But at her last words, he spoke sharply. "Who keeps preventing a solution?"

Miss Simmons spoke out with a clarion voice of her own. "The Russian traitors who have sold out the revolution and asserted themselves the tyrants of the proletariat! Who asked that question? It was a very good one!"

"Wister did," said a girl.

"Oh, you again! Wister, stop disturbing the class!" Miss Simmons led them back outside.

Heller's eyes lingered on a huge statue of a muscular figure that was putting a lot of effort into something.

Heller asked, "What is that statue doing?"

Miss Simmons said, "That is a Russian statue. It is a worker being forced to beat a plowshare into a sword. It personifies the betrayal of the proletariat." She had looked back, moving her glasses off her eyes to see. "Ah, that was a good question, George."

Wister was looking around to see who George was and so were the other students.

She had gathered them together under the Statue of Peace. "Now, today, students, was just a start, an effort to orient this course for you. But I will review why we started here, so pay very close attention.

"All that you will see in our future Sundays of Nature Appreciation is *doomed* by nuclear war. It will make it far more poignant for you, as you admire the beauties of nature, to realize, as you look at every blossom, every leaf, every delicate paw and each bit of soft, defenseless fur, to realize that it is about to be destroyed forever in the horror and holocaust of thermonuclear war!"

Oh, she was right there! If Heller didn't win and a Voltar invasion got turned loose, those crude atomic bombs would seem like a picnic!

"So, class," she went on, "if you do not yet feel, individually and collectively, the craving urge to instantly sign up with the Anti-Nuclear Protest Marchers, I assure you that you soon will—New York Tactical Police Force or no New York Tactical Police Force. Class dismissed. Wister, please remain behind."

The students wandered off. Heller came up to Miss Simmons.

She lifted her glasses up to try to see him. "Wister, I am

afraid your classwork is not improving. You were interrupting and disturbing the others. You were not paying attention!"

"I got everything you said," protested Heller. "You said that if the UN couldn't be made to function, the planet would destroy itself with thermonuclear weapons."

"Weapons made by such as *you*, Wister. My words were far stronger. So you get an F for today. If your daily classwork is a bad average, you know, of course, that even a perfect, INFLUENCED, final examination won't save you. And if you flunk this course, Wister, you won't get your diploma and then nobody will listen to you and you'll never get that coveted job of blowing up this planet. Small as it is, I do my bit for the cause, Wister. Good afternoon." And she stalked off.

Heller sat down.

And how pleased I was! Miss Simmons had him stalled. What a marvelous, brilliant woman! Her straight hair and glasses hid the fact that she was also quite good looking. And even though she obviously hated men, I felt a great tenderness for her, a longing to hug her and tell her what a truly magnificent person she was!

My ally! At last I had found one to give me hope in my sea of chaos!

Oh, it did me good to see Heller just sitting there, staring at the grass.

The fate of empires lay in the delicate and beautiful hands of a woman. But this was not the first time in the age-long histories of planets. I prayed to the Gods that her grip on fate would remain tenacious and strong.

Chapter 6

Heller glanced at his watch and it winked 3:00 P.M. He glanced at the sky: there was a pattern of cloud to the north and a stir of wind.

He got up and, at a fast trot, began to cover the long blocks home.

Suddenly he stopped. Something had caught his eye up ahead. Miss Simmons was just disappearing down a subway stairs, way up ahead.

Heller glanced up and down the street. It was Sunday afternoon and there wasn't anyone about. The usual midtown Sunday desertion. He trotted on. He seemed to be heading for the stairs. It came to me in a flash that maybe he was going to murder Miss Simmons! That is the first plan that would have occurred to me. Apparatus training is always uppermost.

But he passed on by the stairs.

A sharp voice from the bowels of the station! "No! Go away!"

Heller sprang over the rail and dropped onto the steps. He went down six at a time. He burst out onto the platform.

Miss Simmons was standing there, on the other side of the turnstile. A ragged wino was reeling back and forth in front of her. "Gimme a buck and I'll go away!"

She raised her cane to strike at him. He easily grasped it and yanked it out of her hand. He threw it aside.

Heller yelled, "You, there!"

The drunk looked around. He stumbled and scrambled for a

more distant exit stair and went through a steel revolving gate.

Heller fished out a token and went through the turnstile. He walked over to the cane and picked it up. He came back and handed it to Miss Simmons.

"Things are pretty deserted on Sunday," he said. "It isn't safe for you."

"Wister," said Miss Simmons with loathing.

"Maybe I should see you home," said the insufferably polite and courteous Royal officer.

"I am perfectly safe, Wister," said Miss Simmons, acidly. "All week I work cooped up. All week I am mobbed with students. Today the class was finished early and it is the first time in MONTHS I have a chance for a quiet walk alone. And who turns up? YOU!"

"I'm sorry," said Heller. "I just don't think it's very safe for a woman to be walking around by herself in this city. Particularly today when there are so few people about. That man just now———"

"I have lived in New York for years, Wister. I am perfectly capable of taking care of myself. Nothing will ever happen to *me!*"

"You ever walk around alone much?" said Heller.

"I don't get a chance to, Wister. There are always students. Please leave me alone, Wister. I am going to have my walk in spite of you or anybody else. Go away somewhere and play with your atom bombs!"

A train roared up, the doors opened. She turned her back upon him pointedly and entered a car.

Wister trotted down the train a few cars and, steadying an automatic door before it could close, got aboard. The train sped along.

I was trying to figure out what his angle was. He lived only a couple blocks away from the station they had just left. She was definitely in his road on his way to a diploma. It would be greatly to his benefit if she were disposed of. The Apparatus textbook handling would be to do just that. Had I found a real ally only to lose her?

The shuttle train pulled into Grand Central. Heller had his eye on Miss Simmons, seen through intervening car doors. She got out of the train.

Heller also went out of the door.

Miss Simmons probably did not see him. She was following directions which took her to the Lexington Avenue line. Heller followed at a distance.

She got to the Lexington Avenue, IRT uptown platform. Then she walked way on up the platform to where the front end of the train would stop.

She stood there, leaning on her cane, waiting for the next express.

A young man in a red beret walked toward her. Heller started to move forward and then stopped. The young man was a clean-looking youth. He had on a white T-shirt and it said Volunteer Guard Patrol on it.

He spoke to Miss Simmons. "Miss," he said politely, "you shouldn't be riding the front cars or the back cars of a train, especially on Sunday. Ride in the center where there are more people. The gangs and muggers are out real heavy today."

Miss Simmons turned her back on him. "Leave me alone!"

The volunteer guard drifted down the platform. He must have sensed Heller had seen the interplay. He said to Heller as he passed, "Rapes by the trainful and they never learn."

An express roared in and came to a hissing halt with a roar and clang of doors opening. Miss Simmons got into the first car. Heller stepped in to the middle of the train. The doors slammed shut and they roared away, lurching and banging at high speed.

A tough-looking drunk sized up Heller. Heller took his engineer gloves out of his haversack and put them on. It was an effective gesture. The tough one promptly staggered down the swaying train to the next car back.

White tiles of stations flashed by, one after another. They rode and rode and rode, all at very high speed through the dark tunnels, the sound a pounding roar. At each infrequent stop, Heller would half rise to see if Miss Simmons was alighting, would see that she was not and would then sink back.

After a very long time, the signs on the tunnel poles said:

Woodlawn

Miss Simmons got out. Heller waited until the last moment and then got out. Miss Simmons had vanished up a stairs.

Shortly, Heller emerged into daylight. Miss Simmons was striding along northward. He waited a bit. He looked at the sky. It was overcast. Wind was whipping stray bits of paper along roadways.

It was then I realized what he must be doing: he had probably read one of the G-2 manuals, the one about how to tail a Russian spy. He was simply practicing. He had not read any Apparatus manuals and so he would not be well enough trained to know that he should simply murder Miss Simmons. Having accounted for his actions, I felt much easier. Miss Simmons would be quite safe after all and I still had an ally.

Several picnickers were evidently going home, their hair blown about by the wind. Otherwise there was no traffic.

At least two hundred yards behind Miss Simmons, Heller followed along.

She went some distance. A sign pointed:

Van Cortlandt Park

She turned in that direction, striding along in her heavy laced boots, swinging her cane, the perfect picture of a fashionable hiker in the European style.

She made some more turns. They were well into a kind of wilderness interlaced with infrequent bridle paths.

The wind was rising and trees were bowing. Some belated picnickers fled toward civilization. After that it was a deserted expanse of thickets and trees.

Heller was closer to her now but still thirty yards or more behind. Due to the twists and turns of the trail, he was usually masked from her. She was not looking back.

Ahead was a vale. The path went down into a long hollow and then turned up at the far end. It was a totally hidden area, surrounded by large trees.

Miss Simmons got a third of the way up the far slope. Heller stepped forward to go down the path.

Abruptly, from the undergrowth around her, six men sprang up!

One leaped agilely into the trail in front of her, a ragged white youth.

A black jumped into the trail behind her!

Two Hispanics and two more whites blocked her way to right and left!

Heller started to go down the trail toward them.

A harsh, cold voice said, "Hold it, sonny!"

Heller looked back to his left.

Emerged from a tree but still behind it stood an old gray-faced, unshaven bum. He was holding a double-barreled shotgun trained on Heller. He was twenty feet away.

Another voice! "Just stop right there, kid!"

Heller looked back and to his right. Another man, a black, was standing there with a revolver pointed at him, thirty feet away. "We been waitin' all afternoon for a setup like this, kid, so don't make any sudden moves."

The man with the shotgun said, "This is one time, sonny, when you don't get a piece all to yourself. You can have some later, if there's any left."

Excited laughter was coming from the men around Miss Simmons. They were jumping up and down.

She struck at them with her stick!

A black grabbed it and yanked it out of her hand!

The others screeched with laughter and the one with the stick started to dance with it, waving it. The others started to dance around Miss Simmons.

Heller shouted in a strong voice, "Please don't do this!"

The man with the shotgun said, "Take it easy, sonny. It's just a gang rape. Some fun for a Sunday. Me and Joe is a little too (bleeped) out to do more than watch, so you just get smart and be like us and maybe we won't have to kill you."

"What kind of beasts are you on this planet?" shouted Heller.

"You got any money?" said the man with the revolver. "The big H comes high these days."

The crowd around Miss Simmons was dashing in at her and dancing back. They were herding her into a flatter place more masked by trees. She was shouting at them to leave her alone.

Heller reached toward his haversack. "Hold it, sonny. Keep your hands in sight. This is a twelve-gauge and both barrels loaded in front of hair triggers. We can get his money later, Joe. Jesus," he said indulgently, "look at those young devils."

"Only the raving insane do things like that!" said Heller.

"What do you mean, insane?" challenged the man with the revolver. "Pete there taught 'em himself. He really knows his psychology. And every one of those kids got Grade A in psychology. How could they be insane? Jesus, would you look at how hard their (bleepers) are! Great stuff, hey, Pete?"

"Jesus, look at 'em," chortled Pete.

Heller was backing up, I suddenly realized. Inch by slow inch he had been backing up. He was going to use a standard solution. He was going to run away! He was smarter than I thought.

The half-dozen whooping young men, getting wilder and wilder with excitement, had herded Miss Simmons into the flatter area. A Hispanic leaped in and grabbed off her hat!

Another leaped past her and hit at her hair. It came loose and showered around her shoulders.

"Yippee!" screamed a black. "Don't she look wild!"

"Killing a bunch of hoodlums isn't part of my job!" Heller said. Then he shouted, "Please quit this and get away while you still can!"

"The only ones likely to be killed is you and that (bleepch)," said Pete. He shouted down, "Jesus! Start stripping her! Show me some skin! Oh, man, does this beat Sunday TV."

Two of them seized her coat, one from either side, and yanked it off her, danced away and threw it aside.

Two more dashed in past her flailing arms and tore at her shirt!

Heller was backing up, inch by inch.

"Blackie!" howled Joe down into the vale, "get behind her and get that bra off!"

"Ah," sighed Pete in ecstasy.

"Pedrito!" howled Joe. "Get the skirt! The skirt, man! Yank it off her!"

As if in ultra-slow motion, Heller moved back further.

"Heat her up! Heat her up!" shouted Joe. "Grab her from behind and heat her up!"

"Get her down! Get her down!" howled Pete.

Miss Simmons' foot lashed out at a man. He grabbed her shoe with a surging wrench, and tore it off her foot, laces and all. There was a crack.

Miss Simmons' face contorted in agony. "My ankle!"

Pete said, "Oh, Jesus, I like it when they scream!"

Inch by inch, imperceptibly, Heller was backing up. The angle made by two tree trunks was closing. He was getting out of the shotgun's field of fire. In a moment he would be able to escape. Smart.

Joe yelled, "Get her down! Get her on her back!"

Pete shouted, "Strip her total like I taught you!"

Joe let out a sigh. "Oh, wow! Look at that boy paw her!"

Miss Simmons' voice rose to the tops of the trees. "Don't touch me! Don't touch me!"

A Hispanic was watching avidly as Miss Simmons cried, "My ankle is broken!"

Joe licked his lips as Miss Simmons' scream lanced through the glade.

A wild-eyed white heard Pete's shouted order, "Get her begging for it!" He darted forward.

Pete yelled, "Grab her legs!"

Joe jerked as Miss Simmons' scream tore up from below.

"Let Whitey go first!" howled Pete. "The rest of you have got the (bleep)! Whitey first!"

Heller suddenly dived to the ground!

The shotgun blasted with a roar!

Heller was rolling to his left in a blur of motion.

A revolver shot racketed.

The man with the shotgun was trying to get around the tree which now blocked his aim. He pulled back.

Another revolver shot sounded and a spurt of dirt leaped near Heller's head.

Heller was rolling further.

A sudden glimpse of a tree. The shotgun man lunged!

Heller's hands shot out and grabbed the shotgun.

The man screamed, flailing back a broken hand.

Bark leaped from the tree! The racket of a revolver shot!

A sight down the shotgun barrel at the revolver man!

The buck of the shotgun!

The revolver man's chest spurted red and he flew backwards.

The shotgun man trying to get up!

The swinging blur of the stock. The crack as the stock shattered. The shotgun man didn't have a face! Just red flesh and bone splinters!

Heller sprang out into the path.

The group around the girl were spread out, facing up the path, crouched and alert.

A white youth yelled, "It's just one guy! Kill him!"

A black and a Hispanic rushed forward.

A switchblade flashed.

The other four spread out so they could encircle.

Heller's foot struck the switchblade hand. The knife flew. The man screamed!

A man seen between two others. He had a gun.

Heller's foot extended like a battering ram. The man's gun arm crumpled!

A whirl. Another knife! A foot up against the hand. The knife flew into the air!

Heller spun on one foot, the other extended like a scythe. The flat of the foot tore the man's whole face off!

Gods! Spikes! This was why Heller was wearing spikes!

A knife blade glittering. It slashed down on Heller's arm and bit.

A foot up toward the wielder. A down kick! The whole chest of the knife wielder ripped open!

Arms seizing Heller from behind. A darting back of Heller's head, his own arms rising and casting off the grip.

He spun!

Spikes stamped against a thigh and, ripping downward, that foot hit the ground. The other foot coming upward.

The whole throat of the man torn out!

A blur of three men trying to get at Heller.

A woolly head. A spiked foot driving at it. The grind of steel into bones!

A Hispanic face. The blur of a foot kick. No longer a Hispanic face.

A man's heels. He was running, trying to get away.

A rush. A horizontal thrust of two spiked feet. They hit the man in the back. He went down in a skid of leaves. Heller landed upright. Man's head two feet below the spikes. Down came Heller. The soles were held in a V. They stripped the skin, ears and two huge slabs of skull off the head.

Silence.

Heller started checking them. Five were dead, ripped to pieces. The sixth had his whole chest open. Veins and arteries were pumping.

The man came to. He screamed. He collapsed. The body went into the final twitches of the death agonies.

Heller went up the hill. Both Pete and Joe were very dead.

He walked back down, surveying the scene. It looked like a slaughterhouse. Blood was all over and leaves were churned into red mud.

I was terrified. I had never had an inkling as to why he was wearing spikes. But I knew now. In a primitive land where other weapons were not legal, he had been walking around on his! Supposing I had not known this! I myself might have been a target! Oh, I would stay a long distance away from this Heller if I ever had to talk to him. He was *dangerous!*

Miss Simmons, clothes torn, was lying there where they had left her at the first shot.

She was propped on an elbow. She was staring at Heller with wide, round eyes.

He went over to her. He tried to get her to lie back. It must have moved her leg. She screamed in agony! She passed out.

Heller examined her leg. The ankle was a compound fracture with a splinter of bone extending from it.

He got a knife out of his haversack, picked up a broken tree branch and quickly made a splint. He padded the ankle with wads of Kleenex he took from her purse and then taped the splints on with engineer tape.

He tried to get her torn clothes together. He got her into her coat. She was still out cold. He found her glasses and put them in her purse and then tied the purse around her neck.

He gave the churned ground an inspection. His spike tracks were everywhere.

Heller looked down at his baseball shoes. They were coated with blood and fragments of bone and flesh.

He did a tour of the dead men. He chose one of them and took the shoes off the corpse. He took off his baseball shoes and put them on the dead man's feet. Then he pulled on those of the dead man.

It was a bad sign. He had already been reading G-2 manuals, obviously. As I feared, it was likely to make my work that much harder!

After a bit of search, he found Miss Simmons' stick. He went over the scene again—and a gory scene it was, there under the darkening sky, wind now tugging at the hair and clothing of the dead.

He picked up Miss Simmons and looked around again to make sure there was nothing left, apparently. Then he looked up the hill to where the shotgun man still lay, partially in view.

"I wish you'd listened," he said. "I'm not here to punish anybody." He looked down at Miss Simmons' face. She was out cold. Then he looked up at the scudding sky and in Voltarian said, "Is this planet inhabited by a Godsless people? Has some strange idea poisoned them to make them think they have no souls? That there is no hereafter?"

Well, that was Heller. Stupid and theatrical. It served his best interests to just dump Miss Simmons and shove one of those abandoned switchblades into her. You could tell he was not Apparatus trained, so maybe G-2 wasn't going to do me as much harm as I had thought.

Yes. Stupid. He seemed to be casting about for compass directions. Then he began to move swiftly westward and south through thickets and trees, trotting along in a way that seemed to hold Miss Simmons level.

Eventually he emerged from what must have been a vast expanse of parkland. He was soon on some streets.

After quite a distance, a sign loomed ahead in the dusk:

Van Cortlandt Park Subway Station

He bought tokens and the person behind the glass didn't even look at him. He put two tokens in the gate.

He was shortly on a train. It roared along. There were hardly any people aboard. A security guard walked by. Despite the bloody trouser cuffs, the torn clothes on the girl and the splinted ankle, the guard did not even pause as he passed.

Empire Subway Station was there on the white tiles. Heller got off.

Carrying Miss Simmons with no bounce, he moved smoothly along. He was on College Walk. He turned south on Amsterdam Avenue and halted at a door marked:

Empire Health Service

There were no lights on.

He went across Amsterdam Avenue and walked into what must have been the emergency ward of a hospital. He waited a bit and a nurse passing through the waiting room saw him and came over.

"Accident," she said. "Sit right there."

She went off. She came back pushing a wheeled stretcher and patted it.

Heller put Miss Simmons down on it.

The nurse threw a blanket over her and tugged a strap tight over her chest.

The nurse led Heller over to a counter. She got out some forms. "Name?"

"She's Miss Simmons," said Heller. "Empire faculty. You can get the details out of her purse, probably. I'm just a student."

The nurse got Miss Simmons' purse and dug out insurance cards and so on.

A young intern came down the hall and looked at Miss Simmons. "Shock," he said. "She's in shock."

"Broken ankle," said Heller. "Compound fracture."

"You got a slashed arm," said the young intern. He was lifting Heller's sleeve. "Needs handling. Looks like a switchblade wound. Student?"

"Yes," said Heller.

"We'll fix it up for you."

Miss Simmons came to and started to scream.

Another nurse came along with a tray and a hypodermic syringe. The intern got hold of Miss Simmons' arm. The nurse put a rubber tube around the arm. Miss Simmons was threshing about and the nurse couldn't control the arm long enough to get the needle in.

"That isn't heroin is it?" said Heller. "I don't think she's on horse."

"Morf," said the intern. "The purest medical morf. Calm her down."

Miss Simmons was lunging against the strap. She had her other arm loose. She was pointing at Heller. "Get him away from me!" She struggled to draw backwards. "Get away from me, you murderer!"

The intern and the nurse managed to hold her still. The nurse got the needle into a vein.

Miss Simmons was glaring at Heller and screaming. "You murderer! You sadist!"

The intern said, "Now, now, you'll feel better in a moment."

"Get him away from me!" screamed Miss Simmons. "He's just like I thought!"

"There, there," said the nurse.

"Grab him!" screamed Miss Simmons. "I saw him murder eight men in cold blood!"

"Nurse," said the intern, "mark that she's to be placed in an observation ward."

She threshed further. "You've got to believe me! I saw him kick eight men to death!"

"Nurse," said the intern, "change that to psychiatric observation ward."

The morphine must have been biting. She lay back. Suddenly she raised her head and looked venomously at Heller. "I knew it! I knew it all the time! You're a savage killer! When I get well and out of here, I'm going to devote my life to making certain that you FAIL!"

Oh, I was so relieved. I had been afraid all this time that she would be grateful to Heller for his preventing them from raping her, giving her the (bleep) and probably killing her for kicks. But she was true blue to the end.

The grimness was still on her face as she went under the full effects of the morphine and fell back.

I did some rapid calculation. She would not be able to continue as teacher of that course this semester but she certainly would be his teacher again in late winter and the spring. She had ample time to flunk him. Or—oh, joy—hang him sooner with a murder rap!

Bless her crazy, crooked and ungrateful heart!

How wonderful it was to feel I had a real friend!

And even if they put her under psychiatric care, that would change nothing. It never does.

*Does Simmons succeed in
ending Heller's mission?*

Read
MISSION EARTH
Volume 3
THE ENEMY WITHIN

About the Author
L. Ron Hubbard

Born in 1911, the son of a U.S. naval officer, the legendary L. Ron Hubbard grew up in the great American West and was acquainted early with a rugged outdoor life before he took to the sea. The cowboys, Indians and mountains of Montana were balanced with an open sea, temples and the throngs of the Orient as Hubbard journeyed through the Far East as a teenager. By the time he was nineteen, he had travelled over a quarter of a million sea miles and thousands on land, recording his experiences in a series of diaries, mixed with story ideas.

When Hubbard returned to the U.S., his insatiable curiosity and demand for excitement sent him into the sky as a barnstormer where he quickly earned a reputation for his skill and daring. Then he turned his attention to the sea again. This time it was four-masted schooners and voyages into the Caribbean, where he found the adventure and experience that was to serve him later at the typewriter.

Drawing from his travels, he produced an amazing plethora of stories, from adventure and westerns to mystery and detective.

By 1938, Hubbard was already established and recognized as one of the top-selling authors, when a major new magazine, Street and Smith's *Astounding Science Fiction*, called for new blood. Hubbard was urged to try his hand at science fiction. The red-headed author protested that he did not write about "machines and machinery" but that he wrote about people. "That's just what we want," he was told.

The result was a barrage of stories from Hubbard that expanded the scope and changed the face of the genre, gaining Hubbard a repute, along with Robert Heinlein, as one of the "founding fathers" of the great Golden Age of Science Fiction.

Then as now he excited intense critical comparison with the best of H. G. Wells and Edgar Allan Poe. His prodigious creative output of more than a hundred novels and novelettes and more than two hundred short stories, with over twenty-two million copies of fiction in a dozen languages sold throughout the world, is a true publishing phenomenon.

But perhaps most important is that as time went on, Hubbard's work and style developed to masterful proportions. The 1982 blockbuster *Battlefield Earth*, celebrating Hubbard's 50th year as a professional writer, very quickly became an international best seller. From the United States to South Africa, from the United Kingdom to Australia *Battlefield Earth* topped the bestseller lists and received the highest critical acclaim from around the world.

"A superlative storyteller with total mastery of plot and pacing"
PUBLISHERS WEEKLY

". . . swift-moving adventure . . . first class . . . the alien 'Psychlos' are astonishingly convincing . . ."
THE OBSERVER

But the final *magnum opus* was yet to come. L. Ron Hubbard, after completing *Battlefield Earth*, sat down and did what few writers have dared contemplate—let alone achieve. He wrote the ten-volume space adventure satire *Mission Earth*.

Filled with a dazzling array of other-world weaponry and systems, *Mission Earth* is a spectacular cavalcade of battles, of stunning plot reversals, with heroes and heroines, villains and villainesses, caught up in a superbly imaginative, intricately plotted invasion of Earth—as seen entirely and uniquely through the eyes of the aliens that already walk among us.

ABOUT THE AUTHOR

With the distinctive pace, artistry and humor that is the inimitable hallmark of L. Ron Hubbard, *Mission Earth* weaves a hilarious, fast-paced adventure tale of ingenious alien intrigue, told with biting social commentary in the great classic tradition of Swift, Wells and Orwell.

So unprecedented is this work, that a new term—dekalogy (meaning ten books)—had to be coined just to describe its breadth and scope.

With the manuscript completed and in the hands of the publisher and all of his other work done, L. Ron Hubbard departed his body on January 24, 1986. He left behind a timeless legacy of unparalleled story-telling richness for you the reader to enjoy, as other readers have, time and again, over the past half century.

We the publishers are proud to present L. Ron Hubbard's dazzling tour de force: the *Mission Earth* dekalogy.

"I AM ALWAYS HAPPY TO HEAR FROM MY READERS."

L. Ron Hubbard

These were the words of L. Ron Hubbard, who was always very interested in hearing from his friends, readers and followers. He made a point of staying in communication with everyone he came in contact with over his fifty-year career as a professional writer, and he had thousands of fans and friends that he corresponded with all over the world.

The publishers of L. Ron Hubbard's literary works wish to continue this tradition and would very much welcome letters and comments from you, his readers, both old and new.

Any message addressed to the Author's Affairs Director at New Era Publications will be given prompt and full attention.

NEW ERA PUBLICATIONS U.K. LTD
Dowgate, Douglas Road,
Tonbridge, Kent, TN9 2TS, U.K.